THE PRINCE
AND THE MIDWIFE

HIS PREGNANT
SLEEPING BEAUTY

BY
LYNNE MARSHALL

MILLS &
BOON

Welcome to…

The Hollywood Hills Clinic

*Where doctors to the stars work miracles by day—
and explore their hearts' desires by night…*

When hotshot doc James Rothsberg started the clinic
six years ago he dreamed of a world-class facility, catering
to Hollywood's biggest celebrities, and his team are
unrivalled in their fields. Now, as the glare of the media
spotlight grows, the Hollywood Hills Clinic is teaming up
with the pro-bono Bright Hope Clinic, and James is reunited
with Dr Mila Brightman…the woman he jilted at the altar!

When it comes to juggling the care of Hollywood A-listers
with care for the underprivileged kids of LA *anything* can
happen…and sizzling passions run high in the shadow of
the red carpet. With everything at stake for James, Mila
and the Hollywood Hills Clinic medical team their biggest
challenges have only just begun!

Find out what happens in the dazzling

The Hollywood Hills Clinic miniseries:

Seduced by the Heart Surgeon
by Carol Marinelli

Falling for the Single Dad
by Emily Forbes

Tempted by Hollywood's Top Doc
by Louisa George

Perfect Rivals…
by Amy Ruttan

The Prince and the Midwife
by Robin Gianna

His Pregnant Sleeping Beauty
by Lynne Marshall

And look out for another two titles from
The Hollywood Hills Clinic next month!

THE PRINCE
AND THE MIDWIFE

BY
ROBIN GIANNA

Published in Great Britain 2016
By Mills & Boon, an imprint of HarperCollins*Publishers*
1 London Bridge Street, London, SE1 9GF

© 2016 Harlequin Books S.A.

Special thanks and acknowledgement are given to Robin Gianna for her contribution to The Hollywood Hills Clinic *series*

ISBN: 978-0-263-91491-7

Printed and bound in Spain
by CPI, Barcelona

Dear Reader,

I was so pleased to say yes when I was asked to participate in The Hollywood Hills Clinic continuity! Not to mention that I smiled when I saw that my hero was both a prince *and* a doctor—probably not a usual combination, so I knew it would be a fun story to write.

This is the second book I've written with a midwife heroine—the first was for the Midwives On-Call at Christmas series I participated in. The other book— *Her Christmas Baby Bump*—was set in the UK, and this is in the US. There are quite a few interesting differences in midwifery between the two countries, which I found enjoyable to research.

My heroine here, in *The Prince and the Midwife*, works hard and keeps mostly to herself. Her emotions are still raw from a tragedy she hasn't put behind her. I loved the thought of my hero helping Gabby move from her painful past to a new future—but the journey isn't without a few bumps along the way.

Rafael has his own problems, and he's hiding out in LA for a while to deal with one of them—the constant media attention on a few scandals of his that the royal family is none too happy about. He's planning to steer clear of all women until the frenzy passes—but meeting Gabriella makes that feel impossible.

I enjoyed the sparks that fly between Gabby and Rafael from the moment they meet—though the initial sparks are mostly of the annoyed variety! But as they learn to respect one another's work they also learn that perhaps the way they've been living their lives isn't really what they want after all.

I hope you enjoy The Hollywood Hills Clinic books—and Rafael and Gabby's story. You can find out about my other stories, or contact me, at robingianna.com.

Happy reading!

Robin xoxo

This book is dedicated to my friend and neighbour
Betsy Hackett, RN, DSN. Thanks so much, Betsy, for
putting up with my phone calls and numerous questions
about midwifery and birthing babies—smooch!

After completing a degree in journalism, then working in
advertising and mothering her kids, **Robin Gianna** had
what she calls her 'awakening'. She decided she wanted to
write the kind of romance novels she'd loved since her teens,
and now enjoys pushing her characters towards their own
happily-ever-afters. When she's not writing, Robin fills her
life with a happily messy kitchen, a needy garden, a wonderful
husband, three great kids, a drooling bulldog and one grouchy
Siamese cat.

Books by Robin Gianna

Mills & Boon Medical Romance

Midwives On-Call at Christmas

Her Christmas Baby Bump

Changed by His Son's Smile
The Last Temptation of Dr Dalton
Flirting with Dr Off-Limits
It Happened in Paris…
Her Greek Doctor's Proposal

Visit the Author Profile page at
millsandboon.co.uk for more titles.

Praise for
Robin Gianna

'Yet another splendid read from the author…a romance which
should not be missed by everyone who loves medical romance.'
—*Harlequin Junkie* on
It Happened in Paris…

'The story flowed brilliantly, the dialogue was believable and
I was thoroughly engaged in the medical dramas.'
—*Contemporary Romance Reviews* on
Changed by His Son's Smile

CHAPTER ONE

GABRIELLA CAIN ABSENTLY raked her fingers through her hair and stared at the messy room, fighting the deep fatigue that crept quietly into every aching muscle. Her second double shift of the week might be officially over, but as the labor suite department head she wasn't about to leave the disarray for the next midwife to clean up.

Thinking about the twins she'd just delivered to a Hollywood actress and the new mother's proud, beaming husband gave her an energy boost. The suite was a mess for a great reason—the birth of two healthy newborns. After all, just like a kitchen that was never cooked in stayed clean, a spic-and-span labor and delivery suite would mean no new little babies, and wouldn't that be a sad thing?

Gabby finished putting new sheets on the bed, wishing her own at home were as nice as the luxurious Egyptian cotton sheets The Hollywood Hills Clinic provided for its demanding patients, then topped it off with a fresh down blanket. The room was strewn with the various supplies she'd just used, and she figured it made sense to clean that up last so she could note what inventory she might be running low on and get them ordered tomorrow.

She folded clean blankets and stacked them inside the

toasty warming cupboard. Crouching down to finally gather the things on the floor, the sound of the double swinging doors banging open and a gurney being hurriedly wheeled into the room had her pausing in surprise. The other, even more alarming sounds? A woman's moans and the receptionist shouting her name.

"Gabby? Gabby! Are you in here?" Stephanie called.

"I'm here." She stood and stared in dismay when she saw it was Cameron Fontaine lying on the gurney being steered by the hospital's uniformed EMTs, who had doubtless brought her here by helicopter. The famous A-list actress, who was one of Gabby's most difficult patients, and whose baby wasn't due for months. "Cameron? What's wrong?"

"I don't know. I think the baby's coming. It's way too soon, though, isn't it? Oh, God, I'm so scared." She jabbed her index finger toward Gabby, her blue eyes somehow wide with fear and imperiously demanding at the same time. "You've got to do something!"

Gabby's stomach plunged. Yes. It was too soon, and she sent up a deep prayer that Cameron wasn't in labor. That her baby would be fine. That her infant would be born healthy and alive. Her hands suddenly cold, she rushed over to wrap her fingers around Cameron's. "All right. Try to relax. Let's get you into the bed and see what's going on, okay?"

"Just get it stopped! The baby has to cook in there a little longer, right?"

Somehow, Gabby forced a smile, wishing it were that easy. "I believe the proverbial bun in the oven actually bakes, not cooks," she said lightly, proud that she'd managed to keep her tone joking and relaxed. "Let's see what we can do to make sure she gets to rise a little longer, hmm? Try not to worry until we learn more. Maybe baby is just in a mood, wanting a little attention?" She hoped that was the case, and resisted adding that would mean the infant was a chip off the old block.

Cameron's hand squeezed hers tightly, and Gabby frowned when she realized the woman's breath seemed short and gasping as the EMTs carefully moved her to the bed. Thirty-two weeks along was definitely not the optimal time for a baby to decide to come into the world.

"Stephanie, get in touch with whichever OB's on call and get them here, please."

Stephanie gave a nod and ran out, and Gabby barely noticed the EMTs leaving too as she grabbed the blood-pressure cuff. "I'm going to get your vital signs, then do an internal exam, okay?"

"Will you be able to tell if the baby's coming?"

"If you're dilating, yes. Tell me why you think you might be in labor. Are you in pain?"

"Not…not exactly pain." Cameron's hands cupped her belly and her face scrunched up in an unflattering expression Gabby was sure hadn't been seen on any movie screens by the actress's many fans, which proved how distressed she was. "I felt a little crampy, kind of like the Braxton-Hicks contractions you talked to me about. And my belly got sort of hard, and when it didn't go away I knew I had to do something right away and called the clinic."

"You did exactly the right thing, calling for the helicopter to come get you."

"Well, it seemed to take them forever!" She swiped her elegantly manicured hand across her frowning brow. "It was at least five minutes longer than when they came to get me after I hit my head, and every second that passed I got more worried. I called three times, and I think that made them finally hurry."

A smile touched Gabby's lips, as it was pretty easy to imagine how those conversations had gone. "Let's see how baby is doing, all right?"

Gabby pressed her stethoscope to Cameron's belly, and the sound of the baby's steady heartbeat sent the breath she was holding right out of her lungs. Thank God, baby was still alive and moving. She snapped on exam gloves and what she found during the examination was a mixed blessing. "The good news is that your membranes are still intact, so no rupture there. Which means your labor's not advanced, which is also good news. But your cervix is dilated two centimeters, so we're going to have to do something about that."

"Like what? And what do you mean, labor's not advancing? Dilating means labor, right?"

Cameron's voice had gone a little shrill, and who could blame her? Gabby knew she had to help her stay calm—the situation was scary, yes, but with luck it could be managed. "Dilation means early labor, yes, but it can be slowed or sometimes completely stopped with medication. I'm going to get an IV set up to give you a mag sulfate drip right away, and also keep you hydrated with saline and lots of water to drink. We'll do a urinalysis to make sure there's no infection, just to be safe. Then we'll give you steroid injections to help baby's lungs develop in case she decides she just can't wait to get here. Please, try not to worry, okay? We'll be doing all we can to keep her healthy."

"I want to see Dr. Crane. When is she coming?"

Gabby had learned long ago to not be insulted by that demand, which she got from a lot of patients and their husbands. And when it came right down to it, she wanted the obstetrician to get there, too, in case the situation got worse instead of better. "I'll find out." She patted Cameron's shoulder and smiled. "Try to relax. Easy to say, I know, but you don't want your blood pressure all out of whack and make things tougher for baby, do you?"

"Could you get me something to drink before you leave? My breath's been so short for what seems like hours, and I'm beyond parched." She wrapped her fingers around her throat, little gasping sounds coming from her mouth that this time sounded a little forced. "I'd love some artesian sparkling water with a squeeze of lime. You have that, of course, don't you?"

Gabby wanted to say it was more important to get going on the medications she needed first, before wetting her whistle, but figured it would be just as fast to get what Cameron wanted as to point that out.

The small stainless-steel refrigerator in every room was kept well stocked, and Gabby ran the lime wedge around the rim of the crystal glass like a Hollywood Hills nurse who'd been a former bartender had taught her to. Cameron grabbed it like she'd been walking miles through the desert, and Gabby was glad after all that she'd taken a moment to get it for her.

"I'll be right back, okay?" Gabby hurried out to find Stephanie, passing through the halls and out past the beautiful fountain in the center of the glass atrium that made the place feel like a luxury hotel, and breathed in the calming scents of lavender and sandalwood. Except at that moment it didn't do much to slow the current surge of adrenaline that had replaced all her prior fatigue.

"Is the doc on the way to see Cameron, Stephanie? Who is it?"

"Well, as I was about to see who's on call, James phoned. He told me Cameron contacted him while she was on the helicopter to tell him to send her own doctor, because she's convinced Dr. Crane is our best. But she's out of town, so James asked a good friend of his who's in L.A. visiting to come see her. A Dr. Rafael Moreno."

"What?" Gabby stared at her, not comprehending. "Some friend of his? What do you mean?"

"I guess he's some world-renowned OB, and not only that but the prince of some Mediterranean principality, if you can imagine. Isn't that exciting?" Stephanie's eyes were shining, which seemed ridiculous to Gabby since the woman saw superstars in this hospital all the time. "Said he has privileges in hospitals all over the world, including here in California, and thinks Cameron would appreciate the status of having a prince taking care of her."

Gabby gaped. *What in the world?* A *prince* OB? Just visiting the U.S.? *That* was who James thought was the best person to care for this very demanding and famous patient?

She loved working at The Hollywood Hills Clinic but just might have to point out to James Rothsberg that, exclusive and prestigious or not, the number one focus at this hospital still had to be on premier medical care and not the royalty status of some doctor from another country he happened to be besties with. And, yes, she knew James had founded this hospital with that philosophy, demanding every patient receive the best medical care available, but had to wonder about this particular decision.

"Well, send him in as soon as he gets here, please." She headed back to the room, pondering if she should call James right then to talk to him about the seriousness of Cameron's situation and ask about this doctor and his qualifications—if he was really "world renowned," or just famous for being royal.

"The doctor's on the way, Cameron," she said as she got the items she needed. "I'm going to start your IV now." For the moment, she had to ignore the last of the mess in the room she hadn't finished cleaning up yet until the doctor arrived and she was certain Cameron had been stabilized.

"It'd better be Dr. Crane," Cameron said, looking away at the wall with a dramatic wince and yelp as Gabby got the IV needle placed in her arm. "She already knows all about me and my past health scares and situation and I only want to see her."

"I know you do." Gabby tried to find reassurance in the fact that Cameron's voice had become the petulant one she often used when she felt normal. At least she wasn't getting real contractions yet or freaking out. Gabby conjured her own acting skills and infused her voice with enthusiasm, bracing herself for the woman to get upset at the news her doctor was unavailable. "Unfortunately Dr. Crane is out of town. But this doctor is a personal friend of James Rothsberg and is not only an excellent OB but apparently a prince too."

"A prince?" Surprise lit Cameron's face before it relaxed into a pleased smile, thank heavens, instead of outrage. "Well, how nice. If Dr. Crane can't be here, at least a prince will understand how important my baby is to the world."

Because a prince and a self-absorbed actress's baby were more important to the world than most other human beings? Emotions crowded Gabby's chest—disbelief that Cameron obviously genuinely believed that. Annoyance with that attitude. And deeply buried pain.

Because every person's baby was the most important child on earth to them.

She swallowed before she spoke. "I'm not sure when Dr. Moreno is going to get here, and we shouldn't wait to get your mag sulfate drip started. Is your belly still hard and tight? Still feeling crampy?"

"Well, yes. But not too bad. I think we should wait for this prince-doctor." She picked up the television remote, clicked to a movie channel, and beamed the famous megawatt smile she normally reserved for the cameras. "Oh, look, it's one of mine! I loved this one!"

"Cameron." Gabby worked to keep her patience. "Giving you the sulfate drip certainly isn't going to hurt, regardless of what Dr. Moreno has to say, and timing can be critical. Up to three courses of steroids are recommended for the baby's lung health, but have to be given at least twenty-four hours apart, and the sooner we give the first one, the sooner we can give the second one."

"I admit I'm still nervous. I know you're good at what you do. If you think you need to start it now, then let's do it." Cameron's smile disappeared, and Gabby's frustration with her patient evaporated when she saw the tension etched on her face. Probably her wanting to wait and watch the movie, all smiles, was some coping mechanism, telling herself everything was fine now that she was here at the clinic. Deluding oneself was all too easy to do, as Gabby knew firsthand.

She patted Cameron's arm, then gave it a gentle squeeze. "I'll get it started right now. And I bet the doctor will be here any moment." As though her words had willed it, a brisk knock on the door sounded, and she turned as it opened.

To reveal the most physically beautiful man she'd ever seen.

His dark hair was cut fairly short and impeccably groomed, and his olive skin was tanned a golden brown which looked even more swarthy in contrast to his white doctor's coat. The blue dress shirt he wore was crisply starched but left open at the collar without a tie, and it was obvious that beneath it lay a very well-built physique. But the most riveting thing about him was the startling color of his eyes, nearly the same hue as springtime in Seattle after rains had turned the landscape a vivid green.

She felt a little as though all the oxygen had been sucked from the room as those eyes met hers. Though the contact was brief, his gaze seemed to both assess her and dismiss her at the same time. Then his attention moved around the room in a careful scan of the space before finally focusing on their patient.

A smile transformed the aloof expression on his handsome face. *"Buenos días."* He stepped to the bed, reached for their patient's hand and, to Gabby's astonishment, lifted it to his lips. Since when did doctors kiss their patients, even if it was just on the hand? "I do not have to ask if you are the famous Cameron Fontaine. I would recognize your stunning face anywhere. I am Dr. Rafael Moreno."

"It's wonderful to meet you, Doctor," Cameron practically cooed.

"I understand your very special baby is demanding some unexpectedly early attention. I'm told your little one is a girl—what a lucky child. She'll no doubt be as beautiful as you are." Lord. Gabby had to wonder if he'd intentionally ratcheted up the charm, or if it just oozed naturally from the man. "Let us see what she has in mind, shall we?"

"Yes. I'm so anxious to hear what you think is going on and what to do about it."

Cameron's expression could only be described as coy and flirtatious, and Gabby caught herself about to shake her head at the whole scene. Dr. Moreno had instantly sized the woman up, that was for sure, and Gabby was torn between admiration and disgust at how quickly and easily he'd had her eating out of his hand. While not even bothering to introduce himself to Gabby or ask who she was. The man was royal, all right. Royally rude.

"Tell me what's been happening." He sat and directed his attention solely to Cameron, as though Gabby wasn't even there, and the actress told him all about her symptoms as he looked at the vital signs Gabby had recorded. He took his time speaking with her, acting more like they were at a cocktail party than in a hospital room. But of course Cameron, who was always more than happy to talk at length about herself, basked in the attention as he asked all kinds of questions about her life and career in addition to the ones related to her health.

As the minutes stretched on, Gabby fidgeted, wondering when in the world he was going to get on with what needed to be done and have her administer the meds Cameron needed. At the same time, she had to grudgingly give him credit for completely relaxing their patient.

Then that credit evaporated when he reached for gloves, obviously planning to give her an internal exam.

"Excuse me, Dr. Moreno, but did you see in the chart that I just gave her an exam about thirty minutes ago? That she was already dilated to two centimeters?" Gabby asked.

He turned to her with one eyebrow quirked. "And you are…?"

"I'm Gabriella Cain, head midwife here at The Hollywood Hills Clinic."

"Now that I am here to care for Ms. Fontaine, I will take care of future internal exams. I'm sure you know they need to be limited in cases of early onset labor."

What the…? Anger began to burn in Gabby's chest. "Yes, I am aware of that, Dr. Moreno. Which is why I feel you should wait to do another. I was about to get the mag sulfate drip started, followed by the steroids, then do an ultrasound."

"I prefer to not rely on others' examinations and opinions, as that normally isn't in the best interests of my patient. However, if you've done an internal exam, I won't do another at the moment." He turned away from Gabby again, and she stared at the back of his silky dark head, hardly able to believe his arrogantly dismissive attitude. *His* patient? She'd worked with some doctors with domineering attitudes before, but this guy got first place for jerk of the year.

"It's good that you're dilated to no more than two centimeters," he said to Cameron as he looked at Gabby's notes. "Although that is clearly an indication of preterm labor, there are things we can do to try to make that cease, and at the same time give baby a chance to grow more."

"So it is preterm labor. I was so hoping it wasn't." Cameron's white teeth worried her lip, her eyes wide. "Do you think whatever you do to try to stop it will work?"

"It often does, so we will hope for the best." He lifted

his tall frame from the stool he'd been perched on, moving to stand beside the bed and hold Cameron's hand between both of his, a smile on his face some people might think was charming. "And if baby says, *Oh, no, Mama, I'm coming anyway*, we will at least have time to give you steroids to help her little lungs function better when she arrives. So we will do that without delay. Okay?"

"All right. Whatever you think," Cameron said, all grateful smiles. "Thank you so, so much, Doctor."

"Please, call me Rafael."

Whatever you think. Thank you so, so much... Gabby gritted her teeth and told herself she couldn't feel bothered by Cameron's immediate agreement to the same treatment she'd initially refused to agree to when Gabby had told her exactly the same thing. It was no secret doctors got more respect than midwives from many patients, and an über-handsome doctor who, by the way, happened to be a prince too? Jerk or not, it was no surprise that status-conscious Cameron was all too happy to go along with whatever he suggested.

"Bien." He stood and turned to Gabby, and his warm expression cooled to one of professionalism. "I'd assume you have the mag sulfate and steroid ready?" Those startling green eyes slowly scanned the area again before pinning hers again with one dark eyebrow raised. "Except perhaps I should not assume that. When I first walked in I was shocked to see the state of this room, which is, well, I must say, terribly disorganized. I'm frankly very surprised by this, considering the stellar reputation of The Hollywood Hills Clinic and knowing James Rothsberg's perfectionism."

The irritation that had been simmering in her chest burst into a full conflagration of anger that surged through her blood and made her brain burn. Who did this guy think he was? Friend or no friend of James, prince or no prince, he had no right to waltz in like he owned the place, give it his version of the white-glove test, then criticize her without knowing a thing about the patients and medical situations she'd been taking care of for the past ten hours.

"I was in the process of cleaning and reorganizing it from an earlier, lengthy delivery when Cameron arrived in what might have been an emergency situation. I deemed taking care of her and her baby was a lot more important than tidying and prepping a room that could be tidied and prepped later. And the meds *are* ready."

She stalked to the counter, gathering the items together and wishing she could throw them at his arrogant, judgmental face. He reached for them, his hand briefly touching hers, and it ticked her off even more that the feel of his skin brushing hers sent some kind of weird electric shimmer up her arm. The sensation could have been mistaken for attraction, if there had been anything attractive about the man.

Well, there were all those superficially attractive things, but she wasn't a woman interested in slick, glossy men. Or any kind of man anymore, really.

With grudging respect, though, Gabby did have to admire how quickly and efficiently his long fingers administered the drugs, all the while keeping up a smoothly distracting conversation with their patient.

"All set," he said to Cameron, giving her a warm and reassuring smile. "Now we wait, keep you comfortable, and check baby periodically through ultrasound and monitoring."

"Thank you, Rafael. I'm *so* glad you and Gabby are the ones taking care of me."

And Gabby was glad the next shift midwife would

be arriving soon to deal with Cameron and Dr. Moreno. Not to mention that she was way overdue for a major nap.

"How about deciding what you'd like to have for dinner?" Gabby said as she brought her another sparkling water, along with a menu of options for her meal. The onsite Michelin-starred chef was amazing, and even the pickiest patients loved the elegant and trendy foods he prepared. "The midwife on the next shift will be checking on you throughout the night to make sure you're comfortable. Then tomorrow morning I'll be back to take care of you. In the afternoon it'll be time to administer another steroid dose."

"But I don't want another midwife," Cameron said, a twisting pout on her lips that had Gabby wondering how in the world she managed to still look so pretty doing it. "I want you to stay here with me tonight, Gabby."

The fatigue Gabby had felt earlier was back in spades. She had a feeling if she closed her eyes she might fall asleep on her feet like a horse, and the vision of curling up in her own comfy bed and getting a solid night's sleep nearly had her moaning, but she knew Cameron. And Cameron's expectations. The Hollywood Hills Clinic was known for its exceptional medical care, and that included going above and beyond in every way.

Which meant she'd be spending the night here again.

"I appreciate you wanting me with you, Cameron. I—"

"Your staying here is important, since you are familiar with our special patient and her physical condition and worries," Rafael interrupted smoothly. "Here is my contact information. Please don't hesitate to get in touch with me for any reason."

Did the man think he was boss of the world? Gabby

felt like smacking that seemingly sincere smile from his handsome face as he handed her an elegantly embossed card, then turned to give one to their patient. When Cameron reached for hers, she clasped his hand along with it for a lingering moment, practically batting her long lashes at him as she smiled back.

"Thank you so much, Rafael. I can't tell you how much I appreciate your help and expertise during this terrifying time."

"It's beyond my pleasure. It is my calling to help mamas and their babies, whether a pregnancy is smooth and uneventful or high risk and worrying. I promise to take care of you and *bebé* to the best of my ability."

Whereas Gabby and most other nurses and doctors didn't? The guy was pure egotistical arrogance in a white coat, absolutely no doubt about that. And Gabby intended to tell him so, though somehow she'd have to tone down the strength of the language she'd really like to use when she did.

"As I started to say a moment ago, Cameron, I'm more than happy to stay," she said, giving Dr. Moreno a pointed look she hoped he interpreted correctly—which was to tell him to keep his guest-in-this-hospital nose in his own business. "I'll sleep better knowing I can check regularly on how you're doing, and hopefully me being here will help you sleep better too."

"Thank you, Gabby. I will sleep better."

"Why don't you rest now and watch a little TV? I'll be back in a few minutes to find out what you've decided to order for dinner." She turned to Dr. Full-of-Himself and somehow kept her voice cordial. "May I speak to you privately in my office, Dr. Moreno?"

He inclined his head again, and she sensed him following her from the room and down the marble-tiled hallway, past large windows with beautiful views Gabby normally enjoyed, but not at that moment. Right then, she had only one thing on her mind, which was giving Rafael Moreno a piece of it.

She stopped in front of the open door of her office and gestured for him to go inside but he stopped with her.

"Ladies first," he said as he mirrored her gesture.

A man with good manners was usually appealing, but this didn't feel like good manners. It felt more like he was just being controlling again, wanting things to be the way he wanted them and not giving her respect for the fact that it was *her* office. Which meant she should be calling the shots at that moment, even if it was something as simple as who entered the room first.

The smile she stuck on her face was stiff and fake and she didn't care if he saw through it. While part of her knew it wasn't something worth arguing about, he'd irritated her so much already she found herself digging in her heels. "No, I insist. You are a guest here at the clinic, after all." And if that didn't give him a strong hint that he'd overstepped his bounds, she was about to tell him so much more directly.

Those silky eyebrows rose at her, and their gazes clashed for several heartbeats until he inclined his head and stepped into the room. She shut the door behind her, not wanting anyone to overhear their conversation, and when she turned to look at him she had that oxygen-sucked-from-the-room feeling again. His height and the breadth of his shoulders made the room seem to shrink, and his erect posture and the utter self-assurance of his demeanor compounded the effect until she felt she couldn't breathe.

Except breathing was necessary to give him a piece

of her mind. Her mouth suddenly dry as sandpaper, she hoped he couldn't sense her discomfiture as she stepped behind her desk instead of having them sit in the two chairs side by side, wanting to send another message that she was in charge of the maternity wing and its midwives and he should treat her accordingly.

"Please sit," she said as she perched herself in her swivel chair.

But of course he didn't. He simply stared down at her, and she suddenly felt like a bug-eyed hamster being eyed by a hawk. Rafael Moreno, standing there all confident and imperious, had utterly ruined the message she'd tried to send by sitting behind the desk, so now what was she supposed to do? Sit there craning her neck up at him while giving him a dressing-down? Or bob back up like a jack-in-the-box? Either one would make her look foolish and, worse, completely lacking in power and authority.

Damn the man.

"What is it you wish to discuss with me, Ms. Cain?"

She huffed out a breath, trying hard to regain some semblance of equilibrium, and slowly stood again to look him in the eye. Or as much as that was possible, considering he still had a good six or seven inches in height on her. "I know you are James's friend, and I'm told you are good at what you do. Also that you are part of a royal family, which is perhaps why you feel you can do as you please."

"I can do as I please."

The arrogance of the words wasn't diminished by the even modulation of his deep voice. Her heartbeat upped its tempo to double time, and that burning sensation prickled her scalp again. "Maybe you can in a lot of places, but not here, Dr. Moreno. I may be a midwife and not a physician, but I assure you that I'm the person in charge of the day-to-day operation of The Hollywood Hills Clinic's maternity ward. While I am grateful you came quickly to see Cameron when James requested you to, I don't appreciate you walking in and just taking over. Completely ignoring the notes I made on Ms. Fontaine's chart and utterly dismissing my medical opinion and recommendation. Even worse, you said and did it all in front of the patient. That was insulting and rude, and frankly could have very well undermined her confidence in me, my knowledge, and my skills."

The expression on his smooth, angular features didn't change, but in the depths of his eyes there was a sudden, dangerous glint. Her breath caught and held in her chest during the long pause that crackled between them before he finally spoke. "Anything else?"

"Yes, actually."

Gabby slowly walked around from behind the desk, taking that moment to get the air moving in her lungs again, hoping to calm both her tripping heart and her frustration. For the first time in her life she wished she was taller than her five feet six inches, but was so angry she came to stand nearly toe to toe with him anyway.

"I resent you saying that room was a mess, that it was substandard, and by association that *I'm* substandard. Even worse that you said it in front of our patient as well. I work very hard to keep my ward immaculately clean, organized and running smoothly, to keep these rooms as luxurious and beautiful as James insists they be, and our patients expect. But as an obstetrician you should certainly know that when there's any kind of medical emergency, like the difficult twin births I was dealing with prior to Cameron arriving, it tends to mess up a hospital room. Is it possible that you never give that a thought, though, since an OB can often run in, catch a baby, play hero, then leave the cleanup to someone else?"

"I assure you," he said in a silky-soft voice at odds with that glint sparking in his eyes, "I am well versed in hospital room chaos, having worked in all kinds of clinics around the world. *I* resent *your* implication that I'm a spoiled and selfish man unwilling to take on any task required of me. That is an unacceptable insult. Who and what I am is a doctor who prides himself on paying attention to every detail, and the fact is that the disarray of that room was obvious evidence that I had to take control of the situation."

The small gap between them closed, and with his narrowed gaze so close, so intense Gabby found she had to break their eye contact before she got dizzy from it. Which then had her staring at his mouth, at lips that were hard and uncompromising, and somehow at the same time so soft and sensually shaped that her stomach did a strange little flip that didn't feel at all like the anger pumping through her veins.

"And I assure you that was a misconception, and you *taking control of the situation* was both unnecessary and unwelcome." Gabby resisted the urge to stroke her hand down her throat, swiping away the sweat she was sure must be forming there. Why did it suddenly seem so hot in this room? Was it her anger making her heart quiver, and was it her imagination that all that heat seemed to be shimmering right between them, practically pouring from his big, masculine body? "If you end up coming back to see Cameron, and I frankly would prefer a different physician do so, I would appreciate you showing me respect in front of our patient, and I will continue to show you that same respect."

"Oh, I'll be back, Ms. Cain, have no doubt about that. Whether you like it or not. When I make a commitment to a friend like James, and to a patient, I always see it through to the end." His eyes were still narrowed, his words still spoken in that silky, soft tone that sounded odd, coming from lips that had been firmly clamped together the whole time she'd spoken. Then, to her utter shock, he reached for her hand and lifted it to those beautiful lips, pressing them to the back of it.

Both soft and firm, he kept them there for three long seconds, causing that weirdly disconcerting spark to fly up her arm again. Then he released it and, without another word, turned and strode out the door.

Gabby stared blindly at the wall beside her door, absently running her palm from the back of her other hand up her arm, feeling the gooseflesh still making all the little hairs stand at attention. "Well, Gabby, that went well," she muttered to herself, barely able to catch her breath. "When it comes to verbal sparring to handle a problem, that man is clearly way out of your league."

Which left her with a very difficult question. What she was going to do next to keep him from taking over her entire ward?

CHAPTER TWO

"YOU'VE ALWAYS BEEN a workaholic, but your schedule seems insane to me," Rafael said as he sat across from James, glad his friend had finally found time to stop by the cliffside home Rafael was renting. "I thought I might be moving on from L.A. before we had a chance to share another drink."

"Hey, I do things other than work."

"Like what? Are you taking up golf?" Rafael asked with a grin, since he knew the man had zero interest in spending that much time on a game.

That drew a return grin from James. "No, but I do have a date in about…one hour," he said, glancing at his watch. "And what do you mean, you might be moving on from L.A. soon? Is rolling stone Rafael already thinking about leaving? I thought you'd come here to go into hiding for a while."

"Doesn't seem to have worked too well. One or the other of my parents calls me practically daily with disapproving updates on the photos and completely exaggerated stories still showing up in the gossip magazines about me."

"If you didn't date strippers, maybe you wouldn't have that problem."

"I didn't even know she'd been a stripper until it was

splashed across all the papers." He shook his head, wondering why everyone had to make such a big deal out of it anyway. "But if I hear one more word from my family about having to find a 'suitable' girlfriend, I may just become a monk."

"Like there's any chance of that," James said with a smirk. "One of the reasons I always liked hanging out with you was because women flock around a prince like ants to a piece of candy. A good way for me to meet the cast-offs."

"Because you have such a problem with meeting women," Rafael said dryly. "Didn't you just tell me you have a date tonight?"

"Yeah." James's face instantly settled into an oddly serious expression, and it struck Rafael that his friend might be getting back into a relationship with Mila Brightman, his former fiancée.

"I heard you're having to spend time with Mila now you're working with her charity," he said casually, hoping James would talk to him about it if he felt a need to. "Are you seeing her again?"

"No. That was over long ago." James seemed to be studying the condensation droplets on his iced-tea glass very intently, and Rafael wondered if it was to avoid looking him in the eye. "But I do think dating someone new is a good idea to, you know, distract me from thinking about the past."

Rafael frowned. He knew their breakup had been hard on both James and Mila, but it had been James's idea, after all. How much was he still bothered by it? "Maybe you and Mila—"

"I don't really want to talk about it." James set his glass down and put on the cool, professional face Rafael had seen many times when James wanted to put distance between himself and others. "Tell me about how things went with Cameron Fontaine. And by the way, I don't think I've told you how much I appreciate you seeing her."

"I'm glad you asked me. It's what I do. Not to mention that not working and having to lie low in L.A. has been getting a little tedious, so I'm happy to be at the clinic." Oddly, the first thing James's question instantly brought to mind wasn't his patient but a certain gorgeous midwife who was an all-too-attractive combination of warmth and smarts and toughness.

Thinking back, he realized he'd deserved the one-two punch she'd given him in her office. He should have shown her immediate respect instead of making her earn it, but in some of the places he'd worked, it had been important to make sure everyone knew what they were doing before you trusted them to. In spite of the chaotic condition of the room, it had been obvious that she was an expert when it came to the medical care of the patients. And wasn't afraid to point it out in no uncertain terms to anyone who doubted that.

"What's with that smile on your face?" James asked, quirking his eyebrow. "Did you fall in lust with Cameron?"

"No." That would be a snowy day in the desert, and he practically laughed at the question. Cameron Fontaine was the kind of self-absorbed woman he met all too often and had no interest in even for just sex.

He wouldn't admit to James that the woman he'd felt a stirring of lust for had been the clinic's head midwife. A woman with a fiery temper to match the golden fire of her hair. The last thing he needed was the complication of dating someone he had to work with. Not to mention that dating anyone at that particular moment was asking for more trouble from the press and anger and disapproval from his family.

After the tabloids had blown up again with the juicy story of his latest girlfriend, his parents had insisted he stop embarrassing them. It all seemed so ridiculous since he'd dated the woman barely a month before they'd stopped seeing each other, which was how he liked to keep it. Any longer than that and a woman had a tendency to start thinking long term, and he had no intention of doing forever after with anyone. His brother had taken care of marrying to provide heirs, and saddled himself with a woman who didn't even like him much. And the picture-perfect partnership of his parents' arranged marriage? It didn't hint at the cool distance between them, or question why they were on different continents half the time.

No, Rafael was never going to get stuck in some passionless marriage. He liked his freedom and planned to keep it, thank you very much. Lying low to let his parents simmer down a little was the price he had to occasionally pay for that freedom. With any luck, they'd soon stop throwing "suitable" women his way, wanting to torture him with the kind of loveless marriage they had.

"I'm not sure we're going to be able to stop Cameron's labor," he told James, "but I'm hoping to be able to get her at least a second steroid dose before it happens. I'm heading over there soon to see how she's doing."

"Good. You're the best at what you do, and I hope she knows that. I'm guessing she doesn't mind that her doctor is a prince either."

Probably true, but his royal status was something Rafael found to be a far bigger burden than a benefit. "I'll text you with an update after I see her."

"I'd appreciate that." James stood, so Rafael did too. "I'd better get cleaned up for my date."

He had to wonder how Mila would react to seeing photos of James with a doubtless beautiful woman in the media that followed him around as much as they followed him, but it wasn't any of his business.

No, his present business was to keep a low profile and his own face out of the tabloids for as long as possible.

Gabby poured herself another cup of coffee, desperate to somehow keep her heavy eyelids from closing. During the night, when Cameron had slept, she'd managed to grab an hour or two of rest, but had jumped to attention every time Cameron had woken up, both worried that her labor might be advancing. That, combined with her recent double shifts prior to Cameron's arrival, had left her without much in the way of reserve energy.

Gulping at the dark, hot liquid, Gabby moved to Cameron's bedside again. "Any changes in the way you're feeling?"

"No." Cameron folded her arms across her chest and pouted up at Gabby. "And I'm awfully tired of just lying here. The only thing that makes it bearable at all is the good care you're taking of me."

"That's nice of you to say." Her words managed to fractionally perk Gabby up since, inside, she'd become a little tired of catering to the woman's every whim. At least she apparently appreciated it. "I'm doing everything I can to keep you comfortable, and hopefully help baby stay in there a little longer."

"I know I should apologize for being a tad complaining. Even grumpy occasionally. It's just so tiresome being in this bed, but I know you understand that."

"I do understand. Would you like your pillows plumped again?"

At her nod, Gabby complied, thinking it was good the pillows were faux down to prevent any allergens from being in the room, as real down would have been plumped to death by now. Cameron's word "tad" was an understatement, but Gabby was pretty sure the woman truly didn't realize that "Diva" should be her middle name.

"It's not easy getting comfortable, sitting in a bed all day, or to keep from getting bored. I'll bring you another book to read, if you like."

"Maybe later." She leaned back against her pillows with a long-suffering sigh. Just as Gabby was about to creep away, Cameron opened her eyes and started talking again. "And of course the other thing making it bearable to be here is Rafael. He's just the sweetest, dreamiest thing, don't you think? And he's obviously a wonderful doctor."

Dreamy, maybe, when it came to his looks. But sweet? Definitely not. It was an effort, but Gabby managed to keep a smile on her face and sort of agree. "He has an excellent reputation. I'm glad you like him."

"Like him? I just love him! Adore him!" Cameron gushed. "I feel so lucky that he happens to be in Los Angeles right now. It seems like fate, doesn't it?"

Privately, she didn't think it was fate, unless the universe had decided to challenge Gabby by making life at the clinic difficult, having to work with someone as full of himself as Rafael Moreno. But she was a professional and could handle it, no matter what. And, to look at the positive, at least Cameron was happy.

She glanced at her watch. "If you're not going to

sleep right now, I'd like to get another ultrasound of baby, then give your next steroid injection."

"Should we wait for Rafael?" Anxious blue eyes met hers. "He said he'd be here this afternoon, and I'm sure he will be."

Damn the man for insisting he be in charge of everything, and basically telling the patient not to trust her. "I believe Dr. Moreno was simply being cautious because he doesn't personally know me. But midwives are highly trained in all aspects of pregnancy and delivery, including caring for high-risk patients. You can trust me completely."

"Of course I trust you. In fact I'm— I— Oh, my God!" Cameron sat bolt upright in bed, her eyes suddenly wide and scared as she stared at Gabby.

Her heart picked up speed because the look on Cameron's face didn't seem like overdramatic acting this time. She reached for Cameron's hand. "What? What is it?"

"I think… I think my waters just broke!"

Oh, no. Gabby immediately checked to be sure Cameron wasn't experiencing some other sensation that made her think it was her membranes breaking, but there was no doubt about it.

Heart sinking, she prayed the steroids had gotten baby's lungs developed enough for the premature infant to be all right. She perched on the side of the bed and reached for Cameron's hands again. "You're right. Your waters have broken, which means your amniotic sac is no longer intact. And that means baby has to be born, otherwise there's risk of infection. I'll call Dr. Moreno and get him here right away."

"Oh, yes, you must!" Cameron's manicured nails dug into Gabby's skin. "Tell him it's an emergency!"

"I'm sure he'll get here as quickly as possible. Try not to worry, okay? With luck, you'll have a smooth, uncomplicated delivery, and baby will be just fine. I'll be right back."

Gabby managed to extricate her hands from Cameron's grip and made a quick note of the time her waters had broken and an estimation of the amount of fluid before she moved into the hallway to pull up Dr. Moreno's number on her cell. Hopefully, he wasn't at lunch with some bigwig, or with a woman after a date the night before and not answering the phone because of it. And why that thought would make her tummy tighten uncomfortably, she had no idea. Must just be concern for Cameron, because she knew the woman would worry about having a different doctor come to deliver the baby.

But he answered after only two rings, and Gabby let out a relieved breath. "Dr. Moreno, it's Gabby Cain. Cameron's waters broke a few minutes ago and—"

"I'll be right there."

She stared at the now dead phone. Now, there was a man of few words. And questions. Which was probably a good thing since the sooner he arrived, the sooner he'd wield his potent charm on Cameron to keep her calmer in a way Gabby wasn't always able to accomplish.

Back in Cameron's room, she plumped her pillows yet again and checked her vital signs once more. "Dr. Moreno's on his way."

"I knew he'd come right away. I'm just praying he gets here before my baby does!"

"It usually takes a while for contractions to get strong enough for baby to be born. Are you feeling any yet?"

"I… I can't tell for sure. I feel very crampy, like there's a fist inside my belly. It doesn't feel good. And my back really aches. Is it going to get worse? I hate pain! I don't do well with it at all!"

The famous blue eyes staring at her were so scared and anxious Gabby gave her hands another reassuring squeeze. "How contractions feel varies a lot from woman to woman. Some go from feeling cramps that become more intense as labor progresses, and others experience pretty intense contractions. But all that is helping your baby be born, so it's nothing to be afraid of."

"How long will it take?"

"That varies too." Gabby wasn't about to tell her it could be just a few hours or as long as twenty-four or more. If Cameron was stressing now, that would probably send her into a panic. "I'm going to check your cervix to see how much it's thinning and dilating, which may give us a clue how far along you are."

"Okay, but I want an epidural, because it already hurts a lot! So please call whoever does that right away. Unless Rafael will do that himself?"

"Epidurals are done by an anesthesiologist. We'll let Dr. Moreno decide when that should happen." Since he'd wanted to be in charge, Gabby was more than happy to pass the epidural discussion on to him.

It seemed Gabby had barely plumped Cameron's pillows a third time and gotten ice for her to suck on when Rafael Moreno strode into the room as if he owned the place. All tall and powerful and regal, his mere presence seemed to electrify the air. His gaze trapped hers, and everything in the room seemed to fade away except for that intense connection. Suddenly she felt a little unsteady on her feet, but that was probably sheer exhaustion.

"Thank God you're here, Rafael!"

Cameron's voice snapped her back to reality. *Focus*

on your job and patient, silly, not the handsome prince.
Um, what had she been about to do just then? "Hello,
Dr. Moreno. As I told you, Cameron's had PPROM. I
was about to check her cervical thinning and dilation."

"What's PPROM?" Cameron sounded alarmed, and
Gabby gave her a pat.

"Sorry, I was talking to the doctor. It's just an ac-
ronym for preterm premature rupture of membranes,
which just means your waters broke before baby is full
term."

"Let's check how far along you are, Cameron, okay?"
he asked. Rafael donned gloves and began the internal
exam, smiling at their patient and asking questions as
he did. Somehow he managed to have her smiling back
and laughing at a few of his remarks, and Gabby had to
grudgingly admit he had a wonderful bedside manner,
obviously used to dealing with even the most nervous
and difficult kinds of patients.

When he finished the exam he snapped off his gloves
and seemed to take a moment to think of how he wanted
to present his findings. "Your special little one is, as we
know, very anxious to arrive. You are already dilated
to six centimeters, which is a bit surprising for a first
baby, though of course your *bebé* has been impatient
for some time, hasn't she?"

Gabby stared at him in surprise and had to bite her
tongue to keep from blurting out something like *You're
kidding!* Six centimeters was way further along than
she'd expected, and she had to admit she was glad Rafael was already there, or she would have been concerned that he might not get to the clinic in time, which
would have worried Cameron at a time she didn't need
more worries.

"Oh, my Lord, then I need to get an epidural right

now, don't I?" The blue eyes staring at Rafael quickly became panicky as she apparently experienced a contraction. Panting for a moment, she leaned forward to grab his hand. "I hate pain. You can make sure I don't have any more pain, right? Fix that for me, please."

So used to addressing laboring mother's worries, Gabby opened her mouth before realizing Cameron had asked Rafael, not her. And much as it rankled a bit, since she was used to either delivering babies on her own or being part of a team with the obstetrician, she managed to let him answer instead.

"I have already spoken to the anesthesiologist, as I know you want to be as comfortable as possible," he said in that soothing voice that was also, damn it, incredibly sexy. "Now that we know you're dilated enough to receive the pain relief, we'll get the anesthesiologist here pronto."

He turned the power of his smile on Gabby, and she had to admit to a warmth filling her chest that he'd included her with the "we" word. Though why she should care if he did or didn't give her that lip service, she had no clue.

"Gabriella, would you please ask Dr. Smith to come now?"

"Yes, Dr. Moreno."

"Please, call me Rafael. You and Cameron and I are all friends trusting one another here to bring baby into the world, yes?"

"Um, yes." No. Not friends. Colleagues. Co-workers. But that simple word—*friends*—made her chest feel warmer even as it contracted with pain as she went to phone the doctor. Her last relationship had taught her that counting on true friendship and closeness with a man was a mistake. That trust was a mirage. An elusive shimmer of light that could disintegrate and disappear in an instant when times got tough.

Briefly closing her eyes, she willed away the hurt, stuffing it down into the deep, dark corner where it usually resided, until unexpected moments like this dragged it to the surface. But this moment wasn't about her past. This moment was about helping a mother who would soon hold a new life in her arms, a precious child she obviously wanted with all her heart.

Tears unexpectedly stung her eyes, and she angrily swiped them aside. She delivered babies for a living, and usually felt nothing but joy for the new parents, new families. So what was it about this moment, this delivery that was bringing memories to the surface that were better left behind?

The question made her wonder if, somehow, some way, for some bizarre reason, it was Rafael's presence that was making her feel so strange. But, of course, that made no sense. She didn't even know him. Didn't want to.

She kept her life simple. Worked a lot of hours, taking on as many double shifts as possible. Went out with friends occasionally, but that was pretty much it. Could it be that after such a long time of keeping to herself, being around an exceptionally attractive man, annoying or not, had her neglected hormones all charged up or something?

Yes. That had to be it. And knowing that was all it was helped her get her equilibrium back. Time to quit thinking and remembering and start working. She quickly contacted the anesthesiologist, then headed back to Cameron's room.

"You checked Cameron for her group B beta strep culture, yes?" Rafael asked from his position by Cameron's bedside, holding her hand the way she would have, in a way she couldn't remember ever seeing an OB interact with a patient.

"I did. Status was uncertain, so I gave her a second dose of antibiotics in case it's an issue."

"Good." He nodded and stood, and Gabby found herself fixated on the way his broad shoulders and chest filled out his scrubs, how his tanned forearms looked more like they belonged to an athlete than a man who caught babies for a living. Thankfully, her inappropriate perusal was interrupted as Dr. Smith strode in. Face heating, she turned away, hoping to heck no one had noticed her staring.

The doctors shook hands before the anesthesiologist introduced himself to their patient. "Cameron, I promise I'm not going far, just giving Dr. Smith and Gabriella some room," Rafael said. "I'm sure Dr. Smith will take good care of you, and of course you are in Gabriella's excellent hands as well. See you shortly, okay?"

And Gabby sure as heck needed a little space and a breather from Rafael Moreno. She did her darnedest to focus on only Cameron, but as he walked by her she found it impossible to not be aware of the pull of his green eyes, the angular shape of his smooth, golden features, and the sheer masculine force of his presence.

To cover up her confusion over this odd discomfort, she nearly asked tartly if it was okay for her to do an internal exam now, but resisted the urge. She was pretty certain that antagonizing him would just ratchet up this peculiar sizzle between them, and whether it was animosity or something else, Gabby wasn't sure anymore.

Rafael left her to monitor Cameron's labor progress and take care of her, checking in only occasionally, which Gabby was glad about on more than one level. She couldn't deny feeling pleased that he'd obviously come to trust she knew what she was doing, then inwardly scolded herself for that. He should have assumed she was competent at her job, not the other way around, especially knowing James Rothsberg and what he demanded of everyone who worked at the clinic he'd founded.

Rafael not hovering around the room, monitoring everything she did, was another good thing, though why she kept finding him so distracting she had no idea. The man was an expert at turning his charm on and off at will.

"How long is this going to take, for heaven's sake? I thought she was coming soon." Cameron's voice had gotten steadily more frustrated as her contractions got closer together, and Gabby prayed for both their sakes she was close to being ready to push.

"Your baby has a mind of her own already, Cameron, doesn't she?" she said, keeping her voice light. "First she's in a hurry, then she takes her time." A bit like her mother. "The good news is her heart rate looks perfect on the monitor. Let me check your dilation again. Looks like the epidural is keeping you comfortable, isn't it?"

"I guess. If you can call starving to death comfortable." Cameron sighed dramatically as she crunched another of the tiny round ice cubes Gabby had replaced in her cup three times now. "You'd think that with modern medicine, giving birth could be completely pain-free."

"A few decades back, women were given morphine and scopolamine to put them into a twilight sleep. They'd hallucinate, then not remember the birth at all afterwards. I don't know about you, but I'd want to remember forever the moment my baby arrived in this world."

It wasn't the kind of memory she'd wish on anyone,

but it was still hers. To rail against, to shrink from, to cherish.

She could see him as clearly as if he were even now in her arms. Stillborn. One simple word that perfectly described a lifeless infant.

Motionless. Quiet. Angelic and beautiful.

Every detail of that day was burned into her very soul. And she prayed it wasn't a memory Cameron would ever have to share.

"I suppose," Cameron said grudgingly. "So, how many centimeters dilated am I?"

Grateful for the distraction, Gabby checked and was surprised and more than happy at what she found. "Guess what? You're at ten centimeters and fully effaced. Time for baby to come into the world."

"Oh, my gosh—really? Don't you need to call Rafael? What if she comes out before he gets here?"

Gabby wanted to remind Cameron that she was a qualified midwife, fully capable of delivering a baby on her own, but managed to keep her mouth shut. Besides, she'd be lying if she didn't admit she kind of wanted to see Rafael at work. "I'll give him a call right now."

"No need. I'm here," a deep voice said, and Gabby glanced up to see Rafael looking relaxed yet wired, obviously ready to get to work. "I had a feeling your little *bebé* had finally made up her mind."

"That's because you and I are *simpatico*, don't you think? How much longer?"

"Time to be the strong woman you are and get pushing with the next contraction, *sí*?"

Cameron nodded, and Gabby was surprised at how quickly her next contraction came. Rafael was calmly encouraging as long minutes passed, stretching into a half hour, with their patient becoming more frustrated and impatient with each push.

"My friend had her baby sucked out with something. Can't you just do that?" she gasped.

"Ah, 'sucked out.' That's a funny way to put it, though accurate, I suppose." Across their patient, his amused eyes met Gabby's and she felt her lips curving. "But it is not a good idea to use the vacuum on a premature infant, and you're doing well. Isn't she, Gabriella?"

"Wonderful. Just remember to breathe with the next push, okay?" She reached for Cameron's hand, stroking it. "Puff, puff, puff. In and out. Tuck down your chin when you push to give it some extra oomph, okay?"

"Extra oomph." Rafael's laughing eyes met hers again. "You Americans use amusing words. I must take notes."

"Well, do it some other time," Cameron said tartly. "I'm more interested in getting this baby out than helping you write a thesaurus of American words."

"Just trying to distract you from your hard work, Cameron. Another push now, please."

He turned those green eyes back to their patient and Gabby realized she'd been briefly mesmerized— again—by that gaze. She glanced at the monitor wrapped around Cameron's belly as she pushed again, and the reading jerked her mind back to work. "Fetal monitor is showing a decreased variability, Dr. Moreno."

He glanced at it, too, and his expression turned serious. "Keep an eye on it during the next contractions."

"What? What does that mean? Is something wrong?" Cameron nearly moaned the questions as she pushed again.

"Baby's heartbeat is a little flat. But that may just mean she's sleeping."

"Sleeping? How could she possibly be sleeping when she's about to be born?"

"She's warm and cozy inside her mama, and also tiny because she is early. So sleeping is a possibility, though I agree it seems odd that babies sometimes are sleep before being born, doesn't it?"

His eyes met Gabby's, and she read the message in their serious depths. He wanted her to pay close attention to the monitor, and she gave him a small nod. She pressed the intercom around her neck as she watched the baby's heartbeat. "I'll give Neonatal a quick call to get them here and ready."

As Gabby spoke soothingly and encouragingly, Rafael interrupted. "Baby's head is crowning, Cameron! Not too much longer now. You are doing such a good job."

"Yes, a few more good pushes and hopefully she'll be here! Tuck that chin in again and give us another push, okay?" Gabby wiped Cameron's forehead at the same time she glanced again at the monitor and froze for an instant. "Heart rate's flat on the monitor, Dr. Moreno."

"Stop pushing, Cameron," he said in a sharp tone.

"Stop?" The woman looked at him, her tired eyes wide. "What do you mean? I thought you said her head was crowning!"

"The cord is around her neck. I need to get it off before she can arrive."

CHAPTER THREE

CAMERON LET OUT a long cry full of dismay and fear, and Gabby held her hand tighter. "Hang in there, Cameron. Rafael's getting his fingers under the cord."

Gabby kept her voice calm and quiet but her chest squeezed hard when she saw the cord wasn't just around the baby's neck, it was wrapped round a full three times between her collarbone and her tiny chin. Dear God, this was the last thing a preterm newborn already bound to be in distress should go through.

Throat tight, she watched Rafael carefully wiggle his fingers between the cord and the baby's neck. Gabby was pretty sure she didn't breathe at all as the long, tense seconds passed while he worked gently to loosen it.

"What's happening?" Cameron asked in a high-pitched voice. "Is...is she okay? Oh, God."

"Working on it. Hold on."

His fingers finally loosened the cord enough to slip it over the baby's head, and air spilled from Gabby's lungs in a relieved whoosh. "Cord's clear now, Cameron. Get ready."

"Looks like she's been doing synchronized swimming in there to get so tangled up," Rafael said as he flashed a quick grin.

How he managed to look so completely collected,

Gabby wasn't sure, and hoped she always exuded the same calm confidence whenever she had to deal with a tricky situation. "Rafael has her head and shoulders now. One more big push, okay?"

"Good. Perfect. And…here she is!" Rafael had the infant in his hands, his dazzling smile lighting up the room as he held her. "You were *magnifico*! *Bravo!*"

Gabby quickly laid a towel on Cameron's chest so Rafael could briefly place the baby there for Cameron to see her for just a moment as the neonatal team swooped into the room. Cameron looked down at the tiny little face, not a good color yet, still too purple, but Gabby's heart lifted when she saw the infant was already pinking up.

"My sweet precious," Cameron whispered. Two wide eyes stared back at her, and the new mother promptly burst into noisy tears that pulled hard at Gabby's heart. "I love you so much. Please be okay. Please be healthy and normal and not damaged because I didn't eat enough and worked too much and squeezed my belts too tight when you were growing. Worrying about myself instead of you. Please, Skye. Please be the perfect angel I dreamed you would be."

Skye. Cameron had airily claimed she had no idea what she'd name her baby, but Gabby had always suspected she just hadn't been ready to share it. And as she looked at the tiny, scrawny baby's blue eyes, she got choked up herself, knowing so well the guilt Cameron felt. Worries she hadn't shared with Gabby. And she understood. Because she, too, didn't share her guilt with anyone.

Skye was exactly the right choice for the new life in front of her. A pure and precious gift, like any baby was to its mother. Even those who never had their chance to grow up.

"Skye is a beautiful name." Gabby gently wiped Cameron's perspiring brow once more, thinking how the woman looked more beautiful at that moment than all the times her makeup was immaculate and her hair perfectly done by her professional stylists. Having worked so hard to bring her baby into the world, she looked vulnerable and scared and more like a real person than Gabby had ever seen her—not at all the ultra-confident screen persona and diva actress she projected to the world most of the time.

For a moment, she let herself watch a little longer. To see Skye whisked to the heat lamp by the neonatal team, a bulb suction quickly clearing her nose before the small oxygen mask was placed over her head. To marvel at the little body being cleaned up and swaddled tight as Gabby would have done if the baby hadn't had the stress of the cord scare added to her being so premature.

Then she didn't want to watch anymore. She turned to focus back on Cameron and caught Rafael's eye. An eye that seemed to be searching right into her very soul, seeing far too much, and she quickly turned away from that unnerving green gaze.

"She is so beautiful, Cameron," she said, wishing her voice wasn't tight with unshed tears. "Hard work bringing her into the world, I know. But now she's here, you can spoil her rotten."

"Yes," Cameron said in a wobbly voice as she watched the neonatal team take Skye from the room to the NICU. "Yes, I plan to do just that."

"You did great," Rafael said. "I'm not surprised that the real Cameron Fontaine is even more of a warrior than the parts you play." The smile he gave the actress looked so sincere, Gabby wasn't sure if he meant it or if he was as good an actor as their patient.

"Thank you," Cameron said, but without the preening she usually responded with when given a compliment. "But what if she's not all right?"

"No worries until we have to worry, right? What is it you Americans say? Don't borrow trouble?" Another flash of white teeth. "I will get you fixed up, then we'll see if we can sneak you in to see your *bebé*, and ask the doctors how she is doing. Okay?"

Cameron simply nodded, her lip trembling, and Gabby wanted to distract her from her worries. Maybe distract herself a little too. "You must be hungry after all that hard work. How about I get you a bite to eat? What sounds good?"

"Just crackers or something. And maybe juice. Do you have orange juice?"

"You want it, we've got it." Which was pretty much true, as the clinic had more different kinds of food and drinks to offer patients than the biggest restaurant in L.A.

Trying to think about food instead of everything else occupying her mind, Gabby could hear Rafael's deep voice chatting with Cameron as she left the room. She'd already seen he was good with patients, seeming to know when they needed to be firmly told what to do, and when they needed comfort or distraction instead. And, yes, she'd also seen he wasn't *all* arrogant, full of himself princely fluff. That might be a part of him, but there was no denying he was an excellent medical doctor too.

Which, dang it, were all unfortunate realizations, because it had been much easier to ignore the man's overwhelming mojo when she'd thought he was just a handsome, royal jerk.

She concentrated on figuring out what might appeal to Cameron, to focus on *work*, which was how she always coped when something happened to yank her back in time. But how could she deny that concentrating on Rafael Moreno for a moment instead was an awfully appealing distraction?

Promising herself she wouldn't look at said distraction as she walked back to the room with a tray, she stopped dead in the doorway. For one heart-stopping moment she thought Rafael and Cameron were in an embrace, and she stared as a horrifying thought followed. Which was that the man was taking advantage of his beautiful patient at a vulnerable time.

Then her heart jerkily started up again when she realized that Cameron was sobbing, tears streaking down her cheeks as she rested her head against Rafael's broad shoulder, her hands clutching his scrub shirt. That his large hand gently stroking her damp hair back from her face was meant to comfort and soothe. Soft and beautiful Spanish words were coming from his beautifully shaped lips, and though Gabby's knowledge of the language wasn't as good as it should have been, she recognized them as words of praise and reassurance.

Oh. My. In her years as a midwife, working with doctors of all kinds, she'd seen many who were wonderful with patients. But this? This was something entirely new to her experience. This man was one lethal combination of excellent medical skill, patient care, and soothing empathy, with movie-star good looks on top of it all.

A sudden vision of his big, tanned hand pushing back her own hair, cupping her jaw before lowering those sensual lips to hers nearly stopped her breath. At that moment, he seemed to realize she'd come just inside the door and looked up. Still holding Cameron, patting her shoulder, his attention somehow seemed to be one hundred percent on Gabby as his eyes met hers. His lips curved in a slow smile, and his head inclined toward her ever so slightly in a subtle but obvious compliment. Giving her his respect and silent kudos that he thought she'd done a good job.

Somehow she managed to break that mesmerizing eye contact, breathe, and get her feet moving to the side of the bed. Her heart pounded hard in her ears, but thank heavens he couldn't hear it. Could he?

She shook her head at herself and tried to keep her attention on just Cameron, but that was nearly impossible since her face was buried in Rafael's neck, and she was hanging on to him like a barnacle to a rock. "I brought you a few different things to eat." Other than Rafael. Gabby found herself momentarily distracted, wondering how, exactly, his neck smelled. Tasted. She'd bet pretty darned good on both counts. "Try a few, and if you think of something else you'd like to have, I'll be happy to get it for you."

Cameron slowly eased away from Rafael, her hands releasing his scrub shirt to swipe at the tears on her face. Rafael reached for a tissue to hand her and she gave him a grateful smile. "Thank you. Both of you. You've been just wonderful to me through all this, and I really, truly appreciate it."

"It has been a privilege to be a part of it, Ms. Fontaine." Rafael stood from his position by the bed. "I need to make a few notes and talk to the pediatrician about when we can see *bebé*. I'll be right back."

Gabby watched Cameron dig into her food with surprising gusto, considering how emotional she'd been a moment ago, and how she'd mostly picked at her food before then. "I'm glad you're eating. It'll help you get your strength back faster."

"I'd thought I'd felt starved before, all the times I'd hardly eaten, trying to stay skinny to get into my costumes. But this time I'm honest to goodness famished!"

"Anything else you want, just let me know."

"I want to see Skye." She put the fork down and tears welled in her eyes again. "Rafael said he'd get me there as soon as possible."

"I'm sure they'll let you go to see her very soon. They know how important it is for a new mother to be with her baby."

"I hope so." Cameron sighed, and this time it sounded less worried and more dreamy. "Rafael's the sweetest, isn't he? Just wonderful. Gorgeous. Edible."

Edible? Apparently, Gabby wasn't the only one who'd had that passing thought. Then immediately had a vision of Cameron nibbling on the man's sexy lips. Lips she couldn't deny any woman would like a taste of.

Was Cameron planning on making a play for him once she was out of the hospital? Gabby had to wonder if he'd be more than happy to take the A-list actress up on anything she might offer. Then again, she'd just given birth, so they wouldn't...

She drew herself up short and stuffed down those ridiculous and plain awful thoughts. What in the world would make her start thinking about the sex lives of either one was beyond her. She didn't do relationships anymore. Sex either, and maybe that was why it had come to mind at all. It had been a long time and, hey, she was only human, right? What warm-blooded woman wouldn't think about sex at least briefly when sharing the same air as Rafael Moreno?

Thankfully, the man entered the room at that moment, so she didn't have to respond to Cameron's comment. Or maybe she wasn't thankful, because her wayward thoughts sent her gaze straight to his lips and, yes, she couldn't deny they looked very edible indeed. She quickly moved her attention to the bronze color of his throat visible in the V of his scrubs, then on to the broad, powerful chest stretching his scrub shirt taut.

His eyes met hers with something unnerving glimmering in that startling green, and she had that *can't breathe* feeling again. Lord, did he know, somehow, she'd been thinking about his nibble-worthy lips?

"Has our patient had a bite to eat?" he asked in a low, rumbling voice meant for Gabby's ears only. Also meant to make women swoon, if the shivers currently skittering down Gabby's spine were any indication.

"Um, yes." Gabby cleared her throat. "Did NICU say she could see Skye now?"

"*Sí.* They've given us the green light, and transport is coming to get her as we speak." He turned to smile at Cameron, speaking louder now. "Ready to see your beautiful girl now?"

"Yes, I'm so ready!" Cameron shoved aside her food. "Is she okay? Is she going to be fine?"

"Be prepared that she is in an incubator, being given extra-special care. So don't be scared when you see that a few tubes are attached to her. The neonatal specialist will talk with you, but I can tell you she is optimistic."

Gabby noted that he stopped short of committing to the baby being fine, which was wise, considering how premature Skye was and the multiple wraps of the umbilical cord around her little neck. He moved to the bed to pat Cameron on the shoulder again, leaving his backside turned to Gabby's view. A tight, prime backside that filled out his scrubs all too well. Not that she was looking.

"Well, what's taking them so long to come get me so I can see her?"

Gabby hadn't thought she'd ever welcome Cameron's demanding tone, but this time she was glad to hear it. Far preferable to how upset and vulnerable-sounding she'd been earlier.

As if her imperious voice had commanded it, transport arrived seconds later. Gabby moved to help Cameron down from the bed into the wheelchair, but to her astonishment Rafael simply lifted their patient up and gently deposited her in it, as though she weighed little more than her newborn.

"Are you coming with me, Rafael?" Cameron asked, clutching his arm. Her blue eyes were wide and imploring, and her lips were quivering again. Gabby had spent a lot of hours with Cameron, and had a sneaking suspicion the woman was pulling out her acting skills.

Curious to see how Rafael would react, Gabby nonchalantly glanced at him out of the corner of her eye.

"I will join you as soon as Gabriella and I finish up here."

It must have been Cameron's exhaustion that had her simply nodding instead of arguing. An evil part of Gabby that she hadn't even known was inside her had her smiling, wondering how Cameron would react if she said, *I'll join you and Rafael as soon as possible too!*

Then felt horribly guilty about that when Cameron reached for her hand, holding it until the transport guy had to stop wheeling her. "You've been so wonderful in every way, taking care of me and my little Skye long before she was born, and I'm so grateful. I hope you know that."

"Oh, Cameron." The sweet words touched her, especially coming from someone who'd seemed oblivious to many of Gabby's ministrations throughout these long hours. "It's been my pleasure and honor. And of course I'll be checking on you and Skye while you're still here at the clinic."

Cameron squeezed her hand, and she squeezed back just before the wheelchair moved on out of the room. She thought of the new mother seeing her baby again, touching her small body through the incubator ports, and knew exactly how overwhelming that maternal love felt. The only kind of forever love, no matter what the circumstances.

She turned to see Rafael Moreno studying her, his eyebrows twitched together questioningly. She wondered what he was seeing, and put on a bright smile. "Congratulations, Dr. Moreno! You dealt with everything very impressively. So scary that the cord was wrapped around her neck three times—I've rarely seen that. She pinked up fast, though, so I think you got it handled before she'd suffered any oxygen deprivation."

"I hope so. We'll see what the blood gases show."

"Are you worried?" The man looked oddly serious, and Gabby wondered for a second if he'd seen something more alarming than she had.

"No. I agree with you that she looks remarkably good, considering everything. But I owe you an apology."

"For what?" The intense way he was staring at her made her stomach feel strangely twisty and her skin warm and tingly. Hoping he wouldn't notice, she tried for a joke. "Telling me I'm a lousy housekeeper?"

A slight smile alleviated some of the ultra-seriousness from his face. "Yes. And also that I implied you were incompetent."

"Less of an implication than a statement, Dr. Moreno. I believe you said the condition of the room was obvious evidence you had to take control of my ward and care of my patient."

"And I was wrong. Something that rarely happens." His smile grew wider. "I have seen you are excellent at what you do, both with patient care and medical care. I was glad to have you working with me today, keeping me informed of the variables on the monitor, which had me looking for complications when baby's head had barely crowned. Cameron and Skye have much to thank you for."

"Well." What was it about this man that sent her breathing haywire with a simple compliment? Or was it more the way those green eyes caught and held hers? "I appreciate you saying that. And I've seen you are an excellent doctor."

And wasn't standing there giving one another kudos beyond awkward? Gabby quickly turned to tidy the room. "I'd better get to that housekeeping before you report me to James," she said lightly, hoping to get back the equilibrium he seemed to throw out of whack every time she was near him.

"What I will report to James is that you are exceptional at dealing with patients like Cameron Fontaine. He did well to hire someone like you for a clinic catering to the rich and famous."

A club he doubtless belonged to very comfortably. "Thank you again. Likewise." Fumbling with the equipment, she managed to drop the suture kit, and items skittered in every direction across the floor.

Lord. She crouched to gather everything, feeling like a teenager hanging out with the high school football star, utterly clumsy and tongue-tied. When would the man leave so she could finish and go home to finally get more than a couple of hours' sleep? Maybe then her brain would function better around Rafael Moreno, instead of strangely short-circuiting.

Then she had a complete brain freeze when he crouched next to her, his thick shoulder bumping hers as he helped her to pick things up. "Do I make you feel nervous, Gabriella? If so, I'm sorry."

The soft rumble of his voice drew her gaze to his. She couldn't move as she stared at the closeness of his lips. At the sculpted cheekbones and jaw. At the interesting gold and brown flecks within the green staring back at her. As she breathed in the scent of him—a mix of masculinity and antiseptic soap that on him smelled so sexy, her mouth went dry.

"Nervous? No, of course not."

"I think that's a lie. That needs to change, though, as it looks like we'll be working together for the foreseeable future. So we will have dinner together, and you can educate me more about how the clinic and the maternity ward run." He dropped the items onto her tray, then gently stroked his fingertip beneath her eye. "See if you can get in a short nap before your shift ends. That's at six, *si*? I'll be back here at seven."

Before she could formulate a single response to his astonishing suggestion he was gone, leaving her to stare openmouthed after him. When she'd gathered her wits, she stood and studied herself in the mirror, twisting her lips as her finger slowly traced the skin he'd just touched. Nothing like being told, basically, that you looked like a baggy-eyed wreck.

A wreck completely unready for a dinner date with a prince.

CHAPTER FOUR

RAFAEL STUDIED THE woman sitting across from him, nearly smiling as he watched the gusto with which Gabriella attacked her meal. No Hollywood starlet starving herself here, or one of the many jet-setting socialites he knew who ate as little as possible to save their calories for a martini or three. Not that she wasn't every bit as beautiful as those kinds of women, just harder working, spunky, and no-nonsense. Far more down to earth than the women he usually dated.

How had he never noticed the appeal of a woman like Gabriella?

"I trust that your dinner was tasty enough to overcome your doubts about sharing it with me?" he asked.

"I'm sure you've noticed that I'm practically licking my fork, and it's so yummy I'm not even embarrassed about that. So you know the answer is yes."

"Good. James recommended this restaurant, and I'm happy it lives up to its billing. And also happy that I now know the best way to persuade you is through your stomach."

"As opposed to your overbearing insults of the past?" The twinkle in her light brown eyes belied the words, which he hoped meant they'd sent their first impressions of one another into the past. "And the recent one too.

And here I thought you were supposed to be a suave sophisticate with a vast knowledge of women."

"What makes you think I'm not?"

"No smart man wanting a woman to go on a dinner date tells her she should take a nap first because she has bags under her eyes. Then at dinner implies she's making a pig of herself."

He had to laugh. "I apologize profusely if that was how my words came across. Even after several long days of work, you still look amazingly beautiful. And as for the pig part, if that is you, it's now my favorite type of creature. Watching you take pleasure in your dinner has made mine that much more enjoyable."

Even in the candlelight he could see her luminous skin turn pink, which was something else attractive about her. He couldn't think of another woman he knew who would blush at a simple compliment.

"Thank you. For the dinner and the flattery. Both of which have me wondering why you invited me here tonight. What exactly are you wanting from me?"

What did he want from her? He'd thought it was simply a cordial working relationship, learning from her the nuances of how The Hollywood Hills Clinic worked. But her words suddenly had him thinking about something entirely different, and his body stirred with a surge of testosterone.

There had to be legions of men who reacted to her the same way. He had to wonder if she had a man in her life. If she didn't that would be surprising, but perhaps he'd caught her between boyfriends. Except he couldn't be "catching" her at all, since the whole reason he was in L.A. was to steer clear of women and keep his face out of the papers until the heat from his parents cooled off. Their attitudes annoyed the hell out of him, but he still cared about them. It was probably part of his duties as a son to avoid giving either one of them apoplexy.

"All I want is for us to work well together, the way we did with Cameron this afternoon. And to learn a little about the clinic from you." He stuffed down the wayward thoughts pushing him to ask about her personal life and sent her a smile he hoped was blandly professional. "Tell me why you became a midwife and where you trained."

"I'm from a family of several generations of midwives, which isn't as common here in the U.S. as in some other countries. I always knew that was what I wanted to do. Trained at a nursing school, then a midwifery program near Seattle, which is where I'm from."

"And you came here after training?"

"No. I worked at a private midwifery unit there for quite a while. Came here two years ago."

Was he imagining the shuttering of her eyes? That the relaxed smile on her face just moments ago had stiffened into something else? "Was it the appeal of working with famous people that drew you here?" He didn't think so—she just didn't seem like the type to care about that, but it wasn't as though he really knew her.

"No. They'd approached me a few years before I came, then I...decided I wanted a change, and let them know I was available. How about you?" Her brown eyes held something—sadness maybe?—along with a clear determination to change the subject. "I have to admit it's surprising to me that someone born a prince would decide to become a doctor."

"Unless that prince is the second born. My parents saw my role within the kingdom as leading charity work, and while that's worthwhile, I felt there were plenty of others who would happily take on that job.

I wanted a career helping people in my own way, and my parents never understood that. Also, they got very annoyed the times I ducked out of various superficial royal duties."

"What kind of royal duties?"

"Number one would be cutting a ribbon for the grand opening of a museum or concert hall or school. I was taught from a young age how to keep my scissors sharp."

He was glad she laughed at his joke, but there was a nugget of truth to it. His parents couldn't fathom why he'd become a doctor, and Gabriella no doubt wouldn't be able to understand that attitude, since she was a medical professional too. God knew, he'd spent years trying to figure out why they disapproved of him and his choices, and he had finally given up worrying about it.

"Since you could be anything you wanted to be, how did you decide to go into medicine?"

"From the time I was small, I was fascinated with anatomy, dissecting worms and frogs with my tutors. Later, I insisted on studying the animals butchered on our land to feed the royal household and its guests, much to my mother's horror."

Her dazzling, real smile came back, lighting the darkness of their corner table. "I can imagine that might be alarming. Did she think you might grow up to be an axe murderer?"

"Probably. Or, worse, a livestock farmer. Facing the options of her son's occupation being murderer, farmer, or doctor, she reluctantly accepted the latter."

"A wise woman. So how did you decide to become an OB/GYN? Or is that something personal I don't want to know?"

Her soft laughter had him staring at her mouth, and

he wished that, just once, he could taste it. Just to see if it was as soft and sweet as it looked like it would be. "My reputation isn't as bad as you might have heard, so it's not the reason you're thinking. You of all people should know the amazement and joy of assisting a new life. I had that experience totally by accident, when I was visiting a sheikh friend whose wife went into labor unexpectedly. Being there with my friend and his wife to bring their newborn into the world was such an amazing experience, I knew that was what I wanted to do."

"That's a wonderful story. You could have just spent your life traveling the world in search of fun, but instead want to make a difference in people's lives. I really respect that."

The way her eyes shined at him in genuine admiration had him nearly confessing to the many failings he was all too guilty of, but letting her think he was wonderful was far preferable. "I went to medical school with James Rothsberg. We learned what hard work and drive could accomplish, no matter which world you're born into." Especially when that world always looked to find the worst in you, instead of the best. Set examples he had no interest in following, like tethering yourself to a permanent marital relationship for no reason other than convenience.

Her expression turned even more admiring, and as she opened her mouth to ask another question he realized he'd already said too much in terms of true confessions for the night. "Would you care for coffee? How about a look at the dessert menu? I'm guessing you're still not quite full."

"Again, your comment could be interpreted as an insult instead of an offer. But I'll let it slide, since I did put teeth marks on my spoon."

"And the price of a replacement spoon will doubtless be added to the bill, but just this once I'll take care of it. So, dessert?"

"No, thank you." Her fingertips covered a small yawn that morphed into a big one, until she laughed about it. And what was more adorable than a woman who could poke fun at herself? "I'm sorry, but I'm really, really tired. Worked several double shifts, then stayed with Cameron for the past two days. And she needed a thing or two over all those hours that interrupted my dozing."

"I can only imagine," he said dryly, picturing Cameron wanting any number of luxuries as she'd lain in that bed. "And can also imagine you giving her the best of care, regardless of the way it was requested."

"Do I deserve all that credit if I was sometimes secretly irritated in the midst of it?" Her grin was interrupted by another yawn, this one audible. "Oh, my gosh, I'm so sorry. I need to get home to sleep."

"Yes, you do." He quickly scribbled on the check and rose to take her elbow, helping her from the chair to guide her out the door. It was apparent she'd been pushing herself past her limit for days, and he was struck with a sudden, surprising desire to take care of her. A wish that he was close enough to her to have the right to tuck her into bed for a long, well-deserved rest.

But he wasn't and couldn't be. Problem was, only moments after she settled into the leather seat of his car, she fell fast asleep.

So what was he supposed to do now? He drove toward the clinic, the original plan being to drop her off so she could drive her car to her own home. If he had any idea where that was, he would simply drive her there himself. But he didn't have a clue if she lived east or west or north or south of the clinic.

He glanced at her for the tenth time, noting the way the peach-blonde fire of her hair had slipped across her face. Tangling in her long lashes, the silken strands caressed her cheekbones and lay across the corner of her lush lips. Pulling to a stop in the clinic lot, he reached over to gently smooth her hair back, letting his fingers linger on the softness of both her cheek and hair.

"Gabriella? Gabby?" For the first time he used her nickname and found he much preferred her given name, which he'd enjoyed the sound of the moment it had first rolled off his tongue. *Gabriella.* It suited her. Beautiful and feminine. Strong and intelligent. "Wake up. Do you want me to take you home, instead of you driving there? Where do you live?"

No response at all. Just the sound of gentle breathing through slightly parted lips. He did the usual things. Shook her slender shoulder. Asked the same questions louder. And when she still slept like an angel, he made up his mind.

Instead of rousing her enough to get her in her car to drive home, possibly still dangerously half-asleep, he'd take her to his house and tuck her into one of the comfortable guest suites. That way, she'd be sure to get the long sleep she obviously desperately needed. After all, it was his fault she wasn't already in bed, having insisted she dine with him tonight.

Hopefully the paparazzi weren't lurking around the house he was renting. He was pretty sure they'd only watched him the first couple of weeks after he'd arrived in L.A., then moved on to more exciting prey when he'd behaved himself.

He studied her delicate profile. Her straight nose and

a slightly stubborn jaw that suited her. The appealing dip above her pretty lips, soft and sweet in sleep. Yes, getting her to his house was the best way to handle the situation. Gabriella would sleep well and be grateful in the morning, ready to tackle her day at work with her usual energy.

But, a little later, as he swung her soft, warm body into his arms, carrying her fast asleep into the house, that surge of testosterone hit him even harder than before. The feel of her sweet curves pressed against him shortened his breath and sent his heart rate into double time, and neither had anything to do with the exertion of carrying her dead weight. It was then he realized, too late, the big downside of his decision.

Gabriella would get a good night's sleep. But he had a feeling she'd be the only one in the house who did.

The sensation of silky-soft sheets and light, cozy down wrapped Gabby in a snug cocoon as her senses slowly came to consciousness. Feeling more comfortable than she'd ever felt in her life, she lay there in tranquil warmth, a small smile on her face. Feeling wonderful. Feeling indulged and pampered, but why that was, she wasn't sure.

Her palms slowly stretched across the linens, over the fluffy comforter enveloping her, eventually wrapping her arms around herself, savoring the sensation.

Where was she? Not in her little apartment. On a vacation in some exotic place? No, she hadn't been vacationing. Obviously this was some hedonistic dream and she'd be waking soon.

Somehow she managed to crack open her heavy eyelids. And realized it wasn't a dream. She really was in this ridiculously comfortable bed, but where that bed was, she had no clue.

Abruptly, her eyelids shot wide open and, heart tripping, she sat up, trying to get her eyes accustomed to the darkness. Trying to figure out whether or not her beautiful, comfortable dream was really some horrible nightmare.

And realized this was, for certain, most definitely not her bed. So whose was it? Dragging in a rattling breath, she uttered an involuntary shriek and leapt out of the bed, blindly stumbling toward the shadowy door she thought she could see across the room. Fumbling with the latch, she yanked it open, through it into freedom, only to smack right into something large looming across the threshold.

Something hard but smooth. Something warm to the touch, with a rough covering that felt like hair. Something immovable that grasped her arms, holding her. Imprisoning her.

A full-fledged scream tore from her lips. "Let me go!" She writhed to free herself from the monster, to no avail. "Let. Me. Go!"

"Good Lord, Gabriella." The words were tense but soft as the hold on her loosened. "It's me, Rafael. Please stop screaming. It's all right."

Another scream about to rip from her throat, she blinked up to see a sculpted jaw, and though the mouth above it was tightened into a thin line, they were obviously the sensually shaped lips of Rafael Moreno. Relief had her sagging against him. "Oh, my heavens. I woke up and…didn't know where I was." And still didn't, and that realization brought her fully alert. "So…what in the world happened? Where am I?"

"In my home. You were sound asleep in my car. In a near coma really—I couldn't rouse you."

His lips had softened into a smile, and his eyes gleamed at her through the darkness. The bizarreness of the situation finally sank in, and she started to get suspicious then angry. What grown woman would fall asleep so completely she wouldn't wake up when someone tried to, as he'd said, "rouse" her?

She realized her palms were pressed flat against his hard pectorals and soft, hair-roughened skin. Heat seemed to pump from that wide, masculine chest, enveloping her and making it hard to breathe. She yanked her hands off like she'd touched the sun, flinging them to her own chest to do a quick check of what exactly she was—or wasn't—wearing, then jerked out of his hold completely. Relief that she still had on the clothes she'd worn on their dinner date didn't temper the anger making her start to physically shake.

"I can't believe you brought me here, then inside your house to…to put me in bed like a child. Why would you do that? I thought for a minute you must have drugged me or something. And…and taken advantage of me."

Infuriatingly, instead of looking contrite or insulted, his arrogantly amused smile widened. "Believe me, *belleza*, I don't have to drug women for them to wish to come home with me, nor do I have to take advantage of them. They are, instead, quite happy to take advantage of me."

She parted her lips to say something caustic in response, but nothing came out. Because she'd just realized he stood there not only shirtless but was wearing only boxers on his bottom half. Boxers that hung low on his hips, and even in the darkness she could see the ripples of muscles across his middle and the big, sculpted quadriceps of his legs beneath the hem that stopped well above his mid-thigh.

It had been a long time since she'd been with a man. And never one with so much potent masculine appeal, it should be illegal. She sucked in a breath so she could finally talk, but unfortunately brought his scent inside her nose and nearly felt dizzy from it. "Well, I'm not one of them."

"Sadly, I'm aware of that. In fact, you've crushed my ego. Never have I had a woman fall asleep in my company unless it was after a long night of making love."

The rumble of his voice combined with his deliciously drawling accent and his inappropriate mention of lovemaking sent shivers across her skin. Or maybe she was just cold, having left the comfortable bed and the heat of his body. A peculiar tension curled through her body, and she had an almost irresistible urge to snuggle up against that firm, warm chest, imagining how good it would feel against her.

Which was ridiculous. The man had all but kidnapped her. "I doubt if anything could crush your ego, Dr. Moreno. But now that I've woken from my *coma*, I'd appreciate it if you'd take me home."

"If you insist." The polite inclination of his head was regal, despite the fact he stood there practically naked. "But it's four a.m. and I, for one, would like to get a few more hours of sleep before work. Surely it would be best for both of us to go back to bed for a few hours."

Back to bed. What in the world was wrong with her that his words made her think of something very different from sleep? Involuntarily, a slightly hysterical giggle left her lips.

"Something amusing?"

"Just that I was thinking that, since you're a prince,

you should have tried kissing me when I was asleep. I wonder if that would have worked, like in the fairy tales?"

Lord, she must be delirious. Appalled that she'd blurted her thought out loud, the feeling faded as their eyes met. His seemed to blaze at the same time his lids lowered in a look that made her quiver. "Excellent question, *bella*. Next time, I'll try that to find out, hmm?"

"There won't be a next time. But I guess you're right about it being silly to go home right now." She gulped, searching for her common sense. Time to shut down this sensual back and forth between them that she had a feeling could easily get out of control. "I'll just get back to sleep and we can leave for work in the morning. I always keep extra clothes there, anyway."

He inclined his head again. "*Bueno*. We will leave here at eight. Sleep well."

And then he was gone, taking all that heat and testosterone that had shimmered in the room with him.

Gabby shoved her fingers through her hair with a sigh and sank back into the bed, pulling the covers to her chin. She should be glad the bizarre interaction between her and Rafael was over with. Instead, she felt revitalized but at the same time there was an odd hollow in the pit of her stomach. A disappointment that he hadn't responded to her ridiculous remark about a prince kissing her awake with an actual kiss. And why had she said it, anyway? Probably because, unconsciously, she'd been thinking about it all evening as she'd stared across that candlelit table at his beautiful lips.

She flopped onto her side, trying to ignore the tense, letdown feeling around her heart, deciding not to make too much of it. The man was physically gorgeous enough to make any woman swoon, right? And she was a woman who hadn't felt much of anything for a man besides disillusionment in a long, long time.

CHAPTER FIVE

"READY FOR WORK?" Rafael asked, breaking the silence between them as he drove them to the clinic in the powerful car she barely remembered getting into after dinner last night, which made her blush all over again. "I trust your middle-of-the-night awakening didn't interfere too much with the sleep you obviously needed."

"No, thank you. I slept well." Which was a total lie. She hadn't gotten a wink after he'd left her room, imagining how awkward it would be in his house together in the morning and on the way to work. And awkward was an understatement. She'd taken the world's fastest shower in the stunning bathroom attached to the room she'd slept in, wondering if the man might not be the gentleman he seemed but instead a prince who thought he had the right to walk in on her. Then, nervous and uncomfortable, she'd stood in his kitchen, nerves twitchy, clutching her purse and ready to go, while he'd sat relaxed, drinking coffee and having a croissant.

She'd steadfastly declined his invitation to join him, partly because she'd wanted to get going and partly because he'd had a vaguely amused expression on his face. Obviously he wasn't used to women wanting to dash out his door. She didn't doubt it was usually quite the opposite.

He swung out of the car, looking smooth and handsome and not even remotely tired, like she knew she unfortunately still did. She pushed open her own door, about to get out and hurry inside as fast as she could, when he appeared, holding out his hand to her, eliminating any chance of a quick escape. She tried to walk fast, but he simply kept pace with her at her side. As they walked together to the clinic's big double doors, she blushed scarlet from head to toe.

The walk of shame. This was what friends of hers had talked about in the past! Out on a date, spend the night, and show up somewhere wearing the same clothes for all the world to see. Except she hadn't even enjoyed what people would think she had, damn it. Shamed without reason.

"I'm late for work. I'll…um…see you around." She walked faster, trying to get inside and to her locker fast, praying no one had paid attention to what dress she'd worn the night before.

Rafael caught up with her. She stared straight ahead, but he dipped his head to look at her, drawing her gaze to his. To green eyes that now danced with amusement. "Are you worried people will talk, *bella*, if they see us arrive together?"

"Yes!" she hissed. "So please go wherever you need to go and goodbye."

"Not goodbye. We're seeing a patient together in twenty minutes. Until then." He reached for her hand, his eyes twinkling above it as he pressed his lips to it. She snatched it away and practically ran down the corridor toward the women's locker room. The imprint of that quick kiss still tingled on her skin, and she had a bad feeling that meant she was in for a very long day.

Freya Rothsberg, the clinic's PR guru and also James's sister, raised her eyebrows at Gabby as she tore down the hallway, and she forced herself to slow down.

"Good morning, Gabby," Freya said.

"Good morning." Was it her imagination, or was Freya's voice a little questioning? Or was she just being completely paranoid? "I…need to get into scrubs to see my first patient. Have a great day."

Finally able to hide in the locker room, Gabby flung off her dress, quickly hung it up, then got her scrubs on. Breathing a sigh of relief, she leaned against her locker door. Clearly she wasn't up for middle-of-the-night adventures, innocent or not.

Ten minutes later, she felt almost normal and composed, putting a smile on her face as she went into her patient's room. Then every ounce of composure slid away when she saw Rafael standing there, talking with the woman.

"Ah, Gabriella." His eyes met hers, and that darned twinkle still lingered, making her feel embarrassed all over again. "I hope you don't mind, but I took the liberty of seeing your patient before you arrived, as my first patient isn't here yet."

She could feel hot color rushing into her cheeks again, annoyed as all get-out at her reaction to seeing him there. Somehow she bit back the words she wanted to say, which were, *Yes, I do mind, as a matter of fact. I'm trying to stay away from you!*

"Of course not. How are you feeling, Megan?"

"Absolutely great! I was just telling Dr. Moreno that my yoga instructor is so impressed with my workouts.

I mean, I'm doing every bit as much at eight months along as I did before I got pregnant."

"As long as you're feeling good when you exercise, that's very healthy for you and your baby." She made herself turn to Rafael, and the power of that green gaze nearly choked her.

"I'm sure I'll be fit enough for the minor role Daddy has in mind for me in the film he's starting this summer. I told Rafael he should come to the set."

"Megan's father's films are among my favorite thrillers," he said. "I particularly enjoyed that scene in his last movie where one of the main guys showed up in the heroine's bedroom, and she didn't know until then that he wasn't her friend but the terrifying killer instead. Scary stuff."

The wicked glint in those green depths was both irritating and unnerving, since it sent her thoughts right back to what she'd been trying so hard not to think about. Which was the feel of his hard, warm body against hers, and how he'd looked in those boxer shorts.

"So," she said, desperately trying to change the subject, "have you examined Megan yet, Dr. Moreno?"

"I thought I'd leave that to you, along with getting her vital signs. Just wanted to introduce myself before the big day arrives."

"Surely you won't still be working here in another month, will you?" If her voice held a trace of panic, she couldn't help it. "I thought this was a brief pit stop in your life."

"I expect I will be staying a while. I'm enjoying my time in L.A. and here at The Hollywood Hills Clinic. The staff is most…interesting, and I hope to get to know everyone much better."

Gabby dropped the blood-pressure cuff on the floor,

then had to take the reading twice she was so distracted by Rafael's teasing. Which she knew full well it was—for some reason, he was enjoying yanking her chain and making her blush again.

"I'm about to do your internal exam now, Megan, okay?" She turned to Rafael with a saccharine-sweet smile, hoping her narrowed eyes told him exactly how irritated she was without showing, again, how he rattled her. "So you're free to see if your patient has arrived, Dr. Moreno."

"Why do I get the feeling the boss is tossing me out on my ear?" He turned that lethal grin on Megan. "See you next time you're in. You have my contact information if you need me."

Remarkable how the minute the man was out of the room, Gabby was able to focus on her patient and her job without dropping or forgetting a single thing. Pitiful. Which meant that, if Rafael was really going to be sticking around for a while, somehow, some way she'd have to get a handle on her ridiculous, distracted hormones.

Chuckling to himself as he walked down the hallway to see his patient, Rafael reflected on how easy it was to get under Gabriella's skin, and how much fun it was. She was such a complex mix of characteristics combined in a fascinating way, all bundled up inside a beautiful, touchable package. Sweet and smart, feisty and a little shy all at the same time, he wanted to spend more time with her. Learn a lot more about what made her tick.

He might have gotten off on the wrong foot with her initially, but he knew she found him attractive now as well. Last night when he'd held her in his hands and her wide eyes had looked up at him in the dark bedroom, he'd seen the way her lips had parted; had felt her quickened breaths skating warm and fast across his skin. The rise and fall of her chest had been less about her fear and more about sexual attraction—he knew because he'd felt the same hot vibration. Then she'd tried to cover up the zing happening between them with pretend indignation. Zing that had been a two-way street—it had taken all his *won't*-power to resist the urge to pull her closer for a kiss, to see where all that heat shimmering between them might lead.

Except he'd then figuratively smacked himself with the reminder that he was supposed to be lying low in L.A. "Behaving himself," to quote his parents, and dating "appropriate" women, whatever the hell that meant. Apparently not strippers, or those whose faces graced the gossip magazines, and why any of that was a big deal, he didn't understand.

It wasn't as though a single one of them would ever get an engagement ring from him. Seeing the various loveless marriages in his family, not to mention what James's parents' relationship had been like, Rafael figured that kind of commitment would be sheer purgatory. Why in the world would he want to handcuff himself to one woman forever if he didn't have to?

Short-term handcuffing, though? Now, that he was all for. Thinking about something short, sweet and hot with Gabriella put the smile back on his face, only it quickly faded because, damn it, he couldn't let that happen, with the media and his parents breathing down his neck.

Seeing his next patient got his thoughts back on track, and as he was about to go to the nurses' station to discuss her chart, the sound of his name on the large, wall-mounted television in the patient's room stopped him in mid-step. He looked up at the screen to see what ridiculous, untrue story was being spread on the TV gossip shows now.

To his shock, the photos were of the cliffside mansion he was renting, with two people in front of it. Pictures of him carrying a sleeping Gabriella inside, then of the two of them leaving in the morning, with sensational-ized questions and speculation about who Prince Ra-fael Moreno's late-night booty call might be this time.

Damn it to hell. What had he just said about his par-ents breathing down his neck? This time they'd prob-ably be belching pure fire. He glanced at his patient and her nurse, glad they were too busy talking to pay at-tention to the stupid television. He wiped his suddenly sweaty hands on his lab coat, thankful the photos were distant and grainy enough that nobody would likely be able to figure out who the woman was. He hoped Gabriella didn't get wind of the story, and hoped even more that she wouldn't suffer any embarrassment from it. Already, he knew she wasn't the kind of woman who would appreciate being part of a media frenzy, which was one of several good reasons he'd been telling him-self he had to keep his hands off her.

Anger surged into his veins on her behalf. The hard-working, exhausted woman couldn't even fall asleep in his car without untrue rumors being spread, and he wished he could contact the TV programmers with a vehement rebuttal, telling them to lay off.

But experience had taught him that kind of thing just inflamed the gossipmongers even more. With any luck, the hounds would back off when they couldn't figure out who she was, and the story would die a quick death.

For Gabriella's sake, and for his too, he hoped like hell that was exactly what would happen. Seeing the photos in his mind again as he strode from the room to update the charts, he nearly ran into Freya.

"Rafael." A smile played about Freya's lips and she lifted an eyebrow. "I hear your patients love you, so thanks for stepping in. Also sounds like you're very much…enjoying your time in L.A.?"

"Not as much as I'm given credit for, I can tell you that," he said, somehow keeping his voice cool and amused, even as his stomach felt a little queasy. "The story of your life and mine, isn't it?"

"Stories aren't always fiction." Her smile widened, and she walked away without another word.

Trying to get the annoying voice of the TV host out of his head, along with the blurry images he hoped Gabriella wouldn't have to see, he concentrated on the computerized patient charts until his phone interrupted him.

Then he knew the day was going downhill even faster when he saw it was his mother, and his gut clenched with the certain knowledge that their palace spies had informed her of the latest gossip fest.

"*Buenos días,* Mother. It's wonderful to hear your voice." Or would be, if their conversation was going to be about the palace horses or her latest fundraiser or something else pleasant and benign, but he was pretty sure he wouldn't be that lucky.

"Rafael. What do your father and I have to do to make you understand your position in life? Your responsibilities? We might not have liked that you chose to do something like doctoring instead of accepting your traditional role here, but we have learned to live with it. That doesn't give you the right, though, to disregard your family's status completely and do whatever you wish! I thought the latest scandal had taught you that. You said that's why you went to L.A. for a while, to behave! And yet here you are, the subject of gossip again. When are you going to marry a nice girl and be done with this? When—?"

"Mother." He'd gritted his teeth and held the phone from his ear during her long diatribe, but finally managed to cut her off when she took a breath. "If you're talking about the stupid TV news, I can assure you it's nothing. I'm working for a time in James's clinic, and a co-worker and I had work to discuss. She fell asleep and…" This time he cut himself off. Why the hell should he have to defend himself to anyone, including his mother, about something completely innocent? Was it his fault he'd been second born into a royal family, and because of that was a chronic disappointment and annoyance to his parents? His fault that the paparazzi liked to stalk him? As for getting married, she might as well save her breath, because that was never going to happen. "You know, I'm done with this conversation. Is there something else you'd like to talk about?"

"We need to get this ironed out first. If you—"

"Goodbye, Mother. Call me if you want to talk about something besides how much my being a doctor and a heathen embarrasses you."

Under normal circumstances, he would have felt bad hanging up on his mother, even when she was scolding him. But this subject had been beaten to death for months, and he'd moved here to escape the gossip his parents despised. He couldn't handle one more minute of being accused of something he hadn't done. Hadn't he been doing his best to be the outstanding representative of his country his parents wanted him to be?

Anger and frustration had him wanting to punch something, and he knew he needed a calming distraction. And the one thing that always gave him perspective and helped him remember what was really important was spending time with innocent new babies, some of whom were struggling with far more serious problems than he had. Much more important than parental disapproval and gossip and damned fabrications that shouldn't be more than an inconvenient annoyance to be ignored.

Just three steps into NICU he stopped, struck by the picture in front of him. The beautiful profile of Gabriella Cain as she sat next to Skye's incubator, her fire-streaked golden hair tucked behind her ears. Unaware that anyone was looking at her, every emotion was visible. Her eyes and lips, her posture, and the way her fingers gently stroked the infant's tiny arm exposed a mix of emotions so raw his chest tightened to see them. Sadness and anguish. Guilt. And a longing so naked he knew this was far more than a woman simply looking at the miracle of a newborn.

What had happened to Gabriella to bring this kind of pain to her life?

He watched her for long minutes, uncertain whether to approach her with comfort or quietly leave her alone. His feet seemed to make the decision for him, and he found himself right next to her, his hand reaching to slowly stroke down her soft hair then rest on her slumped shoulder with a gentle squeeze.

She didn't react immediately. It seemed to take her a moment to emerge from whatever dark and private place she was in. Then she turned and looked up at him. Her professional mask slipped across her face, covering all that starkly haunted emotion.

"Have you come to see Skye? She's doing really well." Gabriella stood to give him room to move closer to the incubator, and his hand fell from her shoulder. But he didn't want to see the baby now as much as he wanted to be there for Gabriella. "I left Cameron a short time ago," she said. "She's resting, but asked me to check on Skye and report back. Not that she hasn't gotten reports about every fifteen minutes from various members of the nursing staff. But she isn't quite convinced that's enough."

Her smile seemed forced and it didn't banish the sadness from her eyes. He wanted to reach out to her. He wanted to hold her close and console her for whatever hurt she was holding inside. He wanted to tell her it would be okay, that all pain faded and nothing was forever. And as his eyes met her somber brown ones, he knew.

He wanted to know Gabriella a whole lot better, and to hell with lying low and living like a saint. He couldn't care about gossip or stupid photos or even his mother's embarrassment and worries. Right then, the only thing he cared about was spending time with Gabriella and finding a way to make her smile again.

"My updates from the pediatricians have been good enough that I think we can move Skye into her mama's room," he said. "That would keep Cameron happier and save some time and footsteps by the nursing staff, don't you think?"

"Yes. But of course I don't mind checking on the baby. She's beautiful, isn't she? I'm so happy she's all right."

That wistful look crept across her face again, and Rafael found himself reaching for her hand before he even realized it. "I have a favor to ask of you."

"A favor?"

"Yes. Freya told me that all the recent high-profile

operations for Bright Hope patients have the cream of L.A. society lining up to hold exclusive fundraisers, so she's asked if I can attend a charity ball. Since I'm new to Los Angeles and have no one to ask to go with me, would you please come? I'm sure you know all the great things the clinic does for people who don't have easy access to good medical care. Including pregnant women. Wouldn't attending the fundraiser together be a great way for both of us to help continue creating awareness for a good cause?"

The eyes staring at him were wide and stunned. Why, he wasn't sure, since they'd dined together the night before. Surely if she'd heard about the photo and gossip, she would have said so. Still, she just stood there, her lips parted but mute.

"Is my English not as good as I think it is? I asked if you'd attend a party with me. Did I accidentally ask you to eat worms?" he teased, hoping to get a real smile and a yes from her.

"Um, no. Your English, as you well know, is better than most who speak it as a first language." The smile she gave him was strained, but it was a start. "But I'm afraid I can't come with you."

"Why not?"

"It just…wouldn't be right. Excuse me while I check back with Cameron."

He watched her tear from the room as though that gorgeous hair of hers was actually on fire and not just shimmering with flaming hues. He wasn't used to being turned down flat and wondered if it just might have to do with her running from the barely banked-down heat they'd shared last night.

Remembering that the whole reason he'd come to NICU had been to find some inner calm, he turned to

little Skye, sweetly and innocently lying in her crib. But
he wasn't really seeing her. He was seeing Gabriella's
expression as she'd looked at the infant, and he knew
without a doubt that whatever had caused that anguish
was something she'd been carrying for too long.

Yes, he'd been given orders from headquarters—
which meant his parents—to hide from the past, unwelcome limelight for a while. And maybe it would be
a mistake to expose Gabriella and whatever secrets she
carried to the heavy weight of that microscope along
with him. But thinking about her somehow told him
with absolute certainty that hiding wasn't the answer.
Not for him, and not for Gabriella. It was time for both
of them to put their pasts behind them, and the first
steps to making that happen would take place at a certain charity ball. A ball with plenty of supporters. Al-
lies who'd be more than happy to convince her to attend
with him.

CHAPTER SIX

"EVERYTHING LOOKS GREAT, Freya, with baby the perfect size for a healthy fetus, four months in gestation," Gabby said, smiling. "And you look wonderful too. Your skin is positively glowing. Can I admit to being jealous?"

She'd said the words to make Freya happy, but right after she'd spoken them, the unpleasant, unexpected, and unwelcome cloud weightily slipped over her head again. Why were the memories becoming more frequent, instead of more distant? She had no idea, but dwelling on it accomplished nothing, and she did her best to shake off the gray gloom, because Freya deserved the true joy Gabby felt for her friend and employer.

"I do feel wonderful, honestly." Freya's smile was big enough to banish some of Gabby's moping and make her smile too. "Though several friends have told me to enjoy it while it lasts, because after it arrives I'll be so sleep-deprived I'll forget the baby's name."

Freya's words dashed the final remnants of gloom, and Gabby had to laugh. "Maybe not quite that much. But no matter how many times I warn new mothers that a lot of babies refuse to sleep, no one really hears it until they're living it."

"Well, either way, sleep or no sleep, I'm beyond excited." Freya sat up and adjusted her exam gown. "Half-dressed isn't the way to talk business, but since we're both so busy I'm going to take advantage of this time alone to chat."

"About?"

"The charity ball. Rafael Moreno told me he asked you to go with him, but you told him you didn't want to." Her voice became chiding. "Really, Gabby, why in the world would you say that?"

Her stomach plunged and tightened as she stared at Freya in surprise. How was she supposed to answer that? *Oh, I find him too sexy and attractive, that's all, and my life is devoted to my work now.*

"Well, he's a little overbearing, don't you think? And arrogant."

And unbearably hot.

"I think it's confidence more than arrogance," Freya said with a smile. "But you don't have to be best friends with him, or even particularly like him, to attend the ball with him, Gabby. The purpose of the fundraiser is to raise awareness and money for the Bright Hope Clinic. When one of our own obstetricians, temporary or not, who happens to also be a *prince* attends the ball, that's news. Like it or not, that's the way the world works. Rafael pointed out to me that if the head midwife at the hospital is the prince's date for the night, that's even bigger news, and exactly the kind of public relations opportunity I'm always looking for."

How weird was it that Freya's words sent Gabby's stomach sinking in dread at the same time her chest lifted in excitement and her darned subconscious immediately imagined what kind of dress she should wear to such an event? Clearly Rafael Moreno's arrival at

The Hollywood Hills Clinic had sent her sanity a little off-kilter, since she really should be annoyed that he'd gotten Freya involved, using that kind of manipulation to get her to attend with him. Another example of the man's colossal ego!

But even if her entire body had been filled with dread instead of that peculiar mixture of emotions, it wasn't like she could say no. She believed in what the Bright Hope Clinic was doing, and if she could contribute in any way, big or small, she wanted to.

"Fine. I'll go." She hoped Freya didn't notice that her gruffly sighed answer was charged with anticipation too. After all, what woman in her right mind—or even confused one—wouldn't want to be Cinderella for just one night, attending a ball with a handsome prince?

She'd just have to be sure to leave her glass slippers buried deep in her closet at home.

When Gabby had decided to install a new top-to-bottom door mirror in her closet, she'd never dreamed that she'd be needing it to look at herself in a long gown. A gown she'd be wearing to attend a ball with a handsome prince. Gabby snorted and shook her head at herself, wondering how a grown woman could feel so wrapped up in thinking about a party and what she'd be wearing, like a teenager going to the prom. Ridiculous.

She studied the lines of her dress. Turned side to side, looked at the back, then the front again. And sighed. Because she knew full well that the majority of women attending the ball tonight would be wearing designer dresses that cost more than her month's rent, not to mention that there wouldn't be a single one there who'd made her own gown.

Filled with jitters of doubt now, she worried that

maybe she shouldn't have done that. Why had she been so convinced she shouldn't just buy one off the rack? The answer was because she knew anything she could afford would be made from substandard fabrics, compared to the glamorous, designer dresses the rich and famous would be wearing tonight. And she knew how to sew, didn't she?

Her strong, female ancestors had not only studied midwifery and spent their lives helping others, they'd been talented seamstresses. Hadn't learning at her grandmother and mother's knees given her the skills to pull this off? Staring at her dress now, she wasn't so sure. The ring of her doorbell…a loud, silly horse whinny the previous avid horseracing fan tenants had installed…made her jump. Then laugh out loud. Clearly Cinderella's carriage had arrived, except the prince was already on board, not waiting at the ball.

Resisting the urge to wipe her suddenly sweaty hands down the emerald-green fabric of her gown, she opened the front door. Then stared, her breath hitching.

She'd thought Dr. Rafael Moreno had been attractive in the scrubs that showed his strong physique? In a dress shirt and pants at the clinic, and when they'd gone to dinner? Those Rafael Morenos had nothing on this one, who exuded royal arrogance from head to toe in a tuxedo that fitted him so perfectly she knew it had to have been tailor-made for him. His shirt was so white it was practically blinding, his classic black bow tie perfectly placed beneath his strong, tanned throat. The late evening sun gleamed on his dark, glossy hair and sculpted jawline, and a slow smile curved his lips.

She gulped. There was one perfect way to describe how her body was reacting to his mouthwatering beauty.

Tuxedo libido.

She fought down a nervous giggle. How had the room gotten so warm? Clearly, May in Los Angeles meant it was time to adjust the thermostat.

"Hi," she said, knowing she sounded a little breathless, but since she *was* breathless it was the best she could do. "I'm ready. I just need to grab my purse."

"I'm relieved, I have to say."

"That I'm ready? Is that another comment about what you think of my organizational skills?"

"No. As I drove here, I wasn't sure what to expect, having several scenarios that came to mind. In the first, I was afraid you'd open the door wearing sweatpants, planning to ditch me to lounge at home instead, since you hadn't wanted to come with me tonight."

"I wouldn't ditch you, even though you'd have deserved it if I did, since it was pretty sneaky of you to get Freya involved as your date planner. However, I always honor my commitments. Though I admit that lounging in sweatpants holds a certain appeal."

"To me as well. You would look very sexy in sweatpants."

"Uh-huh. Pretty sure sexy and sweatpants are mutually exclusive."

"Not true. I'm picturing you in them right now." Something about the way he was looking at her had her wondering exactly what he was picturing, and her breath hitched all over again. "The other, even worse scenario I envisioned was you wearing a more casual dress because you were planning to go on a date with someone else. In which case, I'd have to fight him when he came to pick you up, and my parents rarely appreciate that kind of scene."

Despite the absurd words, there was something serious in the gleam of his eyes that had her laughing in surprise. "I can't see you fighting over a woman. There are too many fish in the sea who'd fall at your feet for a date, because they don't know what a shark you are."

"But you're willing to risk a date with a shark for a good cause, hmm? And there's only one woman as beautiful and interesting as you are. That dress is exquisite on you, by the way. My mother would be impressed with your designer."

She laughed. and at the same time a bubble of satisfaction and relief that she didn't look ridiculous filled her chest. "Don't tell anyone, but the designer is someone who works for a dress-pattern company, and I made it myself."

"You made it yourself?" The astonishment on his face was comical. "That's incredible! Beautiful, compassionate, and talented as well. Every man at the ball tonight will envy my good fortune to have you on my arm."

It was a line, she knew, but her stomach flipped inside out anyway. "They'll probably envy you for a lot of other reasons, like that whole prince thing that makes you think you can do whatever you want whenever you want." Okay, she didn't really think he was an overbearing jerk anymore, but it was probably a good idea to keep up that charade.

She also wouldn't add all the other reasons men would envy him. Like his incredible good looks and confidence and sense of humor and everything else about him that made every part of her body tingle a little. She turned jerkily to grab her evening bag from the chair, willing herself to act normal and calm. After all, this wasn't a real date. The only reason he'd asked—no, manipulated—her to join him tonight was because it was good PR for the clinic, and more publicity about the ball would result in more donations.

His grasp on her elbow was light, but Gabby still felt the warmth of it clear to her toes as he tucked her into the car. Her heart seemed to thunder as much as the car engine as it accelerated around the mountain curves. Excitement pumped through her veins, and she realized she hadn't felt this…this *alive* in a very long time. Not since her life, which she'd thought had been so steady and planned out, had been obliterated with one, selfishly bad decision.

She determinedly squelched those thoughts. No point in dwelling on something she couldn't change when she had a few hours to enjoy what she knew would be a very special evening. She stole a look at the man sitting so very close to her and he must have felt her gaze because he glanced at her with a smile that suddenly faded.

"There's one thing I must warn you about," he said, turning his attention back to the road. "I'm frequently followed by the press, looking for a juicy story. I would guess there will be photographers outside the hotel anyway, wanting to get pictures of the various stars attending this event. Some will doubtless take pictures of us too, so don't let it worry you."

"Do you often give them juicy stories?"

"If you asked my parents, they'd say yes. In fact, I'll tell you the truth. I came to stay in L.A. for two reasons. To see James and to hide from the press after an unfortunate incident."

"I can't imagine you hiding from anyone."

"I don't like to. But there are times that even I have to bow to family pressures, and this was one of them. But I've decided I don't care. That being out with you tonight is important to me—and I hope you won't let any media coverage bother you either."

"The media won't care who I am, so I'm not worried about it."

"Don't count on that."

His expression looked almost grim as he pulled the car up to the front doors of the hotel. Gabby stared in shock at the swarm of people wielding cameras and standing on both sides of the huge double doors, kept back by red velvet ropes curving between golden stanchions. A valet opened her door and in mere seconds Rafael appeared by her side, reaching for her hand. The camera flashes were so bright and constant it was like being hit in the face with a strobe light, and she blinked and instinctively reeled back. Rafael's hand dropped hers to move to the small of her back, firm and steady. He seemed unfazed by it all, leading her forward in an even, unhurried pace until they were safely inside the hotel doors held open by employees.

"Oh, my Lord, you weren't kidding!" She stared at him. "Is it like this wherever you go?"

"Not always. When there's an event they know I'll be showing up for, yes. But sometimes, as you saw when we had dinner the other night, they're not around. Or it can seem that way, though sometimes I'm wrong about that."

As they moved farther into the room, she quickly looked around, expecting cameras to be closing in on them at that very moment. Thankfully, all she saw was a room filled with beautifully dressed men and women, all smiling and talking against the gorgeous backdrop of an old-style hotel, built in the days when Hollywood had been all glitter and gold and extravagance.

"Gabriella, there is something I need to talk to you about regarding the paparazzi," Rafael said.

She turned to him, wondering what was causing that crease between his brows, but whatever he'd been about to say was interrupted by the arrival of several people eager to talk to him. Then others. More as they wandered through the crowds, taking bites of amazing hors d'oeuvres and sips of champagne, and it was obvious that more than one woman admired her date for the night, and were looking at *her* with envy, not the other way around, as Rafael had flatteringly predicted.

"Rafael, Gabby, I see my sister nudged you into coming tonight," James Rothsberg said as he appeared next to them. Held in the curve of his arm was the stunning woman Gabby had recently seen photographed with him in a few tabloid spreads.

"Does Freya ever nudge anyone into anything?" Rafael said with a grin. "Strong-armed is more like it, but I'm glad to be here for such a great cause, and I know Gabriella cares a lot about underprivileged children too."

"I'm so happy to be helping spread the word about the Bright Hope Clinic," Gabby said. "Not to mention getting to eat all the wonderful food here tonight." She stopped there, even though she would have liked to note that Rafael was pretty good at strong-arm tactics himself.

"Freya's a force of nature, for sure. I'm glad you were able to make it." James grinned and introduced them to his date, who seemed to study Rafael with extreme interest before glancing at Gabby.

"Such a pretty dress," she said with what looked like an oddly amused smile, and Gabby froze, wondering if it was obvious she'd made it herself. "Did you choose the color of it to go with your date's eyes? Quite a striking color."

Well, that was even worse than noticing it was homemade. Embarrassment streaked through Gabby's whole body, ending with her cheeks scorching as she realized her dress really was almost exactly the same color as Rafael's eyes. Would anyone else think she'd done it on purpose, like they were attending a high school homecoming dance together or something? Or, worse, had she chosen the fabric unconsciously thinking of his mesmerizing gaze?

"My goodness, you're right! I hadn't even noticed that," she managed to say, struggling to make her tone sound light and amused too. "My mother drummed into me that people with strawberry blonde hair like hers and mine should wear green whenever possible and avoid red so as not to look like a spark plug."

"She looks amazing in green, doesn't she?" Rafael said smoothly, before turning to Gabby. "Though there's no possibility that tall, slender you could ever resemble a spark plug."

The seeming sincerity joining the gleam in his eyes made her blush all over again. "Thank you."

"You probably know how lucky The Hollywood Hills Clinic is to have her running the maternity ward, James. She's not only a skilled midwife, she has a way with patients that makes every one of them more than glad they're there. Thanks for giving me the opportunity to work with her."

"Gabby's the best. And you'd better not think of stealing her away to some hospital in the Mediterranean when you leave, Rafael, or I'll have to tell secrets about you that you wouldn't want shared."

Obviously just kidding, James's eyes twinkled as

he spoke, but Rafael seemed a little more serious when he looked down at Gabby. "We all have secrets, don't we? Sometimes sharing them is a good thing, don't you think?"

Heart skittering, she didn't answer, wondering what he meant. Could he somehow know about her past and her mistakes?

No. Impossible. Freya knew she'd had a bad breakup before coming to work at the clinic, but not the reason for it, and that was the way Gabby wanted to keep it.

"Sometimes. But usually it's best to keep our secrets to ourselves." James's smile had flatlined too, as he and his date said their goodbyes and went to mingle with the crowd.

"Let's dance, shall we?"

Oh, goodness. Dance? Close to him? "I don't think—"

But in typical Rafael fashion he didn't wait for her to finish her answer before setting his glass on the tray of a passing waiter then wrapping his hand around hers to move to the dance floor. When he turned to face her, his other palm slid from her waist to the small of her back. She slipped her hand up the soft fabric of his jacket to rest it on his shoulder, and her breath caught in her throat as she looked up at him.

The orchestra struck up a new tune, and they began to move. "Thank you for coming with me tonight."

"Thank you for inviting me. It's been lovely."

"Even though you didn't want to at first?"

"Even though." She wasn't about to tell him why, and at the moment that seemed unfathomable. Because being so close to him, with all that heat from his body skimming across her bare arms and décolletage, felt wonderful.

On a slow turn, he brought her close enough that her

breasts brushed his chest, and he lowered his mouth closer to her ear. "So why didn't you want to, Gabriella?"

"Because you're arrogant and bossy."

"Yes. Among other things." The chandelier cast light and shadows across his chiseled face and the bow of his lips as he smiled. "I thought we worked out a few of those issues when we went to dinner together. Which reminds me, I have to tell you something."

"What?"

His smile had disappeared and when he opened his mouth to answer he hesitated. Then, to her surprise, the words that came out were, "Uh-oh," and his attention seemed to be grabbed by something behind her.

She turned to see James standing mostly hidden at the back of the room behind the band. With him, instead of his date, was Mila Brightman and even from this distance it was obvious that Mila was hopping mad about something, and giving it to James with both barrels.

"Oh, dear. What do you think is wrong?"

"I don't know. I hope it's not— Never mind." A deep frown creased Rafael's brow as he shook his head. "I was about to tell you—"

But before he could finish, the band stopped playing and Freya stepped onto the platform to speak into the microphone about the event and why they were all there tonight. After thanking the hosts and giving some details about the Bright Hope Clinic, she advised everyone to enjoy desserts and drinks as there would shortly be a video presentation about some of the patients who'd been helped there.

"I don't know about you, but I think we've done our duty," Rafael said, leaning close to speak in her ear. "What do you say to a little dine and dash?"

"Dine and dash? Do princes do that? I have to admit the mental image of you gobbling food then furtively sneaking out the door is hard to picture." Since she hadn't seen him any way but tall, proud, and very visible, that was an understatement. "But I can't say I'd complain about leaving soon. I'm about talked out."

"You know how it is, trying to say goodbyes and exit an event like this. Takes at least another hour, so let's get the process started."

She didn't, really. If she walked out the door that second, she was quite sure not a soul would bother her, but she'd already seen the attention Rafael garnered, and could well believe he'd be stopped by half the crowd en route.

Which was exactly what happened. And each time he was stopped he took pains to draw her into the conversation. Not only did he introduce her to everyone with glowing compliments about her skills as a midwife, stating again how lucky The Hollywood Hills Clinic was to have her, there was something else in his eyes and expression as he did so.

Something that didn't seem like simple professional admiration. Instead, it felt much more personal.

That odd mix of excitement and dismay rolled around her belly all over again, which was dangerous. Yes, it was a magical night. But she couldn't let the magic of it allow her to forget. She couldn't risk a relationship with any man, even one as amazing as Rafael. And, yes, she knew a man like Rafael Moreno would want only a fling, but even that would be too much.

Why was she even thinking he'd want that, anyway? Must be the Cinderella feeling she'd had all evening, wearing a dress far fancier than she'd ever worn before, on a date with pretty much the world's most handsome bachelor prince. The feel of his big, possessive hand holding hers or resting on her lower back. The compliments. The way he looked at her for long moments as though they were totally alone.

She shook her head fiercely at herself. The man doubtless acted like that with all women at parties, and especially those on a date with him, and to read anything more into it was plain foolish. Probably flirting came to him as naturally as the charm he'd exuded all evening. As naturally as the arrogant rudeness he'd bestowed on her when they'd first met.

Any woman would be intrigued by a multifaceted man like Rafael Moreno. None of it meant a thing—not his flirting and not the googly eyes she caught herself making at him. Tomorrow she'd be wearing her scrubs again, they'd go back to their normal, cordial working relationship and tonight would be forgotten.

Trying to bring her mind back to the conversation, she watched his mouth move as he talked to friends of James he obviously knew, and the sensuality of his lips pretty much obliterated all her previous self-scolding. Her ability to converse. Her thoughts instead drifted to all wrong ones that gave her tummy a different kind of funny feeling. A feeling that she'd give her next paycheck to kiss him once, just to see how it would feel. Just once. Once before the strike of midnight—was that so much to ask?

She stared in fascination as he took a sip of his drink and his tongue licked a tiny drop from his lip. And with breathless certainty she knew. The man would be one amazing kisser.

"You probably agree with that, don't you, Gabriella?"

Rafael had turned fully to her, the slight curve of his lips fading as their eyes met, and she foggily realized the people he'd been talking to had moved on. Several beats passed as they just stared at one another, and Gabby wished she had some idea how to answer him but had no clue.

His lids lowered slightly, and something hot and alive flickered inside that deep green. "You weren't listening at all, were you, *bella*?" He stepped closer, his voice a low rumble. "Something else on your mind?"

Yeah. Oh, yeah, but I'm not saying what. Except she had a bad feeling it was written in red neon on her forehead for him to see anyway. Frantically trying to come up with an answer that wasn't incriminating, she managed one word. "Sweatpants."

A slow smile creased his face and made his eyes gleam. "Mine too, Gabriella. Let's get out of here."

"I don't believe you even own sweatpants."

"Not true. I have all the latest designers' versions in every color, like any prince should."

"Now you're making fun of me. I wasn't saying you wouldn't have any because you're a prince, it's because…because…oh, never mind." He might have been saying sweet and complimentary things about her all night, but it still felt strange to tell him what she'd been thinking. Which was that he exuded a regal confidence all too well suited by the tuxedo he wore. Then again, that same presence filled any room he was in at the clinic, even wearing scrubs, so clearly it had nothing to do with what he wore.

Or what he didn't.

Shocked at the sudden fantasy of what he might look like naked, which she sort of, kind of almost knew, she pinched her lips closed so she wouldn't say anything completely embarrassing as he opened the car door. So focused on her thoughts and, well, truthfully, on *him* and his sheer, breathtaking masculinity as he held her hand, she barely noticed the dozens of flashbulbs lighting the night. His big body shielded her from the cameras as he tucked her into his car before sliding into the driver's seat.

"Seat belt on?" The engine roared to life as he turned the key in the ignition, pausing to look at her with one eyebrow quirked.

"Yes."

"Good." The car rolled slowly forward for about ten feet, then took off like a rocket down the curve and onto the main road.

CHAPTER SEVEN

THE GROWLING SPORTS car's sudden acceleration shoved Gabby back into the sumptuously curved leather seat, and she gasped then chuckled. "You must be in a hurry to get into those sweatpants."

He didn't answer. Just looked at her with that glint in his eyes. A gaze so unnerving she felt like he might be seeing something clear down in her soul she didn't want him to see. He was close, so close to her inside the small confines of the car it seemed he'd sucked every bit of oxygen completely out of the space, making it very hard to breathe.

"Um, you're making me nervous," she finally said. "If you're looking at me, that means you're not looking at the road, and if I have to die, I want equal billing in the headlines."

"Equal billing?" His gaze finally moved to the road, and she let out a relieved breath. "What do you mean?"

"You know, instead of 'Prince Rafael Moreno and some other person die in car crash,' I'd like to at least get 'Joe Schmoe and Gabby Cain plunge into a canyon to their deaths.'"

He laughed. "And here I would have thought you didn't crave publicity, like most of our patients do."

"I'm kidding, of course. Believe me, the last thing

I would ever want is my name splashed in the papers for any reason." Not that it would ever happen to her. But she'd seen enough times when patients got publicity they'd originally wanted, only to have it result in reporters digging deep into details of their lives they didn't want shared.

"I've been in the media since the day I was born. You get used to it."

"I didn't get what that might be like, not really, until all those cameras flashed in my face. It may be just a part of life for people like you and Cameron Fontaine, but I bet it's still not fun." And suddenly it struck her that someone just might want to put a name to *her* face. Some unknown woman attending tonight's party with a Mediterranean prince. Her stomach tightened at the thought, until she remembered that Freya had made a big, public deal out of her being a midwife at The Hollywood Hills Clinic. Surely that's all they would report. Probably no one would feel a need to look beyond that.

The car ground to a halt against the curb in front of her apartment. Rafael turned off the engine and the sudden quiet seemed to ring in her ears along with her rapid heartbeat. He had that look in his eyes again. The one he'd had all evening, as though he thought she was special. Beautiful, which he'd said, but men so often didn't mean what they said, she knew. Sometimes their words were a thoughtless, casual compliment, or a tactic to get sex, or a way to distract a woman from starting important conversations.

And yet when Rafael complimented her, it didn't feel like any of those things. It struck her that, other than the appreciation she often got from her patients, she hadn't felt special to anyone in a very long time.

The last time she had, it had proven to be a mirage.

Evaporating when she'd messed up so badly. Her mistake had broken her heart. Then, along with being heartbroken, she'd been suddenly alone, just when she'd needed support and love more than at any other time in her life.

She drew in a breath, shoved the pain of those negative memories aside, and stomped on them for good measure. Wasn't she Cinderella, just for tonight? Maybe she didn't really deserve happiness, but this evening Rafael had made her feel wonderful and carefree, and she wasn't quite ready for the evening, and those good feelings, to end.

"Would you…like to come in for coffee?"

The eyes that seemed to be studying her with questions in them warmed, crinkling at the corners as he smiled. "I'd like that very much."

Once inside, she ushered him to sit down, and her belly quivered with a maelstrom of nerves and excitement. She'd lived in L.A. for two years but had never had even one man in her apartment. There'd been good reason for that, and there still was, but tonight was a fairy tale, right? One evening before her life went back to normal at midnight.

"Feel free to change into those sweats so you're more comfortable," he said, slipping off his tuxedo jacket and settling himself onto one side of her sofa. "I would if I could."

She watched his long, tanned fingers pull the end of his bow tie, sliding it off before slowly unbuttoning his top shirt buttons, revealing a bronzed throat. Then realized she was just standing there motionless, practically mooning over the man.

Yep. Tuxedo libido all right.

"I think I'll do that. Be right back."

Alone in her room, she felt a twinge of regret at having to take off the dress that had made her feel like she was floating as they'd danced around the ballroom. But it would feel silly, not to mention uncomfortable, to be sitting in her living room in a long gown. As she slid off her clothes, the brief thought of Rafael walking into her room and sweeping her into his arms shortened her breath, but at the same time she laughed at herself. Definitely too much fairy-tale fantasy going on in her head tonight! One thing she was sure of—arrogant or not, playboy reputation or not, he wasn't the kind of man to do something inappropriate like that.

She quickly slipped into a T-shirt and the shapeless, comfy sweatpants they'd joked about, feeling even more unisex in them than the scrubs she wore most days. But if she put on jeans to look at least marginally attractive, he might know why. As the thoughts pinged around in her brain she rolled her eyes at herself and snorted. "Get a grip on yourself, Gabby. He's probably just here to be polite."

But when she emerged to walk across the living room, the way his gaze tracked her made her feel like she still had that gown on after all. Heart thudding, she made coffee in her small kitchen that opened to the living room so she could still see him, watching her in a way that was unnerving but exciting.

"Do you take cream or sugar?"

"Just black."

She handed him the cup, hyperaware of the feel of his fingers sliding against hers as he took it. Then stood there hesitating, probably looking like a fool, as she pondered whether or not to sit next to him on the sofa or several, discreet feet away in a chair.

The decision was made for her when he reached for

her hand and gave it a gentle tug. "Sit by me. You can curl up in comfort a lot better here than over there."

"How did you know this is my curling-up corner? Was I eyeing it longingly?"

"You could say that."

Oh, Lord. Maybe he'd spotted her eyeing *him* longingly. Breaking eye contact with that amused green, she took longer than necessary to slide her cup onto a coaster before scrunching up in the corner as far away from him as possible. Which was still just a couple feet from him. She needed a distraction, and picked her cup up to take a sip, eyeing him over the rim, wondering if the heat radiating through her body was from his nearness or the coffee. She had a bad feeling it had nothing to do with her drink.

Despite loosening his top shirt buttons, there was no way he could be described as being able to "curl up in comfort."

"I feel bad you're still in your starched finery, but I don't think anything I have here would fit you."

"Which is a good thing, as I always feel a little strange when I'm at a woman's home and she opens a wardrobe of men's clothes for me to choose from."

"Does that really happen?"

"More than you'd guess. Which is one of the many reasons spending time with you is like breathing in fresh air."

"Does that line usually work for you?"

"It's one I haven't used before, because I meant it." His eyes gleamed. "Maybe you can tell me how well it works."

She gulped. Should she tell him that just hearing that deep, sexy voice of his recite the alphabet might make her jump into his lap? If she'd been a different kind of woman, that was. A woman interested in being with a man. "I'm not much of an expert on lines men use, so I'm not a good person to ask."

"If that's true, the men in Los Angeles must not be very bright. You're not only beautiful, in the short time I've known you I've seen you're smart and caring and feisty and damned special. And I promise that's not a line."

The amusement had left his face, and his expression was utterly serious as he looked at her. Gabby felt her heart melting and thudding and had no idea what she was supposed to say in response. Maybe compliment him too?

"And I've seen that you're not the arrogant jerk I thought you were. Just a doctor who does what it takes to make things right for a patient, whether it's good medical care, empathy, or humor. Princely attitude notwithstanding."

"Thank you. I think." He smiled again. "Is that what's called a backhanded compliment? But I probably deserve both the good and bad from it. So tell me. Why do you work so much? So many double shifts? And when you're not working, why do you keep mostly to yourself?"

Startled by the turn of the conversation, she found herself hesitating, for a split second feeling a shocking need to share her past, her mistakes. Her pain. But that was ridiculous. She didn't talk to anyone about it. She barely knew Rafael, and he probably wouldn't want their evening together to be spoiled by a depressing conversation. Not to mention that the last thing she needed was for everyone at the hospital to know who she really was. "I love my job. And who says I keep mostly to myself?"

"Freya. James. Even if they hadn't, I've seen it just in the short time I've been here. Seen a sadness that you carry with you." He reached to grasp her hand again, his touch warm and comforting and somehow arousing all at the same time. "What makes you sad, Gabriella?"

"I... Nothing." Just the bittersweet part of her job, bringing babies into the world to loving parents who wanted them. Praying they never had to know how it felt to lose one. "How about you? What makes Rafael Moreno travel the world, working hard and playing hard?"

"Different reasons. But one I just found out? Once in a very long while I'm lucky to meet someone remarkable I enjoy being with." He moved closer, his fingers slipping beneath her chin to bring her gaze to the darkening green one staring at her. "Someone who makes me feel strangely happy in a way I didn't even realize I wanted to."

She stared in breathless fascination as his mouth slowly lowered to hers, giving her time to protest or pull away, but she found she wanted his kiss. Wanted it with a desperation new to her experience. Had wanted it, if she was honest, all the hours they'd spent together.

His lips touched hers, warm and soft and gentle. Not demanding or insistent or aggressive, as she would have expected a man like him to kiss. No, it was the sweetest kiss she'd ever experienced in her life, his mouth moving slowly and surely on hers, giving and taking, and the longer it went on the more her heart liquefied into a puddle of want for him.

The fingers beneath her chin slipped across her jaw, his wide palm cupping her cheek as the kiss deepened, heated, and Gabby was glad she was half lying down or she was sure she'd have fallen down.

"Gabriella." His usually almost nonexistent accent thickened slightly as he spoke against her mouth. "I knew you would taste *delicioso*."

"It's…the coffee."

She could feel him smile even as he kept pressing soft kisses to her lips. "No, *belleza*, it's most definitely you."

A sigh of pleasure left her lips as the kiss went from slow and sweet to hot and wet and so earth-shattering she found herself clutching his muscled shoulders and hanging on for dear life. His palms had moved from her face to tangle in her hair, turning her head to the perfect angle for a deep, mind-blowing kiss. Dazed, she realized one hand had moved down to slip beneath her T-shirt, tracking across her skin in a slow caress that made her shiver, finally resting on her breast through her bra.

"I…see now why you wanted me to change out of my dress."

"I was just thinking of your comfort. And I still am." He surprised her by moving his hand off her breast to caress her ribs again, pressing another soft kiss to her mouth, and she quivered at the tenderness of it. "Obviously, I want you. But not if the Gabriella who mostly keeps to herself will regret it tomorrow. You know I'm here for only a little while, and I have a feeling you're not a woman comfortable with making love with a man who's not able to stick around long."

"Not normally, I admit." But she'd learned not to expect someone to stick around, hadn't she? And as she looked into the green of his eyes, dark and questioning and filled with the same intoxicating desire she was feeling, she knew with certainty that tonight was the one time to change that. "I'm content with my life as it is. But I want you, too. And tonight I feel like being Cinderella, making love with you before I turn back into plain old Gabby Cain at midnight."

"That's the worst description of you imaginable." He seemed to study her a long moment, and she wasn't sure what he was seeing, or looking for. His fingertips traced her cheekbone as his thumb caressed her bottom lip. "You, Gabriella Cain, take my breath away."

Then he kissed her again, slowly and deeply, taking her breath away, too. The kiss held so much promise of delicious, incredible sex she uttered a sound of protest when he stopped. "Are you absolutely sure? Because I need to know now or it might kill me to stop."

"I'm sure, okay?" He appeared so suddenly hesitant she was afraid he'd leap up and leave, which might kill *her*. "Take my word for it. The last thing I want is to end up in a Mediterranean prison for killing a prince."

He chuckled against her mouth. "The prisons at home don't have as many rats as they used to, but it's probably still wise to stay out of them."

"That's my plan."

"Good. Coincides well with mine." She gasped as his lips moved to her jaw, down to her throat, touching the sensitive spot beneath her ear as he deftly flicked the front clasp of her bra open. "I'm wondering if you're perhaps overly warm. I know I am."

Before she could even form an answer, he'd somehow managed to slip her T-shirt over her head and her bra straps down her arms and was staring at her nakedness. His eyes were dark and slashes of color rode high on his cheekbones as his gaze scorched her. Her heart thumped so hard against her ribs she thought he might actually be able to see it pounding.

"You are even more beautiful than I envisioned, *mi*

ángel." The glide of his touch across her breasts felt nearly reverent as his gaze returned to hers, and even as she was shocked that she was doing this, letting herself be with a man again, with *this* man in particular, she wanted him more than she could ever remember wanting anyone.

He kissed her again, hotter and more intense, lying nearly on top of her now, pressing her into the cushions, and the small groan that left his mouth and swirled into hers just about set her on fire. Knowing he was as aroused as she was had her arching her back for more, pressing her breasts against him, only to discover it wasn't enough to feel his shirt there. She wanted his skin against hers, and fumbled to get the shirt open and off.

Except she hadn't done this for a long time, and never with a tuxedo shirt, which she was learning had aggravatingly difficult buttons, and couldn't manage to make it happen. Her sounds of frustration made him smile against her mouth before he leaned back.

"Let me, *bella.*"

In a slow striptease, he worked the buttons one by one, his lips curved at the same time his eyes smoldered, intently focused on her as she watched him. Inch by torturous inch, he exposed a chest even more muscled than she remembered, his bronzed skin covered with dark hair that looked as soft and silky and outrageously manly as the rest of him.

Mouth dry, she knew with certainty that this was truly a Cinderella night. That she'd never again be with a man as physically perfect as Prince Rafael Moreno, and she still couldn't quite wrap her brain around the fact that he wanted to be with her as much as she wanted to be with him.

Then she couldn't admire his chest anymore because he lowered himself to her, his bare and scorchingly hot torso pressed against hers. He kissed her again, and she practically drowned in the deliciousness of it all. Her bones turned to utter liquid when he skimmed that talented mouth down her throat, across her collarbone, then on to her breasts. Gasping, her hands burrowed into the thick softness of his hair as he ministered to one nipple, then the other, and she didn't care that she was making little sounds and moving beneath him and pressing against him because control had gone out the window and all she wanted was to experience the incredible way he was making her feel.

Vaguely, she was aware of wide, warm palms slipping inside her sweatpants to cup her rear, then more aware of his hot mouth tracking from her breast down her belly as the pants and panties disappeared off over her feet, leaving her naked. Strong hands slid back up her legs to caress her thighs, his mouth following.

"Rafael." She didn't know what she was going to say, exactly, and wasn't sure she could talk at all—her breath was so choppy she feared she might hyperventilate.

"Gabriella." His teeth nipped her knee, followed by a teasing lick, moving up to her hipbone, and she jumped with a laughing gasp. "Shall we take this to the bedroom?"

"No. I might combust before then."

A low, masculine laugh full of satisfaction swept across her skin. "*Bueno*. Me as well."

Licking across her quivering belly, he touched her right where she wanted to be touched, and she gasped and wriggled against his talented fingers, until finally she couldn't wait any longer. She reached for him, only to realize his darned pants were still on and completely in the way, just like his shirt had been. "What are your pants doing on? Get them off, fast."

He gave a short laugh. "And you call me bossy?"

"I'm assertive when I need to be. And, believe me, right now I need to be."

His eyes blazed at her with both amusement and heat. "My pants are on because I keep a condom in them. But not for long."

"I appreciate a prepared prince," she managed to say.

Another husky chuckle left his lips as he shucked his pants and took care of the condom, thankfully seeming to be in as much of a hurry as she was. He lowered his body to hers, and she gasped at the amazing sensation as he gently, slowly joined with her body, arching helplessly as they began to move together.

"Cariña. Mi ángel." His whispered words had her blinking open her eyes, and his were the greenest she'd seen them, focused and gleaming and locked on hers. More Spanish words left his lips, first in whispers then louder as they rocked together until she cried out, and he joined with her in a long, low groan that reverberated in her chest.

The way he gathered her against him, tangling his fingers in her hair to tuck her face against his warm throat, felt tender and protective, and Gabby let herself absorb the intimacy and wonder of it. She tried hard not to think about how good it felt, how right, and how, when midnight came, Cinderella would be back in her corner all alone once again.

CHAPTER EIGHT

RAFAEL LISTENED TO the sound of his footsteps echoing across the marble-tiled foyer and wished he'd worn his scrubs and crepe-soled shoes instead, planning to change out of his regular shirt and dress pants if he'd needed to deliver a baby. Then cursed lightly under his breath at himself as he caught himself glancing around guiltily.

When was the last time he'd felt like a boy trying to sneak around undetected? Not since he'd been in primary school, since even before high school most people in authority hadn't felt comfortable disciplining the second-born prince of their country. It was no wonder he'd run a little wild at times.

His various sports adventures, dating adventures, and foolish errors in judgment had been so well documented by the press over the years, he'd believed he was immune to caring about it. And he was immune, really, except that he had to care for Gabriella's sake.

Yes, there were the occasional non-sensationalized stories. Ones that talked about medical school, and the years of study he put in to become a doctor and his actual work. But articles like that didn't seem to hold as much interest for most people as the simple fact that he'd been born under the blessing and curse of royalty.

Not that it was only the public who felt that way, since his own family was pretty uninterested in his accomplishments. There were those times when he was happy about the press coverage, if it brought attention to the needs of the many women around the world who were underserved by proper medical care—or didn't have access to care at all. But those kinds of stories were unfortunately few and far between.

As he skulked through the clinic, he felt ridiculous. And selfish. Spending time with Gabriella while he was in L.A. was more than good for him, but for her? Not so much. Being out in public with him definitely exposed her to potential embarrassment, with the media sniffing around. To having things publicly spread about her, and whether they were truth or lies wouldn't matter.

He'd dated plenty of women who liked having their faces in the tabloids, holding on to his arm. But Gabriella wasn't like other women. In so many ways. Something about her had grabbed his insides and tugged hard at his soul from the first second he'd met her. Her fiery temper had matched that beautiful hair of hers, then the next second she'd been endearingly sweet and caring with their very difficult patient. Add to that a sexiness she seemed barely aware of and a sadness in the depths of those brown eyes, and she was fascinating with a capital F.

The vision of the smile in her eyes and on her lips as they'd danced last night, the sight of her beautiful naked body as they'd made love, the memories of how her skin had felt against his, had him closing his eyes to hold it all inside. Had him wanting to find her right then, pull her into an empty room, and kiss her breathless.

But she deserved better than him. Deserved more than a man who would only be around for a month or two. Deserved the kind of man who was capable of offering her a commitment and a future, if that was what she wanted. And he wasn't that man.

No. For her sake, he should steer clear of her from now on. Let last night be one great memory for both of them. The last thing he would ever want would be to add to the sadness in her eyes after he'd moved on.

He sighed and, feeling a little bruised, rubbed his chest. Knew that the bruising was inside, not out, but it would heal. At least, he assumed it would. He'd never felt quite like this before, so he couldn't be sure. But it would be far worse to keep seeing Gabriella and bruise her, too.

Time to stop moping and get to work. He stopped at the computer outside one of the nurses' stations to check some charts, and decided to see Cameron Fontaine first. Medically, she was absolutely fine. But she'd wanted to stay at the hospital a little longer, both so she could be near baby Skye and because she didn't want to be seen in public while she was losing her "baby fat."

Rafael and everyone else had reassured her it was hardly noticeable, though he knew many of the new mothers giving birth at the clinic worried about the same thing, having to live in the very close scrutiny of the public eye. Cameron was happy to be eating healthy spa food specially prepared to have the nutrition she needed, while helping her lose weight as she worked with personal fitness trainers. And, Lord knew, a happy Cameron made the lives of everyone in the clinic easier.

Including Gabriella's, and he again marveled at her amazing patience and even empathy with a woman who could be pretty demanding. Then realized his every thought seemed to lead right back to Gabriella. How had his head become so consumed with her in such a short period of time?

Deep in thought on his way to Cameron's room, the woman on his mind seemed to practically materialize out of thin air. She'd probably come out of the door he'd been about to walk by, but since her face had been what he'd been seeing and not the hallway, it gave him a start to see her actually there.

From the expression on her face, he'd startled her, too. Her face seemed to flush as she stared at him, and she swept her hair behind her ears in a nervous gesture he'd only seen that night in his house when she'd run into his naked chest. The night he'd wanted to kiss her to see how she'd react.

Which reminded him all over again what it had been like to kiss her the night before. Along with all the other things they'd done together over the course of the night, and he had a feeling his face was flushed, too, but not with nervousness. With a heat he'd had a hard time banking down every time he'd thought of her since leaving her in the wee hours of the morning.

"Good morning, Ms. Cain."

"Um, good morning, Dr. Moreno."

Her voice was husky, and her tongue flicked out to lick her lips, and he was damned if all his resolutions to the contrary moments ago didn't fly straight out of his brain. Replaced by that desire to grab her up, take her to the nearest empty room, and kiss her until neither of them could breathe.

"I was about to see Cameron Fontaine," he said, forcing his mind away from the thoughts that were actually making his body hard as they stood there in public. "Have you checked on her this morning?"

"Yes. She's in the gym with the fitness trainer right

now, so you'll have to see someone else first. Speaking of which, I have a patient waiting in my office. She's feeling nervous about some pain and wants to talk to me about it. Excuse me."

She turned without another word and hurried down the corridor. He watched her slim rear in her scrubs swaying slightly, which immediately took his thoughts back yet again to last night and how she'd looked in her sweats. Then out of them. Which he'd sworn to himself he'd stop thinking about.

Maybe he needed to hit the clinic gym himself for a long workout, then a nice cold shower.

"Dr. Moreno! Rafael!"

Gabriella's urgent voice had him turning to see her running back in his direction. "What's wrong?"

"We have a precipitous delivery. My patient thought she might be imagining things, but she's already eight centimeters dilated. Would you go and see to her while I get the pre-cep pack? My office."

Rafael strode to the room. Knowing Gabriella knew what she was doing should have prepared him, but he was still surprised to see a woman lying on the floor of Gabriella's office, practically wedged between the chairs in front of her desk, writhing and moaning, with blood beneath her on the floor. He cursed under his breath, because it was pretty obvious it was too late to move her to a birthing suite. He gave her knee a quick, reassuring pat. "It's going to be all right. I'm Dr. Moreno, and Ms. Cain is getting what we need to help you, okay?"

He shoved the desk against the wall then grabbed the chairs. As he carried them into the hallway to give them all room, he could see Gabby tearing toward him with a big bowl in her hands.

"Everything should be in here. Clamps, scissors, bulb suction, sutures. Syringe for delivering intramuscular Pitocin. Blankets."

"IV bag?"

"Yes."

He and Gabriella shared a look. It was clear she'd experienced this before, and also knew the potential hazards of delivering a baby under these conditions. A shriek of pain drew their attention to the patient, who was gasping and clutching her belly.

"I want… I want an epidural now."

"I'm afraid it's too late for that," Gabriella said in a gentle, soothing voice. "The baby's coming fast, Trina, but that's good news, because it won't hurt for long, right?"

"Then let's get the C-section done fast. But you can't do the C-section here, can you?" Trina sucked in a few heavy breaths. "I… I don't think I can walk. Can you get me moved to wherever you do that, maybe in a wheelchair?"

"C-section?" Gabriella glanced at Rafael with a question in her eyes, obviously asking if he'd somehow had a conversation with the woman about a Caesarean in the minute she'd been gone. He shook his head but since it was her patient kept quiet to let Gabriella handle it as she saw fit.

"Yes. I talked to my doctor about a C-section so I wouldn't have any changes in my, you know, down there, and he agreed."

"Trina, a vaginal birth is always preferable to a Caesarean section, both for the baby and for the amount of time your body needs to heal."

"I don't care. That's what I want. I know the scar would be low and not noticeable."

The mulish expression on her face contorted into pain as she had another long contraction. Rafael placed his hand on her belly. He could feel the muscles pushing hard, and was sure the baby was on its way. Gabriella must have thought the same thing, as she efficiently set up an IV line in the woman's arm.

Deciding that nature was making the decision for this woman about how her baby would be born, he figured an argument was unnecessary.

"Let's see how much you're dilated now, Trina," he said, giving her what he hoped was a comforting smile. "Do you want me to do the internal exam? Or would you prefer Ms. Cain to?"

"You, please," the woman gasped.

He glanced at Gabriella, and had a hard time not grinning at her narrowed eyes and the expression on her face that was just about the equivalent of her sticking her tongue out at him. But there was a twinkle in those eyes too so he knew she wasn't going to yell at him again.

He snapped on gloves and knelt in front of the woman. "All right. You'll feel a little pressure as I check. You're doing great." Gabriella got the IV taped down, then moved to hold one of Trina's knees.

Then their eyes met in surprise, and the plan changed again. Because the top of baby's head was clearly visible—as he'd guessed, nature had decided when this baby was going to be born. "Guess what, Mama? Baby's decided the time is now. We can see the top of its head. Push hard next time you have a contraction."

"Oh, God! No! I'm… I don't want it to be this way."

Gabby had turned to speak into the microphone around her neck, presumably to call Neonatal and get the troops ready, but now reached to squeeze Trina's hand as she moaned again. "I know, I'm sorry. But, ready or not, here he comes. Breathe now, it's going to be just fine. Give us a push, okay? Another one."

"Great job. Here he comes! I've got his head now." He gently grasped the infant's head, sliding his fingers up to hold the tiny shoulders. "Another push."

As the mother labored, Gabriella kept up her encouragement. "You're doing an amazing job, Trina. Remember to breathe. Puff, puff, puff. One more. Oh, my, you've done it! He's here, and so beautiful!"

The baby was a good color and seemed to be under no stress at all, and the usual, spontaneous satisfaction hit Rafael square in the chest. He grinned at the mother then at Gabriella. Their eyes met for the briefest moment, but it was long enough to see she felt exactly like he did, which was that he wanted to pump his fists in the air that all had gone smoothly, despite the not-very-normal situation.

"You can be front-page news if you want to be, Trina," Gabriella said as she did a quick bulb suction on the baby before handing him to his mother. "I think you might be the first woman to give birth on the floor of the clinic midwife's office."

Trina, obviously tired but now beaming, laughed. "Being on the front page is always one of my goals."

Something Rafael couldn't imagine, and he'd be glad to have her take his place the next time it happened.

Neonatal arrived to take the baby and get him cleaned up and swaddled.

"Your body was obviously perfectly made for this, Trina, with baby coming so fast and easy, and with no complications at all." Rafael had learned that it was always good to distract his patients with chitchat and jokes while he took care of post-birth necessities. "You might consider doing it another ten times or so. What do you think?"

Predictably, Trina laughed at the same time she scowled at him. "Easy for you to say when you're not the one who went through the pain or got your body all stretched out. Besides, every woman's body is made for birthing babies, right? It's our curse in life, though I have to say he just might be worth it."

He smiled at the happy, adoring look she was giving her baby, then glanced at Gabriella, wanting to enjoy her smile, too.

Except she wasn't smiling. Her eyes held the sadness he'd seen in them before. No, this time he'd even call it anguish, and her slender shoulders were slumped with the weight of something heavy but invisible. Seeing her pain, that same heavy weight seemed to settle in his own chest as it ached for her, and he knew that, damn it, he had to learn what was making her feel this way.

To hell with keeping his distance. With keeping her safe from him. He might not have much to offer her other than the here and now and an ear to listen and a shoulder to cry on, but he could at least offer that. Or whatever it was she needed from him.

God knew, he was well acquainted with what it felt like to not have anyone close who particularly cared who you really were.

Dios. He wanted, right then, to take her in his arms and kiss away that sadness. To whisk her off somewhere to talk about it right now, to find out the source and show her that, whatever it was, it would be all right. Except they were at work, caring for a new mother and a new life. Waiting wasn't his strength, but patients had to come first.

Gabriella must have felt that he was watching her,

maybe even sensed the intensity and turmoil inside him at that moment, because she turned to look at him. Their gazes fused for a long moment of charged connection before she blinked, then turned away. He saw a smile force its way to her lips as her face became a smooth mask. She chatted with Trina as she was helped onto a gurney to transport her to a room, and cooed over the baby the neonatal team had placed back in its mother's arms.

Anyone who hadn't been looking at Gabriella exactly when he had might have seen only the pleased, warm midwife caring for her patient. Giving them the kind of heartfelt attention and empathy any pregnant woman would be lucky to receive from her nurse.

Gabriella seemed to be pointedly directing her attention to anywhere and anyone but him as she and a technician got the room cleaned up. Just before the new mother was wheeled out, she thanked him and he turned to smile at her, chucking the little newborn under his chin but still thinking of Gabriella busying herself behind him. He pondered how exactly to approach her. His phone rang, and the screen told him it was James.

He stepped into the hallway, keeping an eye on Gabriella's office door to make sure she didn't escape before he had a chance to talk to her.

"Hello, James, what's up?"

"Can you take a couple of days to go to a special destination?" James asked.

"Depends on the destination."

"A sheikh friend and his wife and extended family are staying in Vail, Colorado. He came here to take care of some business in L.A., and they were planning to leave the U.S. day after tomorrow. Except it looks like she might be close to delivering earlier than expected. Any way you can head to the mountains to see what's going on?"

He didn't have to ask why they didn't just go to the local hospital or see a doctor there. He knew a number of Middle Eastern princes, and they didn't "do" local hospitals without having some connection, along with a guarantee of privacy.

"Any way they can get here?"

"No. He's worried, and doesn't want her to travel. So, can you?"

"Yes." For the first time in half an hour he felt like smiling. "Though I'd need assistance, which means you'll have to adjust Gabriella Cain's schedule so she can come with me."

"Those are your terms?" A low laugh came down the phone line. "Fine. But I hope you know what the hell you're doing, and why you're doing it."

Rafael wasn't too sure he knew either of those things, but he was going with it anyway.

CHAPTER NINE

Swooping down then back up and around on the winding road that had been cut through sheer rock cliffs, the powerful rented sedan effortlessly handled the mountain curves Gabby was sure her own little car would have struggled with mightily. With any other driver at the wheel, she might have been a little nervous at the speed with which he was taking the sweeping turns, but Rafael's supreme confidence was evident, just like it was at work. Or anywhere else, for that matter.

She couldn't help but wonder if her coming along on this work trip had been James's idea or Rafael's. Somehow, she had a feeling it was the prince wielding his powers of persuasion, which was a nice way to say he was manipulative. But how could she be sorry about that?

She glanced at the man and his gorgeous profile, a smile playing at the corners of his mouth.

"Spectacular, isn't it, Gabriella?"

"Yes." And she wasn't about to tell him she was thinking of his looks as well as the scenery. "But I'm surprised you wanted to take the time to drive from the airport, instead of using a helicopter. I thought the Sheikh was worried to death."

"The chopper would only cut about twenty minutes

off the trip. And I talked to both the Sheikh and his wife on the phone. Between you and me, I'm almost positive this is false labor, and maybe not even that. She's taking every twinge or odd feeling as something catastrophic. But of course we need to confirm that, which is why we're here."

Gabby stared out the window, suddenly not seeing the craggy rock cliffs and tumbling river below. She was remembering the odd twinges. Peculiar, off sensations that she too had assumed were nothing, focusing on her patient instead. A stupid error in judgment that had ended up being catastrophic indeed. "I hope we're seeing her as soon as we get there. Just in case."

"Don't worry. We are."

He must have sensed something in her response, because his voice had changed from pleased at enjoying their drive to more serious.

"If you think it's unlikely to be labor, why did you want me to come?"

"I don't know this man, and some sheikhs can be difficult to deal with. Traditional attitudes being what they are, it can be helpful to have a woman who's an experienced midwife helping care for his wife."

"I guess I can see that. How often has Dr. Jet-Setting OB run into problems with that?"

"A few times. When I do, I put on a wig and a dress. Solves everything."

He flashed her a quick grin, and Gabby laughed at that amusing and absurd vision. As though putting on those items would in any way disguise the potent masculinity that exuded from the man.

The road flattened and soon the wilderness gave way to houses and large apartment buildings alongside the highway, then the town of Vail itself came into view.

Rafael swung the car through a roundabout and on into the village, where cobbled walks and charming buildings lined the streets, many designed to look like they belonged in an old Swiss town.

"Like I said, we'll stop at the hospital first, then check into the hotel."

Unable to shake the unease she felt about the pregnant woman's condition, Gabby was just about to ask how far it was to the hospital when she saw signs for it and they swung into the parking lot. "Wow, I'm surprised the hospital is so close to the main town. And how did you know where it was?"

"I've been here a few times. It's a good gig to combine skiing with working."

"I'd think you'd do that in Switzerland and Austria."

"There, too. Among other places. Like I said, it's a good gig." That grin again, then he was out of the car and coming over to her side to open the door, reaching for her hand.

"You don't have to open my door, you know. I'm an open-my-own-door kind of woman."

"Sorry if it bothers you. But as you noted the first day we met, I do as I please. And it pleases me to be a gentleman."

The words held a tinge of that arrogance that was just part of him, but his eyes were warm and sincere. Even as she rolled her eyes a little, she had to laugh. "I guess it's impossible for a prince to not believe he can do as he pleases. And since you haven't asked me to kiss your ring, I guess I'll indulge you by letting you assist me out of the car."

"The only reason I haven't asked you to kiss my ring is because I don't wear one. But I would like you to kiss something else." And with that, he leaned into the car and pressed his mouth to hers.

For a split second she stared into half-closed moss-green eyes before her own flickered shut. And just like that her heart began to pump in slow thuds as she savored the taste of him in her mouth, as she breathed in his scent, letting herself slowly sink into the kiss until he broke the delicious contact and pulled back.

The eyes staring at her this time had darkened, and it seemed his chest rose and fell in several deep breaths before his lip quirked at one corner. "Air's thin up here, isn't it? Let's go."

He held out his hand, and she didn't say a word as she slipped hers into it. Then kept it there as they walked into the hospital, and she had the same bad-good feeling she'd had when James had first told her she needed to come on this trip.

She'd never get truly involved with a man again. Never fully trust that kind of relationship. But if she had to briefly fall off that wagon, wasn't Rafael the perfect man to do it with? Okay, yes, she already had, figuring it would be just that one time. But she was beginning to see that, as long as he was still working at the clinic, there was no way she could resist letting their professional time together turn personal.

She wanted him. Again. And it looked like he wanted her the exact same way.

Her lips hadn't stopped tingling, and she willed herself to look normal as they stopped at the front desk to get directions to the seventh floor. Still holding her hand, he led her to the elevator. "I didn't hear what the room number was."

"That's because there's no need to know it. They've paid big money to basically rent out the whole floor."

"The whole floor?"

"Not uncommon. The Sheikh wants privacy and discretion. He'll likely have flown in his own staff to prepare food for everyone and to tend to his wife. Possibly brought comfortable furnishings for their stay here. I had one patient in Morocco whose family brought twelve place settings of fine china from their palace to the hospital."

"Wow." That was about the only thought she could conjure, though she wasn't sure if it was because she was so amazed or because her brain could only focus on one thing at a time, and at that moment it was still thinking about his lips and the feel of his hand wrapped around hers. About the rest of their stay here together and where it all might lead.

Rafael punched the elevator button and the doors closed. Alone in the enclosed space, their recent kiss sizzled in the air between them, so hot she could practically feel it burning her skin. And from the slight flare to his nostrils, the way his skin seemed to tighten over his cheekbones he felt every bit as much heat as she did.

The elevator pinged open just in time, since her fantasy of grabbing him and pushing him back against the wall to have her way with him was making her feel a little woozy. Their eyes met, and she saw his lips curved in a half-smile and realized hers were, too. Then he gave her a quick wink, and it was so unexpected from autocratic Prince Rafael Moreno she gave a little breathless laugh.

"We'll hold that thought until later, hmm, *bella*?" he murmured.

They walked down the corridor, and Gabby couldn't help but stare at the number of people around. Some wore uniforms, and others were dressed in elegant clothes. There were even quite a few children, and while some occupied themselves quietly with a board game, several boys were tearing down the hall, kicking a ball and shouting.

"This looks like a hospital, and yet not," she said to Rafael in disbelief. "Does the hospital director know this is going on?"

"I'm willing to bet he's done this drill once or twice so, yes. Also planned ahead and put away any equipment that could be damaged by an errant kick." His eyes twinkled. "Let's see how our patient is doing. I'll find out where she is."

He stepped toward a small group of women and started speaking in some language Gabby had never heard, amazed at him and his various skills. Though she shouldn't have been, really. Probably a prince grew up learning any number of languages. She felt embarrassed all over again at her very rudimentary knowledge of Spanish, vowing to study it more. She hadn't needed it too much in Seattle, but speaking the language even halfway well would come in very handy in California.

"This way," Rafael said. He didn't lead the way, having her follow. Instead, he waited for her to join him, then pressed his hand against her lower back as they walked together.

"More of your gentlemanliness? Waiting for me?" she teased.

"Or maybe I just wanted an excuse to touch you."

The gaze that met hers was twinkling, but hot, too, and Gabby sank her teeth into her lower lip to make sure nothing came out that shouldn't. Something along the lines of *You don't need an excuse, which I'm pretty sure you know.*

Acutely aware of that wide hand on her back, she

had to wonder when she'd gone from being an efficient workaholic uninterested in dating to a woman with sex on her mind in the middle of a hospital. Though she knew the answer, and it was standing right next to her in all its six-foot-plus gorgeous glory.

When they went into the patient's room, Gabby was in for yet another unexpected sight. The place looked more like a plush hotel room than a hospital room. Even more so than The Hollywood Hills Clinic rooms—and, since she'd always thought they seemed right out of a five-star hotel, that was saying something. This had to be one of those situations Rafael mentioned where they'd brought in furniture for their stay. A portable wall between two rooms had been removed, creating a huge space, and comfortable furniture filled the area. The bed was still a hospital bed, but it had beautiful linens, and the bedspread looked like something from a high-end furnishings magazine.

An exotic-looking woman lay in the bed, which surprised Gabby a little. Since she wasn't connected to any monitors or IV at this point, Gabby would have expected her to be sitting in one of the deep, upholstered armchairs, but maybe she felt more comfortable lying down. Or maybe, since Rafael had said her husband was worried, everyone thought she should stay in the bed to be safe.

Rafael made introductions, then focused his attention on speaking with the Sheikh, which also surprised Gabby. Normally, getting information and history directly from the patient was important, but since Rafael knew that, it must be part of the typical protocol in this very atypical situation. Maybe this was exactly why he'd wanted her to come, so she could speak directly to the patient without going through her husband first. If she spoke English, that was.

Of course, she couldn't deny that she hoped Rafael had wanted her along for another reason, too. Then scolded herself for having that sex subject dive back into her mind when she had work to do.

"Hello, Amala, I'm Gabby Cain, a nurse midwife from The Hollywood Hills Clinic. I understand you're having some pain, and are worried about the baby?"

"Yes." Thankfully, Amala spoke excellent English, and Gabby smiled in relief. "I keep having pains. Contractions, I think."

"Have you timed them at all? To see how far apart they are?"

"No. But they happen often."

"Okay. I'm going to take your pulse and blood pressure to check those—is that all right?" She pressed her fingers to the woman's delicate wrist. "Tell me about the pain. Where is it, exactly?"

"My belly. Low. And down…there as well."

The woman seemed uncomfortable even using a euphemism, and Gabby smiled wider to hopefully relax her. "The good news is that your pulse and blood pressure are normal. So, are you feeling any pain in your back? Up high in your belly?"

"No. Not my back. I am not sure about how high. But they go away sometimes if I lie down."

Sounded like Rafael might be right about this being false labor, but it was too soon to say for sure. She glanced up to see him finishing his conversation with the Sheikh, then he came to join her on the other side of the patient's bed.

"I'm Dr. Rafael Moreno. It's my privilege to come

see you today. I understand you're thirty-four weeks pregnant. Can you tell me about your symptoms?"

Amala repeated what she'd told Gabby, and more as he asked additional questions. Finally, he nodded. "Let's take a look at what baby is doing inside you, using ultrasound. You have it ready, Gabriella?"

"Yes."

"Good." He reached to lift the patient's shirt over her belly, but she stopped him.

"I'd like Gabriella to do it. Please."

The surprise on his face was gone in a blink, replaced by a calm smile. "Of course. Gabriella is excellent with ultrasound, and I can read them later as well, if you want. I'll be back in a little bit."

His gaze lifted from their patient and his eyes met Gabby's. She absolutely could not control the gleeful little smile quivering on her lips that the tide had turned, and this time the patient trusted her to do the job instead of him.

Gabby slowly ran the wand through the warm jelly she'd squeezed on Amala's abdomen, and carefully studied the pictures on the monitor. Seeing that everything looked one hundred percent normal, and that baby seemed healthy in every way, Gabby's knees got a little jelly-like, too, as relief for the woman swept through her. "Baby looks absolutely perfect in there, all snug and happy. I'm going to go over my findings with Dr. Moreno, but I'm confident that the pain you've been experiencing is false labor, which can be very hard to distinguish from true labor."

"Oh, I hope so. I want my baby to be born at home, so this is good news. Thank you so much."

"So glad to be here to help you." And she was. Glad, in a strange kind of way, that she knew exactly how this pregnant woman had felt, which made her a better caregiver. A better nurse and midwife. She cleaned off the gel and got the patient's top back in place. "Let me see what Dr. Moreno thinks, okay?"

She found him sitting at a round table, playing the board game with the kids there, all of them laughing. Struck by how boyish he looked, too, so unlike the arrogant prince or the dashing date, she slowed her steps and just looked at him, her heart feeling all warm and squishy and starstruck.

He glanced up and grinned at her. Unfolding himself from the chair, he came over to her. "False labor?"

"Yes." She cleared her throat and went over the results with him, and for the first time in her professional life a tiny corner of her mind was on something other than her patient and her work. It was on him, and the scent of him, and how close his head was tipped to hers. Afraid everyone in the room could see how she was feeling and what she was thinking, she again went for a joke to cover it all.

"So, Dr. Prince Rafael Moreno, how does it feel to have your patient doubt your skills and send you out of the room, leaving someone else to do the tests?"

"First, she did not doubt my skills. I'm sure she just knew her husband might be jealous because I am so handsome."

The gold flecks sparkling in his green eyes showed he was teasing, and didn't believe that for a minute. Probably it had been more about modesty, but Gabby was going to rib him about it anyway.

"Uh-huh. All I can say is it made me pretty happy for you to get a taste of it, considering how mean you were the first day we met."

"Mean?" All humor left his face as he looked at her

searchingly. "You thought I was mean? I'm sorry if that's how I came across."

"Okay, mean isn't the right word." A man as empathetic as he was didn't have a mean bone in his body. "Dismissive. Disrespectful."

"And for that I apologize too. Only a fool would disrespect or dismiss someone like you, and sometimes the fool in me comes out when it shouldn't."

"Never mind." Lord, she'd meant it really as a joke, and now he looked so contrite, ashamed, even, she was sorry she'd even mentioned it. Who would have thought the man was even capable of feeling that way? "I'm teasing you, really. Like you do me sometimes."

"I know exactly how to make it up to you in about…" he glanced at his watch "…half an hour. Let's talk to the Sheikh and his wife, hmm?"

Walking beside him, she couldn't help but glance up at him more than once, wondering what he'd meant about making it up to her, and her toes and a lot of other things started to tingle as she imagined what it could be.

You're at work, Gabby! she scolded herself. And work was not the place where her mind could be wandering to bad thoughts.

She stood on the opposite side of the patient's bed as Rafael recommended they stay one more day. He told Amala to write down when she had contractions and how long they lasted, and to be ready for Gabby to do one more ultrasound tomorrow. Gabby tried to listen, but since she knew everything he was going to say, watching his lips move seemed far more fascinating. As did wondering what in the world he had in mind to "make it up" to her.

Those darned thoughts of sex came right to the forefront of her brain again. When in the world was that going to stop?

Probably only after Rafael Moreno was long gone back to the Mediterranean or wherever he was headed next. Her life could get back to normal. The life she'd chosen where she worked a lot and stayed relationship-free. Since it was apparent that she couldn't seem to help but be dangerously distracted by him, she knew that day couldn't come soon enough.

Yet she also had a bad feeling it would also come far, far too soon.

CHAPTER TEN

ADVENTURES IN THE sky were nothing new to Rafael. He'd enjoyed hang gliding, glider planes, and skydiving many times all over the world. At the time, he'd thought every one of those adventures was enjoyable, but nothing came close to the evening he'd just spent with Gabriella.

Holding her close as they'd stood in the basket of a hot-air balloon, able to see for miles across the awesome expanse of the Rocky Mountains, they'd floated through a quiet so deep he'd felt it all the way to his soul. Filled with a tranquil contentment he couldn't remember ever feeling in his life.

Listening to her cries of delight as she'd pointed at beautiful blue-green lakes below, at the snow still covering the jagged peaks, at mountain goats picking their way across vertical rocks in a feat that seemed nearly impossible, he'd smiled and laughed and held her closer.

Her hair had blown across her face, and he'd tucked it behind her ears more than once, both to feel its softness within his fingers and so he could better see the joy on her face and in her eyes.

Joy he'd wanted to see there from the moment he'd observed them shadowed with sadness when she'd sat next to Skye's incubator. Joy he'd known was a big part of who she was, or had been until something had chipped away at it. Minimized it. Maybe even crushed it.

As the balloon had sunk back to earth, they'd watched the sun set in a blaze of glorious red and gold behind the mountains. Colors so vivid they'd almost rivaled the strands highlighting Gabriella's beautiful hair.

He'd wanted to have her to himself for a little while longer, away from L.A. and whatever was there that might be the reason she carried that sadness around. Again, he knew that was damned selfish of him, but he'd been having a tough time battling it. And since fate had seemed to give him exactly what he'd wanted, did he really have to fight it?

All he knew was that he didn't seem to have a lot of fight left in him when it came to keeping away from Gabriella.

He opened the door of the hotel restaurant, sliding his hand around hers before they meandered out onto the huge stone patio, warmed by several fire pits surrounded by cushioned chairs. And, lucky for him, it was nearly deserted.

"Would you like to sit out here? Or are you too full to sit after you ate a steak big enough for two people?" he couldn't help but tease.

"Haven't we already discussed how not at all suave it is to talk about how much I eat?" Her eyes gleamed up at him. "All women need iron in their diets. The occasional steak is good for me. But I'm not sure what your excuse is, because you ate even more than I did."

"Fresh out of excuses." That was true for pretty much anything he did around Gabriella, and he didn't care anymore. "Where would you like to sit?"

"By the fire. It's getting chilly, don't you think?"

"We can go inside if you like."

"No. It's so beautiful, I want to stay out here." He followed her gaze over to the timeless mountains, silhouetted by the darkened sky that was still slightly lit with pale pink streaks. Across the creek covered with small chunks of ice and snow, slowly melting in the springtime temperatures. "I can't believe there's no one around to enjoy this."

"May is off season for Vail. Too late to ski and too cold for most other sports."

"Except hot-air ballooning. Bundling up in a ski coat, gloves and hat were part of the fun." Her eyes smiled at him through the darkness. "And since I don't even own a coat, it's a good thing the hotel keeps winter stuff guests have left behind for people like me to borrow."

"I'm sure you're not the only Southern Californian to come here unprepared."

"Unprepared?" He nearly laughed at her indignant expression. "I was a Girl Scout. Believe me, I know how to be prepared."

"If you say so. How about we sit here?" He tugged her down to a thickly pillowed settee, and he could feel the warmth of the fire reaching out to him. Much like Gabriella's warmth did, touching him in ways he couldn't remember being touched before. "I'm glad you liked it."

"I loved it. It was the most special thing I've ever done. Thank you."

"The most special thing I've done too. So thank you." And the reason it had been so special was because he'd done it with her. How he felt about her was something he couldn't quite figure out, but he suspected that feeling might not happen again for a long time. Or maybe ever.

"I know that can't be true, but it's sweet of you to

say so." She laughed softly. "You've been all over the world, but I haven't left L.A. in two years."

"You haven't?" He couldn't wrap his brain around not getting out of town even once in all that time. "That's got to be a record. I haven't *stayed* in one place more than two months since I graduated from medical school."

"Yours is more likely to be a record than mine."

He saw her shiver a little in the crisp mountain air, despite the orange flames licking upward, ending in gray smoke that disappeared into the starlit sky. He wrapped his arm around her shoulders and tugged her close to his side, and the way she snuggled against him felt damn good. "Cold?"

"A little. My Washington State blood, used to damp, chilly weather, must have thinned after living in California."

"I've been wanting to ask you something." If she was feeling even a little of the closeness, the intimacy he was feeling right now, sitting next to her in this beautiful place, maybe now was the right time to learn what secrets she might be keeping to herself. Secrets she might need to unload.

"What?"

"I've noticed that sometimes when you look at newborns, or after you've helped bring a baby into the world, that there's a sadness in your eyes. Why?"

"Sadness?" She made a sound that was probably supposed to be a laugh but didn't get there. "I don't know what you're talking about. There's nothing more joyful than a successful delivery and healthy baby, and you know it."

"But sometimes a pregnancy doesn't end successfully. Or with a healthy baby," he said quietly, his gut telling him there was some kind of history for her that was tied to that reality.

"True."

She stared fixedly at the fire, her relaxed expression more tense now. He hesitated, wondering if asking her more questions would ruin her evening. And his too. But he'd wanted to provide an ear in case she wanted to unload on him, so he'd try just once more. "Why did you leave Seattle to come to L.A.?"

More staring into the fire, and just when he was regretting ruining the intimate comfort they'd been feeling by digging into her life, instead of keeping it light and superficial like he usually did, she sighed and started to talk.

"I was engaged to be married. Thought I had it all—a job I adored, a family who supported me, a man who loved me. But it turned out he didn't love me, at least not enough. Something…bad happened, and he left me. I decided to start fresh in L.A., and that's it in a nutshell."

He wanted to say that any man who had her in his life, planning on forever, then left was a fool and an idiot. But he knew that was just the way relationships turned out most of the time. Unfortunate for people who believed in that kind of love, but it was reality. Either someone left, or a couple stuck together long past the time they should have gone their separate ways.

Her boyfriend's abandonment, causing her pain, was just more proof that relationships weren't meant to last for the long haul, and that planning to get married was just a road leading to unhappiness.

"I'm sorry. That must have been hard for you."

"It was. But I'm over it now."

Somehow he didn't believe that. But he knew her well enough to know she was done talking about it, even though he was sure it couldn't be the whole story. He slipped his fingers beneath her chin, tipping her face up to his, and all he could think of to do for her was kiss away the sadness on her face, replacing it with the desire he'd seen there on and off all day. Desire that he'd battled with a whole lot of effort, because he didn't want to hurt her. A battle he had to win now that he knew her ex had already caused her pain. But just as he was about to draw back and start some unimportant chitchat, she wrapped her cold hand around his nape, brought his face close, and pressed her mouth to his.

He could see her eyes closing just before his own did, and the way she sighed and sank into him knocked every good intention out of his head and had him gathering her close. He cupped her soft cheek in his hand, angling her mouth to his, and when she sighed again it felt like a siren song, driving him a little crazy. He couldn't help but deepen the kiss. The wet slide of her warm tongue against his felt as erotic as full sex with any other woman, and it was only through some miracle that he managed to remember that, deserted or not, they were in a public place and pulling off her clothes right then and there wasn't an option.

Or a good idea. He absolutely was not going to be the next man to hurt her.

"Gabriella." He sucked in some much-needed air. "It's too cold out here to be comfortable. Let's go inside and talk in the lounge."

"I'm very comfortable."

Well, damn. What was he supposed to say to that? She pressed her chest to his, and while he couldn't really feel her breasts against him, knowing what softness lay under all the layers of clothes they wore nearly made him moan. Her cold hands cupped his cheeks and she brought his face to hers again for another mind-blowing kiss that had him thinking about risking arrest and getting naked with her right there after all. Thank God the murmur of other voices on the patio cut through his fog and helped him get his libido at least marginally in check.

Which then helped him remember the paparazzi and how he needed to keep Gabriella safe from the media. While he hoped they hadn't gotten wind of them coming to Vail, he'd learned not to count on that.

He dragged his lips from hers and sucked in a deep breath of chilly mountain air that barely cooled the heat pouring through his veins. "Bad idea to do this out here. Cameras, you know?"

The brown eyes that met his looked a little dazed, but she nodded. "Cameras. I remember. How about we go to the room?"

Knowing she wanted that, too, made what he had to say nearly impossible. But he forced himself. "Gabriella, it's better if—"

"Stop." She pressed her fingertips to his lips. "You asked me things. There are things I want to ask you too."

He braced himself, not being in the mood for true confessions. Mostly because he hated to see her shock and disappointment and disapproval. But she probably had a right to know.

"Ask away."

"Why are you hiding out in L.A.?"

"What makes you think I'm hiding? I'm visiting."

"I don't live under a rock, Rafael. I know there was a scandal with some woman."

The way she smiled and cupped his cheek in her hand relaxed him a little. At least she knew that much, and was still there with him. He turned his face to press his mouth to her palm for a moment, deciding what he wanted to say.

"Then you know I dated a woman who some people thought was not the kind of person a prince should be dating. It wasn't as though we had anything more than a casual relationship, but the media hounds ran with it, as they love to do. Since my face had been plastered on television and tabloids quite a lot the past couple years, there was more uproar than usual back home."

"Do you care about it? And if you do, why do you do things you know the media will have a field day with?"

At first, he thought she was judging him, and the pain of that stabbed his chest. But when he looked into her eyes, really looked, he could clearly see that she was just asking, not judging. Her hand still softly caressed his cheek, and the touch weakened him. Or made him stronger, he wasn't sure which. Either way, he realized he actually wanted to talk to her about it, which surprised the hell out of him.

He drew in a fortifying breath before he spoke. "First, half the stuff said about me isn't true. Or is greatly exaggerated. Second, if I read that stuff and worried about it, I'd spend all day doing it and I have more important things to think about."

"So why hide out at all?"

Good question, and one he wasn't sure how to answer. "My parents get upset about it. And this time the hubbub was so loud they demanded I lie low and keep my face out of the press. And since I'm a grown man and can do as I please, my only explanation of why I did so is that I care about their opinion of me. Because their opinion's been pretty low for a long time, and I guess that's always bothered me."

His words rang in his ears, and it was like being

given a good whack on the side of the head. Apparently there was some part of him deep inside that was still that boy who was the second prince. The spare heir. The one who didn't always follow rules and had embarrassed his parents when he'd left the kingdom to become a doctor. The one who refused to ever marry, despite having very good reasons for that.

The son they were always disappointed in, whether he lived up or down to his reputation in the media. Pathetic that it hurt that they felt that way, but there it was. The truth.

"What do you mean, their opinion of you is low? That's ridiculous."

"Not ridiculous." He pressed his lips to her forehead and let them stay there, because the simple connection felt good. "I told you before that they wanted me to stay in the family business, so to speak. They never understood or approved of my wanting to be a doctor, and were more than disappointed when I did it anyway."

"Rafael." She grasped his face in her hands, and he felt a little like he was drowning in the sweet sincerity of the brown eyes staring into his. "I don't know your parents. But I have to believe you're wrong about a lot of this. Maybe they wanted you to do more traditional duties at home, but surely they're proud of the hard work you put in to be a doctor. Of the lives you save and the good you do. When you go home, promise me you'll talk to them. Share how you've felt, and clear the air. I bet you'll be surprised at how they respond."

Gabriella knew a lot about human nature—hadn't he seen it first hand in so many ways? That didn't mean she knew a thing about his family situation, but he realized he didn't have anything to lose by talking things over with his parents. Who knew, maybe they could come up with a relationship less full of stress and more full of the kind of closeness he'd seen in other families. Including royal ones like those of the Sheikh they'd met today, who obviously cared deeply about his extended family.

"I don't expect anything would change, but for you I'll think about it."

"Not for me, for you. Because after another week or so we won't see each other again."

A good thing for her. Not so much for him. She was the most special woman he'd ever known, and he wished they could spend more time together. But he was a man who generally disappointed the people in his life, and she was a woman who'd already been badly disappointed by someone else. She deserved someone who believed in love and happy-ever-after. He definitely didn't, but maybe she'd somehow find that one day.

The thought made his chest feel oddly tight and he stood to end the torture of being with her when he shouldn't be. "We have an early morning. The Sheikh wants to get going as soon as we check once more that his wife's not in labor."

Her gaze stayed on his as she slowly pushed to her feet. Searching. Questioning. Not a surprise, since moments ago he'd been kissing her like a man on a mission to get horizontal with her as soon as possible.

Much as he still wanted that more than his next breath, she deserved better.

They walked in silence to their rooms, which were connected by an interior door, and Rafael knew he wouldn't get much sleep, thinking about her warm, soft body curled into a bed so close to his. The same way he'd been unable to sleep the night he'd tucked her into the guest room of his house, and he hadn't even known her then.

Now that he did, now that he knew the attraction was mutual, staying away from her would require Herculean strength, but for her sake he could do it.

Stopping at the door to her room, he somehow managed to kiss only her cheek, though he knew his lips lingered there too long. "Good night, Gabriella."

"This is totally unfair, you know."

"What is totally unfair?"

"Getting James to include me on this trip, then making me sit close to you, look at you, feel the touch of your hand while we drove, and it was all so distracting I barely noticed the gorgeous scenery. Then you took me on a romantic balloon ride with your arms around me, which was the most incredible thing I've ever done. More romance and kissing and touching by a fire under the stars. And now you dump me like a hot rock in front of my door?"

The flash of fire in her eyes, the annoyance in her voice and her words were so surprising and adorable he couldn't help but laugh, even though having to leave her now wasn't in the least amusing. "Dumping is a strong word. I'm simply dropping you off after a wonderful day together."

"Why?" A challenge in her brown eyes joined that single word.

"For the reasons we just talked about outside, Gabriella," he said quietly, hoping she'd understand. "You deserve so much more than someone like me can give you. I'm leaving soon, and I don't want to be another man who disappoints you."

"You can't disappoint me if I'm not expecting anything." Her fingers slid up the front of his jacket to grasp his neck again, on up to trace his jaw and cheekbones, and even that simple touch made him want her even more. "You've made me see that I've been living in a co-coon this past two years. Hiding. But unlike you've had to do in these past weeks, I haven't been hiding from outside forces. Haven't been hiding because someone asked me to. I've been hiding from myself, and now I know it's time to change that." Her eyes softened, and her voice dropped to a whisper. "Being with you tonight is all I want. Breaking out of my shell to enjoy just one more incredible night with an incredible man. Is that so much to ask?"

He didn't even realize he'd wrapped his arms around her until his hold tightened and he couldn't make himself let her go. He warred with himself about the right thing to do. "Gabriella—"

She rose on tiptoe and buried her hands in his hair. Pulled his mouth to hers for a kiss so long and sweet and hot it fried every last working brain cell he had left.

He somehow broke the kiss and stared into her beautiful eyes. "You promise you won't regret it when I leave? That you won't feel hurt that I can't stay?"

"I won't regret it. I won't be hurt. Unless you walk away this second. In which case I'll have to become like autocratic Rafael Moreno was the first day we met and 'take control of the situation.'"

How a woman's eyes could be amused, sensual, and flashing all at the same time he had no idea, but it was an irresistible combination. He loved how Gabriella made him smile and laugh and want her so much he ached. "You already know I hate to give up control of any situation, *mi ángel*," He touched his mouth to hers and began to walk her backwards ten feet down the hallway to his own door. "So how about we take control of it together?"

"I like that idea a lot."

And with that she plastered her body close to his, wrapped her arms around his neck and kissed him, which was so distracting he had a hard time remembering in which pocket he'd stuffed his room key. "Can you wait for just two seconds while I find my key?"

"I don't know. But I'm happy to help you look."

She peppered kisses on his face at the same time she put her hand caressingly into his pants pocket, obviously looking for something other than his room key, and he laughed then nearly moaned.

"I'd never have dreamed that charming midwife Gabriella Cain could be such a vixen." Thank God he finally found the key in his jacket pocket, because she was driving him crazy and they were both still fully clothed. He shoved the door open and nearly stumbled as he backed her inside because now that they weren't in a public hallway and he'd abandoned all worries of hurting her, he couldn't get his hands and mouth on her fast enough.

"I've never been a vixen, I don't think." She pushed his jacket off at the same time he was unzipping hers. "Apparently, you bring her out in me."

"I'm about to show you what you bring out in me. Didn't you say you felt like Cinderella at the charity ball? I think I may be turning into the Beast." And while it was a joke, it wasn't far from the truth. He'd already stripped off her sweater and was in the process of unbuttoning her pants, and couldn't remember a time he'd felt as desperate to make love with a woman as he felt right now.

"You're mixing up your fairy tales. But since you are a prince, I guess that's okay."

She lost him on the conversation because he'd gotten her pants off and he took a moment to look at her, holding his breath at the vision before him. At her slim body, her luminous eyes, her hair a little tousled and her beautiful lips parted. He reached to unclasp her bra and as she stood there in near-naked perfection, he felt humbled. Incredibly lucky to be the man she'd chosen to break out of her shell with.

"Gabriella." He drew her close and kissed her, drinking in the taste of her and the sweetness of her, then scooped her up against his chest. A couple of steps to the bed and he'd deposited her in it, stripping off the last of his clothes to slide in next to her, loving the feel of her skin against his.

He captured her wrists in his hands and raised them above her head, letting his other roam in a gentle touch over her breasts and down her ribs as his mouth captured her nipple.

"I guess you were serious about taking control." She gasped. "How can I touch you if you're holding my hands?"

"Later. First, I want to make you feel good." So good, so special for her that she'd never feel regret. Just memories of what it had been like between them, which he knew he'd never forget.

He moved his mouth back to hers, slipping his hand between her legs to feel the wetness there, caressing her for long minutes, and with any other woman he might have joined with her right then. But this was Gabriella, and he wanted to touch her all night. Could listen to her little moans forever as she writhed and gasped, but finally her hands broke free of his hold and she reached for him.

"I thought we agreed we were going to share control tonight, hmm?" she said, grasping and stroking him until he was the one moaning.

"Take pity on me, *bella*. The truth is I have little control around you."

He could feel her smile against his lips. "That's what I like to hear, Dr. Moreno. And remember how I said I was a Girl Scout? Always prepared?"

He laughed when he saw she had a condom in her hand, and where she'd grabbed it from he had no clue. Didn't care either, because after she slid it in place she rose up and sheathed herself on him. Rafael had never seen anything so beautiful in his life as this woman moving gracefully above him, looking down at him through eyes shining with the same intense desire that clawed into his very soul, leaving him weak. He held her hips, moving faster, wanting to see her expression as she came undone. When she did, arching her back and crying out, he was again filled with awe that he'd been privileged enough to be the one to put that look of ecstasy on her face. Then he followed her with his own cry of rapture as he gathered her close to his pounding heart. A heart he knew would never be quite the same again.

Rafael awoke to the feel of a slender shoulder pressed against his collarbone and a round, firm bottom spooned against him, and instantly began to harden at the sweet sensations and memories of last night's incredible lovemaking. Never had he experienced something so beyond the physical with a woman. Something that had demanded engagement from his heart and mind and soul every bit as much as his body.

He softly kissed Gabriella's hair, the hair he so loved to look at and touch. The golden fire that was such a part of who she was both inside and out, feisty and angelic, determined and dazzling. He moved his lips to the soft curve behind her ear, which he'd learned was a sweet spot she particularly enjoyed him kissing, but she didn't stir. Apparently she felt as worn out by their time together as he did. Worn out by the emotion of sharing their secrets with one another as much as their late-night lovemaking.

Finally hearing her story about her ex had been satisfying. Not completely, because he had a feeling there was more to the story than she'd wanted to talk about last night. But knowing she'd trusted him enough to share at least part of the reason she confessed she'd hidden away the past two years felt good. He wanted to be the person she danced with in the sunlight now that she'd decided to come out to play.

But he couldn't be that person, couldn't risk hurting her, and that reality blasted his sense of triumph to smithereens. He wouldn't be here for her. Couldn't be her forever love, because such a thing didn't exist.

He tucked her warm, captivating body closer, closing his eyes to breathe her in, and the ache in his chest told him one thing for certain. At least one person would hurt like hell when he moved on from L.A., and it would be the first time in his life that ending a fling would make him feel anything but guilt or relief.

The muffled tones of his cellphone had him searching for it in the bed, finally finding it when he slid his hand beneath Gabriella's pillow. This time she did stir, and his good morning murmur in her ear got cut off in mid-word when he saw who was calling.

His brother.

What could he possibly want? His brother's life was full of responsibilities that Rafael was more than happy to not have. Also more than happy that his brother rarely called, because when he did it was usually to scold him for embarrassing the royal family, as if it wasn't enough to hear it from both his mother and his father.

He nearly ignored the call, but finally swung his feet to the side of the bed and stood, striding to the bathroom so as not to disturb Gabriella. "To what do I owe the honor, Alberto?"

"Unfortunately, I have bad news. Mother has had a heart attack, and you need to come home right away."

CHAPTER ELEVEN

GABBY DID HER best to focus on work but, despite repeatedly yanking her attention back to her job, she kept making silly mistakes. Thankfully none had been too important, but still. How often did she normally drop things? When was the last time she'd walked into the storage room before completely forgetting what she'd needed? It had happened twice already. And giving a patient still water when she'd asked for sparkling...? Never.

And she knew it was because Rafael and his family were weighing on her mind. When he'd told her he had to leave and why, he'd sounded very matter-of-fact, but she knew him now. Knew that behind that suave and confident exterior was a man with a sensitive heart who cared passionately for others. No matter what he'd said about his family, about his conviction that they were disappointed in him, that he'd let them down when he'd decided to take a different path than what they'd planned for him, she could see he wasn't indifferent to it. That he cared about that more than he'd ever let on. And when she'd looked into his eyes after he'd told her his mother was ill, the calm mask on his face hadn't concealed the worry in his eyes.

Of course he'd been worried. No matter what kind

of relationship anyone had with their parents, they were still important. Still loved.

She stared, unseeing, at the tray of supplies in her hands. Love. Such a complicated and confusing thing. She'd been so sure she'd loved Ben, had made a baby with him and had been planning to marry him. But now? Now she knew the truth. That it had all just been easy. They'd dated, he'd seemed like a good, stable man, and when she'd gotten pregnant had figured it was time to get married. Wasn't that what most people would have done?

But she'd never really loved him.

She knew that now. Knew because she was crazily in love with Rafael Moreno. Arrogant prince, excellent doctor, and tender lover. The knowledge balled her stomach, and her heart swelled at the same time it pinched tight. How had she let herself fall in love with the man? A notorious playboy, an international jet-setter who didn't stay in one place very long, and a man who freely admitted he didn't believe in forever-after love.

Truth was, though, she couldn't blame herself. It hadn't been a question of letting herself fall for him. It would have been like trying to stop an ocean wave as she swam in the Pacific, because Rafael was a force of nature every bit as mesmerizing and powerful.

She loved him. And when he'd kissed her goodbye, she'd known there was a good chance he might never be back.

The ball in her stomach rolled and her knuckles whitened on the tray, but she lifted her chin as she picked up her pace down the hallway. Somehow she had to focus on what she did best, which was work. It wasn't Rafael's fault she'd fallen so hard for him. If he called to report back about his mother, which he'd promised to do, she'd do everything in her ability to listen like a friend would and not let him know how much she missed him. How much she hoped he'd come back to L.A., but at the same time part of her hoped he wouldn't.

The love, the connection she felt with him seemed huge and overwhelming and uncontrollable. But the thought of having a real relationship with someone again? Something more than the short fling she'd decided to allow herself with him? Just the idea of it scared her to death.

"Why do I even care, Freya?"

Gabby hesitated at the sound of Mila's upset voice, not wanting to walk by the open lounge door while she was obviously having a personal conversation. "He already broke my heart once—shouldn't that have been enough to make my feelings turn to stone where he's concerned?"

"We can't just turn our feelings on and off like a faucet, Mila," Freya said in a soothing tone. "It's okay to feel the way you do."

"I mean, it almost seems like he's flaunting his new girlfriend, doesn't it? Like he's deliberately waving her in my face to upset me."

"I think James…well, he might be having his own struggles, Mila. He's never been one to let emotions control him, you know? Maybe his behavior is some unconscious reaction to seeing you again. I don't know what else to say, except you should tell him what you just told me and give him some time to think about it."

Now tearful, Mila continued to talk, and Gabby pivoted, deciding to go back the other way so as not to embarrass her. Her already aching heart hurt a little more, feeling bad that Mila was so upset. Why did life have to be so hard? Why did love have to hurt?

Giving your heart to someone made you horribly vulnerable, she knew. So where, exactly, did that leave her when it came to Dr. Rafael Moreno?

Everyone walking the hospital hallways drifted toward the walls to leave an open path as Rafael strode through, murmuring to one another and bowing as he passed, and his lips twisted at the sure sign he was home. He'd grown up with that kind of deference. Hadn't really even noticed it until he'd left the country. Now most people just saw him as a doctor, and it struck him how much he greatly preferred that to this kind of respect, based only on his birthright and not his accomplishments.

Something his parents and brother still didn't understand.

He pressed his lips together and forged on until he got to his mother's room. Then surprised himself when he had to stop outside it to inhale long calming breaths, fighting for composure. It wasn't as though he didn't practically live in hospitals. Between medical school and residency and working around the world, doing basic medicine and not the specialized obstetrics he did elsewhere, he'd seen thousands of sick people. Had seen plenty of them die. Had seen patients make miraculous recoveries too.

But none of them had been his mother.

Yes, she aggravated him, insulted him, berated him and lectured him. But she was still his mother and, damn it, he loved her. She'd been so angry about the recent press brouhaha and the various photos and lurid details, half of which had been made up, and he wasn't proud of the things he'd said back to her when she'd scolded him about it. He couldn't remember what they were, exactly, but he knew his words had hurt her feelings.

All that felt pretty unforgivable now that she was lying in a hospital bed in Intensive Care. Even though her heart attack had been fairly mild and the prognosis was good, he also knew things could go downhill fast.

Bracing himself, he forced his feet to go through the doorway. Then stood feeling slightly off balance at the end of the hospital bed, gripping the railing tight, because the pale woman hooked up to machines, with an I.V. in her arm and an oxygen hose in her nose, didn't look like his mother at all. She looked a good ten years older than the last time he'd seen her, and in that very second he vowed to never let so much time go by again between visits.

He swallowed hard then looked past the scary things to the one thing that seemed normal and familiar. Her hair was remarkably well coiffed and tidy for someone lying in the ICU after a heart attack, and it helped him manage a smile. Yes, this woman was his mother after all. The vain queen of the land who was always perfect and regal from head to toe.

Her eyelids flickered open and took a moment to focus on him. Then she smiled and slowly extended her hand. "Rafael."

The heavy tightness in his chest loosened at the way she said his name. At the way her smile, weak as it was, lit her tired eyes. He quickly stepped around the bed to grasp her hand. "Hi, Mother. Your hair looks nice. I'm surprised, though, that you're not wearing lipstick."

Her smile widened into a slightly wheezy chuckle. "Had one tucked under my pillow, but I think the nurse took it when they changed the sheets." The squeeze she gave his hand was weak but stronger than he'd expected, and he began to relax.

"Isn't this a rather drastic way to get me to come home?"

"You make me do drastic things. You've been like that since you were a little boy, and you're apparently never going to change, even if it kills me."

"And apparently you aren't going to change either, scolding me while flat on your back in a hospital bed." Her acerbic tone was that of the queen and mother he knew well, but her eyes held a new vulnerability that made him feel guilty as hell for all the things he'd done wrong in his life that had caused her anxiety and stress. He leaned over to kiss her cheek. "I checked all your test and lab results. Has your cardiologist been in to talk to you about it?"

"Yes. But I'd like to hear what you think."

She wanted to hear what he thought? Since when? "You have some mild blockage in your right coronary artery. They're going to do angioplasty to cross through the area that's narrowed by cholesterol plaque, and put in a stent to bridge that narrowing. The procedure has been done for years now, and results are usually good. So, assuming it goes well, you should be your old, bossy self soon."

"I'm never bossy. I'm simply assertive and direct."

"Rafael!"

He turned at the sound of his father's booming voice to see him striding into the room. Unlike Rafael's mother, he looked exactly like he always did, posture erect and the picture of health with his skin tanned from golfing and his silver hair thick and wavy. But his eyes held a worry Rafael had never seen before.

His father's arms enfolded him in a hard hug. "What

do you think about your mother? Is she going to be all right? Is what they want to do a good idea? I've talked to the doctors here, but I trust you to know what's really going on."

Rafael stared at him in shock. Again, this was entirely new. He couldn't remember the last time they'd trusted him about anything, let alone his doctoring skills.

"I was just explaining the test results to Mother." He repeated what he'd told her, and as he stood there, beyond surprised at the intent interest on both his parents' faces as he spoke, Gabriella's words came back to him. Saying that he should talk to them, should share how he felt about their opinion of him. He'd told himself for years he didn't care if they respected him or not. But the peculiar mix of emotions filling his chest as he stood there looking at them told him loud and clear he'd been lying to himself.

Maybe Gabriella was right, and it was time to see if the air could be cleared between them, at least a little. "But I have to be honest. I'm surprised you're asking my opinion. You've expressed nothing but disappointment that I decided to become a doctor."

"I admit we wanted you to stay here and help your brother with various royal duties, but when you became a doctor? That wasn't a disappointment, Rafael." His father grasped his shoulder in a strong grip. "We were proud of you."

"Always, Rafael. And I'm sorry we never really told you that," his mother said. Her eyes held some look he couldn't be sure of—guilt, maybe? Contrition? "As I've been lying here, I've thought about you. Realized that perhaps we've been wrong to object to you living your life the way you want to."

"I'm sorry, too," his father said. "In case you don't know, your mother regularly brags about your work. When she's not apologizing for the stupid things you do sometimes, that is." His father's grin took any sting out of his words, and he squeezed Rafael's shoulder before releasing it to hold his mother's hand tight. And when his parents' eyes met both were filled with softness, an obvious connection that he'd never seen between them before.

That rocked him back on his heels as much as what they'd just said. They were proud of him? Even *bragged* about him? He found it nearly impossible to believe, but it was becoming clear he'd been wrong about a lot of things, so maybe it was really true.

His mind filled with a vision of Gabriella and her insight about his family that he hadn't truly thought was a real possibility. Insight that had been pretty incredible, since she hadn't even met his parents. She'd figured out something in just a few minutes of conversation with him that he hadn't seen in thirty-one years.

She was one special woman, no doubt about that. Someone who understood human nature in a way he was obviously still trying to figure out, which was just one reason she was an amazing midwife.

Just one reason why he'd been so attracted to her that very first day they'd met.

A need to talk to her that moment, to call her and tell her he'd taken her advice, had him opening his mouth to tell his parents he'd be back in a short time when a nurse came into the room.

"Time to check your vital signs, Your Majesty," she said, before coming to a dead stop to stare at Rafael.

A good excuse to make his exit. "Then I'll leave you for the moment, Mother. I'll be back in a little while."

He scooted past the nurse, who still hadn't moved, on down the long hallway to an exit door so he'd be sure to get a good signal on his phone. Just the thought of hearing Gabriella's voice made his chest feel lighter than it had since the second his brother had called him in Vail.

Gabby wandered restlessly out of her kitchen with a cup of tea in her hand and plopped onto her sofa. The sofa where she'd made amazing love with Rafael, and thinking of it made her breath short and her heart heavy. If she was going to feel this way every time she sat on it, she might have to sell it and buy a new one. Something a completely different style and color. Maybe rearrange the whole room while she was at it.

Then again, her memories of being in Vail with him—their hot-air balloon ride, their intimate conversation beneath the stars, their lovemaking there too were all etched in her mind forever. And since being hundreds of miles away from Colorado didn't seem to be doing much to dim those memories, rearranging her living room probably wouldn't help much either.

She grabbed the TV remote and skimmed through some channels, not finding much that grabbed her attention. Why hadn't she taken on a third shift instead of just a double to keep her mind occupied? To keep her mind off Rafael and his mother and wondering how she was and if he was upset and if he'd ever come back to Los Angeles.

Wondering if she'd ever hear from him again.

If she did, she'd try to act normal. Cool. Like the kind of woman he usually dated, who didn't expect anything more than a quick fling. Not that she did expect more than that, or even wanted more than that, and had to somehow make sure he knew that, but still.

Lord, she was a confused mess. She sighed at the same time her phone rang and her heart nearly flipped over in a loop-the-loop when she saw it was him on the line.

"Is your mom okay? Are you okay? Is everything all right? Where are you?"

She winced even as the last words were coming out of her mouth. So much for being calm and cool.

"I'm at the hospital. I've just left Mother for a bit and am glad to say she's doing well. They'll be doing an angioplasty later today, and hopefully that will go smoothly and she'll be heading home soon."

"That's wonderful news! Thanks so much for letting me know. I've been so worried."

"I knew you would be, *bella*, because you care about everyone, even people you've never met. In fact, I have to tell you I took your advice and I'm impressed with your amazing insight. How is it you understand the inner workings of my parents' brains when you don't even know them?"

"What do you mean? What advice?"

"You told me you thought I must be wrong about them not being happy that I became a doctor. And you were right. I just about fell over when they were asking my opinion about Mother's health and the upcoming procedure, and decided then to ask them, to tell them my perspective on it. Only because you'd suggested I do, so I thank you for that. They assured me they aren't unhappy that I became a doctor, and I suspect my relationship with them will be a little less...turbulent now."

"Oh, Rafael. I'm so glad you did." She'd known his parents had to be proud of who he was. How could they not be?

"Me too."

Gabby bit her lip, feeling the silence stretch awkwardly between them but not wanting to say anything that showed how much she'd been missing him. Definitely didn't want to ask what his plans were, and prayed he'd tell her so she wouldn't have to either ask or stay anxiously in the dark about it.

"Anyway, I just wanted to give you an update," he said, his voice low and warm and not all that different from the way it had sounded when they'd made love, and she quivered in spite of herself. "I'm not sure exactly when I'll be back. I'll be staying here at least until she's stabilized from the procedure—I'll let you know how that goes."

"I'd like that. And I'll be thinking of all of you."

"And I'll be thinking of you, Gabriella Cain, both when I'm awake and asleep. You can be sure of that. *Adios* for now."

"Bye." She hoped her voice wasn't shaking at his words as much as her heart was. "Talk to you soon."

She hugged the phone to her chest and grinned like an idiot. Then, seconds later, a niggle of fear jabbed her in the solar plexus. When he came back, would she ready to put herself out there again? Let herself be in a relationship with a man, if that was what he'd been hinting at? Risk getting hurt all over again? There was a part of her that said no. The scared, wimpy part Rafael didn't know about. He thought she was feisty and brave and wasn't that who she wanted to be? Who she used to be?

Rafael had risked his family's disapproval to go for what he wanted, which was to become a doctor. Wasn't the chance to maybe, possibly be happy with him worth even more of a risk?

Yes. There was absolutely no doubt about that. It was worth that and a whole lot more.

She didn't have to be at work for another eight hours. She felt beyond antsy, but it was a little too late to go out somewhere. How in the world was she going to fill the time?

Forty minutes of cleaning her apartment left it unfortunately immaculate. Chewing her lip, she had an *aha* moment. "My knitting stuff and the DVD on how to do it!" Surely learning something new would take up at least an hour, wouldn't it? Then, with any luck, she could get some sleep.

Like that was going to happen.

She pulled the knitting things from a drawer she'd stuffed them into and was crouching down to stick the DVD into the player when one of the shows featuring stories about musicians and movie stars came on the TV. About to switch it off, she stopped dead when Rafael Moreno's face filled the screen.

"And in other news, remember Prince Rafael Moreno and his former stripper girlfriend? Looks like he's gone to the opposite end of the spectrum, dating a wholesome nurse midwife."

Heart pounding, Gabby's legs felt so wobbly that she tumbled back onto her rear as she stared at the bubbly blonde host of the show. How had they found out about her?

"But wholesome and midwife might not always go hand in hand, at least when it comes to Gabriella Cain, who works at the famous and prestigious Hollywood Hills Clinic.

"Our reporters have been busy doing in-depth research on the prince's newest fling and found out that just two years ago she was not only pregnant with another man's child but her utter disregard for her health led to her child being stillborn. A tragedy that could have been avoided, sources say, if she'd been focused on her unborn child instead of herself.

"Not something you would expect from a midwife who takes care of pregnant women every day, is it? We're the first to bring you this breaking report and we are pretty sure that Rafael's parents, and many others in the palace, will be furious all over again about his taste in women. After all, someone like Gabriella Cain isn't the best choice to be the prince's girlfriend or future wife, is she?"

A sickening, icy numbness crept across every inch of Gabby's skin as she watched and listened. Saw the photos of her and Rafael together coming out of his house the morning after the night she'd fallen asleep. Photos at the charity ball. Photos in Vail. Heard the lies, and the truth too, about her mistakes and her loss and how Ben had left her because of her terrible choices. There was even a photo of her baby's grave marker, and seeing it made her feel like she was dying inside.

She was shaking so badly it hurt physically, but she found she couldn't move to turn it off. Had to watch the entire train wreck of her life unfold in garish Technicolor for all the world to see. And just when she was sure it couldn't get any worse, it did.

Because some person, she had no idea who, was offering a loud opinion that someone like Gabby, a woman who'd neglected to pay attention to signs there might be a problem with her own pregnancy and baby, was totally unsuited to be a midwife anywhere, let alone at The Hollywood Hills Clinic, where patients had come to expect the very best.

Dear God.

She should have told Rafael. Should have told him their night together in Vail, when she'd only touched on the truth, telling him about Ben. Had decided she would when the time was right, if there'd been a time that was right. If she'd seen him again.

And now he'd find out this way. In this horrible, lurid, appalling way with exaggerated detail that made her sound like a monster. Not a woman who'd made a bad mistake and had had her heart broken because of it.

She had no idea if Rafael had planned for them to possibly be together as a couple, but it didn't matter. Even if he had, after he heard about this he'd drop that thought fast and run as far as he could. And as she stared at the screen, the nasty things being said about her sounded very far away. A light year's distance.

The same distance she now felt between herself and Rafael.

It made her realize that, even though she hadn't let herself admit it, deep inside her stupid, lonely heart she'd thought maybe, possibly the two of them had something special. Something that might bud into a real relationship, even bloom into a forever-after. But her pathetic heart should have known better than to keep clinging to those Cinderella dreams.

As a prince, the man would surely need an heir. And even if, somehow, he still wanted to be with her after all this, it would be impossible. She could never go through the nightmare of losing a baby again. Never get pregnant again. Because the pain ripping through her heart at that moment felt, impossibly, even more torturous than the day she'd held her beautiful, lifeless baby in her arms.

A damp saltiness touched her lips, and she realized

tears were streaking down her cheeks in stinging water-falls. With shaking hands she slowly swiped them away.

Somehow she had to start a new life. She'd done it two years ago and, as hard as it had been, she could do it again. After this horrifying media exposure she couldn't imagine a single patient would trust her any-more. She didn't want James and Freya to feel bad about having to let her go. And even if, somehow, they didn't want her to leave, she couldn't face the looks and se-cret whispers about her past and her baby from patients and staff alike, whether it was criticism or sympathy.

No. It was time to cut the cord, so to speak, and be reborn. Again. Start over someplace where people didn't know her past and, somehow, try for a new future.

A future that could never include Rafael, and of all the things ripping out bleeding pieces of her heart that was the very worst.

CHAPTER TWELVE

"RAFAEL!"

His father's bellow carried all the way down the hospital hallway, and Rafael took off in a dead run to his mother's room, fearing the worst. His heart practically stopped when he saw the bed was empty, and his father was pacing the room like an agitated grizzly bear.

"What? Has something happened to Mother?"

"She's all right, for now at least. They took her to prep her for the surgery. I hate to think, though, how your damned latest scandal is going to upset her. The woman has already had a heart attack, Rafael—how is it that you don't care how your actions will affect her recovery? Why don't you give a damn about anyone but yourself?"

"I don't know what you're talking about, but I wouldn't be here if I didn't care about Mother and her health and recovery." He fought down his anger, which was rising to match his father's, because he didn't understand what had enraged the man again.

"You told us you'd go to L.A. to stay out of the news for a while. And now this! Who knows, maybe the last few scandals were part of the reason your mother had her heart attack in the first place. Maybe you should think about her health and recovery first instead of last."

"Again, I don't know what you're talking about, so please enlighten me." He wanted to add, *Before I put a fist through this wall, or even your face.* Which, of course, he'd never do, but visualizing how good that would feel after being accused, again, of something he doubtless hadn't done helped calm him down.

"This." His father flicked on the TV, and a news station blared with chatter and photos. Rafael stared in horror. These pictures weren't dim and blurred. These showed him holding Gabriella's hand as he'd helped her from the car outside the charity ball. The two of them going into her apartment afterwards. The two of them kissing—hotly kissing—by that fire pit in Vail.

Damn it to hell.

"So I dated a woman? A nice woman. A few casual dates. Since when is that an embarrassment that would give Mother another heart attack?" He tried to keep his voice cool, but it was hard with his breath short and his anger flaming higher. Did his parents expect him to stop living?

"Nice? Not according to this. This shows why she's not a good choice for you. Are you ever going to find someone to settle down with and marry who's appropriate? Who would make your mother happy and proud?"

Proud. There was that word. They'd said they were proud of him for being a doctor, but obviously it stopped there. They weren't proud of his private life, of who he was outside the hospital. He'd told himself he didn't care but, like the rest of it, knew now that wasn't true.

He shifted his gaze back to the TV monitor and listened to the story in all its garishness, his gut burning and his heart feeling like someone had driven a scalpel straight through it.

A stillborn child. This was the source of the pain he'd

seen on Gabriella's face as she'd watched little Skye in the incubator. When new mothers had held their infants close to their breasts. And now all that pain was being blasted out there for all the world to see. Lurid details he knew had to be killing her to hear and see splashed in the media, and even unbelievable, nasty comments implying she was unfit to be a midwife.

And that it was happening at all was completely his fault.

His fault. There was no doubt he'd made the torment she obviously carried inside even worse. And as bad as that felt, there was something else digging a hole into his chest. The fact that she hadn't told him any of this, hadn't shared it when they'd been talking about their pasts and their secrets, made him wonder if there were other things in her past she didn't want to share. Other things she wanted to keep hidden.

It seemed most everyone he got involved with had a past that was better left buried. Over and over, his notoriety ended up causing whatever it was to become unearthed. And that hurt everyone. His mother, now ill and fragile. His father, angry about that, and who could blame him? Whatever woman Rafael had been seeing at any moment. And even his career, when a few scandals had threatened to derail his reputation as a doctor, making a few people see only that part of him, and not his skills as a physician.

No wonder he ended up being a disappointment to some of the people closest to him. And not only because of the media. Because he'd never wanted to commit to anyone. Still didn't believe in love and forever-after, though for a brief moment being with Gabriella had made him wonder if he could possibly be wrong about that. He had learned not to fully trust anyone, and felt ashamed that a small part of him felt that way about Gabriella, wondering what might come out next that would upset his mother while she was in Intensive Care. And what kind of son would risk his mother's health and recovery for a fling?

God. What did it say about him that he would even let that cross his mind about Gabriella? Obviously, he couldn't see her anymore. For her sake. For his mother's. The damned selfish man inside him argued with that decision, but Rafael resolutely struck him down. Gabriella had already been through so much terrible heartache. She deserved someone who knew how to trust completely. Who wouldn't expose her to public scandal. A man who could offer her something she might believe was real love, forever wiping away the pain of her old boyfriend leaving just when she'd needed him.

"No, Father, I'm never going to settle down and get married, which I've told you before. I'm sorry that's a disappointment to you and Mother, but that's just the way it is. I'm going to stay here for a while, though, until Mother gets well. Because I do care about her, even though you've thought some of the things I've done make it seem like I don't."

He turned and left the room, heading back to the door opening to the outside, needing to suck some air into his lungs that wasn't vibrating with anger. And to call Gabriella again.

His last promise to his father would be the easiest to keep. Staying away from women wouldn't be an issue, because he had no desire to date anyone besides Gabriella or make love with anyone other than her. And he knew that would be true for a long, long time.

Rafael wasn't sure how long he stood there on the small hospital balcony, staring across the landscape of the place where he'd grown up. The place he'd left for too long, searching for something. When he'd met Gabriella, a part of him, an unconscious part, had felt a little like he might have found it. But that part was the selfish part, and he was kicking that guy out of his life for good.

He knew he needed to stay here for now. Lie low. Really lie low this time, being the poster boy for a good prince doing his duties. Even embrace the good that might come of that, bringing his knowledge of health-care needs around the world to charitable work here at home. Be here for his mother, keep an eye on her medical care as her health improved. Not upset her. Be here for his family.

He held his phone in his hand, staring at it, but couldn't make himself phone her. He'd ended things with a woman more times than he could count, but it had never felt painful like this did. Nearly impossible, in fact. But he couldn't be the man she needed. He couldn't be his old, selfish self.

He made himself phone her number. It went straight to voice mail, and his heart fell when he realized he wouldn't get to hear her voice again. At the same time, the cowardly part of him felt relieved to be able to just leave a message.

He hesitated over what to say, then decided to keep it short. Without detail, or comments about her pain that he'd just learned about. Anything that might hurt her more, or make her try to contact him. Weaken his resolve to keep her safe from him.

"Gabriella? Rafael. Listen, I'm... Mother is so far still fine, so don't be worried about that, but...well, I don't think I'll be coming back to L.A. I need to stay here until she's stronger. It was great knowing you, and

I wish you only the best for your life. Truly." His voice shook on that word, but he couldn't help it. The last ones he whispered, so she wouldn't know. *"Adios, mi bella."*

Gabby sat on the damp, green grass in the Seattle cemetery, not caring that her pants were getting wet and cold. She couldn't care about her clothes or anything else when she'd lost everything she cared about all over again.

Her baby lay under this earth where she'd just placed a small bouquet of spring tulips. The pain of losing him had slowly faded with time, and even more in the past weeks when she'd realized that shutting herself in a box by working all the time was no way to honor the tiny, beautiful baby who had been her son. Who should have had a chance to grow up into a boy and then a man. Seeing Rafael live his life on his own terms had opened her eyes to the realization that she wanted to live the same way. Without hiding, without fear of what others might think of her if they learned the truth.

But, oh, how wrong she'd been that could be possible. Her past mistake would always be there. Ben had blamed her, and she'd blamed herself. Now others did too, and she thought maybe they were right. Maybe she wasn't fit to be a midwife anymore. A woman who didn't listen to her own body probably shouldn't be listening to anyone else's.

So if she couldn't be a midwife anymore, where did she belong? What would she do with her life? God, she just didn't know. But she did know one thing. She could never be a wife and mother, because there was no way she could go through that kind of heartache all over again. She'd gone back into hiding from that, at least, and this time she was never coming out.

Staring down at the small stone carved with her baby's name, she became aware of a movement next to her and turned her head, only to have her heart completely stop in shock.

Ben.

For a moment she could barely process it. She opened her mouth to speak, but nothing came out. He gave her a twisted smile then knelt on the grass next to her. "Hi, Gabby. Rough day, huh?"

He'd seen the news. "Yeah. Pretty rough."

"All that garbage on TV made me think about you and this little guy. Gave me a strangely strong need to come here, and now that I see you're here too, I figure that's the reason why."

"What do you mean?"

"Because the universe knows I need to make things right with you."

"Make what right?"

He stared at her a long moment, his hand gripping the back of his neck before he dropped it, placing it on top of hers. "Hell. I... I'd been thinking that maybe I'd call you after I stopped here today, but now that you're right in front of me, all the things I know I should say to you seem a lot harder than I thought they would."

Since she didn't have any idea what to say to him either, she kept quiet and just looked at him, waiting. Bracing herself for the worst.

"I know I treated you badly when our baby died inside of you," he finally said. "I was hurt at losing him and angry at the world about it. I took that anger out on you."

"No, you didn't. You didn't say much about anything." And in some ways that terrible silence, his inability to talk about it, had been worse to take than if he'd ranted at her.

"Maybe not. But when you blamed yourself I didn't tell you it wasn't your fault. I felt the same horrible loss you did, and it pushed me to act in a way I'm not proud of. I let you believe I blamed you, but I never did. Not really."

Again, she didn't respond, having no idea how to process what he was saying. How to feel about it. She'd held his blame, along with her own, so close to her bruised and battered heart. Had let it live there, a sharp splinter that had stabbed and festered, and she hadn't even tried to remove it because she'd believed she deserved the pain.

"There's more, and I want to tell you about it," he continued, still wearing that wry smile. "I'm married now. Have a baby on the way, and after what happened to us I admit I've been damned scared. I've asked her doctor lots of questions, and he's explained things to me. So even if there was a part of me that wasn't sure back then, I know now. You working late that day, assuming the pains you felt were nothing? That didn't have a damned thing to do with losing our baby. It was just one of those really bad outcomes that happen sometimes."

Gabby's throat closed, and tears burned the backs of her eyes as she looked at Ben. The man who two years ago she'd expected to share her life with. Who had in one second of hardship left.

This was proof he was the good person she'd thought he was. That he'd been perhaps as immature and unprepared as she'd been in trying to deal with their loss. "Thank you for telling me this. It's been…very hard to know how to feel about it."

"I know. But here's something else I want to tell you.

We both had a bad time of it, but I've finally found happiness again. I love my wife and can't wait until our baby is born. I don't know what's going on with you and this prince guy in the news, but you know…?" His smile broadened to become a real one. "It's worth taking a risk. It is. And he'd be one lucky guy to have you."

Unable to say another word, stunned by all he'd said, Gabby just stared at him. He reached out to squeeze her shoulder before he stood, and after a lingering look at their baby's headstone he was gone.

Gabby sat for long minutes, processing it all. The knowledge that he didn't blame her seeped slowly into the fog in her brain. Pushed out some of the guilt she'd carried for so long. And as that guilt eased from her chest it was replaced by cautious optimism.

Maybe she could put the past behind her, the way Ben had. Maybe she could be happy again, and maybe that happiness could come from being with Rafael. Hadn't she decided, before the shock of the media mess, that she needed to try to be more like her old self? That spending time with him to see where it might lead was worth the risk of future pain?

A gusty breeze moved her hair, and she had to smile. She could feel it. A shift in the wind, both literally and figuratively. No more guilt. No more hiding. No more self-protection. Time to move on, and what better way than to reach for the hand of a certain handsome prince who, from what he'd told her about his relationship with his parents, just might be experiencing a little shift in the wind himself?

She looked down at the small gravestone. She kissed her fingertips then slowly caressed the name and date etched there before standing tall. As she walked to her car she knew that part of this healing, part of moving forward would come from sharing everything with Rafael. Talking about it over the phone wouldn't be the way to do it, but with any luck his mother would improve and he'd be back soon.

Her chest filling with a buoyancy she hadn't felt in a long, long time, Gabby fished her keys from her purse and got into the car. Then her heart smacked into her ribs when she saw Rafael had called and left a message.

A giddy feeling of joy bubbled through her, and she quickly brought up her voice mail. His voice was odd, not warm like it usually was. Not even filled with its normal confidence, and in seconds the bubble deflated and flattened completely.

Her ears rang as she listened to the classic brush-off. "It was great knowing you, and I wish you only the best for your life…" Then his final quiet words felt like a hard slap of reality. *"Adios, mi bella."*

Adios, mi bella.

She wasn't sure how long she sat in the car, hands still holding the phone limply in her lap. Her pants, damp from the grass, now chilled her to the bone, and somehow she finally managed to lift her hands to the steering wheel to get the engine running and the heat on.

What a fool she was. Thinking Rafael, a man who'd stated more than once that he didn't believe in long-term relationships and forever-after, would want to be with her longer than a few days or weeks. But even as that knowledge felt like a huge hole in her heart she straightened her spine. Looked into the rearview mirror, swiped away the tears leaking from her eyes, and saw the new Gabby. A stronger Gabby. A woman who was moving on from the past to a new future. A person who deserved someone who loved her—hadn't Ben said any man would be lucky to have her? She'd thought maybe Rafael was that man, but that had been a pipe dream. A fairy tale.

Her cold hands gripped the steering wheel. Once she found a new job she'd find a way to balance work with finding a life that included other things. Maybe she'd even get lucky like Ben and find someone to love who'd love her back.

The hardest thing she'd ever done had been dealing with the loss of her baby. The next hardest thing?

Forgetting all about Rafael Moreno.

CHAPTER THIRTEEN

"SO YOU AGREE that your mother looks good? That she's recovering well?"

Rafael looked at the anxiety in his father's eyes as they walked to his mother's room, surprised all over again at the intensity of it. Though he supposed he shouldn't be. Even if his parents didn't have a particularly close relationship, they'd still been married for over thirty-five years, so that had to mean something.

"The angioplasty went well, and every test so far shows she's doing very well. I'm sure they told you they're planning to release her tomorrow for some T.L.C. back at the palace."

"Yes. But I wanted to make sure you agreed with that."

Just yesterday, his father's words would have pleased him. At that moment, though, he didn't seem able to feel much more than a heavy emptiness. "I agree with it. I'm guessing you've scheduled more nursing care than she wants, and she'll be chafing at the bit about everyone fussing around her."

His father chuckled. "She's already chafing. You know your mother."

They entered the room, and his mother promptly frowned at him. "You're giving me that disapproving look," he said. "Never thought I'd miss it, but at least it shows you're feeling pretty good."

"I'm wondering what's happened with your latest scandal. Really, Rafael, it's unbelievable."

"Why do you always pick the wrong women, son?" his father chimed in. "It's like you do it on purpose."

He stared at his father. Maybe he did. Maybe he'd always chosen women he knew were "inappropriate" as part of keeping his distance from them. But Gabriella? He hadn't really chosen her.

He'd been irresistibly drawn to her.

"Maybe I've done that in the past, Father, but Gabriella Cain is different from any woman I've ever known." He might not be able to be with her again, but he wasn't about to tolerate anyone saying nasty things about her. "She's not only beautiful, she's smart and good at her job and beyond caring to her patients. I don't know the whole story the media's been throwing out there, but I do know it has to be sensationalized and maybe even totally wrong. If you met Gabriella, you'd love her."

His mother's frown lifted into raised eyebrows, and she cocked her head. "Sounds like maybe *you* love her."

He stilled. Pictured Gabriella's sweet face and fiery hair and the tenderness in her eyes, and knowing he'd never see any of that again physically hurt.

Love her? Maybe he did. What he felt for her was unlike anything he'd felt before. But love was fleeting, he knew.

Both his parents were looking at him expectantly, but he didn't want to talk about Gabriella unless he had to, and changed the subject. "How does the surgical entry wound feel, Mother? Has the pain lessened?"

"Yes. It's not too bad."

"I've seen them change the bandages, and it looks

bad to me," his father said. "Your mother's just tough. Always has been." As he looked at his wife the man's eyes were filled with a warmth and softness Rafael had rarely seen.

"Is that a compliment or something else?" His mother reached for his father's hand and smiled at him.

"A compliment. As though I'd give anything else to my very special wife." He held her hand tight, leaning to give her forehead a lingering kiss.

Rafael stared at the way his parents looked at one another. At the…the *love* in his father's eyes as he gently stroked her skin, bruised from the needle sticks and IV.

His parents *did* love each other? Even though their marriage had been arranged and the time they spent together seemed to be far less than the time they spent apart? All Rafael had ever noticed had been cordial respect between them, but maybe because they were his own parents he hadn't really been looking.

All those questions and revelations jumbled around in his head until everything settled into a new order and a clear focus. And with that focus came another vision of Gabriella.

Until this very second, once his mother was completely well, he'd planned to keep living his life the way he always had, moving from place to place and from woman to woman and from job to job. Never dipping his toe deeper than the shallow end of the pool for fear of becoming trapped and emotionally entangled, ending up in a long-term loveless situation like his parents and brother.

Except, apparently, he'd been wrong about that. And could that mean he might be wrong about his sibling's marriage too?

It didn't really matter. What mattered was that he'd

closed his mind and heart to any possibility of real love. Had shut it tight, not even realizing he'd been doing it. But wanting to see inside Gabriella's heart and mind for the time he was with her had cracked his heart and brain open instead, just enough to let in a sliver of light. Instead of learning her secrets, she'd gently but directly gotten him to spill his own. To explain that he was the black sheep and always would be. Instead of judging him, she'd believed in him. Believed his parents must, too.

And he was damned if she hadn't been absolutely right.

He watched his father cup his mother's cheek in his palm, and their stunning love and deep connection struck him all over again.

At that moment he knew he looked at Gabriella exactly the same way. Looked at her in a way he'd never before looked at a woman, and if he was as lucky as hell, she just might look back at him the same way. He didn't have to worry about protecting her from him, because she'd turned him into a different man. He didn't have to worry about exposing her to media rumors, because he was ready to make a commitment to her he'd never dreamed possible until now.

"I'm in love with her." He actually said the words out loud he was so shocked. And rocked back onto his heels yet again.

"What did you say?"

He blinked to see both his parents looking at him quizzically. "I said I'm in love with her. Gabriella Cain. I'm in love with her, and I'd like to talk to you about it."

Normally, on a long flight Rafael could get some sleep in the comfortable bed on his family's jet. But that had proved impossible. He'd read medical journals he needed to catch up on, checked the stock market, and even worked on some crossword puzzles, which he hadn't done in years. But no matter what he did, his mind was only partly there. Gabriella occupied most of his thoughts, and all of his heart, and every hour that passed before he could tell her how she'd changed him and ask her to be his wife felt like extended torture.

Finally, the early evening lights of L.A. stretched across the horizon and he found himself wondering which golden light, of the millions of lights switching on at that moment in the city, was the one lighting her cozy living room.

The jet's wheels had barely touched the runway when he switched on his cellphone to call her. He saw that he had a voice-mail message from James, and, much as he was desperate to talk to Gabriella, figured he should find out what James wanted, in case it had something to do with her. When he pulled it up to listen to it, he stopped smiling and stopped breathing at the same time.

Then listened to it again.

"Rafael, it's James. Do you happen to know where Gabby went? Give me a call."

What the hell? What did James mean?

He quickly punched in her number, and a cold dread began to seep through his veins when a recorded message said the number was no longer in service. He stared hard at the phone as if, somehow, he could reach inside to conjure Gabriella straight out of it.

What had he said in his voice-mail message to her? He couldn't remember exactly, but he didn't think it was anything that would have made her take off. Was it? Which probably meant, if she'd left L.A., it was because the horrible media story had driven her away.

If she was hurting and gone, the blame lay squarely at his feet and, damn it, he was going to make it right.

As the jet taxied down the runway, Rafael called James, cursing when he didn't answer. It seemed forever before the jet had parked and he could leave it to run to his car, which he'd arranged to have dropped off there for him. If Gabriella had been nervous about the speed he'd driven in the mountains, she'd have closed her eyes for sure if she'd been in the car with him now, taking curves like the devil was on his heels. And he could practically feel it nipping, because a deep sense of foreboding had filled his chest. A feeling that this wasn't going to be as simple as showing up at her door, sweeping her into his arms and telling her that her past didn't matter and that he would always be there for her.

He skidded to a stop in front of her apartment and banged on her door. But of course there was no answer. Was she in there, or had she gone? He should have called James to see if he'd come here looking for her. He banged some more, until her neighbor's door opened.

"What's all the racket out here?" the man asked.

"Do you know if Gabriella Cain is home?"

"Saw her leave yesterday. Had a few suitcases with her."

Damn it! "Thanks." Rafael spun on his heel and pushed his car even harder to get to the clinic, parking it practically sideways before he ran inside.

Desperately hoping that somehow she'd shown back up after James had left his message, he checked her office first but it was quiet and empty. Now it was just a room, with all the life and energy gone from it. He put his hands on her desk and leaned on it, needing that support when he saw that her usual tidy stacks of papers were gone, and so were the few personal items he'd noticed there before.

"She handed in her resignation."

Rafael swung around at the sound of James's voice. His friend stood there looking grim and angry, rubbing the back of his neck with his palm.

"When?"

"Yesterday. That's why I'm here so late, trying to find a replacement. Not that it'll be easy to replace someone like Gabby. I've been trying like hell to figure out where she went so I could talk her into coming back, but no luck so far."

"Why did she leave?"

"Because the damned news outlets were splashing photos of the two of you everywhere, and along with that some people were running their mouths about her past making her unfit to work here as a midwife. I'm tempted to call the news outlets who've run this damned story, but since they're always looking for a way to throw the media spotlight on me, too, I'm afraid it would just make it worse. Did you warn her this could happen if the two of you spent time together?"

"Not enough, obviously." Damn it, this was what he'd wanted to avoid all along, and he should have told her about the grainy photos from that first night together, when she'd fallen asleep at his house. Maybe she'd have been more prepared for this if she'd known they'd been dogging both of them from the start.

But things were different now. She wasn't just another fling, she was the woman he loved. He'd be more than happy to have that be headline news, if she loved him back.

The thought that she might not made it hard to breathe.

"I'm going to get with some of my people from the

palace. See if they can find out where she's from, where her family is, or who her old friends are. I'll start there."

"All I know is that she's from Seattle. I'll keep working on it and let you know. I want her back too. Good luck."

James gave Rafael a quick, hard hug, then left and Rafael sat in Gabriella's chair to get started on the most important hunt of his life.

Gabby sat on the dock near her childhood home and stared out at the Pacific Ocean, pulling her jacket closer around her to keep away the penetrating evening chill. Always, whenever she'd had problems in her life, she'd felt soothed by the sound of the surf. By watching the rhythmic waves slide up and down the sand. By seeing the orange sun gleaming lower in the sky to finally dip below the horizon. All of it usually left her feeling like she was ready to take on whatever challenge she had to face.

Her current challenge, forgetting about Rafael Moreno, felt pretty impossible. Taking the positive step to begin sending out applications for jobs had helped a little. Maybe once she moved somewhere to start afresh, met new people and didn't hide away like she had the two years she'd been at The Hollywood Hills Clinic, it would get better. Maybe forgetting him would be easier than she expected.

And maybe the seagulls would start swimming and fish would fly across the sky.

A sigh filled her chest. Surprised by a movement next to her, she looked up, and her heart ground to a complete halt.

"So, *querida*, you are here." Rafael dropped down next to her, and in his quiet voice was a note she hadn't heard before. "Should you ever become a felon, be glad to know you're very hard to find."

"Rafael. How…? Why…? Is your mother okay?" Her heart started up again in lurching thuds against her ribs, and she just stared in disbelief that he was actually there. And why, when he'd given her the brush-off and basically said goodbye, have a nice life?

"My mother is fine. Tell me why you left L.A." He reached for her hand, but she pulled it away. Somehow he couldn't have seen what was on TV.

She licked her lips, and her gut churned with dread, but she had to tell him. "The media ran a story. About me, and…and how I gave birth to my stillborn son. Talked about how I should have done things differently. Why I shouldn't be a midwife and…it's all true. Except that it wasn't my fault. I realize that now, and I know I'm still good at what I do."

"I know. I heard the story." He reached for her again, and this time she let his warm hand engulf her frozen one. "Of course you're still good at what you do. Better than good. I'm so sorry this difficult part of your life has been thrown out there for all the world to see. It's all my fault, and I feel very badly about that."

So that was why he was here. To apologize for the media, which wasn't really his fault at all.

She stared back at the horizon because she couldn't bear to look at his face. "I don't think it's your fault any more than my losing the baby was mine. Don't worry, I'll cope."

"I know that too. You're a strong woman, not to mention talented and caring and so beautiful you make me ache." He took her face in his hands, the green eyes meeting hers filled with tenderness as he turned her toward him. "Tell me about your baby. Tell me what happened."

God, she didn't want to talk about it. But maybe telling the story would be part of the process to continue to heal. To truly put it in the past. "I was working late. Had finished a long shift, and my patient had been in labor a long time. She was very upset and exhausted, and even though I'd been feeling odd pains all evening I really felt I should stay with her, be there for her until her baby was born. She developed complications and ended up having surgery, and I couldn't just leave her with an OB she'd never met before. So I stayed, and her baby was born healthy."

She closed her eyes, not wanting to remember the rest of it. Rafael's hands slipped to her shoulders as he rested his cheek against hers. "And then what happened?"

"By then I was feeling really bad. I went to my office, and the pain was so overwhelming I collapsed. By the time someone found me I was in premature labor." She pulled her cheek from his and opened her eyes, barely able to squeeze out the rest of the story. "I'll never forget the moment when they listened for his heartbeat, but there wasn't one. They attached the monitor to be sure, but nothing. My baby was dead. I had to deliver him, knowing he was gone. And never, as long as I live, will I forget how it felt to hold his small, motionless body in my arms, eyes closed, an incredibly peaceful look on his tiny, perfect face. The face of an angel."

Her voice broke as the memories flooded her. Rafael had said she was strong. Now he knew otherwise.

"I'm so sorry," he said, folding her close against him. She let herself cling to him for a long moment. Pressed her face to his neck. Let herself soak in his warmth one last time. "I've delivered stillborn babies, and I've seen the parents' pain. I can't imagine it. But I'm glad to hear you know it wasn't your fault. That probably your baby wasn't growing normally. Most likely, your pains came after he had passed away inside you, and whether or not you'd gone to see someone earlier about it wouldn't have made any difference."

His hand stroking slowly up and down her back felt even more soothing than watching the ocean. "I know. I do. But it's hard not to feel like somehow, if I'd done things differently, he'd be here now."

She could feel his face move against her hair in what she took to be a nod before he pulled back. "Thank you for sharing this with me. Now I'd like to share with you the second reason I'm here."

His face was so serious she readied herself for some other thing even worse than the first media blitz, though surely that wasn't possible. "What is it?"

"I'd decided I should stay at home for a while. Figured I'd been running from there for too long and hurting others in the process." His wide palms cupped her face again. "Hurting you, both with the media focus and because I knew I couldn't give you the kind of love you deserve."

Oh, God. And here he was, hurting her now by stating the obvious. She tried to turn away from him, but he held her gaze.

"Then I found I was wrong. Again. I've been wrong about so damn many things, but the biggest was believing that there's no such thing as real love. Lasting love. I know I was wrong because I'm very much in love with you, Gabriella. And I know that I'll love you forever."

"Rafael." Her heart thundered in her ears so loudly it drowned out the sound of the ocean waves. What was he saying, exactly?

"I love you. Like I've never loved anyone before."
This time he whispered the words. "And I hope and
pray that, even though I sure as hell don't deserve it,
you might love me back."

Tears stung her eyes and spilled over, and his thumbs
slowly slid across her cheeks to wipe them away.

"I do love you. But it's me who doesn't deserve you.
And someday you'll want children. Will need an heir
for your country. I don't think I can go through losing
a baby again."

"I don't need to produce an heir. My brother's wife
is expecting as we speak, and since I know she wants a
big brood, there will be more than enough Morenos running around the palace to satisfy the entire kingdom."

That vision managed to make her smile a little, even
through her tears, because she could just see green-
eyed, dark-haired Morenos who looked like Rafael,
loudly tearing up and down marble hallways and breaking priceless antiquities. And with that vision came
the longing again to have a child, but hadn't she gone
through enough pain already?

He must have seen something in her face, because
his usual arrogant confidence seemed to be on shaky
ground as he drew her closer. "The only thing I need
in my life is you, Gabriella. I need you to help me see
things I can't otherwise see on my own, except through
your beautiful eyes. And because my parents are happy
that I'm crazily in love with a wonderful woman, and
thrilled at the thought of me never again embarrassing
them, they gave me something to give to you. If you'll
accept it."

The tenderness and intensity and even a shocking
vulnerability in his eyes stole her breath, and it took her
two attempts to find her voice. "Accept what?"

"This thing in my pocket that's digging into my ribs, and I hope you'll help me relieve my pain." His fingers stroked her cheeks once more before leaving them to pull a surprisingly worn-looking box from his jacket.

"That looks about a hundred years old," she said through sniffles she knew had to be awfully unattractive, but she couldn't seem to do a thing about the tears that kept leaking from her eyes.

"Four hundred, actually. My great-great…some big number of greats-grandmother was given this ring by some great-great-grandfather." He surprised her by folding his fingers back around the box, and she nearly begged him to let her at least look inside. His other fingers tipped her chin up to meet his eyes. "Will you marry me, Gabriella? Be my wife? My princess? Please say yes."

Gabby stared, unable to fully process his words, unable to speak, and he pressed his lips softly to hers before pulling back again. "You're scaring me here, Gabriella. Will it help to see the ring?"

He flipped open the box, and she gasped at the huge, square-cut emerald surrounded by diamonds. An emerald that dazzled almost as much as Rafael's eyes. As Rafael himself. But not quite.

"It's beautiful," she whispered, "but I didn't need to see it to say yes. Yes, I love you and, yes, I'll marry you."

"Thank God," he whispered back. He pulled her close, and she could feel his body relax as he pressed his cheek to hers. "I promise you won't regret it. I'll do everything I can to make you happy."

Long seconds ticked by as they just held one another, and she knew he was feeling the same unbelievable connection radiating between them without another spoken word. When they slowly parted, he pulled the ring from the box and slipped it onto her finger. As she looked down at it, a bubble of happiness ballooned in her chest so big she thought she might just float away. At the same time she realized there was one important thing they hadn't talked about.

"I assume you want to go back to your country to live? Would I…if we're married…be able to work?"

"I'm not going to lie," he said, his lips twisting. "Being my wife will require helping with some charitable work I'd like to start in the kingdom, and public appearances. But we can live anywhere you want, and you can do whatever you want, including be a midwife. We can work together, if you like, or not. It's up to you."

"I don't know. You can be awfully overbearing and bossy."

"Another reason I need feisty and amazing Gabriella to keep me in my place." He gave her another lingering kiss then stood, holding out his hand to help her to her feet. "What do you say we go back to L.A. for now, until we make a plan?"

"Yes." She twined her fingers with his, hardly able to believe this was really happening. "I think I'm finally ready to move on to wherever life takes me next. With you."

CHAPTER FOURTEEN

"Here's some news I think you'll want to read with your breakfast, Gabriella," Rafael said, sliding several newspapers in front of her on the table.

"I'm enjoying being pampered by you in this beautiful house." She scowled and took a fortifying swig of the delicious coffee Rafael had made. "Why would you want to ruin that for me by making me read the news?"

"I don't think this news will ruin your morning." He refilled her cup and she looked up to see his lips were curved and his eyes were dancing.

Moving on from her past didn't mean she wanted to read the awful stuff that had continued to be plastered in all the media but she had to admit his expression made her curious. She glanced at the headline and her heart stumbled.

"What…is this?" She slowly picked up the paper, staring.

"The world is defending you, *querida*," Rafael said. "Shall I read a few of the quotes? *'Gabriella Cain is the best thing to ever happen to The Hollywood Hills Clinic.'* I like that one, since she's definitely the best thing to ever happen to me." He dropped a kiss on her head. "And how about this? *'Anyone who knows mid-*

wife Gabriella Cain knows this trash being said about her can't possibly be true.'"

"Oh, my gosh." She stared up at him, her heart somehow squeezing and swelling at the same time. "This is incredible!"

"And my favorite, from Cameron Fontaine," Rafael continued, flicking through another paper. *"'If Gabriella Cain isn't hired back by The Hollywood Hills Clinic there will be a boycott. And if there isn't an immediate retraction from the media, taking back all those ridiculous and inflammatory statements, influential actresses and studio directors like me are going to sue the hell out of every single one of them.'"*

Gabby put her hands to her cheeks and laughed. "Oh, my gosh, that's so Cameron. I guess she liked me after all."

"Loved you. As I do." He leaned down to kiss her cheek, moving on to her mouth, and just as Gabby was clutching his shirt and sinking into another delicious kiss, the doorbell rang.

"Well, who could that be? Maybe it's the media come to apologize."

"Like that would ever happen." There was something odd, secretive even, about the smile playing on his lips, and Gabby had to wonder why.

"You never know, when a woman like you has so much clout behind her." He winked and headed for the door, and when he returned a moment later a familiar voice came with him.

"Gabby. You've got to help me out," James said. "There's a near-riot at the clinic!"

"A near-riot? What are you talking about?"

"Several of your pregnant patients are refusing to see anyone else, and they're threatening a sit-in if you don't come back. They're mad as hell that you're gone and they're blaming me." James threw his arms wide, and she nearly laughed at the look of alarm on his normally cool, impassive face. "Will you come back? Please? Tell me what it would take and I'll make it happen."

The swelling of her heart grew so much she could barely hold in all her joy. Then remembered she wasn't living her life alone anymore. That there were two of them now. Someday, maybe, she might even be ready to add a few more to the wonderful life she and Rafael would share.

She turned to him, and her face must have told him exactly what she was thinking because he stepped close, pulled her into his arms and kissed her forehead.

"The clinic is a pretty great place to work, isn't it?" He tipped her chin and his beautiful eyes smiled into hers.

"Yes. It is." She pressed her palms against his chest and smiled back. "How would you feel about us both working there?"

"You already know, Gabriella Cain," he said, his warm gaze a steady promise, "that wherever it is you want to be, I'm right there by your side."

* * * * *

Look out for the next great story in
THE HOLLYWOOD HILLS CLINIC

HIS PREGNANT SLEEPING BEAUTY
by Lynne Marshall

And if you missed where it all started, check out

SEDUCED BY THE HEART SURGEON
by Carol Marinelli

FALLING FOR THE SINGLE DAD
by Emily Forbes

TEMPTED BY HOLLYWOOD'S TOP DOC
by Louisa George

PERFECT RIVALS...
by Amy Ruttan

All available now!
And there are two more fabulous stories to come...

HIS PREGNANT SLEEPING BEAUTY

BY
LYNNE MARSHALL

Published in Great Britain 2016
By Mills & Boon, an imprint of HarperCollins*Publishers*
1 London Bridge Street, London, SE1 9GF

© 2016 Harlequin Books S.A.

Special thanks and acknowledgement are given to Lynne Marshall for her contribution to The Hollywood Hills Clinic *series*

ISBN: 978-0-263-91491-7

Dear Reader,

It's always fun to be part of a continuity with seven other authors—especially such a talented group! When I met my characters Joseph and Carey I immediately fell in love. Joe is the kind of hero you want to throw your arms around and never let go. The problem is he doesn't want to let anyone close enough to do that. He has his reasons, believe me, and they're doozies. Carey is a glass-half-full kind of girl, even though life has thrown her some tough issues with which to deal. From the moment Joe sees Carey he assigns himself as her guardian—and what a lucky girl she becomes! I rooted for their happily-ever-after right from the start!

His Pregnant Sleeping Beauty is the first time I've ever written about a paramedic hero. Fortunately I had some wonderful personal resources, and therefore I feel my scenes are authentic. In fact you could say I'm proud of them. What a tough job first responders have! And writing about Carey took me back to my RN roots. I just love nurse heroines! So I guess you could call me a happy camper all round, being the lucky lady to write their story in Book 6 of The Hollywood Hills Clinic series. Why not check them all out?

Dear readers, if you read a book and enjoy it please consider writing a short review to help spread the word. Or give a shout-out about it on social media. We authors really appreciate that. Oh, and if you're on Facebook 'friend' me, I'd love to keep in touch.

Until next time,

Lynne

PS Visit my website to keep up with all the news: lynnemarshall.com. You can also sign up for my author newsletter there.

This book is dedicated to the two paramedics
who helped me make my character, Joe, a true hero.
Thank you, John-Philip Maarschalk and Rick Ochocki, for your expert
input and help. What would the world be without our first responders?

Lynne Marshall used to worry that she had a serious problem with
daydreaming—then she discovered she was supposed to *write* those
stories! A Registered Nurse for twenty-six years, she came to fiction-
writing later than most. Now she writes romance which usually
includes medicine, but always comes straight from her heart. She is
happily married, a Southern California native, a woman of faith, a
dog-lover, an avid reader, a curious traveller and a proud grandma.

Books by Lynne Marshall

Mills & Boon Medical Romance

Cowboys, Doctors...Daddies!

Hot-Shot Doc, Secret Dad
Father For Her Newborn Baby

Temporary Doctor, Surprise Father
The Boss and Nurse Albright
The Heart Doctor and the Baby
The Christmas Baby Bump
Dr Tall, Dark...and Dangerous?
NYC Angels: Making the Surgeon Smile
200 Harley Street: American Surgeon in London
A Mother for His Adopted Son

Visit the Author Profile page
at millsandboon.co.uk for more titles.

Praise for
Lynne Marshall

'Heartfelt emotion that will bring you to the point of tears, for those
who love a second-chance romance written with exquisite detail.'
—*Contemporary Romance Reviews* on
NYC Angels: Making the Surgeon Smile

'Lynne Marshall contributes a rewarding story to the *NYC Angels*
series, and her gifted talent repeatedly shines. *Making the Surgeon
Smile* is an outstanding romance with genuine emotions and
passionate desires.'
—*CataRomance*

CHAPTER ONE

CAREY SPENCER HAD never felt more alone in her life than when she got off the bus in Hollywood.

Joseph Matthews, on that night's shift for the prestigious Hollywood Hills Clinic, had just delivered one of the industry's favorite character actresses to the exclusive twenty-bed extended recovery hotel. It was tucked between Children's Hospital and a smaller private hospital on Sunset Boulevard, and the common eye would never guess its function. Joe had agreed to make the Wednesday night run because James Rothsberg himself had asked. After all, the lady *had* won an award for Best Supporting Actress the year before last.

As the lead paramedic for the ambulance line he owned, Joe had attended the not-to-be-named-aloud patient during the uneventful ride to the recovery hotel. She'd been heavily sedated, her IV was in place, her vitals, including oxygen saturation, were fine, but she'd had so much work done on her face, breasts and hands she looked like a mummy. When they'd arrived, you'd have thought he'd delivered the President to Walter Reed National Military Medical Center the way the abundant staff rushed to the ambulance and took over the transfer.

Now, at nine p.m., back sitting in the front of the private ambulance, Joe switched on some music. Jazz, his favorite station. Yeah, he owned this bus—hell, he owned all six of them—so he could play whatever music he wanted. But that also kept him thinking about work a lot. It was the first of the month and he'd have to make copies of the June shift schedule for the EMTs and paramedics on his team before they showed up for work tomorrow morning.

"I'm hungry," Benny, his EMT, said from behind the wheel.

Why was Joe not surprised? The kid had barely turned twenty and seemed to have hollow legs.

Restless and out of sorts, a state that was nothing new these days, Joe nodded. "How about that Mexican grill?" They'd just made their last run on Friday night, without plans for later, so why not?

"You read my mind." Benny tossed him a cockeyed grin, his oversized Afro flopping with the quick movement.

He turned off Hollywood Boulevard and up N. Cahuenga to the fast-food place by the cross-country bus depot, where a bus had just arrived from Who Knew Where, USA. Benny had to wait to pull into a larger-than-average parking space. Joe mindlessly watched a handful of people trickle off the bus.

A damn fine-looking young woman wearing oversized sunglasses got off. Sunglasses at night. What was up with that? She was slender and her high-heeled boots made her look on the tall side. She wore jeans and a dark blue top, or was it a sweater? Her thick hair was layered and long with waves and under the bus depot lights looked brown. Reddish? He wondered what her story was. Probably because of the shades at night. But he didn't bother to think about ladies these days. Yet, still, dang, she was hot. And stood out like a rose in a thorn patch.

Benny backed the private ambulance into the space at the farthest end of the restaurant lot, and Joe got out the passenger side, immediately getting hit by the mouthwatering aroma of spicy beans and chipotle chicken. He stretched, eager to chow down. A sudden movement in his peripheral vision drew his attention. Someone sprang from behind a pillar and snagged a lady's purse strap and wrist, pulling her out of the crowd and toward the nearby alley. It was the woman he'd just been gawking at! The other travelers had mostly dispersed. She put up a fight, too, and squealed, yet the few people left lingering didn't seem to notice...but he did.

Joe ran to the mouth of the alley. "Hey!" Then sprinted toward the young woman, who was still fighting to hold on to her purse.

The tall but skinny, straggly-haired dude dragged her by the shoulder strap and wrist deeper down the alley. *Why doesn't she just let go? Ah, wait, it's one of those over-the-torso jobs.*

"Hey!"

This time the guy turned and whacked her with his fist, knocking the young woman to the ground. Her head hit with a thud. He ripped off the purse, hitting her head on the pavement again, then stepped over her to get to Joe with a wild swing.

Joe blocked the first punch with little effort—the dumb punk didn't know what he was dealing with as he boxed for his workouts—but the guy pulled a knife and lashed out. Joe threw another punch and landed it, even while feeling a hot lightning-quick slice across his ribs. Now he was really ticked. The guy ran deeper into the alley with Joe in pursuit, soon disappearing over a large trash bin and tall crumbling brick wall. Joe skidded to a brief stop and watched in disbelief. For a scumbag the man was agile. Probably from a lot of practice in assaulting innocent people.

The girl! Holding his side, he sprinted back to where she lay. Out cold.

Benny met up with him. "I called the police. You okay?"

"Just a superficial wound." Still, he checked it briefly since an adrenaline rush could mask pain. The last thing he wanted to find out was that the cut was deep enough to cause evisceration and he hadn't noticed. Fortunately the only thing he saw was oozing blood, nothing gushing. He'd throw a thick absorbent pad over his middle as soon as Benny got back with the trauma kit, oxygen bag and backboard. He didn't want to bleed all over the poor lady. "Bring our equipment, okay?" He grabbed a pair of gloves from Benny's belt, and knelt in front of the young woman as Benny took off for the ambulance. "I'm a paramedic, miss. Are you okay?" he said loudly and clearly. She didn't respond.

She'd hit her head hard when she'd fallen—correct that, had been punched to the ground. He tried to rouse her with a firm hand on her shoulder. "Hello? You okay, you awake, miss?"

He watched the rise and fall of her chest. At least she was breathing normally. He felt her neck for the carotid pulse and found it. Rate and strength normal. Good. He scanned her body for bleeding or other signs of obvious injury. Maybe the scumbag had stabbed her too. Then he used the palms of his gloved hands to sweep the underside of her arms and legs to check for bleeding, and did the same beneath both sides of her back. So far so good.

There was a fifty-cent-sized pool of blood behind her head, but he didn't move her neck, not before he and Benny had placed a cervical collar on her. Her assailant had run off with her purse and she didn't appear to have any other form of ID. He checked her wrist and then her neck to see if she wore any emergency alert jewelry. No such luck. They'd have to wait until she regained consciousness to find out who she was.

Even under the dim lights in the alley she had an obvious black eye, and because the dirtbag had yanked off her torso-anchored purse strap the sweater she'd been wearing had been pulled halfway down her left arm… which was covered in bruises. She'd just been mugged, but these marks weren't fresh. Anger surged through him. She'd been beaten up long before today.

What kind of guy treated a woman like that?

He shook his head. Of all the lousy luck. She hadn't stepped off the bus five minutes ago and had already gotten mugged and knocked unconscious. The only thing she had going for her on this nightmare of a Friday night was him. He shuddered for the young stranger over what might have played out if he hadn't been here.

Maybe it was those thick eyelashes that seemed to glue her eyes shut, or her complete vulnerability, being unconscious in an alley, or maybe it was the obvious signs of abuse, but for whatever reason Joe was suddenly struck with an uncompromising need to protect her.

From this moment on tonight he vowed to take responsibility for the out-of-luck Jane Doe. Hell, if anyone had ever needed a guardian angel, she did.

Benny had moved the ambulance closer, and brought the backboard and equipment. Joe let Benny apply a large sloppy dressing around his middle as he checked her airway again, noting she had good air exchange. He worried, with the head injury, that she might vomit and wanted to be near if she did to prevent aspiration.

"We're going to give you some oxygen and put a collar round your neck," Joe said calmly, hoping she might already be regaining consciousness and hear him explain everything they did to her. They worked together and soon had Jane on the backboard for stability. Joe secured her with the straps, never taking his eyes off her. She had definitely been knocked out cold, yet still breathed evenly. A good thing. But he knew when unconscious people woke up they could often be combative and try to take off the oxygen and cervical collar. Hell, after what she'd just been through, could he blame her if she woke up fighting?

With her long dark auburn hair spread over her shoulders and her hands strapped to the transport board, she made the strangest image.

An urban Sleeping Beauty.

"Ready for transfer?" Joe said, breaking his own thoughts.

"Don't you want to wait for the police?"

"If they're not here by the time we get her in the back of the van, you call them again and tell them to meet us at the clinic. She might have a skull fracture or subdural bleed for all we know, and needs medical attention ASAP." He knew the next forty-five minutes were all she had remaining in the golden hour for traumatic head injury. "I'm going to call Dr. Rothsberg and let him know what we've got."

He jumped into the back of the van first to guide the head of the gurney on which they'd placed the long spine board and patient as Benny pushed from the back, then he rolled the gurney forward and locked it in place with sprung locks on the ambulance floor.

He'd ride in the back with her. If she woke up, confused and possibly combative, he wanted to be there. Plus it would be his chance to do a more thorough examination.

Joe did another assessment of Sleeping Beauty's condition. Unchanged. Then he made the call. Unexpectedly, Dr. Rothsberg said to bring her to the clinic instead of county. Which was a good thing, because Joe would have taken her home before he'd consider delivering a Jane Doe to county hospital to potentially slip through every conceivable crack due to their overstretched system.

He stripped off the makeshift dressing and his shirt to assess his own wound, which was long and jagged, still wept blood and would definitely need stitches. Now that he was looking at it, it burned like hell. Benny had a short conversation with the police, who'd just arrived. Great timing! He showed them where they'd found her and where the attacker had fled over the wall then left them to look for witnesses as Joe cleaned and dressed his own wound. Damn, the disinfectant smarted! One of the policemen took a quick look inside the ambulance, saw the victim and Joe with his injury, nodded and took off toward the alley.

Benny closed the back doors of the van, got into the driver's seat then started the ambulance. "They'll take our statements at the clinic later."

"Good," Joe said, taping his dressing, constantly checking his patient as he did so.

As Benny drove, with their lights flashing, Joe checked her vital signs again, this time using a blood-pressure cuff then a stethoscope to listen to her lungs.

He opened her eyes, opening the blackened eye more gingerly, and used his penlight to make sure she hadn't blown a pupil. Fortunately she hadn't, but unfortunately he'd had to move a clump of her hair away from her face in order to do so. It was thick and wavy, and, well, somehow it felt too intimate, touching it. It'd been a while since he'd run his fingers through a woman's hair, which he definitely wasn't doing right now, but the thought of wanting to bothered him.

By the status of her black eye, it'd been there a few days and definitely looked ugly and intentional. Someone had punched her. That was a fact. There was that anger again, flaming out of nowhere for a woman he knew zero about.

He decided to insert a hep-lock into her antecubital fossa so the clinic would have a line ready to go on arrival. A head injury could increase cranial pressure and so could IV fluid. He didn't want to add to that, and so far her blood pressure was within normal limits. While he performed the tasks he thought about everything that had happened to his patient prior to winding up in that alley.

She'd gotten off the bus and hadn't waited to collect a suitcase, which meant all she'd carried with her was in that large shoulder bag. And that was long gone with the punk who'd knocked her cold and jumped the wall. He tightened his fists. What he'd give to deck that guy and leave him in some alley.

If Joe added up the clues he'd guess that the lovely Sleeping Jane was running from whoever had bruised her arms and blackened her eye. She'd probably grabbed whatever she could and snuck away from…

"Who are you?" Joe asked quietly, wondering if she could hear him, knowing that unconscious people sometimes still heard what went on around them. "Where did you come from?"

He lifted one of her hands, that fierce sense of protectiveness returning, and held it in his, noticing the long thin fingers with carefully manicured but unpainted nails, and made another silent vow. *Don't worry, I'll look out for you. You don't have to be afraid where I'm taking you.*

They arrived at The Hollywood Hills Clinic, nestled far beneath the Hollywood sign at the end of narrow winding roads with occasional hairpin turns. The swanky private clinic that hugged the hillside always reminded him of something Frank Lloyd Wright might have designed for the twenty-first century, if he were still alive. The stacked boxy levels of the modern stone architecture, nearly half of it made of special earthquake-resistant glass, looked like a diamond in the night on the hillside. Warm golden light glowed from every oversized window, assuring the private clinic was open twenty-four hours. For security and privacy purposes, there were tall fences out front, and a gate every vehicle had to clear, except for ambulances. They breezed through as soon as the gate opened completely.

Benny headed toward the private patient loading area at the back of the building. Joe put his shirt back on and gingerly buttoned it over his bandaged and stinging rib cage.

He still couldn't believe his good fortune over landing the bid as the private ambulance company for James Rothsberg's clinic only two short years after starting his own business. He'd been an enterprising twenty-three-year-old paramedic with a plan back then, thanks to a good mind for business instilled in him by his hard-working father. James must have seen something about him he liked when he'd interviewed him and Joe had tendered his bid. Or maybe it had had more to do with the nasty info leak the previous ambulance company had been responsible for, exposing several of the A-list actors in the biz on a TV gossip show, making Joe's timing impeccable. He used to think of it as fate.

James's parents—Michael Rothsberg and Aubrey St. Claire—had had enough info leaks in their lives to fill volumes. Everyone, even Joe, remembered the scandal, and he'd only been in his early teens at the time. Their stories had made headlines on every supermarket rag and cable TV talk show. Everyone knew about their private affairs. After all, James's parents had been Hollywood royalty, and had been two of the highest-paid actors in the business. Watching them fall from grace had become a national pastime after a nasty kiss-and-tell book by an ex-lover had outed them as phonies. Their marriage had been a sham, and their teenage children, James and Freya, had suffered most.

James had told Joe on the day he'd hired him that loyalty to the clinic and the patients was the number-one rule, he wouldn't tolerate anything less, and Joe had lived up to that pledge every single day he'd shown up to work. He'd walked out of James's office that day thinking fate was on his side and he was the luckiest man on earth, but he too would soon experience his own fall. Like James, it hadn't been of his own making but that didn't mean it had hurt any less.

These days Joe didn't believe in fate or luck. No, he'd changed his thinking on that and now, for him, everything happened for a reason. Even his damned infertility, which he was still trying to figure out. He glanced at the hand where his wedding ring had once been but didn't let himself go there, instead focusing on the positive. The here and now. The new contract. His job security.

The clinic had opened its doors six years ago, and two years later, right around the time James's sister Freya had joined the endeavor, Joe's private ambulance service had been the Rothsbergs' choice for replacement. Having just signed a new five-year contract with the clinic, Joe almost thought of himself as another Hollywood success story. Hell, he was only twenty-eight, owned his own business, and worked for the most revered clinic in town.

But how could he call it true success when the rest of his life was such a mess?

James Rothsberg himself met the ambulance, along with another doctor and a couple of nurses, and Joe prepared to transfer his sleeping beauty.

A little bit taller than Joe, James's strong and well-built frame matched Joe's on the fitness scale. Where they parted ways was in the looks department. The son of A-list actors, James was what the gossip magazines called "an Adonis in scrubs". Yeah, he was classy, smooth and slick. He was the man every woman dreamed of and every man wanted to be, and Joe wasn't afraid to admit he had a man crush on the guy. Strictly platonic, of course, based on pure admiration. The doctor ran the lavish clinic for the mind-numbingly affluent, who flocked to him, eager to pay the price for his plastic surgery services. Well, someone had to support the outrageously luxurious clinic and the well-paid staff. In fact, someone on staff had recently commented after a big awards ceremony that half of the stars in attendance had been through the clinic's doors. A statement that wasn't far from the truth.

"James, what are you still doing here?"

"You piqued my interest," James said. "I had to see Jane Doe for myself."

Joe pushed the gurney out of the back of the ambulance, and Rick, one of the evening nurses, pulled from the other end.

James studied Jane Doe as she rolled by. "She didn't get that shiner tonight."

"Nope," Joe said. "There's a whole other story that went down before she got mugged."

James nodded agreement. "That reminds me, I got a call from the police department. They'll be here shortly to take your statement." He tugged Joe by the arm. "Let's take a look at your injury before they get here, okay?"

Joe was torn between looking after Sleeping Beauty or himself, but knew the clinic staff would give her the utmost medical attention. Besides, it wasn't every day the head of the clinic offered to give one-to-one patient care to an employee.

"Thanks, Doc. I really appreciate it."

"It's totally selfish. I've got to look out for my lead paramedic, right?" James said in a typically self-deprecating manner. That was another thing he liked so much about the guy. He never flaunted his wealth or his status.

Joe glanced across the room at the star patient of the night, Ms. Jane Doe, still unconscious but breathing steadily, and felt a little tug in his chest, then followed James into an examination room.

After the nursing assistant removed Joe's dressing, James studied it. "So what happened here?"

Joe explained what had transpired in the alley as the doctor applied pressure to one area that continued to bleed.

"Oh, you're definitely getting a tetanus shot. Who knows what was on that guy's blade."

"Well, he *was* a scumbag."

"Good thing you've got a trained plastic surgeon to stitch you up. I'd hate to ruin those perfect washboard abs."

Joe laughed, knowing his rigorous workout sessions plus boxing kept him fit. Boxing had been the one thing he could do to keep sane and not beat the hell out of his best friend during his divorce. "Ouch," he said, surprised by how sensitive his wound was as the nursing assistant cleaned the skin.

"Ouch!" he repeated, when the first topical anesthetic was injected by James.

The doctor chuckled. "Man up, dude. I'm just getting started."

That got an ironic laugh out of Joe. *Yeah, sterile dude, man up!*

"You won't be feeling much in a couple of minutes."

Joe knew the drill, he'd sutured his share of patients in his field training days, but this was the first time in his entire life he'd been the patient in need of stitches. Hell, he'd never even needed a butterfly bandage before.

"So, about the girl with the black eye," James said, donning sterile gloves while preparing the small sterile minor operations tray. "I wonder if she may have had any prior intracranial injuries that might have contributed to her immediately falling unconscious."

"I was wondering the same thing, but she hit that pavement really hard. I hope she doesn't have a subdural hematoma."

"We're doing a complete head trauma workup on her."

"Thanks. I know this probably sounds weird, but

I feel personally responsible for her, having seen the whole thing go down, not getting there fast enough, and being the first to treat her and all. Especially since she doesn't have any ID."

"You broke a rule, right? Got involved with your patient?"

"Didn't mean to, but I guess you could say that. I know it's foolish—"

James turned back toward him. "And this might be foolish too, but when the police come we'll tell them we'll be treating *and* letting our Jane Doe recover right here."

Touched beyond words, as the cost for staying at this exclusive clinic would be astronomical, Joe wanted to shake the good doctor's hand but he wore sterile gloves. "Thank you. I really—" He was about to say "appreciate that" but quickly went quiet, not used to being the patient as the first stitch was placed, using a nasty-looking hooked needle, and though he didn't feel anything, he still didn't want to move.

"If I stitch this up just so, there'll hardly be a scar. On the other hand, I could make you look like you've got a seven pack."

As the saying went, it only hurt when he laughed.

A couple of hours later, the police had taken a thorough report, and also told Joe they hadn't found anyone matching the description a couple of witnesses had given for the suspect, they also said they hadn't recovered Jane Doe's purse.

Joe sighed and shook his head. She'd continue to be Madam X until she came to. Which hopefully would be soon.

"We do have one lead, though."

He glanced up, hopeful whatever that lead was it might point to Jane's identity.

"The clinic staff found a bus-ticket stub in her sweater pocket. If she used a credit card to purchase the ticket, we might be able to trace it back and identify her."

"That's great. But what if she paid cash?"

"That might imply she didn't want to be traced."

"Probably explain those bruises, too."

The cop nodded. "The most we could possibly find out is the origin of the ticket. Which city she boarded in, but she's bound to wake up soon, right?"

Joe glanced across the room. Jane was now in one of the clinic's fancy hospital gowns and hooked up to an IV, still looking as peaceful as a sleeping child. "It's hard to say with concussion and potential brain swelling. The doctors may determine she needs surgery for a subdural hematoma or something, for all I know."

The young cop looked grim as he considered that possibility, and Joe was grateful for his concern. "Well, we'll be in touch." He gave Joe his card. "If she wakes up, or if there's anything you remember or want to talk about, give me a call. Likewise, I'll let you know if we find anything out."

"Thanks."

An orderly and RN rolled Jane by Joe. "Where's she going?"

"To her room in the DOU. She's in Seventeen A."

The definitive observation unit was for the patients who needed extra care. Dr. Di Williams ran the unit like a well-oiled machine. Jane would be well looked after, but… He made a snap decision—he wasn't going home tonight. If James and Di would let him, he'd wait things out right here.

Fifteen minutes later, Sleeping Beauty was tucked into a high-end single bed in a room that looked more like one in a luxury spa hotel than a hospital. The only thing giving it away were the bedside handrails and the stack of monitors camouflaged in the corner with huge vases and flower arrangements. The tasteful beige, white and cream decor was relaxing, but Joe couldn't sleep. Instead, he sat in the super-comfy bedside chair resting his head in the palm of his right hand, watching *her* sleep. Wondering what her story was, and pondering why he felt so responsible for her. He decided it was because she was completely vulnerable. He knew the feeling. Someone besides a staff nurse had to look out for her until they found out who she was and could locate her family.

Sporting that black eye and those healing bruises on her arms, it was likely she had been in an abusive relationship. Most likely she'd been beaten up by the man she'd thought she loved.

His left thumb flicked the inside of his vacant ring finger, reminding him, on a much more personal level, how deeply love could hurt.

CHAPTER TWO

A FIRM HAND sent Joe out of a half dreaming, half awake state. He'd been smiling, floating around somewhere, smiling. The grip on his shoulder made a burst of adrenaline mainline straight to his heart, making his pulse ragged and shaky. He sat bolt upright, his eyes popping open. In less than a second he remembered where he was, turned his head toward the claw still grabbing him, and stared up at the elderly night nurse.

Cecelia, was it?

"What's up?" he said, trying to sound awake, then glancing toward the hospital bed and the patient he'd let down by falling asleep. Some guardian he'd turned out to be. She'd been placed on her side, either sound asleep or still unconscious, with pillows behind her back and between her knees, and he hadn't even woken up.

"Your services are needed," Cecelia said with a grainy voice. "We have a helicopter transfer to Santa Barbara."

"Got it. Take care of her."

"What I'm paid for," Cecelia mumbled, fiddling with the blanket covering her patient.

Joe stood, took one last look at Jane, who still looked peaceful, and walked to the nearest men's room to freshen up, then reported for duty in the patient transitioning room.

Rick, the RN from last night, was at the end of his shift and gave Joe his report. "The fifty-four-year-old patient is status post breast reduction, liposuction and lower face lift. Surgery and overnight recovery were uneventful. She's being transferred to Santa Barbara Cottage Hotel for the remainder of her recovery. IV in right forearm. Last medicated for pain an hour ago with seventy-five milligrams of Demerol. Dressings and drainage tubes in place, no excess bleeding noted. She's been released by Dr. R. for transfer." The male RN, fit and overly tanned, making his blue eyes blaze, gave Joe a deadpan stare. "All systems go. She's all yours." Then, when out of earshot of the patient, Rick whispered, "I didn't vote for her husband."

Joe accompanied the patient and gurney to the waiting helicopter on the roof and loaded the sleeping patient onto the air ambulance. He did a quick head-to-toe assessment before strapping her down and locking the special hydraulic gurney into place. He then made sure any and all emergency equipment was stocked and ready for use. After he hooked up the patient to the heart and BP monitor, he put headphones on his patient first and then himself and took his seat, buckling in, preparing for the noisy helicopter blades to whir to life then takeoff.

After delivering the patient to the Santa Barbara airport and transferring the politician's wife, who would not be named, to the awaiting recovery hotel team, he hoped to grab some coffee and maybe a quick breakfast while they waited for the okay to take off for the return trip.

Two hours later, back at the clinic, Joe's only goal

was to check in on Jane Doe. He hoped she'd come to and by now maybe everyone knew her name, and he wondered what it might be. Alexis? Belle? Collette? Excitedly he dashed into her room and found her as he'd left her…unconscious. Disappointment buttoned around him like a too-tight jacket.

The day shift nurse was at her side, preparing to give her a bed bath. A basin of water sat on the bedside table with steam rising from the surface. Several towels and cloths and a new patient gown were neatly stacked beside it. A thick, luxurious patient bath blanket was draped across her chest, Sleeping Beauty obviously naked underneath it. He felt the need to look away until the nurse pulled the privacy curtain around the bed.

"No change?" he asked, already knowing and hating the answer.

"No. But her lab results were a bit of a surprise."

"Everything okay with her skull?"

"Oh, yeah, the CT cranial scan and MRI were both normal except for the fact she's got one hell of a concussion with brain swelling. Well, along with still being unconscious and a slow-wave EEG to prove it."

Joe knew the hospital privacy policy, and this nurse wasn't about to tell him Jane Doe's lab results. Theoretically it wasn't any of his business. Except he'd made a vow last night, and had made it his business to look after her. As he hadn't signed off on his paramedic admission notes for Jane last night, he suddenly needed to access her computer chart to do so.

He headed to the intake department to find a vacant computer, but not before running into James, who looked rested and ready to take on the day. Joe, on the other hand, had gotten a glimpse of himself in the mirror when he'd made a quick pit stop on arriving back at the clinic a few minutes earlier. Dark circles beneath his eyes, a day's growth of beard… Yeah, he was a mess.

"What are you still doing here?" James asked.

"Just got back from a helicopter run to Santa Barbara for one of your patients."

"Cecelia told me you stayed here last night."

Damn that night nurse. "Yeah, well, I wanted to be around if Jane Doe woke up."

He didn't look amused. "This is an order, Joe. Go home and get some sleep. Don't come back until your usual evening shift. Got it?"

"Got it. Just have to sign off my charting first."

Several staff members approached James with questions, giving Joe the chance to sneak off to the computer. He logged on and quickly accessed Jane Doe's folder. First he read her CT scan results and the MRI, which were positive for concussion and brain swelling, but without fractures or bleeding, then he took a look at her labs. So far so good. Her drug panel was negative. Good. Her electrolytes, blood glucose, liver and kidney function tests were all within normal limits. Good. Then his gaze settled on a crazy little test result that nearly knocked him out of the chair.

A positive *pregnancy* test.

His suddenly dry-as-paper tongue made it difficult to swallow. His pulse thumped harder and his mind took a quick spin, gathering questions as it did. Did the mystery lady know she was pregnant? He wondered if the father had been worried out of his mind about her since she'd gone missing. Or was the guy who beat her up the father…because she was pregnant?

Had she been running away? Most likely.

Shifting thoughts made bittersweet memories roll through his mind over another most important pregnancy test. One that had changed his life. He wanted more than anything to make those thoughts stop, knowing they never led to a good place, but right now he was too tired to fight them off.

He'd once been on that pregnancy roller-coaster ride, one day ecstatic about the prospect of becoming a father. Another day further down the line getting a different lab test irrefutably stating there was no way in hell he could have gotten his wife pregnant. Any hope of becoming a father had been ripped away. The questions. The confrontations. The ugly answers that had finally torn his marriage apart.

Hell.

He needed to leave the clinic. James had been right. He should go home and get some sleep because if he didn't he might do something he still wanted to do desperately. Give his best—strike that—*ex*-best friend the beating he deserved.

On the third day Joe sat in his now favorite chair at the mystery lady's bedside, thumbing through a fitness magazine. Di Williams, the middle-aged, hardworking head of DOU, had shaken him up earlier when she'd explained Sleeping Beauty's condition as brain trauma—or, in her case, swelling of the brain—that had disconnected the cerebral cortex circuits, kind of like a car idling but not firing up the engine. She'd also said that if she didn't come around soon, they'd have to consider her in a coma and would need to move her to a hospital that could best meet her longer-term needs.

The thought of losing track of the woman he'd vowed to look after made his stomach knot. The doctor had also said she'd be getting transferred to a specialist coma unit later that afternoon for an enhanced CT scan that would test for blood flow and metabolic activity and they'd have to go from there, which kept Joe's stomach feeling tangled and queasy.

Time was running out, and it seemed so unfair for the girl from the bus. What about her baby?

Jane moved and Joe went on alert. It was the first time he'd witnessed what the nurses had said she often did. He'd admitted, when no one had been around, to flicking her cheek with his finger from time to time to get some kind of reaction out of her, but nothing had ever happened. The lady definitely wasn't faking it. She moved again, this time quicker, as though restless. A dry sound emitted from her throat. He held his breath and felt his heart pump faster as he pushed the call light for the attending nurse.

Jane Doe was waking up.

Tiny sputtering electrical fuses seemed to turn on and off inside him as his anticipation grew. He stood, leaned over the hospital bed and watched the sleeping beauty's lids flutter. Instinctively, he turned off the overhead lamp to help decrease the shock of harsh light to her vision as her eyes slowly opened.

They were dark green. And beautiful, like her.

But they'd barely opened before they snapped shut again as her features contorted with fear.

Carey fought for her life, flailing her arms, kicking her feet. Someone wanted to hurt her. It wasn't Ross. Not this time. She ran, but her feet wouldn't move. She tried to scream, but the sound didn't leave her throat. Fear like she'd never felt before consumed her, but she couldn't give up, she had to protect herself in order to protect her baby.

Someone shouted and ran toward her. She knew he

wanted to help. Broad shoulders, and legs moving in a powerful sprint. "Hey!" His voice cut through the night. That face. Strong. Determined. Filled with anger over the man trying to take her purse. She fought more. She had to break away from the smelly man's grip.

"Hey!"

Fight. Fight. Get away.

"Hold on, everything's okay. You're safe." Did she recognize the man's voice? "I've got you." Hands gripped her shoulders, kept her still. She held her breath.

More hands smoothed back her hair. "It's okay, hon." A woman's voice. "Calm down. You're in the hospital."

Hospital? Had she heard right?

Carey shook her head. It hurt. She was hit by a wave of vertigo that made her quit squirming. She lay still, waiting for the hands to release her. It felt like she was in an extremely comfortable bed. She relaxed her tight, squinting eyes and slowly opened first one then the other. She turned her head to a shadow looming above her. It had features. The face she remembered from her dreams. Strong. Brave. Was this *still* a dream?

She stared at him, her breathing rapid, waiting for her eyes to adjust to the light. He was the man who'd taken on her attacker. She scanned his face. Kind brown eyes. Short dark hair. A square jaw. Good looking.

"You're in the hospital and you're safe," he said in a low, comforting voice.

She looked beyond him to a gorgeous room. A hospital? It looked more like an expensive hotel with muted colors and modern furniture, chic, classy, a room she'd never been able to afford in her life. Was she still dreaming? Since she'd stopped protesting, it was quiet. Oh, and there was an IV in her arm. Being an RN herself, she recognized that right off. A catheter between her legs? And she wore a hospital gown. But this one was silky and smooth, not one of those worn-out over-starched jobs at the hospital where she worked.

Everything was so strange. Surreal. As she gathered her senses she couldn't remember where she was other than being in a hospital. She couldn't figure out why she'd be here. Wait. Someone had attacked her. She'd been pushed down. *Oh, no!* Her hand flew to her stomach, and she gasped.

"My baby!" Her voice sounded muffled and strange, as if her ears were plugged.

"Your baby's fine," the woman said. "So you remember you're pregnant."

Her hearing improved. She nodded, and it hurt, but she smiled anyway because her baby was fine.

The attractive young man smiled back at her, and the concern in his eyes was surprising. Did she know him?

"My baby's fine," she whispered to him, and a rush of feelings overcame her until she cried.

Then the strangest thing happened. The man that she wasn't sure if she knew or not, the man with the kind brown eyes...his welled up, too. "Your baby's fine." His voice sounded raspy.

She cried softly for a few moments, his eyes misty and glistening as he gave a caring smile, and it felt so good.

"Where am I?"

"You're in the hospital, hon," the nearby nurse said.

"But *where* am I?"

"Hollywood," he said. "You're in California."

She thought hard, vaguely remembering getting on a bus. Getting off a bus. It was all too much to straighten out right now. She was exhausted.

"What's your name, honey?" The nurse continued.

"Carey Spencer." At least she remembered her name. But she needed to rest. To close her eyes and…

"She's out again." The kind man's voice sounded far, far away.

"That's what happens sometimes with head injuries," the nurse replied.

Dr. Williams cancelled the plan to transfer her to a coma unit since it was clear Carey Spencer was waking up. Joe assigned another paramedic to cover his shift and stayed by her bedside, hoping to be there when she woke up again. The next time, hopefully, would be permanently. He had dozed off for a second.

"Where am I?" Her voice.

Had he slept a few minutes?

He forced open his eyes and faced Carey as she sat up in the bed, propped by several pillows. Her hair fell in a tangle of waves over her shoulders. Those dark green eyes flashed at him. She'd already figured out how to use the hand-held bed adjuster. "Where am I?" she asked more forcefully.

He'd told her earlier, but she'd suffered a head trauma, her brain was all jumbled up inside. Because of the concussion she might forget things for a long time to come. She deserved the facts.

"You're in the hospital in Hollywood, California. You got off a cross-country bus the other night. Do you remember where you came from?"

"I don't want anyone contacting my family."

He rang for the nurse. "We won't contact anyone unless you tell us to."

"I'm from Montclare, Illinois. It's on the outskirts of Chicago."

"Okay. Are you married?"

She shook her head, then looked at him tentatively. "I'm pregnant." Her eyes captured his and he could tell she remembered they'd gotten emotional together earlier when she'd woken up before. "And my baby's okay." She gave a gentle smile and odd protective sensations rippled over him. Those green eyes and the dark auburn hair. Wow. Her blackened eye may have been healing, but even with the shiner she was breathtaking. In his opinion anyway.

"Yes. Everything is okay in that department. How far along are you? Do you know?"

"Three months."

"And you came here on the bus for...?"

She hesitated. "Not for. To get away." She lifted her arms, covered in fading bruises. "I needed to get away."

"I understand." The uncompromising need to protect her welled up full force again. "Are you in trouble?"

She shook her head, then looked like it hurt to do so and immediately stopped.

The nurse came in, and asked Joe to leave so she could assess her patient and attend to her personal needs. He headed toward the door.

"Wait!" she said.

He turned.

"What's your name?"

"I'm Joseph Matthews. I'm the paramedic who brought you here."

"Thank you, Joseph. I owe you my life. And my baby's," she said from behind the privacy curtain.

He stared at his work boots, an uncertain smile creasing his lips. She certainly didn't owe him her life, but he was awfully glad to have been on scene the night she'd needed him.

The police were notified, and Joe didn't want to stick

around where he had no business, though in his heart he felt he deserved to know the whole story, so he went back to work. Around ten p.m., nearing the end of his shift, James approached. "Did you know she's a nurse?"

"I didn't. Interesting."

"She won't tell us how she got all banged up, but the fact she doesn't want us to contact the father of the baby explains that, doesn't it."

"Sadly, true."

"So, since she's recovering, if all goes well after tonight, I'm going to have to discharge her."

Startled by the news, Joe wondered why it hadn't occurred to him before. Of course she couldn't live here at the clinic. Her identity had been stolen along with her purse and any money she may have had in it. She was pregnant and alone in a strange city, and he couldn't very well let her become homeless, too. Hell, tomorrow was Sunday! "I've got an extra room. I could put her up until she gets back on her feet."

Joe almost did a second take, hearing himself make the offer, but when he thought more about it, he'd meant it. Every word. Even hoped she'd take him up on it.

"That's great," James said. "Though she may feel more comfortable staying with one of our nurses."

"True. Dumb idea, I guess."

"Not dumb. Pretty damn noble if you ask me. I'll vouch for you being a gentleman." James cast him a knowing smile and walked away.

Joe fought the urge to rush to Carey's room. She'd been through a lot today, waking up after a three-day sleep and all, and probably had a lot of thinking and sorting out to do. The social worker would be pestering her about her lost identification and credit cards and helping straighten out that mess. The poor woman's already bruised brain was probably spinning.

He needed to give her space, not make her worry he was some kind of weird stalker or something. But he wanted to tell her good night so he hiked over to the DOU and room Seventeen A, knocked on the wall outside the door, and when she told him to come in, he poked his head around the corner.

"Just wanted to say good night."

She seemed much less tense now and her smile came easily. She was so pretty, the smile nearly stopped him in his tracks. "Good night. Thanks for everything you've done for me."

"Glad to be of service, Carey."

"They're going to let me go tomorrow."

"Do you have a place to stay?"

"Not yet. Social Services is looking into something."

He walked closer to her bed and sat on the edge of his favorite chair. "I...uh... I have a two-bedroom house in West Hollywood. It's on a cul-de-sac, and it's really safe. Uh, the thing is, if you don't have any place to go, you can use my spare room. It's even got a private bathroom."

"You've done so much for me already. I couldn't—"

"Just until you get back on your feet. Uh, you know. If you want. That is." Why did he sound like a stammering, yammering teenager asking a girl on a date? That wasn't what he'd had in mind. He just wanted to help her. That was all.

She was the vision of a woman trying to make up her mind. Judging him on whether she could trust him or not, and from her recent experience Joe could understand why she might doubt herself. "Um, Dr. Rothsberg will vouch for me."

"I'll vouch for who?" James walked in on their awkward moment.

"I was just inviting Carey to stay in my spare room, if she needs a place to stay for a while."

James nailed Carey with his stare. "He's a good man. You can trust him." Then he turned and faced Joe and looked questioning. "I think."

That got a laugh out of Carey, and Joe shook his head. Guys loved to mess with each other.

"Okay, then," she said, surprising the heck out of Joe.

"Okay?"

"Yes. Thank you." The woman truly knew how to be gracious, and for that he was grateful.

He smiled. "You're welcome. I'll see you tomorrow, then." It was his day off, but he'd be back here in a heartbeat when she was ready for discharge.

He turned to leave, unusually happy and suddenly finding the need to rush home and clean the house.

CHAPTER THREE

Joe had worked like a fiend to clean his house that morning before he went to the clinic to bring Carey back. He'd gotten her room prepared and put his best towels into the guest bathroom, wanting her to feel at home. He'd stocked the bathroom with everything he thought she might need from shampoo to gentle facial soap, scented body wash, and of course a toothbrush and toothpaste. Oh, and a brush for that beautiful auburn hair.

Aware that Carey only had the clothes on her back, he'd pegged her to be around his middle sister Lori's size and had borrowed a couple pairs of jeans and tops. Boy, he'd had a lot of explaining to do when he'd asked, too, since Lori was a typical nosy sister, especially since his divorce.

Once, while Carey had been sleeping in the clinic, he'd checked the size of her shoes and now he hoped she wouldn't mind that he'd bought her a pair of practical ladies' slip-on rubber-soled shoes and some flip-flops, because she couldn't exactly walk around in those sexy boots all the time. Plus, flip-flops were acceptable just about everywhere in Southern California. He was grateful some of the nurses had bought her a package of underwear and another bra—he'd heard that through the grapevine, thanks to Stephanie, the gossipy receptionist at The Hollywood Hills Clinic, who'd said she'd gone in on the collection of money for said items.

Now he waited in the foyer for the nurse or orderly to bring Carey around for discharge, having parked his car in the circular driveway. Careful not to say anything to Stephanie about the living arrangements, knowing that if he did so the whole clinic would soon find out, he smiled, assured her that Social Services had arranged for something, and with crossed arms tapped his fingers on his elbows, waiting.

She rounded the corner, being pushed in a wheelchair—clinic policy for discharges, regardless of how well the patient felt, but most especially for someone status post-head injury like her. She was dressed the way he'd first seen her last Wednesday night, and she trained her apprehensive glance straight at him. Even from this distance he noticed those dark green eyes, and right now they were filled with questions. Yeah, it would be weird to bring a strange lady into his home, especially one who continuously made his nerve endings and synapses react as if she waved some invisible magnetic wand.

He wanted to make her feel comfortable, so he smiled and walked to pick up the few things she had stuffed into a clinic tote bag, a classier version of the usual plastic discharge bags from other hospitals he'd worked at. It was one of the perks of choosing The Hollywood Hills Clinic for medical care, though in her case she hadn't had a choice.

It was nothing short of a pure leap of faith, going home with a complete stranger like this, Carey knew, but her options were nil and, well, the guy *had* cried with her that first day in the hospital when she'd woken up. The only thing that had mattered to her after the mugging was her baby, and when she'd been reassured it was all right, she'd been unable to hold back the tears. Joseph Matthews was either the easiest guy crier she'd ever met or the most empathetic man on the planet. Either way, it made him special. She had to remember that. Plus he'd saved her life. She'd *never* forget that.

When Dr. Rothsberg had vouched for him, and she'd already noticed how everyone around the clinic seemed to like the guy, she'd made a snap decision to take the paramedic up on his offer. But, really, where else did she have to go, a homeless shelter? She'd been out of touch with her parents for years and Ross was the reason she'd run away. She had zero intention of contacting any of them.

Recent history proved she couldn't necessarily trust her instincts, but she still had a good feeling about the paramedic.

When they first left the clinic parking lot Joseph slowed down so she could look back and up toward the hillside to the huge Hollywood sign. Somehow it didn't seem nearly as exciting as she'd thought it would be. Maybe because it hurt to turn her head. Or maybe because, being that close, it was just some big old white letters, with some parts in need of a paint touch-up. Now she sat in his car, her head aching, nerves jangled, driving down a street called Highland. Having passed the Hollywood Bowl and going into the thick of Hollywood, she admitted to feeling disappointed. Where was the magic? To her it was just another place with crowded streets in need of a thorough cleaning.

It was probably her lousy mood. She'd never planned on visiting California. She'd been perfectly happy in

Montclare. She'd loved her RN job, loved owning her car, being independent for the first time in her life. She still remembered the monumental day she'd gotten the key to her first apartment and had moved out once and for all from her parents' house. Life had been all she'd dreamed it would be, why would she ever need to go to Hollywood?

Then she'd met Ross Wilson and had thought she'd fallen in love, until she'd realized too late what kind of man he really was.

Nope. She'd come to Hollywood only because it had been the first bus destination she'd found out of Chicago. For her it hadn't been a matter of choice, but a matter of life and death.

Back at his house, Joe gave Carey space to do whatever she needed to do to make herself at home in her room. She'd been so quiet on the ride over, he was worried she was scared of him. He'd probably need to tread lightly until she got more comfortable around him. He thought about taking off for the afternoon, giving her time to herself, but, honestly, he worried she might bolt. Truth was, he didn't know what she might do, and his list of questions was getting longer and longer. All he really knew for sure was that he wanted to keep her safe.

The first thing he heard after she'd gone to her room had been the shower being turned on, and the image that planted in his head needed to be erased. Fast. So he decided to work out with his hanging punchbag in his screened-in patio, which he used as a makeshift gym. He changed clothes and headed to the back of the house, turned on a John Coltrane set, his favorite music to hit the bag with, and got down to working out.

With his hands up, chin tucked in, he first moved in

and out around the bag, utilizing his footwork, warming up, moving the bag, pushing it and dancing around, getting his balance. With bare hands he threw his first warm-up punches, *slap, slap, slap*, working the bag, punching more. The stitches across his rib cage pulled and stung a little, but probably wouldn't tear through his skin. Though after the first few punches he checked to make sure. They were healing and held the skin taut that was all.

As his session heated up, so did the wild saxophone music. He pulled off his T-shirt and got more intense, beating the hell out of the innocent bag where he mentally pasted every wrong the world had ever laid at his feet. His wife sleeping with his best friend, the lies about her baby being his. The divorce. He worked through the usual warm-up, heating up quickly. Then he pounded that bag for women abused by boyfriends and innocent victims who got mugged after getting off buses. *Wham*. He hit that bag over and over, pummeling it, his breath huffing, sweat flying. *Thump, bam, whump!*

"Excuse me, Joseph?"

Jolted, he halted in mid-punch, first stabilizing the punchbag so it wouldn't swing back and hit him, then shifted his gaze toward Carey. She had on different jeans, and one of his sister's bright pink cotton tops, and her wet hair was pulled up into a ponytail, giving her a wholesome look. Which he thought was sexy.

"Oh. Hey. Call me Joe. Everything okay?" he asked, out of breath.

"That music sounds like fighting." She had to raise her voice to be heard over the jazz.

"Oh, sorry, let me turn it off." That's why he liked

to work out with Coltrane, it got wild and crazy, often the way he felt.

Her gaze darted between his naked torso and his sweaty face. "I was just wondering if I could make a sandwich."

"Of course. Help yourself to anything. I've got cold cuts in the fridge. There's some fruit, too."

"Thanks." Her eyes stayed on his abdomen and he felt the need to suck it in, even though he didn't have a gut. "You know you're bleeding?"

He glanced down. Sure enough, he'd tugged a stitch too hard and torn a little portion of his skin. "Oh. Didn't realize." He grabbed his towel and blotted it quickly.

"Did you get hurt when you helped me?"

"Yeah, the jerk sliced me with his knife." Still blotting, he looked up.

Her eyes had gone wide. "You risked your life for me? I'm so sorry."

"Hey, I didn't risk my life." Had he? "I was just doing my job."

"Do paramedics usually fight guys with blades in their hands?"

"Well, maybe not every day, but it could happen." He flashed a sheepish grin over the bravado. "At least, it has now."

Her expression looked so sad he wanted to hug her, but they hardly knew each other.

"Thank you." He sensed she also meant she was sorry.

"Not a problem. Glad to do it." He waited to capture her eyes then nodded, wanting to make sure she understood she deserved nothing less than someone saving her from an alley attacker. They stood staring at each other for a moment or two too long, and since he was the one who always got caught up in the magic of her eyes, she looked away first. Standing in his boxing shorts, shirtless, he felt like he'd been caught naked winning that staring match.

"So… I'm going to make that sandwich." She pointed toward the door then led into the small kitchen, just around the corner from the dining area and his patio, while he assessed his stitches again. Yeah, he'd taken a knife for her, but the alternative, her getting stabbed by a sleazebag and maybe left to die, had been unacceptable.

The woman had a way of drumming up forgotten protective feelings and a whole lot more. Suddenly the house felt way too small for both of them. How was he going to deal with that while she stayed here?

Maybe one last punch to the bag then he promised to stop. *Thump!* The stitches tugged more and smarted. He hated feeling uncomfortable in his own house and blamed it on the size. He'd thought about selling it after Angela had agreed to leave, but the truth was he liked the neighborhood, it was close enough to work, and most of his family lived within a ten-mile radius. And why should he have to change his life completely because his wife had been unfaithful? Okay, one last one-two punch. *Whump, thump. Ouch, my side.* He grabbed his towel again and rubbed it over his wringing-wet hair.

One odd thought occurred to him as he dried himself off. When was the last time a woman had seen him shirtless? His ex-wife Angela had left a year ago, and was a new mother now. Good luck with that. He hadn't brought anyone home since she'd left, choosing to throw himself into his expanding business and demanding job rather than get involved with any poor unsuspecting women. He was angry at the world for being sterile, and angrier at the two people he'd trusted most, his wife and his best friend. Where was a guy supposed to go from there? Ah, what the hell. He punched the bag again. *Wham thud wham.*

"Would you like a sandwich?"

Not used to hearing a female voice in his house, it startled him from his down spiraling thoughts. A woman, a complete stranger no less, was going to be staying here for an indeterminate amount of time. Had he been crazy to offer? Two strangers in an eleven-hundred-square-foot house. That was too damn close, with hardly a way to avoid each other. Hell, their bedrooms were only separated by a narrow hallway and the bathrooms. What had he been thinking? His stomach growled. On the upside, she'd just offered to make him a sandwich.

Besides everything he was feeling—the awkwardness, the getting used to a stranger—he could only imagine she felt the same. Except for the unwanted attraction on his part, he was quite sure that wasn't an issue for her—considering her situation, she must feel a hell of a lot more vulnerable. He needed to be on his best behavior for Carey. She deserved no less.

"Yes, thanks, a sandwich sounds great." Since the bleeding had stopped, he tossed on his T-shirt after wiping his chest and underarms, then joined her in the kitchen.

"Do you like lettuce and tomato?"

"Whatever you're having is fine. I'm easy." His hands hung on to both sides of the towel around his neck.

"I never got morning sickness, like most women do. I've been ravenous from the beginning, so you're getting the works."

She was tallish and slender, without any sign of being

pregnant, and somehow he found it hard to believe she ate too much. "Sounds good. Hey, I thought I'd barbecue some chicken tonight. You up for that?"

She turned and shared a shy smile. "Like I said, I'm always hungry, so it sounds good to me."

He got stuck on the smile that delivered a mini sucker punch and didn't answer right away. "Okay. It looks like it'll be nice out, so I thought we could eat outdoors on the deck." He needed to put some space between them, and it wouldn't feel as close or intimate out there. *Just keep telling yourself she's wearing your sister's clothes. Your sister's clothes.*

He'd done a lot with his backyard, putting in a garden and lots of shrubbery for privacy's sake from his neighbors, plus he'd built his own cedar-plank deck and was proud of how it'd turned out. It had been one of the therapeutic projects he'd worked on during the divorce.

The houses had been built close together in this neighborhood back in the nineteen-forties. He liked to refer to it as his start-up house, had once planned to start his family in it, too. Too bad it had been someone else's family that had gotten started here.

Fortunately, Carey interrupted his negative thoughts again jabbing a plate with a sandwich into his side. He took the supremely well-stacked sandwich and grabbed some cold water from the refrigerator, raised the bottle to see if she'd like one. Without a word she nodded, and put her equally well-stacked sandwich on a second plate. As he walked to the dining table with the bottles in one hand and his sandwich in the other, he called out, "Chips are on the counter."

"Already found them," she said, appearing at the table, hands full with food and potato-chips bag, knocking him over the head with her smile—how much could a lonely man take? Obviously she was ready to eat.

It occurred to him they had some natural communication skills going on, and the thought made him uneasy. Beyond uneasy to downright uncomfortable. He clenched his jaw. He didn't want to communicate with a woman ever again. At least not yet, anyway, but since he'd just had a good workout and he was hungry, starved, in fact, he'd let his concerns slide. For now. Carey proved to be a woman of her word, too, matching him bite for bite. Yeah, she could put it away.

After they'd eaten, Carey asked to use his phone to make some calls.

"What'd I say earlier? *Mi casa es su casa.* It's a California rule. Make yourself at home, okay?" Though he said it, he wasn't anywhere near ready to meaning it.

"But it's long distance."

"I know you've got a lot of things to work out. All your important documents were stolen." This, helping her get her life back in order, he could do. The part of living with a woman again? Damn, it was hard. Sometimes, just catching the scent of her shampoo when she walked past seemed more than he could take.

"The clinic social worker has been helping me, and my credit cards have been cancelled now. But I couldn't even order new ones because I didn't have an address to send them to."

"You've got one now." He looked her in the eyes, didn't let her glance away. He'd made a promise to himself on her behalf that he'd watch over her, take care of her. It had to do with finding her completely helpless in that alley and the fierce sense of protectiveness he'd felt. "You can stay here as long as you need to. I'm serious."

She sent him a disbelieving look. In it Joe glimpsed

how deeply some creep back in Illinois had messed her up and it made him want to deck the faceless dude. But he also sensed something else behind her disbelief. "Thank you."

"Sure. You're welcome." Though she only whispered the reply, he knew without a doubt she was really grateful to be here, and that made the nearly constant awkward feelings about living with a complete stranger, a woman more appealing than he cared to admit, worth it.

Later, over dinner on the deck in the backyard, Joe sipped a beer and Carey lemonade. Her hair was down now, and she'd put on the sweater she'd worn that first night over his sister's top. In early June, the evenings were still cool, and many mornings were overcast with what they called "June gloom" in Southern California. She'd spent the entire dinner asking about his backyard and job, which were safe topics, so it was fine with him. Since she'd been asking so many questions, he got up the nerve to ask her one of the several questions he had for her. Also within the safe realm of topics—work.

"I heard at the clinic that you're a nurse?"

She looked surprised. "Yes. That was the call I made earlier, to the hospital where I worked. I guess you could say I'm now officially on a leave of absence."

"So you'll probably go back there when you feel better?" Why did this question, and her possible answer, make him feel both relief and dread? He clenched his jaw, something he'd started doing again since Carey had moved in.

She grimaced. "I can't. I'll have to quit at some point, but for now I'm using the sick leave and vacation time I've saved up and, I hope you don't mind, I gave them your address so they could mail my next check to me here."

"Remember. *Mi casa es tuya.*" He took another drag on his longneck, meaning every word in the entire extent of his Spanish speaking, but covering for the load of mixed-up feelings that kept dropping into his lap. What was it about this girl that made him feel so damn uncomfortable?

His practiced reply got a relieved smile out of her, and he allowed himself to enjoy how her eyes slanted upward whenever she did. It was dangerous to notice things like that and, really, what was the point? But having the beer had loosened him up and he snuck more looks than usual at her during dinner. "The clinic is always looking for good nurses. What's your specialty?"

"I work, or I should say worked, in a medical-surgical unit. I loved it, too."

"See..." he pointed her way "...that would fit right in. When you feel better, maybe you should look into it. I can talk to James about it if you'd like." *Yeah, keep these interactions all about helping her, and maybe she'll skip the part about asking you about yourself.*

"James?"

"Dr. Rothsberg."

"First I have to get my RN license reissued from Illinois since it was stolen along with everything else."

So maybe she did have plans to stay here and seek employment. Now he could get confused again and try to ignore that flicker of hope he'd kept feeling since she'd walked into his life. He ground his molars. "Would your license be accepted in California?"

"I did some research on the bus ride out and I'll have to apply here in California. That'll take some time, I suspect."

"Well, I'm working days tomorrow, so you can spend the whole day using my computer and phone and maybe start straightening out everything you need to."

She nodded. "I do have some people I owe a call." Deep in thought, she probably went straight to the gazillion things she'd have to do to re-create herself and begin a new life for her and her baby in a new state. He wouldn't want to be in her shoes, and wished he could somehow help even more. Would that go beyond his promise to watch over her?

At least the social worker and the police department had started the ball rolling on a few things. But, man, what a mess she had to clean up, especially since she hadn't wanted her family notified of her whereabouts. Why was that?

Joe wanted to ask her about her living situation back home, but suspected she'd shut down on him like a trapdoor if he did this soon, so he tucked those questions into his "bring up later" file. With an ironic inward laugh, he supposed they had a lot in common, not wanting to bring up the past and all. "You feel like watching a little TV?" He figured she could use something to distract her from all the things she'd have to tackle tomorrow.

"I'd like that but only after you let me clean up from dinner."

"Only if you'll let me help." Hell, could they get any more polite?

She smiled. "So after we do the dishes, what would you like to watch?"

"You choose." Yeah, he'd let his guest make all the decisions tonight. It was the right thing to do.

"I like that show about zombies."

"Seriously?" He never would have pegged her as a

horror fan. "It's my favorite, too, but I didn't think it would be good for your bambino."

"Ha," she said, picking up the dishes from the bench table on the outdoor deck. "After what this little one has been through already, a pretend TV show should be a walk in the park." She glanced down at her stomach while heading inside and toward the kitchen. "Isn't that right, sweetie pie."

There he went grinding his molars again. He followed her in and watched her put the dishes on the counter and unconsciously pat her abdomen then smile. That simple act sent a flurry of quick memories about Angela and how excited they'd once been when she'd first found out she'd gotten pregnant. They'd been about to give up trying since it had been over a year, had even had fertility tests done. They'd rationalized that because they were both paramedics and under a lot of stress, and he worked extended hours trying to make a good impression with Dr. Rothsberg, that was the reason she'd been unable to get pregnant.

So they'd taken a quickie vacation. Then one day, wham, she magically announced she was expecting. Joe had practically jumped over the moon that night, he'd been so happy. They'd finally start their own version of a big happy family. Since Angela's body had gotten the hang of getting pregnant, he'd planned to talk her into having a few more kids after this one. He'd walked on air for a couple of months…until his fertility report had dropped into the mailbox. Late. Very, very late.

What a fool he'd been.

Trying to give his overworked jaw a break, Joe went to town scrubbing the grill from the barbecue as if it was a matter of life and death. By the time they'd finished with the cleanup, he didn't know about Carey any more, but he definitely needed the distraction of some mindless TV viewing.

She sat on the small couch, passing him along the way, and he caught the scent of her shampoo again. It was a fresh, fruity summer kind of smell with a touch of coconut, which when he'd bought it for her had never planned for it to be a minor form of torture.

Mixed up about his feelings for the smart and easy-going nurse from Illinois, he intentionally sat on the chair opposite the couch, not ready to get too close to her again tonight. It brought up too many bad memories, and he so did not want to go there. There was only so much boxing a guy could do in a day. Torture sounded better than reliving his failed marriage. He clicked on the TV right on time for the show they both liked to escape to. If zombies couldn't make him forget how attracted he was to the lovely stranger living in his house, nothing could.

Carey put her head on the pillow of the surprisingly comfortable guest bed, thinking it was the first time she could remember feeling safe in ages. Things had gotten super-tense living with Ross those last few weeks, and, talk about the worst timing in the world, she'd gotten pregnant right around the time she'd known she had to leave him.

She didn't want to think about that now, because it would keep her awake, and she was really tired. It'd felt so normal and relaxing to sit and watch TV with Joe. He'd made the best barbecue chicken she'd ever eaten and she'd made a pig out of herself over the baked potato with all the toppings, but she chalked it up to his making her feel so welcome. The only problem was she couldn't get the vision of him in his boxing shorts, working out with the punchbag, out of her mind. Wow, his lean body had showcased every muscle in his arms and across his back as he'd punched. His movements had been fluid and nothing short of perfection. Not to mention his washboard stomach and powerful legs. The guy didn't have an ounce of fat on him.

What on earth was she thinking? Her life was in a shambles. She had an unborn baby to take care of. The last thing she should be thinking about was a man.

A naturally sexy man with kind brown eyes and a voice soothing enough to give her chills. She squeezed her eyes tight and shook her head on the pillow.

When she finally settled down and began to drift off to sleep she realized this was the first day she'd ever felt positive about her and the baby's future in three months. Things would work out for her, she just knew it. Because she, with the help of Joe, would make sure they did.

A slight smile crossed her lips as a curtain of sleep inched its way down until all was dark and she peacefully crossed into sweet dreams. Thanks to Joe.

CHAPTER FOUR

ON MONDAY, AFTER working all day, Joe insisted Carey come out with him for dinner, which was fine with her because she'd felt kind of cooped up. They ate at a little diner, then he showed her around Santa Monica, like the perfect host. She got the distinct impression it was to get them, and keep them, out of the house, because sometimes things felt too close there.

At least, that's how it felt for her, and sometimes she sensed it was the same for him. The guy seemed to bite down on his jaw a lot! But she soon ignored her worries about him not wanting her around and went straight to loving seeing the beach and the Pacific Ocean, and especially the Santa Monica pier.

On Tuesday Joe had the day off, and he dutifully took her shopping for more clothes at a place called the Beverly Center. They checked the directory and he guided her to the few stores she'd shown interest in, then he stood outside in the mall area, giving her space to shop. Clearly he wanted nothing to do with helping her choose clothes, rather he just did what he thought he should do out of courtesy to her situation. She protested all the way when he insisted on paying for everything. She sensed his generosity was based on some sense of charitable obligation, and she only accepted his offer when he'd agreed to let her repay him once she was back on her feet. She'd be sure to keep a tally because things were quickly adding up!

Wednesday morning, before he started an afternoon shift, he chauffeured her around to the Department of Motor Vehicles for a temporary driving license, and since she'd received a check from her old job he also helped her open a bank account. She decided the guy was totally committed to helping her, like he'd signed some paper or made some pact to do it. And she certainly appreciated everything he'd done for her, but…

Even though he was easy enough to be around, she felt it was out of total obligation to treat people right in life. Far too often she sensed a disconnect between his courtesy and that safe distance he insisted on keeping between them. Well, if that's what he wanted, she knew exactly how to live that way. Her parents had, sadly, been perfect role models in that regard.

Joe got home on Wednesday night to a quiet house. Carey had said hello, but now kept mostly to herself in her room. It made him wonder if he'd done something to offend her. He'd been trying his best to make her feel at home, though admittedly he may have been going about it robotically. But that seemed the only way he could deal with having a woman in his life again. Since he worked the a.m. shift the next day, he didn't get a chance to ask Carey if he'd put her off or if her withdrawal had nothing to do with him. Something was definitely on her mind, and under the circumstances, being battered, bruised, mugged, homeless, and completely vulnerable, not to mention living with a stranger, he could understand why.

Maybe he'd come off aloof or unapproachable at

times. But she had no idea how nearly unbearable it was to fix meals with her when it reminded him how much he missed being married. And having Carey there twenty-four seven, with her friendly smile and naturally sweet ways, was nearly making him come unhinged. She deserved someone to share things with, to talk to, but it couldn't be him. Nope. He was nowhere near ready or able to be her sounding board. All he'd signed up for was offering her a place to live.

Maybe he could arrange for some follow-up visits with the social worker at the clinic. That way she could get what she wanted and needed and he wouldn't have to be the person listening. Because when a woman vented, from his past experience with Angela, he knew she always expected something in return. Nope, no way would he unload his lousy past on Carey, no matter how much she might think she wanted him to. The lady had far too much on her plate as it was, and, truthfully, re-living such pain was the last thing he ever wanted to do. The social worker was definitely the right person to step in, and he planned to ask Helena to follow up the next day.

On Thursday evening, Joe came home to find Carey scrubbing the kitchen floor. From the looks of the rest of the house, she'd been cleaning all day.

"What's up?" he asked.

She was so focused on the floor-scrubbing she didn't notice him. He stepped closer but not onto the wet kitchen tiles.

"Am I that much of a slob?" he tried to joke, but she didn't laugh. Something was definitely eating at her. "Carey?"

Finally she heard him and shook her head as if she'd

been in a trance and looked at him. "Hi." Not sounding the least bit enthusiastic.

"Everything okay?"

She stopped pushing the mop handle. "Just trying to pay you back for all you're doing for me."

Damn. She may as well have sliced him with a knife. "You don't have to be my house cleaner, you know."

"What else can I do?" The obvious "else" *not* being to sleep together.

Why was that the first thought to come to his mind? Cripes, she had him mixed up. He used her clear frustration as a springboard to what his latest mission on Carey's behalf had been. "I, uh, spoke to the social worker today—the one who helped you while you were in the hospital—and she said she'd love to keep in touch." He'd totally reworded their true conversation, trying to make it sound casual, not necessary, but the truth was he'd talked at great length with Helena at work about Carey's precarious situation. The social worker wanted to keep connected with Carey and promised to call her right away.

"Yes. Thanks. She called earlier today. I'm going to have a phone appointment with her on Monday."

"That's great." He almost said, *I hope it helps you snap out of your funk,* but kept that thought to himself because a sneaky part of him worried he'd put her there. He knew too well how unhelpful being told to snap out of it could be, especially when a person was nowhere near ready. He would protect Carey in any way he could, and felt she shouldn't be nervous all the time. But he'd never been in her shoes, and…

Then it dawned on him. Why hadn't he thought of it before? The woman was a nurse. Nurses were always busy on the job. She was used to helping people, not the other way around. She was probably going crazy with so much time on her hands and nothing to do but watch TV or read while he was away every day. But she'd had a head trauma and needed to heal. "Do you feel ready to go back to work?"

She shifted from being intent on cleaning to suddenly looking deflated. "That's the thing, I can't until the California RN license comes through. Plus I still feel foggy-headed from the concussion. At this point I'd worry I might hurt some poor unsuspecting patient or something. But on another level my energy is coming back, and I'm feeling really restless."

That damn mugger had not only stolen her identity and money but also her confidence. He thought quickly. It was early summer, people went on vacations. "I think there might be some temporary slots to fill in while people go on vacation. Jobs that don't require a nursing license."

She stopped mopping and looked at him, definite interest in her eyes.

"For instance, I know of a ward clerk on the second floor who's getting ready to visit her family back east for two weeks. Maybe you could fill in on something like that. Sort of keep your hand in medicine but in a safer position until you feel back to your old self."

She rested her chin on the mop handle. "How can I just walk in off the street and expect to get a job in a hospital like The Hollywood Hills Clinic?"

He flashed an overconfident grin he hadn't used in a long time. "By knowing a guy like me? I could put in a good word to Dr. Rothsberg for you. What do you say?"

The fingers of one hand flew to her mouth as she thought. "That would be great. But it would also mean

I'd have to quit my job back home." Worry returned to her brow.

Joe was sure he was missing out on another story, probably something huge. Like, who she was running away from, and would they come after her? If only he could get her to open up. This was stuff he needed to know if he expected to protect her. Rather than press her right then, he let her finish her task and went to his room. Besides, he needed time to figure things out for himself, like the fact that he both totally looked forward to seeing her each day but dreaded how it made him feel afterwards.

After he changed into workout clothes, he headed to the back porch for some boxing, since it was the one sure way to help him blow off steam. Well into his usual routine, while she was in the other room, watching TV, he wondered if, in fact, the guy who'd given Carey her shiner might come after her, and an idea popped into his head. "Hey, Carey, come out here a minute, would you?"

Within seconds she showed up looking perplexed, and maybe like she'd rather be watching TV. Yeah, she'd probably already had it with living with him.

"Since you were mugged recently, and I'm sure you never want to go through that again, would you like me to show you a couple of moves?"

She looked hesitant, like learning a few self-defense maneuvers might bring back too many bad memories.

"Maybe it's too soon," he quickly.

"No, I can't keep hiding out at your house. I know there's a bus stop right down at the end of your street, and I shouldn't be afraid to use it." She nodded, a flicker of fight in her eyes. "Yeah, show me how I could have kept that creep from dragging me into the alley that night."

"That's the attitude," Joe said with a victorious smile. She smiled back, that spirited flash intensifying.

"Okay." He clapped his hands once. "I saw the guy grab you by the wrist and pull you away that night. So, first off, a lot of the information that's on the internet for ladies' self-defense is bogus. Here's something that works. When that guy grabbed your wrist, you could have used your other hand to push into his eyes, or, if he wore glasses, you could have gone for his throat. With either move you also could have included a knee to the groin. That stuff hurts the attacker and surprises them. Knocks them off balance. Let me show you."

He grabbed Carey's right wrist and immediately felt her tense, making him think maybe he was right and it was too early to do this lesson with her. But he was committed now and pressed on, and she had enough anger in her eyes to put it to good use.

"Okay, use your left hand and go for my face," He showed her how to make an open, claw-like spread with the fingers and how to jab it at a person's face to do the most damage. "Get those fingers on my eyes and press with all your might."

She followed his instructions and went for his eyes.

"Ow!" He reacted and pushed her hand back to keep her from injuring him.

"Sorry!"

"Don't be sorry, fight for your life. It's up to me to keep you from hurting me. You just caught me off guard. Got it?"

She gave one firm and committed nod.

"That's the spirit. If the guy foils that move with his other hand, like I just did, make sure you put your knee to his groin at the same time." He flashed a charming grin. "Don't actually do that one now, okay?"

She laughed, and it felt good to get her to relax a little.

"Just knee him in the groin area and later you can practice kneeing the heck out of that boxing bag."

"Got it, boss." Yes, she was really into this now.

He said, "Go!" and grabbed her left wrist this time, and she moved like lightning for his face and eyes, driving her knee into his groin at the same time. Being prepared for the move, in case she got overzealous, which she obviously had, he brought his own knee up and across to protect himself, letting her full force hit his thigh. If he hadn't, he'd have been on his hands and knees, riding out the pain, right now.

He didn't want to discourage her efforts but, damn, that could have hurt! "Good." Up close, their eyes locked. He could hear her breathing hard and felt the pulse in her wrist quicken. The fire in her green-eyed stare made him take notice. He stepped back, releasing her wrist. "That was good."

She rubbed her wrist and searched the floor with her gaze, making a quick recovery. This wasn't easy to relive, he understood that, but keeping the same thing from ever happening again was more important than her current comfort zone.

"Now do the same thing, going for my throat." He showed her the wide V of his hand between the thumb and index finger and demonstrated how to drive it into the Adam's apple area of the attacker's neck. "Since most guys, like that scumbag the other night, will be taller than you, force your hand upward with all you've got. Okay?"

Carey agreed and he immediately grabbed her hand, trying to catch her off guard. Something clicked, like she'd gone back in time. She went into attack mode and because he wasn't ready for it she got him good in the throat. He coughed and sputtered and backed away to recover, and only then did she realize she'd shifted from demonstration to true life.

"I'm sorry!" she squealed, grabbing her face with her hands, as if just snapping out of a bad dream.

He swallowed, trying to get his voice back. "That's the way. See how it works? I dropped your hand, and that means you could have run off screaming for help at that point."

"Oh, Joe." Carey rushed to him. "I'm so sorry I hurt you." She touched his shoulder and, without thinking, he reacted by opening his arms. Carey threw her arms around him and squeezed. "Can I get you some water? Anything?"

"Maybe a new throat," he teased, though he really liked having her arms around him, the realization nearly making him lose his balance. She smelled a hell of a lot better than he did, and up close, like this, her eyes were by far the prettiest he'd ever seen in his life, though fear seemed to have the best of them right now.

Surprised, no, more like stunned by how moved she'd been when grappling with Joe, Carey held him perhaps a second too long. Fear still pounded in her chest. At first the lesson had brought out all the bad memories she'd been trying to force down a few months before leaving home and definitely since coming to Hollywood. Ross had changed from attentive boyfriend to jealous predator. He had frightened her. He'd also grabbed her by the wrist like that on several occasions, each time scaring her into submission. Then the creep at the bus station must have seen her as an easy mark, sensed her fear, and grabbed her the same way, pulling her into the alley.

She hated feeling like a victim!

Anger had erupted as horrible memories had collided with Joe's grip on her wrist. She'd never be a victim again, damn it. Never. Suddenly fighting for her life all over again, she'd switched to kill mode and had practically pushed his larynx out the back of his neck. Darn it! She hadn't meant to hurt him, not the man who'd saved her and taken her in, but she clearly had.

Now, being skin to skin with her incredibly fit and appealing roommate had changed the topic foremost in her mind. Being in Joe's arms wiped out her fear and she shifted from fighting for her life to being completely turned on. What was it about Joe?

So confusing. It wasn't right.

Obviously her concussion was still messing with her judgment.

In a moment of clarity she broke away and strode to the kitchen to get him a glass of water, trying to recover before she brought it to him.

"What about pepper spray?" She schooled her voice to sound casual, completely avoiding his eyes, as if she hadn't just survived a flashback and had flung herself into Joe's arms. There was nothing wrong with a decoy topic to throw him off the scent, right? The man had turned her on simply by touching her. Pitiful. Blame it on the head injury.

"First you have to get it out of your purse, right?"

She nodded, quickly realizing the fault in her premise. He stood shirtless, damp from his workout, skin shiny and all his muscles on display. Cut and ripped. A work of art. She handed him the glass. Thought about handing him his T-shirt so he'd cover up and make her life a little safer for the moment, or less tempting anyway. At least it seemed easier for him to swallow now and that made her grateful she hadn't caused any permanent damage. Could she have? If so, he'd just given her a huge gift of self-protection. No way would she let herself be a victim. By God, she'd never let anyone hurt her again.

"Plus, I've heard about guys who've been sprayed and didn't even react," he continued. "Also, when you're scared or nervous, you might spray all over the place and not hit the eyes."

She kept nodding, watching him, completely distracted by his physique, unable to really listen, wishing she'd brought herself a cool drink too. Surely her head injury had left her brain unbalanced, taking her back to the worst moments in her life one second and then the next rushing into the realm of all things sensual.

"Your hands and your knees are your best defense. Want to practice again?"

She sucked in a breath and shook her head quickly. This was all too confusing. "I think that's enough for tonight."

He put down his glass on the nearby table, folded an arm across his middle, rested the other elbow on it and held his chin with his thumb and bent fingers, biting his lower lip and nailing her with a sexy, playful gaze. "Chicken, eh?"

Joe had saved her life. He'd also just given her a great gift of learning self-defense. And there *was* that sexy sparkle in his eyes right now...

"Are you challenging me?" Suddenly awash with tiny prickles of excitement again, she moved toward him and grabbed his wrist with all her might. "Let's see you fight your way out of this one, buddy." She knew she didn't have a chance in hell of keeping hold but enjoyed the moment, and especially grappling with the hunk. When was the last time she'd had fun horsing around with a man and not felt the least bit afraid or vulnerable?

She trusted Joe not to hurt her.

He swung his free arm around behind her and pulled her close, pretending to get her in a head lock but quickly moving into a backward hug. "I don't suggest you ever let your attacker get you in this position," he said playfully over the shell of her ear.

"There won't be any more attackers," she said through gritted teeth. "Because I'll kick their asses first."

He tightened his hold, but in a good way, a sexy way. She went limp in his arms, feeling his closeness in every cell and nerve ending, confused by the total attraction she had for him. This was the worst time in the world to fall for someone. She was pregnant with another man's baby, for crying out loud. He must have felt the shift of her mood from fight to flight, or in this case to catatonic, and he quickly backed off. They'd gotten too close. Too soon. That sexy, challenging gaze in his eyes from a second before disappeared and he reached for his water to take another drink as a distraction.

"So," he started again, sounding nonchalant, "another good idea, if a bad guy only wants your wallet, is to reach into your purse, grab your wallet and throw it as far away as you can. He probably wants your money, not you, and will go after it. Then scream like hell and run for your life. Of course, if he has a gun you may want to reconsider that move."

She gave the required light laugh over his obvious smart-aleck attempt to change the focus of what had just gone down. But their eyes met again, his honey brown and inviting as all hell, and it seemed they both knew some line had just been crossed. Though she couldn't tell from Joe's steely stare how he felt, and wasn't about to guess because the thought made her get all jittery inside, she hoped he couldn't tell how shaken she was.

She watched him with a mixture of shame and longing, but mostly confusion. Damn that concussion. "Thanks for the lesson," she whispered. "I'd better get some rest now."

They'd gotten too close, that was a fact.

She turned to head for her room, but a sense of duty stopped her. The man had saved her life then offered to share his home with her. Where did a guy like that come from? The least she could do was tell him what she'd been through, why she'd run away from home. He deserved to know how she'd ended up smack in the middle of his life. And if she shared, maybe she'd find out something about him, too.

"Joe?" She circled back to face him.

"Yeah?" He'd gone back to throwing punches at his punchbag and stopped.

"I ran away from a man who wanted to possess me. Completely. Little by little he clipped away at my life. Half the time I didn't even notice, until one day I realized he'd isolated me from everything I liked and loved other than him." She picked at a broken fingernail. "He wanted to control my life, and when I got pregnant he acted like that would ruin everything and got abusive with me." Carey stared at her feet rather than risk seeing any judgment on Joe's face. "I ran away the night he handed me a wad of money and told me to take care of 'it', as if my baby was a problem that needed fixing. He didn't want to share me with anyone, not even our kid."

She finally glanced up to find nothing but empathy in Joe's eyes. "I fought him and he roughed me up. So when he gave me the money I grabbed whatever I could without being obvious, acted like I was going to do what he wanted, then ran for my life."

Joe stepped toward her but she backed up, needing the distance and to tell him her entire story.

"I came to California because it was the next bus out of Montclare, and I didn't have time to pick or choose. I must have looked like a sitting duck because I stepped off the bus and immediately got dragged into that alley." Frightened to relive that night, and frustrated by the emotion rolling through her, she dug her fingers into her hair. "At first I thought maybe Ross had somehow found me and he was taking me back home. Then I realized I was getting mugged, but it was too late. I didn't know how to protect myself." She removed her hands from her hair and held them waist high, palms upward, beseeching Joe to understand. "If it wasn't for you I don't know where I'd be.

"I owe my life to you, and I've got to be honest and say it's strange to feel that way." She sat on the edge of the nearby dining table chair. "Yet here you are day after day watching over me, making my life better. I'm grateful, I am, but please understand that I'm confused and scared and…" Her voice broke with the words. "And I don't know what the future holds for me. Whether I stay here or go somewhere else, I just don't know, but the only thing that matters right now is my baby." Her forearm folded across her stomach and she blinked.

"I get it," Joe said. "Believe me, I understand how life-changing a baby can be."

"You do? Are you a father?"

"Uh, no." He immediately withdrew.

"So how do you know, then?"

"Look, forget I said that. Right now, all I want is for you to be healthy and safe." He came to her and crouched to be eye level with her. "I'm sorry if I've made you uncomfortable. I can't help but find you attractive, so there, I've said it, and I know that's not acceptable."

How was she supposed to answer him? "It may not be acceptable but I feel the same way." Oh, God, she'd put her secret thoughts into words. "It's just the worst timing in the world, you know?"

"I know. Like I said, I get it." He made the wise decision not to touch her but instead to stand and step back.

"Thank you for understanding."

"Of course."

She stood and started walking, this time without looking back, and headed on wobbly legs to her room. Had she just admitted she found Joe Matthews as attractive as he'd just confirmed he found her?

This was nuts! So she'd blame it on the head trauma.

Joe stood perfectly still, watching Carey make her exit. He half expected to hear her lock the door to the bedroom. He hoped he hadn't made her feel creepy about him. It hadn't been his intention to get her in a hug, but he'd been showing her ways to get out of predatory attacks and had inadvertently become a predator himself.

Great going, Joe. You made your house guest think you wanted to crawl into her bed.

He went back to the porch and punched the bag. "Ouch!" He hadn't prepared his fist and it hurt like hell. And what had gotten into him to let slip that he'd known how it felt to be an expectant parent? That wouldn't happen again. He wound up, wanting to punch the bag again, this time even harder, but stopped himself.

Regardless of how awkward he may have made Carey feel, she'd just opened up to him. Man, she'd had it tough back in Chicago. He couldn't remember the name of the suburb she'd come from, and right now that didn't matter. What mattered was that she shouldn't feel like she'd run all the way across country only to find herself in the same situation again.

She needed to get out of the house. To begin something. To get that job and start some money rolling in before she got so pregnant she wouldn't be able to. His head started spinning with everything that needed to be done for her. He needed to help her get her independence back.

From personal experience he knew about a special class at The Hollywood Hills Clinic. A class that would be perfect for where she was right now in her life. He knew the right people to talk to about it, too. And he'd move ahead with her getting that job, so if she wanted, in time, she could move out.

Maybe he couldn't erase what had happened between them just now, but he sure as hell could make some changes for the better happen, starting tomorrow.

He flipped off the light and headed to his room to take a cold shower and hopefully catch a little sleep.

On Friday afternoon Carey sat on the backyard deck in the shade of the huge jacaranda tree, the flowers falling into piles of light purple and scattering across the wood planks like pressed flowers in a painting. She'd been reading an article about early pregnancy on the internet on Joe's tablet when she heard his hybrid SUV pull into the garage and shortly after he came through the gate in the backyard.

Did he know she was out here? Or, more likely after last night, maybe he wanted to avoid her by coming through the back way, hoping she'd be inside.

"Hey," he said, all smiles, as if nothing monumental had occurred between them last night.

"Hi. You're home early."

He came toward the deck but didn't come up, keeping a safe distance between them, placing a foot on the second step and leaning a forearm over his knee. "One of the perks of owning your own business is that I call the shots. It was a slow day, so I took off early."

"Lucky you." His smile was wide, giving her the impression he had some good news. Maybe he had found somewhere for her to move to? If she was honest, that would give her mixed feelings, though the social worker Helena had said she'd look into housing for her, too, and she'd agreed to it at the time. "But I know you've worked hard to get where you are and at the ripe old age of twenty-eight you deserve your afternoon off. Twenty-eight, that's right isn't it?"

He nodded proudly. Yeah, he'd made something out of himself and he wasn't even thirty yet. "And you are?"

"Twenty-five."

"A mere child." He smiled, pretending to be the worldly-wise older man, but his gaze quickly danced away from hers. Yeah, he was still mixed up about last night, too. "So, listen, about you feeling isolated and stuck here and everything…"

"I didn't say that."

"You didn't have to. I figured it out after you went to your room last night. But let's not rehash that, because I've got some good news."

She shut down the tablet and leaned forward in the outdoor lounger. "Good news? They found my stuff?"

He wrinkled his nose and shook his head. "Sorry, I wish. But here's the deal—the clinic has this prenatal class, they call it Parentcraft and it's starting a new session tomorrow. I hope you don't mind, but I put your name in, and Dr. Rothsberg gave me the okay. I thought you could ride into work with me in the morning, and check it out."

"You signed me up? Isn't there a fee? I…uh…can't—"

"Like I said, James took care of everything. He's a generous man. There's a spot for you and the first session starts tomorrow at ten."

"Joe, I'm really grateful for you doing this, but you're helping so much, I don't think I'll ever be able to repay you."

"Carey, I'm not doing any of this to make you feel indebted to me. Please, don't feel that way. My parents taught me a lot of stuff, and helping folks was big in our family. When you're back on your feet you'll find a way to help someone else in need. That's all. No debt to me, just pay it forward."

"Joe…" She stared at him, trying her hardest to figure him out. Was he a freak of nature or her personal knight in shining armor? She leaned back in the lounger and looked into the blue sky dotted with its few wispy clouds. "It's just hard to take in all this goodness after the way my life had been going this past year." She heard him step up the stairs and walk toward her.

"Well, get used to it." He sat on the adjacent lounger then reached out to touch her hand. "That man you ran away from is ancient history. It may not have been your plan, but Hollywood is your new beginning. Just go with the flow, as my yoga-brained sister likes to say."

Carey laughed, wondering about Joe's family. They must be some special people to produce a gem like him. "Okay. Thanks. I'm excited about the class tomorrow."

"Great, and while you're at the hospital you can fill out the papers for the temporary ward clerk job, too."

"What?"

"I know, too much goodness, right?" He laughed, and she thought she could easily get used to watching his handsome face. "James, uh, Dr. Rothsberg, has taken care of everything. Hey, not every clinic can boast their very own Jane Doe. We just want to help get you back on your feet."

"This is all too much to take in."

"Then don't waste your time." He stood. "Come on, I'll take you to my favorite deli on Fairfax. You like roast beef on rye? They make their sandwiches this thick." He used his thumb and index finger to measure a good four inches.

Well, come to think of it, she was hungry. Again! And what better way to keep her mind off the whirl-wind of feelings gathering inside her about that man than stuffing her face with a sandwich. Otherwise she'd have to deal with her growing awareness of Joe, the prince of a guy who had literally come out of nowhere, protecting her, saving her, taking her in, changing her life in a positive way, and, maybe the most interesting part, forcing her to remember pure and simple attraction for the opposite sex.

Saturday morning Carey was up and dressed in one of the new outfits Joe had bought her, a simple summer dress with a lightweight pastel-green sweater that covered the tiny baby bump just starting to appear. She was nervous about applying for a job, though she knew she really needed to get out among the living again, to prove to herself she was getting back on her feet. Also, having something to do after a week of lying low since being discharged from the clinic was a major reason she looked forward to applying for the job. As for the parenting class, with her huge desire to be a good mother she was eager to start.

Joe had dressed for work, his light blue polo shirt with The Hollywood Hills Clinic logo above the pocket fit his healthy frame perfectly and highlighted those gorgeous deltoids, biceps and triceps. The cargo pants, though loose and loaded with useful pockets, filled with EMS stuff no doubt, still managed to showcase his fine derriere. She felt a little guilty checking him out as he walked ahead to open the door to the employee entrance. How much longer would she be able to blame her concussion for this irrational behavior? In her defense, there was just something so masculine about a guy wearing those serious-as-hell EMS boots!

He glanced at his watch. "You should have enough time to get your paperwork done for the job application first. I'll walk you over to HR."

"HR?"

"Human Resources."

"Ah, we call it Employee Relations back home."

"Yeah, same thing, but first I'm going to show you where your parenting class will be so you'll know where to go when you're through. Follow me."

Carey did as she was told, clutching her small purse with her new identification cards and temporary driving license, while walking and looking around the exquisite halls and corridors with vague memories of having been there before. Though the place seemed more like a high-end hotel than a hospital. And this time she had money from her last pay check from the hospital back home, instead of being completely vulnerable, like before. Ten days ago she'd arrived on a stretcher, and today she was applying for a job and starting a new parenting class. She was definitely getting back on her feet. Who said life wasn't filled with miracles?

"Oh, Gabriella," Joe said, to a pretty woman walking past, "I'd like to introduce you to Carey Spencer. She'll be starting your class later." He turned to Carey. "Gabriella is the head midwife and runs the prenatal classes."

The woman, who looked to be around Joe's age, with strawberry-blonde hair and a slim and healthy figure, smiled at Carey, her light brown eyes sparkling when she did so. They briefly shook hands, then all continued walking together, as the midwife was obviously heading somewhere in the same direction. As Gabriella was just about Carey's height, their eyes met when she spoke. "Oh, lovely to have you. How far along are you?"

"A little over three months."

"Perfect. We're beginning the class with pregnancy meal planning trimester by trimester, plus exercises for early pregnancy."

This was exactly what Carey needed. Just because she was a nurse it didn't mean she knew squat about becoming a mother or going through a pregnancy. "Sounds great." Her hopes soared with the lucky direction her life had taken. Thanks to Joe and Dr. Rothsberg.

"Yes, I think you'll love it." Gabriella cut off into another hallway. "Be sure to bring your partner," she said over her shoulder. "It's always good to have that reinforcement."

And Carey's heart dropped to her stomach, pulling her pulse down with it. Was having a partner a requirement? Obviously, Gabriella didn't know her circumstances.

Joe gave her an anxious glance. "That won't be a problem. Trust me, okay?"

Surely, Carey hoped, in this day and age there were

bound to be other women in the class without partners. Joe was probably right about it not being a problem. But, please, God, she wouldn't be the only one, would she?

Forty-five minutes later, after submitting her job application for the temporary third-floor medical/ surgical ward clerk in HR and feeling very positive about it, Carey had found her way back to the modern and pristine classroom and took a seat. Several hand-outs had been placed on the tables. A dozen couples were already there, and more drifted in as the minutes ticked on. She glanced around the room, seeing a sea of couples. Oh, no, she really was going to be the only one on her own. How awkward would that be?

Fighting off feeling overwhelmed but refusing to be embarrassed, she glanced at the clock on the wall—three minutes to ten—and thought about sneaking out before the class began. She could learn this stuff online, and wouldn't have to come here feeling the odd man out every week. But Joe had gone out of his way to get her enrolled, and Dr. Rothsberg was footing the bill. She went back and forth in her mind about staying or going, then Gabriella entered and started her welcome speech.

She'd sat close to the back of the room, and it would still be easy to sneak out if she wanted or needed to. But, wait, she wasn't that person anymore, the one who let life throw her a curveball and immediately fell down. Nope, she'd turned in her victim badge, and Joe had helped her. She could do this. She forced her focus on the front of the class to Gabriella, who smiled and brightened the room with her lovely personality. The last thing Carey wanted to do was insult anyone, especially after Joe and Dr. Rothsberg had made special arrangements to get her here. But, oh, she felt weird about being the only single mom in the class.

"Why don't we go around the room and introduce ourselves?" Gabriella said.

Soon everyone else would notice, too.

The door at the back of the class opened again. Feeling nervous and easily distracted, Carey glanced over her shoulder then did a double take. In came Joe, his heavy booted steps drawing attention from several people in the vicinity.

"Sorry I'm late," he said to Gabriella, then walked directly to Carey and took the empty chair next to her. "If you don't mind," he whispered close to her ear, "I'll pretend to be your partner today." For all anyone else knew in the class, he could have told her he loved her. The guy knew how to be discreet, and from the way her heart pattered from his entrance he may as well have just run down a list of sweet nothings.

He'd obviously picked up on her anxiety the instant Gabriella had told her back in that hallway to be sure to bring her partner. He was here solely to spare her feelings.

Joseph Matthews truly was a knight in shining armor! Or in his case cargo pants and work boots.

As he settled in next to her his larger-than-life maleness quickly filled up the space between them. Warmth suffused her entire body. Being this close to Joe, having access to gaze into those rich brown eyes, would definitely make it difficult to concentrate on today's lesson.

"You're next, Carey. Introduce yourself and your partner," Gabriella said, emphasizing the *partner* part.

Joe hadn't meant to put Carey on the spot, but after seeing the panic in her eyes earlier, when Gabriella had told her to be sure to bring her partner, he couldn't let her go through this alone. At first he'd wanted to run like hell when he'd shown her the classroom. Coming here had brought back more awful memories. He and Angela had actually started this class before she'd moved out.

Feeling uneasy as hell when he'd dropped Carey off earlier, he'd gone back to his work station, but had soon found he'd been unable to concentrate on the job. His mind had kept drifting to Carey sitting here alone, feeling completely out of place, and he couldn't stand for that to happen. Besides, wasn't it time for him to move on? Determined to put his bad memories aside once and for all—his divorce hadn't been his fault—he'd made a decision. She shouldn't have to attend this class alone. If offering her support could ease her discomfort, he'd take the bullet for her and be her partner. The woman had been through enough on her own lately.

"Oh," she said, as if she'd never expected to have to introduce herself, even though everyone else just had. "Um, I'm Carey Spencer, I'm a little over three months pregnant, I, uh, recently moved to California." She swallowed nervously around the stretching of the truth. Joe reached for her hand beneath the table and squeezed it to give her confidence a boost. "I'm a nurse by profession, a first-time mother, and…" She looked at Joe, the earlier panic returning to those shimmering green eyes. He squeezed her hand again.

"I'm Joe Matthews," he stepped in. "Carey's friend. *Good* friend." He glanced at her, seeing her squirm, letting it rub off on him a tiny bit. "A really close friend." Overkill? He gazed around the room, having fudged the situation somewhat, and all the other couples watched expectantly. "We've been through a lot together, and we're both really looking forward to taking this class and learning how to be good parents."

Okay, let them think whatever they wanted. His

statement was mostly true—in fact, it was ninety-nine per cent true, except for the bit about being "really close" friends, though they had been through a lot together already. Oh, and the part about him ever getting to be a parent. Yeah, that would never happen. The reality hit like a sucker punch and he nearly winced with pain. Why the hell had he willingly walked into this room again? Carey's cool, thin fingers clasped his hand beneath the table, just as he'd done to support her a few seconds ago. The gesture helped him past the stutter in thought.

He'd come here today for Carey. She needed to catch a break, and he'd promised the night he'd found her in the alley that he'd look out for her. If she needed a partner for the parenting class then, damn it, he'd be here.

"I'm a paramedic here at the clinic, so if I ever need to deliver a baby on a run, I figure this class will be good for that, too." He got the laugh he was hoping for to relieve his mounting tension as the room reacted. "It's a win-win situation, right?"

He shifted his eyes to the woman to his left. If taking this class together meant having to really open up about themselves, well, he was bound to let her down because he was far, far from ready to talk about it.

Carey didn't know squat about his past, and if he had his way, she never would. Why humiliate himself again, this time in front of a woman he was quickly growing attached to, when once had already been enough for a lifetime?

CHAPTER FIVE

ON THE SATURDAY after the next Parentcraft class, Carey stood in the kitchen, using her second-trimester menu planner for dinner preparation. She'd had to stretch her usual eating routine to include items she'd never have been caught dead eating before. Like anchovies! Why was Gabriella so big on anchovies? Obviously they were high in calcium and other important minerals, plus loaded with omega three and six fatty acids, but Carey didn't think they tasted so great and smelled really bad. Carey practically had to hold her nose to eat them.

Fortunately this Saturday-night menu included salmon—yay, more omega fats—which Joe was dutifully grilling outside on a cedar plank. Dutiful, yeah, that was the right word for Joe. Everything he did for her seemed to be done out of duty. Sure, he was nice and considerate, but she never sensed he was completely relaxed around her.

She diligently steamed the broccoli and zucchini, and in another pot boiled some new red potatoes, grateful that Joe seemed okay to eat whatever she did. So far she'd managed to keep her occasional junk-food binges to herself. Nothing major, just items that had definitely been left off the Gabriella-approved dietary plan for a pregnant lady, like sea salt and malt vinegar potato chips, or blue corn chips, or, well, actually, any kind of chip that she could get her hands on. She rationalized that if occasionally she only bought the small luncheon-sized bags she wouldn't do the baby any harm. Or her hips.

Her weight gain was right on target, and when she'd seen Gabriella in clinic for a prenatal checkup, thanks to Dr. Rothsberg, she'd complimented her on how well she was carrying the baby. The ultrasound had been the most beautiful thing she'd ever seen, and the first person she'd wanted to share it with had been Joe, and since he'd brought her to the appointment, once she'd dressed she'd invited him back into the examination room. He'd oohed and aahed right along with her, but she'd sensed a part of him had remained safely detached. She could understand why—he was a guy and it wasn't his baby.

It made sense…yet he'd gotten all watery-eyed that day in the clinic when she'd found out her baby was okay, and he'd made that remark that one time about knowing how life-changing a baby could be. She'd asked him point blank if he was a father, but he'd said no and had powered right on. What had that been about? Heck, she'd only just recently found out how old he was, and the only thing she knew beyond that, besides he had a big, kind family, was that he was divorced.

The thing that kept eating away at her thoughts was that Joe didn't seem like the kind of guy who'd give up on a marriage.

Carey popped the top from another beer can and carried it outside to Joe. Being so involved together in the parenting class had definitely changed their relationship for the better, yet she knew Joe held back. She'd opened up about Ross in the hope of getting Joe to share whatever it was that kept him frequently tense and withdrawn.

At first she'd written off that always-present slow simmer just beneath the surface as being due to his demanding job as a paramedic, and also the fact he ran the business. But he clearly thrived on being in charge. It was obvious he loved the challenge. No, that wasn't the problem, it was when they were in the house together, her occasionally indulging in baby talk to her stomach, or discussing the latest information from the Parentcraft classes that she noticed him mentally slip into another time and place. Granted, another person's pregnancy wasn't exactly riveting to the average person, but Joe had volunteered to attend the class with her. If it was an issue, why had he signed on?

Now outside, she smiled and handed him a second beer. "Ready for another?"

His brows rose. "Sure. Thanks." As he took it, their eyes met and held, and a little zing shot through her. The usual whenever they looked straight at each other.

She turned and headed back toward the kitchen, feeling distracted and desperately trying to stay on task.

"You trying to get me drunk?"

"Maybe." She playfully tossed the word over her shoulder then ducked inside before he could respond.

Tonight was the night she hoped to get him to open up. If she had to ply him with beer to do it, she would.

Later over dinner… "Mmm, this is delicious," Carey said, tasting the cedar-infused salmon. "That lime juice brings out a completely different flavor." They sat at the small picnic table on the deck under a waxing June moon.

"Not bad, I must say. What kind of crazy food do we have to prepare tomorrow?"

"Watercress soup with anchovies, what else?" She laughed. "That's lunch, but for dinner we get chicken teriyaki with shredded veggies, oh, and cheese rolls. Can't wait for the bread!" She leveled him with her stare. "I have to thank you for putting up with this crazy diet."

His gaze didn't waver. "I've enjoyed everything so far." He reached across the table and covered her hand with his. "Since I'm your prenatal partner, the least I should do is help you stay on the diet. Your baby will thank me one day."

Sometimes he said the sweetest things and she just wanted to throw her arms around him. But she'd made that mistake once already during the self-defense training and it had mixed up everything between them for days afterwards. Since then he seemed to have shut down like a spring snare, and she'd carefully kept her distance. But he'd just planted a thought she couldn't drop. Would her baby ever know him?

Right now his hand was on top of hers, and she couldn't for the life of her understand why such a wonderful man wasn't still happily married with his own assortment of kids.

She lifted her lids and caught him still watching her, both totally aware of their hands touching, so she smiled but it felt lopsided and wiggly. She stopped immediately, not wanting him to think she was goofy looking or anything. Things felt too close, it nagged at her, and she knew how to break up that uncomfortable feeling pronto. "You mentioned once that you were divorced." She decided to get right to the heart of the conversation she'd planned to start tonight.

He removed his hand from hers and sat taller as ice seemed to set into his normally kind eyes. "Yeah." He dug into his vegetables and served himself more fish, suddenly very busy with eating. "My wife left me."

Why would any woman in her right mind leave Joe? "That must have hurt like hell."

"It was not a good time." He clipped out the words, with an emphasis that communicated it would be the end of this conversation. And why did she know without a doubt that he wasn't telling her anywhere near the whole story? Because he'd hinted at "getting it" and knowing how babies changed lives. Things didn't add up. Had he lost a child?

So she pressed on, hoping that talking about herself some more might help him to open up. "Sometimes people *should* get divorced." She pushed her empty plate away and sipped from her large glass of iced water.

"For instance, my parents were a train wreck. My dad was out of work most of the time, and my mother was always taking on whatever odd jobs she could to make up for it. Instead of being grateful, my typically belligerent father went the macho route, accusing her of thinking him not good enough to take care of the family. Occasionally he'd haul off and hit her, too. I swore I'd never, *never* put myself in the same position."

Joe protested, shaking his head. "You didn't."

"Didn't I? After working my whole life to be independent, I fell for the exact same kind of guy as my dad. A man so insecure about his masculinity that he kept me isolated, insisting it was because he loved me so much. Then he turned violent whenever I stood up to him, and especially when I told him we were going to have a baby. What a fool I was. I didn't learn a thing from my parents' lousy marriage." If she hadn't already finished eating she wouldn't have been able to take another bite, with her stomach suddenly churning and contorting with emotion.

"He must have had a lot going for him to get you interested at first, though. I'm sure he hid his insecurities really well." His hand came back to hers. "Don't call yourself stupid. You have a big heart. You just didn't see the changes coming."

"You give me a lot of credit." She squeezed his hand. "I'm still mad at myself for winding up in this position."

"As crazy as it sounds, I'm kind of glad you did." He squeezed back then let go completely, keeping things safe and distant. "You're better off here."

With you? She wanted to add, *I am better off here but where do we go from here?* "What are we, Joe?"

He screwed up his face in mock confusion. "What do you mean?"

"Are we friends? You can't call me a tenant because I'm not paying you rent." She tried to make an ironic expression, but fell far short because the next pressing question was already demanding she ask it. "Am I one huge charity case that you, in your kindness, the way your parents taught you, just can't bring yourself to send away?"

"God, no. Carey, come on." He wadded up his napkin and tossed it on the table. "You're overthinking things, making problems where there aren't any. We're friends." He shrugged.

"We can't call ourselves friends if you won't open up to me." She stood and started clearing the table. "Friends share things."

Joe shot up and helped to pick up dishes, as usual, and they headed to the kitchen and washed the plates in silence. A muscle in his jaw bunched over and over. Not only had she *not* gotten Joe to open up, she'd made sure he'd keep his distance and would probably never let her close. Major fail.

But what should she expect, being pregnant with another man's baby?

Early on Monday morning the phone rang. Sunday evening had been strained but tolerable between them, and Joe had withdrawn more from Carey by working during the day and later by working out while listening to that aggressive jazz saxophone music while he did so. It made her want to put on headphones. Carey didn't know if she could take much more of him distancing himself from her, but under the circumstances she felt trapped for now. Which felt far too familiar, considering her past.

Joe had the day off and answered, then quickly handed the phone to Carey.

"This is Mrs. Adams from social services. The police department told us about your current situation, and Helena from The Hollywood Hills Clinic Social Services also contacted us. Sorry it took so long, but there is quite a backlog. Anyway, we have found a temporary apartment in Hollywood where you can stay for now."

"Well, that's wonderful. When can I have a look?"

"You can move in this weekend, if you'd like. Or today if you need to. We have a voucher worth a month's rent and this unit has just become available. Would you like me to bring the voucher by?"

"Yes. Of course. Thanks so much."

Carey hung up having made arrangements with Mrs. Adams, glancing up to see Joe watching her skeptically. She owed him an explanation and told him exactly what Mrs. Adams had just said.

"So, if all works out, I'll be out of your hair, maybe as soon as tonight."

"Where is this place? Will you be safe?" There went that jaw muscle again.

"I don't know anything, but would social services send me somewhere unsafe?"

"They're just trying to put a roof over your head." His fingers planted on and dug into his hips, his body tensed. He wore an expression of great concern, making his normally handsome face look ominous. "Safety might not be their number-one goal. I'm going with you."

Every once in a while, thanks to her recent experience with Ross, Joe seemed too overbearing. Yeah, she'd messed up lately, but she was a big girl, a mother-to-be! And she would be in charge of her life from here on. "I can take care of myself. Thanks."

His demeanor immediately apologetic, he came closer. "I didn't mean to come off like that, dictating what I intended to do, but please let me come with you. I'd like to see where you'll be living. I know all the areas around here."

Since he sounded more reasonable, she changed her mind. "Okay, but I make the decision. Got that?"

"Got it. But first off you've got to know that you don't have to move out. You're welcome to stay here as long as you need to."

"Thank you, but as a future single mother I've got to prove to myself I can take care of things. I got myself into this situation, I should get myself out. Besides, I'll be starting the temporary job next Monday, and—"

"Your salary won't be enough to rent an apartment in any decent neighborhood. I'm not trying to throw a wet blanket on your plans, I'm just being honest."

She refused to lose hope. "I'm going to go see that apartment with Mrs. Adams and then I'll decide."

"Can you at least call her back and tell her I'll drive you over there?"

"Okay, but only because it will be more convenient for her."

"Fine."

That afternoon Joe parked on North Edgemont in front of an old redbrick apartment building that was dark, dank and seedy-looking as hell. He clamped his jaw and ground his molars rather than let Carey know what he thought. She'd made it clear it would be her decision, and he'd honor that. The only thing the area had going for it was a huge hospital a couple of blocks down on Sunset Boulevard.

If they'd offered the rent voucher the first week she'd moved in, he would have encouraged her to jump on it. Having a woman in his house again, especially a pregnant woman, brought back a hundred different and all equally awful memories. Having to do things together, like shopping for groceries and fixing meals, was nearly more than he could bear. Plus, with Carey living with him, it seemed Angela had moved back in, just in a different form. So he'd concentrated on Carey being a victim and he was her protector. Keeping it clinical and obligatory had been the key.

Best-laid plans and all, he'd gotten involved with her anyway. Why had he taken it on himself to teach her self-defense, and why in hell had he volunteered to be her prenatal class partner? The problem was there was too much to like about Carey. So he glanced at the dreary apartment building and felt a little sick.

If she decided to take this place, he'd have to find her

a car. Which wouldn't be a problem with his father's business. No way did he want her walking these streets at night, coming home from work and getting off the bus. Pressure built in his temples just thinking about it.

He stood back and let Carey introduce herself to Mrs. Adams, who showed her inside. The term *flophouse* came to mind, but Joe kept his trap shut. Damn, it was hard.

The single room had a tiny alcove with a half-refrigerator, a small microwave and a hot plate. How would she be able to continue with the nutritious meals from Gabriella's class? He'd throw out the mattress from the pullout bed and burn it rather sleep on it, and the rusty toilet in the so-called bathroom made his stomach churn. Not to mention that the constant dripping from the kitchen sink would keep her awake at night.

Caution was as plain as day on Carey's face as she glanced around the place. But he already knew her well enough to know she'd try to make the best out of a lousy situation. Hell, she'd been putting up with him withdrawing every time they'd gotten too close. Probably walked on eggshells around him. But was living with him so bad that she'd choose a dump like this just to get away?

Last night she'd said a real zinger, not realizing it, of course, but nevertheless her comment had hit hard. When she'd talked about her ex being insecure about his masculinity to the point of taking over her life, it had made Joe cringe. He could relate, especially since getting the lab results about him being sterile, and following up later with a urologist as to the reasons why. Was that part of him wanting to protect Carey? Was it some twisted way of making himself feel like a complete man again?

"And you said you have a voucher for the rent here for the next month?" Carey asked.

Mrs. Adams, a tiny African-American woman with short tight curls and wearing a bright red blouse, looked serious. "Yes, we can also provide food stamps and you can move in now or this weekend if you'd like."

Carey was about to say something, and damn it to hell if it meant he was waving around his insecure masculinity or whatever, Joe couldn't let this fiasco continue another second. "What's the crime rate in this neighborhood?" he butted in.

An eyebrow shot up on Mrs. Adams's forehead. Was she not used to being asked that question by people desperate enough to need county social services assistance? "I honestly don't know. It's a busy neighborhood. There's a church right up the street, a hospital down on Sunset. There's a small family-run market on Hollywood Boulevard and the apartment building is really well situated for all of her needs."

Carey stood still, only her eyes moved to watch him. Was it trust or fear he saw there? Was his being concerned coming off as overbearing? He hoped she saw it a different way, the way he'd intended, that he was worried for her safety. He subtly shook his head but she quickly glanced back at Mrs. Adams. "Thank you so much for showing me this place. Do I have to sign anything?"

Joe understood she'd been trying to be a good soldier, stiffening her lip and all, but all it had done was turn her to cardboard. She obviously wanted to make the offer from social services work out, but Joe strongly suspected that in her heart she was scared. And he was pretty sure he saw it in her eyes, too. Those lush meadow-green eyes seemed ready for a storm. How could she not be afraid? Now that he'd identified what was going on with her, he could practically smell that fear. He just hoped it wasn't directed toward him.

She didn't belong here. She belonged with him. Safe. Protected. That's all there was to it. Was he being crazy, like Ross? With all his heart he hoped not, but right at this moment it was hard to evaluate his motives because the lines had blurred and there was no way in hell he'd let this happen.

Joe stepped forward, unable to let the scene play out another moment. He reached for and gently held Carey's upper arm, pleading with his eyes, hoping she wouldn't see a crazed, insecure man. He fought to keep every ounce of emotion out of his voice. "Stay with me." Making the comment a simple suggestion. Then he stumbled, letting a drop of intensity slip back in. "Please."

Carey hadn't given in, though she'd wanted to. Mrs. Adams had gone on alert when Joe had taken her arm in his hand. The poor woman had probably thought he was the guy she needed to get away from. Carey had made sure she knew otherwise. No, Joe wasn't scary, but he had a rescue complex and she needed to help him get over it.

They drove back toward West Hollywood mostly in silence. True, the last thing she wanted was to move into such a depressing place, but rather than cave just because Joe wanted her to she'd asked Mrs. Adams to give her twenty-four hours to make her decision. It had also seemed to calm the woman's sudden uneasy demeanor over the battle of wills between Carey and Joe about moving.

And this had been where Joe had proved he was nothing like Ultimatum Ross. Trusting her decision, he'd agreed that was a smart idea, and Mrs. Adams had smiled again. Inside, so had Carey.

The man was too good to be true, and she couldn't trust her instinct to believe he was what he was, a great guy! She'd thought she'd fallen for a great guy back home, a man who'd gone out of his way to charm her and make her laugh, and above all who'd wanted to take care of her. Look where that had led. But the last two weeks of living with Joe had been little short of perfection. He was patient and friendly, didn't have mood swings, like Ross, had just mostly kept his distance. Sometimes that had been maddening. Joe was tidy and helpful and—oh, she'd tried long enough to avoid the next thought—sexy as hell! The male pheromones buzzing through that house had awakened something she'd tried to put on hold since long before she'd gotten pregnant. Desire.

When she'd taken off her blindfold and finally seen who Ross truly was, she hadn't wanted to be engaged to him anymore. But he was such a manipulating and suspicious guy that she'd pretended to be sexually interested just enough to keep him off the scent. She'd intended to leave him. Had made plans for it, too. Then the unthinkable had happened and she'd gotten pregnant. The only thing she could figure was she'd missed a birth-control pill. Ross had hated hearing that excuse, and he'd accused her of wanting to ruin everything they'd had together. He'd even accused her of being unfaithful.

And he'd gotten violent.

How could she ever trust her instinct where men were concerned?

She needed Joe to open up to make sure he wasn't hiding something awful. Maybe she could use him wanting to rescue her all the time as a bargaining chip to get him to share something personal. She'd been kind of forced to tell him about Ross, what with her bruises and black eye and being pregnant and running away. But her attempt to get him to tell her about his failed marriage Saturday night had fallen flat. Maybe his divorce still hurt too much.

"If you expect me to continue to live with you, we have to actually be friends, not just say we are."

"Of course we're friends." He kept his eyes on the road.

"No, we're not. I've shared some very personal stuff with you, and yet you're nothing but a mystery to me. Friends know things about each other."

"What do you want to know?" He sounded frustrated.

"Why did your wife leave you? What happened? What broke up your marriage?"

He braked a little too hard for the red light, then stared straight ahead for a couple of moments. "If you're thinking I was a player you'd be wrong. In our case it was the other way around."

Carey nearly gulped in her shock. What woman in her right mind would be unfaithful to a guy like Joe? What in the world was she supposed to say to that? "She left you for another man?" She admitted she sounded a little dumbstruck.

"As opposed to a woman?" He gave an ironic laugh and glanced at her with challenge in his eyes. "I guess that might have hurt even more, but yes to your question. It was another man." He could have been testifying in court by his businesslike manner. Just the facts, ma'am.

So Joe was one of the walking wounded, like her.

"I'm so sorry." It was probably a lot easier for him to assign himself the role of protector than to open the door to getting involved with another woman. Especially a vulnerable person like her. Joe had proved to be wise on top of all his other wonderful assets.

Though she knew without a doubt what had gone down today, looking at the apartment, was on a completely different level. Joe had asked her to stay. She'd seen from that touch of desperation in his eyes that he'd meant it, too. She didn't have a clue if once upon a time he'd asked his wife to stay and she'd left anyway, but right at this instant Carey made a decision.

No way would she be another woman walking out on Joseph Matthews. "May I borrow your cell phone?"

While driving, he fished in his pocket and handed it to her. She looked in her purse for the business card. "Hello, Mrs. Adams? This is Carey Spencer. Yes, hi. About that apartment, I am so grateful for the rent voucher and the offer of food stamps, but I have decided to stay where I am."

Not another word was spoken on the drive home, but Carey could have sworn the built-up tension in the car had instantly dissipated as if she'd rolled down the window and let the Santa Ana winds blow it all away.

The following Monday Carey started her new job as a substitute ward clerk and couldn't hide her elation over working again. More importantly, the California Board of Registered Nurses assured her she'd get her RN license in a couple more weeks, just in time to apply for another job, this one as an RN, after the vacationing ward clerk came back. Life was definitely looking up.

The evening shift on the medical/surgical unit was nonstop with admissions and discharges, and she was grateful she'd spent a couple of afternoons learning the computer software and clinic routine with the current ward clerk the week before she'd left.

Joe had offered to rent her a car, but she didn't feel ready to drive the streets of Los Angeles, especially those winding roads in the Hollywood Hills, just yet, so Joe had reworked things and scheduled himself on evening shifts so he could bring her to work and back.

She sat transfixed before the computer at the nurses' station, deciphering the admitting orders from Dr. Rothsberg for a twenty-eight-year-old starlet who'd been intermittently starving and binging herself then herbal detoxing for the last several years, until now her liver showed signs of giving out. She'd been admitted with a general diagnosis of fever, malaise and abdominal tenderness. Though bone thin everywhere else, her abdomen looked to be the same size as Carey's, but the actress wasn't pregnant.

Carey had arranged for the ultrasound and CT studies for the next day, and had moved on to requesting a low-sodium diet from the hospital dietary department, which had a master chef. She could vouch for the great food with a couple of memorable meals she'd had during her stay. The patient would probably never notice the lack of salt amidst a perfect blend of fresh herbs and spices. Then she reminded the admitting nurse that her patient was on total bed rest. She went ahead and read Dr. Rothsberg's analysis and realized therapeutic paracentesis was likely in the petite Hollywood personality's future.

Deep in her work, she glanced up to find Joe smiling at her. "I brought you something," he said, then handed her a brown bag with something inside that smelled out of this world.

She stood to take the bag over the countertop, inhaled and couldn't resist. "Mmm, what is it?"

"Your dinner. I was on a call in the vicinity of Fairfax, so I got you one of those deli sandwiches you gobbled down the last time we were there."

"Turkey salad, cranberries and walnuts with bread dressing?"

"Yup."

"Including the pickle?"

He nodded, as if offended she'd even suggest such an oversight.

"Well, thank you. I'll be starving by the time my dinner break rolls around."

"You're welcome." He got serious and leaned on his forearm, making sure to hold her gaze. "I've been thinking. We'll have to get more organized now that you're working and pack a lunch for you every day. We can still use Gabriella's guidelines."

"Sounds good." Totally touched by his concern for her well-being, she fought that frequent urge to give him a hug. Fortunately the nurses' station counter prevented it this time. "But please let me splurge on things like this once in a while." She held up the deli bag.

He winked, and it seemed a dozen butterflies had forced their way into her chest and now attempted to fly off with her heart. Since she'd decided to keep living with him, he'd changed. He'd become easier to talk to, and though he still hadn't opened up he'd quit grinding his teeth so much. Truth was, the man could only suppress his wonderful nature for so long. Now she was the lucky recipient of his thoughtfulness and loving every second of it.

"See you later," he said, making a U-turn and heading off the ward. The perfectly fitting light blue polo shirt showed off his broad shoulders, accentuating his trim waist, the multi-purpose khaki cargo pants still managing to hug his buns just right, and those sexy-as-hell black paramedic utility boots... She guiltily watched his every move until he was out of sight. Wow, it looked like she didn't have to worry about her sick relationship with Ross at the end before she'd run away, and ruining her natural sex drive. She'd faked interest and excitement with him for her safety. Now, with Joe, without even trying, the most natural thoughts of all had awakened some super-hot fantasies. Like the desire to make love and really mean it. What would that be like with Joe?

"Uh-huh. Nice." One of the other nurses in the area had joined her in staring at the masculine work of art as he'd swaggered out the door. How could a guy *not* swagger, wearing those boots?

Getting caught ogling Joe made Carey's cheeks heat up, especially after what she'd just been thinking, so she tossed a sheepish look at the nurse then delved back into the admission packet for the actress.

Joe went straight to the clinic's paramedic station just off the ER to check on the EMT staff. He knew the emergency nurses sometimes got upset if the guys didn't help out when things got busy. Joe was always prepared to intervene and explain that wasn't their job, and the RNs didn't need to get all worked up about the EMS guys sitting for half a minute, waiting for the next call. On the other hand, he'd insisted to his guys that if a nurse said she needed more muscle, and they weren't doing anything at the time, they should jump to it and help out with lifts and transfers. Keeping RNs happy was always a good idea. He'd also taken to suggesting the guys hang out in their truck on downtime rather than at the tiny desk with two computers designated as their work station, so as not to complicate things in the ER.

Not taking his own advice, he took a seat and brought up the evening's schedule, and in the process sat in the vicinity of James, who was conferring on the phone about a patient he'd just admitted to Carey's floor with liver issues. James nodded and smiled at Joe, and Joe returned the courtesy.

Soon James hung up. "How's that scar doing? Any more tearing with your workouts, you beast?"

Joe laughed. "I'm all healed. Thanks." Joe saw James's sister, Freya, appear across the ER, obviously looking for someone.

"There you are," she said over the other heads, immediately making her way toward James.

James ducked down in an obvious fashion. "Oh, boy. Here we go," he said jokingly in an aside to Joe. "What does she want this time?" He raised his voice to tease his younger sister.

Knowing from their rocky history that the brother and sister's relationship had never been better since Freya had come to The Hollywood Hills Clinic as a sought-after public relations guru, Joe chuckled at James's wisecrack.

"There you are," Freya said, her dark blue eyes sparkling under the fluorescent ER lights. "I know you've been avoiding me, but I need a firm date for when you'll visit the Bright Hope Clinic. Here's my calendar, I've highlighted the best days and times for me and them. What works for you?" She shoved her small internet tablet calendar in front of James, making it impossible for him not to pick a day and time.

Her long brown hair was pulled back into a simple

ponytail that waved down her back, nearly to her waist, yet she still looked like she could be royalty. Hollywood royalty, that was. Joe had heard rumors about her once having had to go to rehab for anorexia, but from the healthy, happy-looking pregnant woman standing before him he'd have never guessed.

James took a deep inhale and scrolled through his smartphone calendar, matching day for day, saying, "No. Nope. Not that one either. Hmm, maybe this one? September the first or the second?"

"Let's take the first." Freya quickly highlighted that day. "It is now written in stone. Do you hear me? There's no getting out of it. You'll show up and do those publicity photos in the clinic in South Central and smile like you mean it."

"Of course I'll mean it. I'm going for the children."

"I know, but you know." They passed a secret brother-sister glance, telling an entirely different story than the simple making of plans for publicity shots. Joe deduced that since Dr. Mila Brightman ran Bright Hope, she was the issue. She happened to be Freya's best friend, and also the woman James had stood up on their wedding day. Or, at least, that was the scuttlebutt Stephanie the receptionist had told Joe one day on a break over coffee in the cafeteria. It had happened before Joe had started working there, she'd said, so all he could do was take Stephanie's word for it. The woman really was a gossip. But, damn, if that was the case, no wonder James hesitated about going. How could he face her after dumping her on the day of her dream wedding?

Having achieved her purpose, Freya rushed off, no doubt wanting to end her day and get home to her husband Zack.

"The last thing I want to do is upset a pregnant lady,"

James said to Joe in passing, "but, hey, you know all about that, right?"

The casual comment took Joe by surprise. At first he thought James was referring to his ex, Angela, but then realized he must have been referring to Jane Doe, aka Carey, who lived with him and happened to be just shy of four months pregnant.

"Tell me about it," Joe said, hoping he'd recovered quickly enough not to seem like a bonehead, and pretending that pregnant ladies were indeed unpredictable and demanding, while knowing for a fact Carey was anything but.

On Friday night, at the end of the first week on the job for Carey, Joe insisted they stop for a fast-food burger on the way home. How could she have been in California for three weeks and not tried one? They didn't even bother to wait to get home but devoured them immediately on the drive. Even though it definitely wasn't on her second-trimester diet list, she'd never tasted a better cheeseburger in her life.

"My parents are having a barbecue on the Fourth of July," Joe said, his mouth half-full, one hand on the steering wheel, the other clutching a double cheeseburger.

A national holiday had been the last thing on her mind lately. Plans seemed incomprehensible. She thought of that dreary apartment she'd almost taken and shivered at the thought of being on her own there, especially on the Fourth of July, grateful to have Joe's sweet house and lovely garden in the back to look at. She'd be just fine.

"Do you want to come? They'd love to have you."

What? He was inviting her to his parents' home?

Why? Out of his usual sense of obligation? "Oh, you don't have to—"

"I want to, and my whole family's going to be there so you can meet my sisters and brothers, too."

"Do they know about me?" Why was he pushing to take her?

"I have a prying mother and a loose-lipped sister. Mom's got this sixth sense about changes in my life, no doubt recently fueled by Lori loaning out some clothes."

"The whole story?" She really didn't want her personal failures shared, especially with Joe's family.

He shook his head and took another bite of his burger. "I wouldn't do that. You know better. But you said you wanted to be friends, and I take my friends to family barbecues."

She'd put her foot down when she'd decided to stay with him. He'd agreed to consider her a friend. If this was his way of proving it, as confusing as it would be for her, not to mention nerve-racking, she really shouldn't refuse to meet his family. It might set things back if she didn't.

"Then I guess I'll have to go." She played coy, but cautious contentment she hadn't felt in ages settled in a warm place behind her breastbone. This was more proof that Joe was *nothing* like Ross. He pushed her to get out and do things, got her a job, and now he wanted her to meet his family on Independence Day no less. Wow, what did it all mean?

Joe finished his hamburger as they neared his house. It'd tasted great, as always, but now his stomach felt a little unsettled. He'd tried not to think about the ramifications of what he'd just done, but couldn't avoid it. Trust, or lack thereof, in women in general and Carey, by reason of her gender, made him have second thoughts about the invitation. The gift of Angela's infidelity just kept on giving.

Maybe he'd jumped the gun in asking her to his parents' Fourth of July party. It was too soon. She might get the wrong impression and he wasn't anywhere ready to get close to her. He pulled into the driveway and rather than pull into the garage he parked under the small carport instead. It wasn't like he could change the date of Independence Day, and for the record he wondered if he'd ever be in a place to trust a woman again, whether next week or two years from now.

But the damage had been done. He'd asked Carey to go along, and he couldn't very well take the invitation back. He'd just have to live with it.

Once home, Carey went directly to her room to change her clothes, planning to watch a little TV to unwind after another busy evening shift at the end of her first week. But not without noticing a shift in his mood since he'd issued, and she'd accepted, the invitation to his parents' Fourth of July barbecue. When she came back, Joe was already working out on the patio, hitting his punching bag like it was a full-out enemy. For someone who'd just wolfed down a double-double cheeseburger, French fries and a large soda, he looked the picture of health.

Feeling a bit guilt-ridden, she wandered into the dining room to have a better look, wondering if he'd taken his T-shirt off for her benefit. She particularly loved watching the muscles on his back ripple whenever he landed a good punch. She stood quietly, taking in the whole workout, admiring every inch of him.

Before she'd run away, she'd worried about ever having normal desire for a man again. Faking love with Ross had scarred her more than she'd ever dreamed.

But it hadn't stopped there. Ross had dominated her entire existence to the point of making her fear for her life. How could she ever desire a man who'd treated her like that?

Yet Joe, without even trying, brought out her most basic feelings. He turned her on. So confusing. Maybe she could blame that on the concussion or the pregnancy. Yet what a relief to know she was still a red-blooded woman with a normal sex drive.

With his back to her, he grunted and huffed as he punched the bag, and she could swear the muscles on his shoulders and arms grew more cut by the moment. Needing to either bite her knuckle to keep from groaning or do something to cool herself off, she chose to head to the kitchen for a bottle of water. When she opened the refrigerator, she grabbed one for Joe, too.

This time making her presence known, she went out onto the patio, setting his water near him. "You're making me feel very guilty about having that burger and not intending to do my preggers exercises tonight, you know."

Joe laughed, and because of it messed up his timing and the punch nearly missed the bag altogether. He went for the bottle. "Thanks." Carey enjoyed watching his Adam's apple move up and down his throat while he gulped the water. A few drops dribbled down his chest. Yeah, she noticed that, too.

Her eyes drifted to the jagged scar running across his ribs, still red and tender-looking. He'd been stabbed rescuing her. The thought seemed surreal and sent a barrage of intense feelings ranging from gratitude to lust to guilt rushing through her. On impulse she walked toward him, reached out and gingerly ran her fingers across the scar. His skin was damp, smooth and...

She slowly lifted her gaze from the fit washboard abs to his chest and the pumped pecs lightly dusted in dark hair, then onward to his strong chin and inviting mouth and last to his intensely brown, almost black with desire, eyes.

The moment, when they were up close and locked into each other's stare like that, shuddered through her.

Feeling absurdly out of character in general, and especially because she was four months pregnant, she ignored her insecurities, focusing only on the consuming pull between them, making a trail with her fingertips across the expanse of his muscled torso, along the broad rim of his shoulder, then upward to his jaw.

She swallowed lightly in edgy anticipation.

He didn't move, just kept willing her into the depth of his eyes, and she knew without a doubt he was as into this moment as she was. So she edged closer, lifted her chin and, though feeling breathy from nerves, she went for it, covering his mouth with a full-on kiss.

CHAPTER SIX

IF JOE LET Carey's kiss continue, he'd have to take her all the way and probably scare her half to death with his need. The mere touch of her lips had unleashed pure desire, like a lightning bolt straight down his spine.

But he knew Carey well enough now, and the woman was trying to show her gratitude for his saving her and taking her in. He didn't want gratitude, or, if she knew his whole story, pity, or anything else. All he wanted was to get lost in her body, to make love.

He broke off the kiss to get things straight. "I don't expect anything from you. You don't have to—"

She didn't listen or give him a chance to call her out, she just kissed him again, and, damn it, those lips he'd so often admired on the sly felt better kissing him than he could ever have imagined. He quit fighting his need and pulled her near, devouring her mouth, half hoping she'd get scared and back off so that what was otherwise inevitable wouldn't happen. But the hard and desperate kiss only seemed to fan her need as much as his as she pressed her body flush with his.

He could handle this, wouldn't lose control. They'd just make out for a while then call it quits. But then there was the feel of her lips, smooth, plump, that inviting-as-all-hell tongue, and the touch of her fingertips at the back of his neck and on his shoulders. The sound of her deep breathing, the scent of coconut in her hair, and especially those little turned-on sounds escaping her throat made it so hard to not completely let go. And, damn, that wasn't the only thing that was hard. Yeah, he was pumped, horny, and making out with a woman who seemed to want him as badly as he needed her.

This was about sex. Against a wall. He needed to look into her eyes, to see if she really was as into this as he was, because he wouldn't take her if she wasn't. Electricity seemed to run through his veins, maybe partly because he was worked up from boxing, but most definitely from holding and kissing her. Surely she felt that electricity too. If she was just looking for some comforting necking, she'd come on way too strong, so it was best to check things out. Figure out where she was at before he let loose. He placed his thumbs in front of her ears, his fingers digging into that thick and gorgeous auburn hair, and though hating to separate their mouths he moved her head back.

Carey seemed dazed and was breathless, so it took a moment for her to connect with his stare. Her eyelids fluttered open and maybe Joe's interpretation was skewed from wanting her so much, but her eyes were on fire. For him.

Her nostrils flared and she breathed quickly. "Please don't stop," she whispered. "This has nothing to do with gratitude, believe me." She kissed him again, and the dam of unspoken longing, secret desire, and flat-out need totally broke.

She wanted him. He wanted her. Tonight he'd have her.

He walked her backwards, reached under the back of

her thighs and lifted her as he did so. She wrapped her legs around his waist, and soon her back was against a well-secluded wall in the corner of the patio. She'd already pulled her top over her head by the time they'd gotten there, and once at the wall, just as quickly, she released her full breasts from the constraints of the bra.

He looked down. The view of their chests mashed together exhilarated him, the hot, soft feel of her breasts even better. But she was hungry for his mouth and wanted all his attention there. So he obliged. He wedged her tight against the wall, sitting her on the edge of a book case, leaning into her, weaving his fingers with hers and lifting her arms flush to the plaster so he could be closer still. She moaned, enjoying the full body contact every bit as much as he did. He inhaled her sweet-scented neck and nuzzled it deep with kisses. She liked it, moaning again and bucking her hips just above his full erection, causing more lightning bolts along his spine.

Soon Carey wiggled off his hips, standing just long enough to tug down his boxing shorts and her yoga pants. She took the time to run her hand along his glutes and give them an appreciative squeeze as she stepped up close and hugged him again.

His erection landed between their bodies and the surge of sensation from her skin to his nearly sent him over the top. God, he wanted her. And she obviously wanted him. Right then.

He may be sterile and she pregnant, but he still knew the purpose of protected sex, and it wasn't all about birth control. Any guy his age had a stash of condoms, even though lately he hadn't been in the least bit interested in getting involved enough with a woman to use them…until Carey.

Living with Carey these past few weeks had made him very much aware of where those condoms were, too. "One second." He stopped pressing her to the wall, and regretfully removed himself from between her gorgeous thighs. "Don't move." He stepped back and his eyes took her in, in all her lush splendor. God, he wanted her.

Joe zipped around the wall to his bedroom and returned in record time, afraid she might have already changed her mind.

She wasn't there. His heart sank.

"I'm in the bathroom. I'll be right there!"

The wall was looking less and less appealing so he went into his bedroom and pulled back the covers on his king-sized bed, finding it hard to believe he'd soon be making love to Carey.

Carey never had expected to be having sex with Joe tonight, but now that she'd started it, and sex was definitely on the table, or nearly against the wall in their case, she wanted to freshen up. Ross may have scarred her but Joe could heal her. She didn't expect anything more than tonight, just the chance to find out she could let go and be with him, someone new, different, better than toxic Ross. If she didn't take this opportunity, she might never get over her past or feel normal again.

She stepped into the hall to find Joe waiting for her, having made the mistake of glancing at her pregnant abdomen just before she did. A wave of insecurity nearly made her back out, but the instant she saw his Adonis-like form, and the unadulterated desire in his eyes, every insecure thought left her mind. She wanted Joe more than she'd ever wanted to be with any man.

She rushed to him and he picked her up again, her

cooler skin crashing with his hot damp flesh. She inhaled his musky scent and grew hungrier for him. He carried her to his bed and, probably because she was pregnant, laid her down gently. Frantic for him, she'd have none of that, pulling him firmly toward her, and impatiently bucked under him.

He had other plans, though, and took his time exploring her body, figuring out what excited her and what drove her wild. Just about everything at this point! On his side, facing her, he rested on one arm, lowering and lifting his head to kiss her mouth, her neck, her breasts, while his free hand cupped her and explored her most intimate area. Breathless with longing, sensations zinging every which way through her body, she never wanted the intensified make-out session to end. Until, very soon, the mounting desire was too much and she needed him, all of him, inside her.

She rolled onto her side, throwing her leg over his hip, straddled him and pushed him back onto the mattress. From his firm feel she had zero worries whether he was ready or not. She slid her awakened center, thanks to his earlier attentions, along his length, thrilling at the feel of it and the thought of him soon being inside her. He'd already made her wet so she skimmed along his smooth ridge with ease, several times, stimulating herself more than she thought she could take. He definitely liked it.

But stopping her in mid-skim, as if he might lose control, he sheathed himself in record time then, taking control, placed her on her side with her back to his chest. One arm was underneath her and that hand cupped her breast while the other dipped between her thighs and opened her, rubbing the amazingly sensitive area, and she was soon straining at the onslaught of arousal. She moaned in bliss and Joe, being definitely ready, tilted her hips back, making her swaybacked, then entered her.

The culmination of sensations as he pressed into her took her breath away. She rolled with him, taking in every electrifying thrust. His hands remained attentive in those other strategic places as friction built deep inside, knotting behind her navel and lower. Heat lapped up the base of her spine, across her hips and over her breasts, flooding the skin on her chest and cheeks. She could feel the fully ignited body flush nearly burning her skin. If possible, he felt even harder now and an absurd thought occurred to her. She was making love with him, Joe! It wasn't a wish or a fantasy or a secret dream anymore. It was really happening.

Maybe it was the added hormones of pregnancy, and more probably it was the undivided attention from Joe, but she'd never, *ever* been this turned on in her life. With her entire body tingling and covered in goose bumps, running hot with sensations—not to mention the involuntary sounds escaping her throat—there would be no guessing on his part about how he made her feel. *Freaking amazing.*

She couldn't take more than a few minutes of the intense sensory overload without completely giving in to it. His pumping into her, slowing down and drawing out every last response, then speeding up at the perfect moment to drive her near the flashpoint soon became her undoing. She turned her head and found his mouth. They kissed wildly, wet and deep.

When she came, her center seemed to explode with nerve endings lighting up, zinging and zipping everywhere as they relayed their ecstatic message deep throughout her body. She gasped and writhed against him, riding the incredible wave for all it was worth, while sensing his time was near. Soon his low, elongated moan became the sweetest music she'd ever heard.

It had taken several minutes for things to settle down between Joe and Carey. He'd briefly jumped out of bed for the bathroom to take care of business, returning to find she'd probably done the same. He smiled when she came back with the fresh flush of lovemaking on her face and across her chest. Though she'd run a brush through her hair, it was still wildly appealing. He continued floating on the post-sex euphoric cloud when she crawled back into bed beside him. He'd just had mind-blowing sex with an amazing lady and he felt great. Beyond great. He pulled her close, delivered a sweetheart kiss then snuggled in, savoring the afterglow between them. But it was late and they'd worn each other out.

Within a few short minutes Carey fell asleep. She'd gone still, wrapped in his arms, then her breathing shifted to a slower, deeper rhythm. It felt right, holding her, breathing in her scented hair, touching her soft skin and womanly body. But sleep wasn't ready to come to Joe.

His hand dropped over her abdomen and the noticeable early second-trimester bump. It jolted him. His mind raced with comparisons with another woman and another time. He'd avoided the thought long enough, now it wouldn't let him go.

What the hell had he just done? He'd ruined everything.

The battle in his mind continued with rival thoughts. He had to be honest, he'd wanted this more than anything, and being with Carey had been on his mind for longer than he cared to admit. She'd knocked every sensible thought out of his head just by being the wonderfully appealing, sweet woman she was. The sexy-as-hell—and who'd just proved it beyond a doubt—mother-to-be.

Yes, she was pregnant with another man's baby, and though the circumstances were totally different, the scenario seemed too damn familiar.

Also, Joe worried that Carey was confusing gratitude with desire. She'd denied it when he'd bluntly asked her, but they were both obviously under some voodoo spell when it came to each other. He wouldn't dare call it love. Hell, she'd just escaped a toxic, abusive relationship. Any decent guy, and Joe considered himself one of the good guys, would be an improvement.

Back and forth he silently argued, feeding his confusion rather than solving anything. He'd essentially been acting like a partner to Carey in all but name—how had he not seen that before? It'd started with the staggering need to protect her and moved on to bringing her home. They'd lived together for almost a month, sharing the little everyday things that true couples did. He was the first person other than the midwife to see Baby Spencer in the ultrasound. He'd secretly teared up, seeing how the fetus already sucked its thumb and had a tiny turned-up nose in the profile. She'd even asked him to go to the next doctor's appointment with her, too, joking she was worried she'd forget something, and he'd been following her pregnancy like an auditor.

Just like he'd done with Angela at the beginning of her pregnancy.

What had possessed him to step into the role of being Carey's partner in the parenting class? He squeezed his eyes tight, avoiding the answer, holding her a little tighter than before. It wasn't out of pity for her being the only one enrolled without a significant other—no, he had to be honest. It was because he'd wanted to. Maybe even needed to.

Did he enjoy getting kicked in the teeth?

Damn it, for one of the good guys he was really screwed up. Losing Angela had nearly done him in, along with getting hit by the hardest dose of reality in his life. He was sterile. He'd never be a father. And Angela had cheated on him, taking the task of getting pregnant to his best friend, Rico.

In time he'd lose Carey and her baby, too, once she got back on her own two feet again. Just like he'd lost Angela and the baby he'd once thought was his for a brief but ecstatic period of time.

He slipped out of bed, unable to stay close another second to the woman who'd just thrown his entire world on its head. He pulled on his boxing trunks, went to the kitchen and drank a full glass of water, then walked to the couch and sat. Being away from her spell helped his body settle down. His mind was another story altogether, though. He folded his arms across his chest, plopped his feet on the coffee table and, using the TV controller, turned to an old black and white movie with the sound muted. Fortunately it dulled his thoughts and little by little, as the dark drama unfolded and minutes passed, he finally drifted off to sleep.

"Joe? What are you doing out here?"

Sunshine slipped through the cracks in the living-room window blinds on Saturday morning. Joe eased open one eye from where his face was mashed against the armrest cushion on the couch. "Huh? Oh, I couldn't sleep and I didn't want to wake you so I came out here."

"I was worried I'd snored or something." She'd obviously tried to lighten the mood, so he laughed easily, as if nothing was wrong at all. She looked nearly angelic, standing with the window behind her, her silhouette outlined by bright morning light. She was wearing an oversized T-shirt with those long, slender legs completely bare. It made him want her all over again, but that was the last thing he should ever do.

"No." He scrubbed his face, trying to wake up, realizing she hadn't bought his explanation, and he needed to be straight with her. "You didn't snore." Yeah, he had to nip this in the bud and, though it might sting today, she'd thank him later for sparing her more pain.

"What's up, Joe? I don't have a good feeling about us having sex and then you sneaking off to the couch."

He wasn't ready to look at her, and when he told her his thoughts she deserved his undivided attention. "I need some coffee." He stood and she followed him into the kitchen. He glanced at her before he got on the job of filling the coffeemaker and saw the frightened and forlorn woman he'd first seen at the bus station. It made him feel sick to do that to her so he stopped avoiding the moment and grabbed one of her hands. "Look." He shook his head. "I'm sorry we crossed the line last night. It was fantastic, amazing, and a huge mistake."

"No. It was totally okay with me. Couldn't you tell?" She searched his eyes, looking for answers. It made him look down at the hand he held. "In fact, it was an incredible night. I never dreamed making love with you could be so wonderful."

He glanced upward, finding those eyes…greener in the morning light. "It was great, but things are too confused between us. You need time to heal from your lousy relationship with Ross, and the most important thing in your life right now should be your baby. Focus on the baby, instead of getting all involved with me. Not that I didn't love what we did in there last night, it's just that we're dangerous for each other right now. I shouldn't take time and energy away from you focusing on what you want to do with your life. I'll just interfere, and you need to think what's best for you, not anyone else."

Who was he kidding, laying all the excuses at Carey's feet? He still wasn't ready to trust another woman, to open up about the pain of his wife's infidelity. And that's what he'd need to do in order to be with someone new. Her. It was why he'd been living like a workaholic hermit all this time. What would she think of him if she knew how scared he was to tell her the truth, and if he wasn't ready to be completely honest, what was the point of being with her?

He pulled her close and held her, and it hurt to feel her stiffen when he wanted to love her. But now he had to push her away because she deserved better. She deserved a future of her own making. All he'd do was mess things up. "We both have a lot going on in our lives right now and it isn't a good time to confuse things even more with sex." He pulled back to engage with her eyes, but she was now the one avoiding eye contact. "And, believe me, that was incredibly hard to say, because I wanted you like I've never wanted anyone else last night."

It seemed she'd stopped breathing, a dejected expression changing her beauty to sadness. He felt queasy, like he'd already finished the pot of coffee and the acid lapped the inside of his stomach. But he forged on because he had to.

"It's not right for us to be together now. Our timing

is off. We just have to face that. And no one is sorrier than me."

Something clicked behind those beautiful eyes. Her demeanor shifted from tender and hurting to world-weary chick. "Yeah, you're right. It really was stupid." She pecked his cheek with a near air kiss. "Now I need to shower."

He watched her walk away, her head high and shoulders stiff. In that moment he hated more than anything having given her a reality check, and the thought of drinking a cup of coffee made him want to puke.

CHAPTER SEVEN

CAREY STOOD UNDER the shower, hiding her tears. Joe's rejection had stung her to the core. She'd given him everything she had last night yet this morning he had closed the door.

She lifted her head and let the water run over her face. He'd made her remember her shameful past, and she wanted to kick herself for trying to forget. If there was one lesson she should have learned by now it was not to ever let herself get close to any man again. Yet here she was a month after running away from Ross, opening her heart to Joe. Could she have been more stupid?

Joe wasn't out to hurt her. It had just turned out that way, and it was her fault. She'd suspected from the beginning that he carried heavy baggage. It may have taken a near stranglehold to get him to reveal one small fact—the tip of the iceberg—that his wife had screwed him royally, and what the rest of the story was, Carey could only guess. One thing was certain, he was hurting and afraid of getting involved again.

Truth was she wasn't the only one with a past not to be proud of. Joe belonged in her league. All the more reason the two of them were a horrible match.

Yet she'd trudged on, defying the truth, letting his

kindness and charming personality, not to mention his great looks, win her over little by little. She'd let him take care of her and he'd quickly earned her trust. She still trusted him. But she couldn't let herself fall any deeper in love with him. Something in her chest sank when she inadvertently admitted she'd fallen for him. No. That couldn't be. She needed to stomp out any feelings she already had for Joe beyond the practical, and she needed to do it now. She lived here because she couldn't afford her own place. Yet. In time she'd be free of him, wouldn't have to be reminded daily how wonderful he'd been at first. Then how tightly he'd shut her out. Yet how much she still cared for him fanned the ache in her chest.

She diligently lathered her body, aware of more tears and that sad, sad feeling nearly overtaking her will to go on. Then her hands smoothed over her growing tummy and she knew she couldn't let anything keep her from the joy of becoming a mother. Her baby deserved nothing less than her full attention. Wasn't that what Joe had said, too?

From now on she'd concentrate on getting her life together and becoming a mother, and forget about how being around him made her feel as a woman. Really, how stupid was it, anyway, that fluttering heart business. It never paid off.

After showering and hair-drying and dressing, with her mental armor fully in place, she marched into the kitchen where she heard Joe puttering around. "I've decided to take you up on that offer to rent a car for me."

"Sure, we can do that this afternoon since my dad owns a rental franchise." He responded in the same businesslike tone she'd just used on him.

"Thanks. In the meantime, may I borrow *your* car? If I don't leave now I'll be late for the Parentcraft class."

He was dressed. He stopped drying the coffee carafe, turned and looked at her dead on. "I'm going too, but you can drive if you want."

He tossed her the keys, and in her profound surprise she still managed to catch them. "Uh, I don't think so."

"Well, I know so, because you forget things. And two sets of ears are better than one, especially since you're probably already distracted from everything I pulled on you this morning."

"It would be totally awkward for both of us. You know that."

"No, I don't because I've never done this before. Besides, no one else needs to know."

He was making her crazy with this line of thinking, and so, so confused. "I can't just give myself to someone then forget about it. What's wrong with you?"

"You're right, I'm totally screwed up, I admit it, but I started this class with you, and I intend to be there for you all the way to the end."

Why was he being so unreasonable? But, honestly, how could she hold against him what he'd just acknowledged? He was the first guy in her life who insisted on sticking something out with her. It seemed a very unselfish thing to do.

Now her head was spinning, and it wasn't because of the recent concussion. "This is all too complicated. I'd rather just go myself." He'd hurt her enough for one day. She couldn't possibly sit next to him in a class for two hours and not think about what had happened. Surely he knew that. What was wrong with the man?

He touched her arm and she went still. Something told her he was about to convince her to let him go, and right this minute—*thanks a million, armor, for abandoning me*—she felt too confused to argue.

"Carey, I know how it feels to be let down by someone. I know you've been let down a helluva lot lately, and I respect you too much to do that with this class on top of everything else I've already fouled up."

She felt like grabbing her head and running away. "Let's just drop this. I'm going now." She turned to leave, but he stopped her again.

"Listen, I may have totally screwed up by letting my body do the thinking instead of my brain last night, but long before that... I'll be honest and say I made a promise to myself about you. That first night I promised I'd look after you. And once I found out you were pregnant, I vowed to be there for the baby, too."

He took her by the shoulders, leveling his gaze on hers, delving into her eyes. She couldn't bring herself to look away. "This class is important. You need to know what Gabriella has to say. I signed on to be your partner, and I intend to stay on. We may have made a huge mistake, sleeping together so soon, but in this one thing I'm going to be the only person in your life right now who won't bail on you. Please let me go with you."

Damn her eyes, they welled up and she had to blink. The man was too blasted honorable, and she hated him for it. Hated him. "I won't be able to concentrate with you there." It came out squeaky, like she needed to swallow.

"You wouldn't be able to concentrate if I didn't go either. All the more reason for me to be there." He patted her stomach. "Little baby Spencer needs us to pay attention. Now, let's go."

He gently turned her by her shoulders then nudged her in the small of her back through the door, and because she couldn't stop the stupid mixed-up tears she handed back the keys. "You'd better drive."

Carey finished the temporary job as ward clerk just in time to interview for a staff RN position in the same ward at the clinic. Having seen her work ethic already, and now that she had her RN license straightened out, they hired her on the spot. Carey was thrilled! Life was looking up. Except for that messy bit of being crazy about Joe Matthews and him being adamant about living by some code of honor. He was so damn maddening!

Ever since they'd made love, and especially after he'd explained how he'd made a promise to look after her, she'd thought she'd figured him out. Basically, he was the guy of her dreams but didn't know it yet. The next big test was to get him to realize that. The guy followed the rules, maybe hid behind them, too. She could live with that for now, but it sure was hard! No deep, dark Joe secret would scare her away. Nothing he exposed could deter her. He was a good man, and she didn't want to lose him, no matter how stubborn he was. But she had to be careful not to let on about her continued and growing feelings for him or she'd blow it. The big guy needed to be handled with the utmost care. For his own good.

Things had been very strained at the West Hollywood house since they had "faced the facts" a little over a week ago. It seemed they'd both bent over backwards to be polite and easy to get along with since then, taking the art of being accommodating to a new extreme, but simmering just beneath the surface was the tension. Always the tension. There was nothing like confusing love with kindness and one spectacular "crossing the line" event to create that special brew. Now she'd clearly seen the error of her ways.

He thought he'd convinced her to only look out for herself and the baby, and she was! But she was also letting her heart tiptoe into the realm of love, the kind she'd never experienced before. The problem was, she couldn't let her champion paramedic know or he'd run. So the question remained, was she being the world's biggest fool or the wisest of wise women?

Only time would tell.

The nursing recruiter spent the entire first day on the new job orienting Carey and preparing her for the transition to the floor. From this day forward she'd remember July the first as her personal almost-Independence Day in California. But first she had to get through the holiday weekend, which included meeting Joe's family at their annual barbecue celebration. Why? Because he was the kind of guy who would never retract an invitation once made. Hadn't he proved that already by continuing with the prenatal classes?

Man, he irked her…in a good way.

Another reason was that purely out of curiosity she wanted to meet the family that had spawned such a unique guy as Joe. If she played her cards right, she might find out a lot more about him. As she'd predicted, so far he'd yet to renege on the invitation, but she thought she'd test the waters anyway.

"Listen," she said, on the night of July third, "I think I'll skip the barbecue tomorrow." Her heart wasn't into the excuse by a long shot. After his incredibly lame but amazingly touching reason for continuing with the parenting classes, she was curious to see how compelling he could be over Independence Day.

"But you've got to come. Mom will hound me for weeks if I back out now."

"You don't have to back out. I'm just not sure I'll go."

"If you don't go, I won't either."

"You can't play me like that."

"Play you? I just gave us both a way out. I'll tell her you don't want to come."

"So I get blamed? Oh, no. It's not that I don't want to go, it's our weird relationship I'm worried about. How would we hide that?"

"By acting like friends. We are still friends, right?"

"In some crazy bizarro-universe sort of way, yes, I guess we are. Besides, your mother would be horribly disappointed if you didn't go."

"Exactly my point."

Darn it, his logic had outsmarted hers once again. "You are so frustrating!"

"So you're saying you want to spend your first Fourth of July in California by yourself? Really?"

She couldn't argue with that line of thinking. He'd invited her into his family, an honor for sure but one that wouldn't come without questions. Probably most of the questions would come from his mother. Did she want to open herself up to that? And, more importantly, why did he? But, on the other hand, did she really want to spend the holiday by herself? "Honestly, I'd rather not be alone, but I don't want to feel on the spot either."

"Trust me, I know how to handle my family, and I promise you'll have a good time. You'll like them."

That's what she was afraid of.

"My parents live close enough to the Hollywood Bowl to see the fireworks there," he said, driving to his boyhood home. "When I was a kid I used to lie flat on my back in the yard so I wouldn't miss a thing."

Carey wasn't sure she'd be able to handle anything about today, but she smiled and pretended to be interested in his story and happy he felt like talking about it. No way would she let on to Joe how tough each and every minute spent with him was for her. She did it to hold out for a bigger reward, but so far he wasn't showing any signs of opening up or changing. Holiday Joe was still By-the-Book Joe.

Carey sat in the car, wearing red board shorts with a string-tie waist to accommodate her growing tummy, a white collared extra-long polo shirt and a blue bandana in her hair. Joe wore khaki shorts and a dark gray T-shirt with an American flag on the chest in shades of gray instead of in color. Still, the point was made. They were celebrating the Fourth of July. With his big family. Oh, joy. Cue butterflies in stomach.

Although they'd made love and had opened up to each other that one night, Carey hadn't learned one bit more about Joe's broken marriage. Evidently he was determined not to ever let her know the whole story. Because of that, she felt stuck in a holding pattern, unable to be a real friend even though he'd insisted they were, definitely not a lover but merely a person who needed a place to stay, biding her time until she could move out. Every agonizing day, since things hadn't changed, it became more evident it was time to make her break.

In the back of her mind she kept assuring herself that with her new RN salary she should be able to save up enough fairly soon to rent a small but decent apartment somewhere and then get out of Joe's hair once and for all. Yet the thought of *not* seeing him every day sent a deep ache straight through her chest. Because she still cared for him.

He glanced at her, taking his eyes off the road briefly and giving a friendly yet empty smile. If only she could read his mind. She returned the favor with a wan smile of her own. What a pitiful pair they'd become. They'd both taken to wearing full mental armor since the morning after their one perfect night. Politeness was killing them. And it hurt like hell.

Joe's parents' home turned out to be in the Hollywood Hills area, not far from Joe's house. He explained while they snaked up the narrow street that he'd grown up in a neighborhood called Hollywood Heights. She could see the Hollywood Bowl to the north and some huge and gorgeous estates to the west, wondering if he might have grown up there and was secretly rich. The thought amused her. Hey, the guy had owned his own business since he'd been in his early twenties. Hadn't he said his father owned a car rental franchise? Maybe his dad was a CEO of one of the major chains. But then they turned into a long-standing middle-class neighborhood instead, and, to be honest, Carey was relieved.

Joe had never mentioned much about his family before, beyond the sister who'd loaned some clothes. Carey thought about that as they pulled into the driveway of a beautifully kept older Spanish Revival home. The front of the one-story, red-tile-roofed house was covered in ivy with cutouts where the living-room windows were and a well-maintained hedge lined the sprawling green yard in front of two classic arches on the porch. The fact that rows of palm trees stood guard on each side of the house made her smile. So Californian.

She had no idea how long his family had lived there,

but he'd just said he'd been a kid here. That made her wonder what it would be like to always have a family home where you went for holiday celebrations.

Joe introduced Carey to his parents, who clearly adored him, and she could see that he'd gotten his soft brown eyes from his mother, Martha, and his broad shoulders and dark hair from his dad, Doug. They both grinned and immediately made Carey feel welcome, though there were questions in their gazes. She wondered if they assumed she and Joe were a couple.

The sister who'd loaned Carey clothes turned out to be named Lori, and she made a point to put it out there right off—Joe was the nice guy he was only because she'd been his middle sister by two years and had often insisted he play dress up and dolls instead of cowboys and Indians. Carey laughed and watched Joe blush, something she'd never seen before. She'd bet a fortune he'd always looked out for his kid sister and younger siblings, too.

Being an only child herself, she'd never experienced the power of a sibling, in this case to put a macho guy like Joe in his place in front of his mysterious new woman friend—who'd once been so desperate as to need to borrow Lori's clothes. Now she was dying to find out who they thought she was and, more importantly, what they thought she was to Joe.

Andrew—Drew to his family and friends—was the taller but younger brother to Joe by four years, and was a fairer version of Joe but had the narrower build of his mother. Where Joe was a muscled boxer, Drew looked more like a long-distance runner. Both looked fit but in different ways.

"We're waiting for Tammy and Todd to arrive before

we begin making ice cream," Martha said, as she gave Carey a quick tour of the house.

Carey soon found out they were the babies of the family at twenty-two, fraternal twins who still seemed to hang out with each other all the time and therefore would be arriving together. Interesting. This family believed in togetherness. Another foreign idea to Carey. Maybe that had something to do with Joe insisting they continue the parenting classes together?

The rest of the four-bedroom house gave the appearance of being lived in but with obvious recent upgrades, like a state-of-the-art kitchen and a family-friendly brick patio and neatly manicured lawn, complete with a small vegetable garden. Now she understood where Joe had probably gotten his idea for his own inviting patio and backyard. He hadn't fallen far from his family tree.

Being in this home, sensing the good people who inhabited it, caused nostalgia for something Carey would never have to sweep through her, pure bittersweet longing. She'd be all the family her baby would ever have. Their home would be each other, small but loving. She vowed her child would always feel loved, no matter where they lived. Seeing good people like Joe's parents with such love in their eyes when they looked at their adult kids gave her hope for her and the baby. She wanted it more than anything for herself, that parent-child relationship.

The moment the twins walked in with a couple of bags of groceries, everything stopped and it was clear they were the wonder kids. The light of their mother's life. Martha made over them as if they were still in their teens, and Joe raised his brows and half rolled his eyes over her ongoing indulgences. *Wow, would you look at that, the babies have just managed to go to the market all by themselves*, he seemed to communicate with that look. Since she and Joe had a strong history of nonverbal communication, she was willing to bet on it. Come to think of it, Lori and Drew had exactly the same expression, and it made Carey smile inwardly. Nothing like a little friendly sibling rivalry, something she couldn't relate to. She also found it interesting that Tammy had dark hair like her father and Todd was nearly a blond—the only one in the family.

"Let's get that ice cream going," Doug said, clapping his hands, reminding Carey of Joe. He grabbed Todd, since his shopping bag contained the essential ingredients, putting him immediately on ice-cream duty. Joe was assigned to grill the burgers on the gorgeous built-in gas stainless-steel barbecue on the patio, and Lori enlisted Carey to help put together some guacamole dip and chips to go along with cold sodas and beers for those partaking, as an appetizer. Except, coming from Illinois, Carey didn't have a clue how to make guacamole, so all she actually wound up doing was mashing the avocados and letting Lori take over from there. With Martha overseeing the condiments and side dishes, already made and waiting in the refrigerator, the early dinner preparation seemed to run like a well-oiled machine.

Carey felt swept up, like a part of the family, and she cautioned herself about enjoying it too much. These were Joe's people, she'd never be a part of them. Today was simply a gathering she'd been invited to take part in rather than be left alone on a huge national holiday. If there was one thing to be sure of in these otherwise confusing days, Joe was way too nice a guy to let that happen. Yet, curiously, no one else had brought a date.

His mother loved to tell tales about her kids, embar-

rassing or not, she didn't care. It was clearly her privilege to share as their mother. Carey learned a whole
history of childhood mess-ups and adventures for all
five of the Matthews kids as the afternoon went on.
Then Lori took her aside and asked her a dozen questions about what it was like to be unconscious for three
days. They wound up having a long conversation, just
the two of them, and Carey could see herself making
friends with Lori if given the chance. It made her feel
special to be taken in so easily, and closer to everyone—
a sad thing since she understood there would never be a
chance to really be close to any of them beyond today.
Unless Joe came to his senses.

Later, as they ate, Carey found out that Drew's lady
friend was in the navy and was currently deployed in
Hawaii. Poor thing, he'd said with a grin, and just as
quickly notified his parents he was planning to take a
trip to see her in August if his dad would be willing to
give him the time off. Hmm. Carey wondered if anyone else worked for their dad.

Just as Carey prepared to take a bite of her thick and
delicious-looking home-grilled cheeseburger, which required both hands to hold the overfilled bun, a gust of
wind blew a clump of hair across her face. Before she
could put down the burger to fix it, Joe swept in and
pulled the hair out of her face, tucking it behind her
ear, a kind but cautious glint in his eyes. The simple
gesture was enough to give her shivers and make her
once again long for that dream she'd had to tuck away.
Fact was, the guy couldn't resist coming to her rescue.
Plus at his parents' house they couldn't very well hide
out in their separate bedrooms, avoiding each other.

Why did things have to be the way they were? Why
couldn't they just go for it? She took the bite of seri-

ously delicious burger, Joe having cooked them to perfection, her mind filled with more secret wishes. But even as she wished it she knew that between the two of them, with all the baggage they held on to, the fantasy of being Joe's woman would probably never be.

Lori, a yoga instructor, soon explained that her significant other was a resident at County Hospital and couldn't get the day off. Martha mentioned that Todd and Tammy would be seniors at the University of Arizona and were living at home for the summer. It made Carey feel like a special person to have the entire family to herself. And they all truly seemed to enjoy having her there.

"This is the most delicious peach ice cream I've ever tasted," she said later to Todd when the homemade dessert was served.

"It's my dad's secret recipe. He wants to make sure I carry on the family tradition."

It made Carey wonder if only the men got to learn the peach ice-cream recipe and she glanced at Joe, her unspoken question being, *Do you know how to make it, too?*

Incredibly, he gave a nod. She looked at Lori, who shook her head. Then she glanced at Drew, who'd made eye contact with her and nodded. Cripes, this intuitive communication business must run in the family, and evidently only the guys got the ice-cream recipe.

"Before you call me sexist." Doug spoke up, obviously noticing all of the subtle communication going on. The mental telepathy gift was beginning to creep Carey out! "I have my reasons," Doug continued. "It's to make sure that once a lady tastes this ice cream, she'll love it so much she'll never be able to leave one of my boys." He gave a huge, self-satisfied grin over the explanation that Carey couldn't argue with. Obviously it had worked with Martha. And from the taste of it, she understood perfectly well why. It was also very apparent Joe had never thought to make any for her.

Then it hit her that Joe's wife had left him, peach ice cream or not, and putting her own feelings aside she worried that Doug had inadvertently brought up a touchy subject for Joe. She glanced at him as he studied his bowl of dessert, though he'd stopped eating it. Martha seemed uncomfortable, too, and sent those unhappy feelings Doug's way through a terse look.

The family was well aware of Joe's heartache, and that was probably why they'd been so delighted he'd brought her over today. Oh, if they only knew how disappointed they'd soon be, but that would be nothing near what she already felt. If only...

As the afternoon wore on into evening one by one the siblings made excuses to leave, and soon it was only Joe and Carey hanging out with Doug and Martha.

"Over the years the trees in the neighborhood have grown so high they block out a lot of the view of the Bowl fireworks." Martha seemed compelled to give Carey a reason.

"I thought you said you could watch the fireworks from your backyard?" she said when she had Joe alone at one point.

"The really big ones we still can, but everyone has plans, you know how that goes."

She guessed she understood, but the thought of families, like trees, outgrowing themselves made her feel a little sad. It didn't seem to faze Martha and Doug, though. After all, the twins would be home for the entire summer.

It amazed Carey that after spending only one afternoon with the Matthews clan she already felt she knew more about their open-book world than she did about Joe, having lived with him for over a month.

"We're staying, though, right?" To be honest, Carey looked forward to seeing those famous Hollywood Bowl fireworks from his family's backyard.

"We sure are." His beeper went off and he checked it. "Excuse me." He got up, walked toward some bushes and made a return call.

She figured it was work related and suspected she might not get to see any fireworks at all today. Her sudden disappointment quickly dissipated when Joe smiled at her.

"Guess what? I've just received a special invitation."

"To what?"

Joe winked. "I must be doing really well at the clinic because James himself just invited me and a guest to his private fireworks viewing tonight."

"At his house?" A flash of pride for Joe made the hair on Carey's neck stand on end, further proving she was still far too invested in the guy. "Why so last minute?"

A satisfied smile stretched Joe's lips, the ones Carey had secretly missed kissing. By the way she'd longingly glanced at them just now, she'd probably just given herself away. "Well, apparently someone cancelled, and I was the first person he thought of."

"So you're a replacement?"

"I'd rather not put it like that but, yeah, I guess I am."

She wanted to hug him. "I didn't mean to burst your bubble. It's really a big honor."

"I know. I've heard that every year he invites a handful of employees to share the evening with him. It's sort of his way of giving a pat on the back to his best-performing department heads." Pride made his smile bright, and Carey quickly realized how rarely he grinned. If only she could put a smile like that on his face again. She had, that one special night.

"That's fantastic, Joe." Without thinking, she touched his arm, immediately being reminded of and missing the feel of his strength. "You're a hard worker and it's good that Dr. Rothsberg has noticed."

He covered his pride with a humble shrug. She wanted to throw her arms around him, but he'd made it very clear that he was never going to let her near again. Yet she'd had a wonderful afternoon and evening with his family and really liked every single one of them, feeling closer to him because of them, and a secret dream to be a part of his life rose up, refusing to get brushed aside again. Stupid, stupid girl.

Joe knew better than to push things any further than they already had, after spending the entire afternoon with Carey and his family. But he'd had a great day. Carey had fit right in with everyone, and they all clearly liked her. It made him wonder if he'd made the right decision to never let anything further happen between them. In so many ways she was right for him. It was all the stuff from before that kept both of them hung up. He hated to admit how scared he was, because it seemed so damn wussy, but he was. And Carey had wounds and scars of her own, yet she seemed more willing to move beyond them than he was. Being here with her made him feel confused again. Needing to keep his distance but not wanting to completely let go.

And here she was, in his old backyard, smiling at him. The Tiki torches lining the patio emphasized the red in her beautiful auburn hair and made her eyes look as green as the lawn. He couldn't seem to stop himself from making another big mistake where Carey was concerned. Knowing he really shouldn't open the door for more, James had told him to bring Carey along when he'd mentioned where he was and who he was spending the holiday with. And right now he couldn't think of a single reason not to.

Letting the moment take control, Joe made a snap decision. "Will you come with me?"

At a quarter to nine Joe pulled into the designated employee parking lot at The Hollywood Hills Clinic, the huge, lighted building as alive with activity as ever. Hospitals never got to take days off, but Carey was grateful she had this one Monday before she started her new job.

He directed Carey to a mostly hidden employees-only elevator by putting his hand at the small of her back. His touch made her tense with longing. *Stop it! Don't get your hopes up.*

Soon they were on the top floor, walking down a long, marble-tiled hallway. Joe opened huge French doors at the end and they stepped onto a balcony. She immediately heard music and loud talking coming from above. In the corner of the small balcony was a spiral staircase leading to the roof. Joe took her hand to show the way. Again, touching him like this set off a million unwanted feelings and emotions with which she wasn't ready to deal. Fortunately, the spectacle of a group of highly gorgeous people on the roof quickly took her mind off that.

Wow! The panoramic view of the entire city of Los Angeles was spectacular from up there, too.

Dr. Rothsberg, the tall and handsome, blue-eyed blond, golden boy of medicine, immediately came to greet Joe. "Hey, great, you could make it." He turned to Carey. "I'm so glad you could come, too."

"Thanks for having me." Carey tried to hide her fascination with the incredible specimen of a man but was worried her dazed stare may have given her away.

Dr. Rothsberg kept smiling as though he was used to people looking at him like that. "Make yourselves at home. There are drinks over there." He glanced at Carey. "No alcohol for you, young lady."

She laughed, perhaps a little too easily, wondering if all women acted this way around the guy, then figuring, *Hell, yeah*.

Joe led her to the bar and got her a root beer, already knowing her weakness for that particular soda, while he grabbed an icy IPA because it wasn't everyday he got a chance to enjoy an imported Indian pale ale.

"See that lady over there?" Joe pointed out a beautiful woman with hair a similar color to Carey's. She nodded. "Her name is Dr. Mila Brightman and she runs a clinic in South Central L.A. It's called Bright Hope. She used to be engaged to James." He'd lowered his voice and moved closer to her ear so she'd better hear him say the last part.

Carey's eyes went wide. It was hard enough being around Joe after only spending one incredibly beautiful night with him, so what must it be like to be on the same rooftop as an ex-fiancé? "What happened?"

"I don't like to spread gossip, but I heard from Stephanie the receptionist that he stood her up at the altar."

Holy moly! Why would she come close to the man if that was true?

"She's best friends with Freya, James's sister," Joe continued.

"Oh, I met Freya one day in the recruiter's office. She's our PR lady, right?"

Joe nodded.

"That should make for some heavy family tension. Wow."

"You've got that right."

He'd moved closer to bring Carey up to date without sharing the info with anyone else, and she'd moved in because of the music and talking, and now they huddled together, sipping their drinks and taking in the incredibly romantic skyline of L.A., and it suddenly overwhelmed her. They'd gotten too close. She couldn't handle it.

"I'm going to get one of those delicious-looking cookies I saw over there." She pointed to a dessert table in a secluded corner that promised to be both a delight and a nightmare for a woman monitoring her baby weight. "Can I bring you one?"

Joe shook his head, a look she couldn't quite make out covering his face. Was he sorry she'd stepped away? Or was he shutting down again? After such a great day, she hoped not.

She crossed to the spread of goodies and wound up having a harder time than she'd thought, making a decision. There was so much to choose from!

On the walk over she'd noticed Dr. Rothsberg surreptitiously watching Mila, who was across the roof, talking to Freya. Then Mila wandered over to the dessert table and stood next to Carey, and though she gave a friendly enough greeting, the woman seemed totally preoccupied with the group where James stood. As Carey continued to decide which two goodies to choose—she'd increased her limit upon seeing all the choices—Dr. Rothsberg also headed for the table.

Not having anything to do with the couple but now knowing their history thanks to Joe via Stephanie,

Carey got nervous for both of them as well as for herself. Yikes. What would happen when they faced each other? She kept her eyes down, studying the huge display of desserts, unable to make a choice or move her feet, willing herself to become invisible.

"Mila," James said, all business, "I'm sure Freya has told you I'll be coming to your clinic for a personal tour in early September."

Carey had wound up being between the two of them but on the other side of the table, and didn't dare move. They didn't seem to notice her anyway, as their eyes had locked onto each other. She chanced a glance upward to see for herself. *Yowza*, she could feel the tension arcing between them, so she distracted herself by first choosing a huge lemon frosted sugar cookie.

"Yes, Freya mentioned it. So thoughtful of you to tear yourself away from your girlfriend to make the trip."

Could the woman have sounded *more* sarcastic? But who could blame her? She'd been stood up on her wedding day. He was lucky she didn't pull a dagger on him! Carey worked to keep her eyes from bugging out and began to slice a large piece of strawberry pie in half so as not to feel too guilty about gobbling it all down. It had whipped cream topping with fresh blueberries sprinkled over it, so it was definitely a patriotic pie. Really, she *should* eat it. For the holiday's sake.

James moved dangerously close to Mila, a woman who looked like she'd claw out his eyes if he got even an inch nearer, and yet he leaned down with total confidence, his mouth right next to her ear. "In case you're interested, I've broken up with her."

Carey couldn't help looking up, but only moved her eyes so they wouldn't see body movement, still praying she was invisible, but the couple didn't seem to see her or care that she could hear their entire conversation. Mila was clearly flustered by his comment. She obviously hadn't known he'd broken up with the other woman. Wow…oh, wow.

Practically impaling Mila with his piercing blue eyes, now that he'd noticed her surprised reaction, he went still. "In the future, why don't you ask me personally how things are going in my life, instead of relying on the gossip pages as your source of information?" The sarcasm was sprinkled over every single word, yet Carey got the distinct impression that a pinch of hurt had been mixed in. She wanted to gasp over their hostile encounter but kept her mouth shut rather than draw attention to herself.

Then she accidentally dropped the knife. They both noticed. "Sorry," she said as she grabbed the pie, put it on the plate with the cookie and rushed away, wondering why Freya hadn't told Mila that James had broken up with his girlfriend, since they were best friends.

She arrived back where Joe stood, casually talking to another employee she'd seen around the clinic over the last couple of weeks. Frank, was it? They said hello and the man seemed friendly enough. Her hands shook as she took the first bite of the cookie. She glanced over her shoulder back to the dessert table but Mila and James had moved away to their respective groups. Even while trying to hide, she'd felt their sexual chemistry.

James may have stood Mila up, an unforgivable thing to do, but Carey could've sworn she'd glimpsed lingering love in his eyes. And though Mila had come off like a hurt and still angry woman toward him, Carey was pretty sure she'd seen relief on her face when James had told her he'd broken up with whoever that other woman was. Then again, Carey did have a huge imagination where love was concerned and may have seen what she'd wanted to see. She glanced at Joe, still chatting with Frank, remnants of her own lost before it ever started love driving home the point.

She promised to keep everything she'd just heard to herself. No way would she want that gossip Stephanie to get hold of this juicy information.

At exactly nine, as if some great force had waved a magic wand, fireworks started popping up all over the valley from the Hollywood Bowl, all the way out to Santa Monica beach. Someone shut off the outdoor lights as the magical display continued. Amazing and mesmerized, having never seen anything as spectacular in her life, Carey stood closer to Joe, and his arm soon circled her waist, and her arm wrapped around his. So natural. And right now there was no fighting her attraction to the man. The constant effort from living with him, plus spending all day long with him today, and especially now with a night filled with sparkles and shimmering colors dripping down the sky, had worn her down. She secretly savored his sturdy, steady build.

Carey gazed up at Joe, who beamed like a kid, nothing like that dutiful mock smile he'd given on the drive to his parents' house earlier today. She offered a bite of the fabulous cookie and was surprised when he took it greedily. Knowing this moment would only complicate things further between them, she ignored caution and leaned into his strength. His fingers gripped her side the tiniest bit tighter and her own version of pyrotechnics exploded in her chest. Yes, this would definitely confuse things. Their eyes locked for an instant. Along with seeing the reflection of fireworks in his darkened gaze, she was pretty sure she saw some regret.

Oh, who was she kidding? She'd just read her own

feelings into those wonderful brown eyes, just like she'd done with Mila and James. She really needed to stop projecting her thoughts and feelings onto everyone else. It would never get her anywhere, just make her feel disappointed. Because no matter how much she might want a second chance with Joe, it didn't matter. He wasn't open to it. But why did he keep glancing at her during the fireworks show? And now his fingertips lightly stroked her side. Funny how holidays could do that to people.

She went back to watching the dazzling and dizzying display of colors across the night sky and became aware of a strange sensation inside her. Had she eaten too much sugar? Or were the gunshot-like sounds of the rainbow-colored rockets popping and crackling through the night causing the reaction?

The feeling was very subtle, yet she couldn't deny it. This had to be *quickening*. She'd learned in her class with Gabriella that primigravida mothers often didn't realize it the first time their babies moved. Who knew? Maybe it had happened before and she'd missed it. But not this time! *Oh. My. God.* Her baby was alive and moving. *Inside. Her.*

"Joe." She nearly had to yell for him to hear her.

Grinning from the bright chaos playing out before them, he glanced down at her. When she knew she had his full attention, she was so excited she could hardly get out the words. "I just felt the baby move for the first time." Her throat tightened with emotion as she admitted it, and the unrelenting firework display went blurry in the background.

His eyes widened and his childlike grin from the fireworks turned to an amazed smile, as if she'd just told him "their" baby had moved. There she went, projecting again. But, in her defense, they had just gone over the information at the last prenatal class. Joe had been there with her, like he'd promised.

He grabbed her full on, pulling her close, then squeezed. "That must feel amazing."

Thankful for his goodness, and her good fortune of feeling her baby move for the first time on the Fourth of July, the blurriness turned to tears. "It did. Oh, my God. How strange and wonderful." She sucked in a breath, feeling like she was floating on air, then pulled away from his shoulder.

His eyes had gone glassy and the dazzling lights sparkled off them as he turned serious. She could have sworn she'd seen a flash of pain, but he quickly covered it up. He shook his head as if amazed and unafraid to show it. Just like the day in the clinic when she'd come to and nearly the first thing she'd asked had been if her baby was all right, and the nurse had assured her it was. She'd cried with joy. So had Joe. The stranger who'd saved her.

He was anything but a stranger tonight. He was the greatest guy she'd ever met.

She hugged him again and promised herself she'd remember the priceless expression on Joe's face for the rest of her life. Then she cried once more as a pang of longing for what she could never have set in deep and wide.

CHAPTER EIGHT

THEY DROVE HOME from the party in silence, still riding the high from the fireworks. Joe kept his confusion to himself. He'd held her in his arms again, and the longing had dug so deep he'd been unable to completely hide it. He was pretty sure she'd noticed his reaction, too. He couldn't continue with Carey like this. She didn't belong to him, her baby wasn't his. She deserved some guy who could love her and give her more children. Not him.

Yet she'd fit in so well with his family, and it had been clear they'd all liked her. It'd made him wonder about possibilities, and he thought he'd given up on those ages ago. Could he actually get over being cheated on by his wife and best friend, or the fact he was sterile? Was he ready, maybe, to finally move on? In his usual rut, the answer came glaring back. No.

Holding her, watching the fireworks together had been a huge mistake. Hell, ever letting her into his life had been a mistake. He'd been the one to point out how much they both had going on personally, and how important it was not to confuse things between them any further. Yet he hadn't had the heart to un-invite her for the Fourth of July celebration with his family. He'd resorted to using the lame excuse of protocol as the reason. Yeah, he was a guy of his word. Besides, his mother wouldn't have let him, and if he hadn't brought Carey, Mom would have spent the entire afternoon badgering him.

Carey's baby had moved, and the truth had knocked him sideways. She had a life to look forward to and she didn't deserve having a guy like him hold her back. Maybe one day he'd be able to forget and move on, but he wasn't there yet, and most days he doubted he ever would be. Their timing sucked. She pregnant. He like one of those zombies on the show they liked to watch together.

If he insisted on continuing to look after her, his job from now on would be making sure she became independent of him. Not to get swept away and continue to confuse and complicate things by grabbing her under the fireworks and holding her like she belonged to him. What the hell had he been thinking? From now on he had to act logically and realistically. It was his only defense for survival. And he really needed to stay out of her way.

Getting her the car from his father's lot had been a start. She could have it as long as she needed it. Now that he knew she'd be working from seven a.m. to three p.m. at the clinic, he'd go in tomorrow and change his schedule to work the evening shift.

The less time he spent near Carey, the better. The alternative was too damn painful.

"Thanks for everything," Carey said once they'd gotten home. She lingered in the living room, a dreamy smile clinging to her face.

He'd been so wrapped up in his thoughts he'd almost forgotten she was there. "Oh. Sure. You're welcome. It was fun." He shoved his hands in his back pockets and kept his distance.

"The best fireworks I've ever seen."

His attempted smile came nowhere near his eyes. "Me too." Empty words. He may as well be talking to a stranger, and she obviously felt his detachment because her expression turned businesslike.

"Well, I'd better get right to bed since tomorrow is my first day on the new job."

He tried a little harder to be part of the human race. "I'm glad you had a good time."

Her eyes brightened. "I loved your family."

That's what he'd been afraid of. "I could tell they really liked you, too." It didn't matter, he needed to step back and let her move on. Without him. "Oh, and good luck tomorrow."

She flashed that genuine killer smile and it took him by surprise. Why did it always do that? Taking every single crumb he offered, she struck him as beautiful and innocent. The sharp pang of longing nearly made him grimace. All he wanted to do was grab her and kiss her, and let his body do the thinking for the rest of the night, so he stayed far across the room, hands shoved in his pockets, and worked on making his smile look halfway real. She noticed his awkwardness and pulled back.

"So good night, then." She turned and headed for her room, her beautiful auburn hair forcing him to watch every step of her departure. That constant ache inside his chest doubled with the inevitable thought.

"'Night," he muttered. *Get used to it, buddy, soon enough she'll be walking right out of your life.*

At the end of the first week of Carey's new job, Joe, after agonizing over how best to handle the situation, told her he had to work on Saturday and would have to miss the next Parentcraft class. His intention was to let her down easily, yet he still dreaded it.

In truth, he'd scheduled the extra shift after he'd talked to Gabriella about helping Carey find a birth coach. He couldn't be the one. The thought of going through labor with her, being there for her at the toughest time, seemed beyond him. He worried he might have an emotional setback because of it, and fall apart on her. Angela and Rico had really done a job on him. He also understood how important it was for a mother-to-be to bond with their birth coach when it wasn't the husband or partner. They'd gone over that very topic the Saturday before. The sooner she found one, the better.

When he got home late that afternoon he saw Carey out on the patio deck, napping on one of the lounging chairs. Though he knew he shouldn't, he tiptoed to the screen door and studied her up close, afraid to breathe so as not to wake her. A real sleeping beauty. It brought back memories of sitting by her hospital bed, watching her, when she'd been unconscious for those three days.

Joe remembered trying to imagine who she was and where she belonged then. Now he knew exactly who she was, how wonderful she was, and how much he wanted her for himself. What a stupid fantasy. He may as well try to sprint to the moon.

She must have felt his presence or she'd been playing possum all along because he turned to leave, then heard her stir.

"Joe?"

"Yeah." He stopped in mid-step. "Didn't want to disturb your nap."

She stretched and yawned, and he didn't dare go out there, just stayed bolted to the floor, wishing things could be different. Knowing they never could be. Yearning to make it so anyway.

"What time is it?"

"Almost five. Want me to get dinner started?"

She swung her legs around and sat, feet on the wooden planks, facing him. "I missed you in class today. We started practicing relaxation techniques and special exercises. She had us work with our partners, but Gabriella worked with me."

"I had to accompany a transfer patient on the helicopter to Laguna Beach today." He'd volunteered. Would he have been able to function getting up close and personal with her in class? He'd definitely made the right decision to work, but he wondered when he'd started becoming a coward.

"The thing is, I talked to Gabriella about our situation, and she said she has access to the local doula registry. Those women love to be birthing coaches, so I asked her to give me some names." She stood and walked toward the screened-in porch door, each standing on opposite sides of the thin barrier. "Bottom line, you don't have to come anymore." With sadly serious eyes, she watched and waited.

He'd wanted to let her down easily because he was a coward. Now she'd beaten him to the task, officially releasing him. He didn't have the right to feel hurt, hell, he'd wanted a way out, but the casual comment—*you don't have to come anymore*—cut to the bone. An ice pick could have done the job just as well.

He resisted reacting, but his skin heated up anyway. He wondered how much she'd told Gabriella about them, if her story fit in any way, shape or form with his. He hadn't expected to feel upset, but he was really bothered, and definitely sad now that she'd come out and said it. Ah, hell, truth was it killed him to stand aside, even though he'd already set the ball in motion to arrange this very thing. He hadn't expected to feel like the air had been kicked out of his lungs and feel a sudden need to sit down. He steadied himself, because he knew one fact that couldn't be denied. "I guess that's for the best."

Clearly feeling let down, if he read her sudden drooping shoulders right, she covered well, too. Just as he had. "Yeah. I guess so, but thanks for being there for me all these weeks."

They'd been reduced to communicating in robotic trivialities.

"You're welcome. It was fun." *While it lasted, which he'd known from the beginning couldn't be long.* He'd just never fathomed the profound pain that would be involved. He'd gotten swept up in emotion and carried away that first Saturday, letting his feelings for Carey blur reality. He couldn't let her be the only one without a partner. He'd let down his usual guard, acted on a whim, and had paid for his mistake every single week since. Sitting beside her, acting like they were a couple, wishing it was so, scaring himself with the depth of desire for it to be so, but knowing, always knowing, it could never be.

His mouth went dry with unexpected disappointment. He needed to get away from her now. "Hey, listen, I'm going to the gym. Don't hold up dinner for me, okay? I'll grab something on the way home."

He left without before he could see her reaction.

The next Friday, Carey admitted a late-afternoon patient. The forty-eight-year-old male had a face everyone who'd ever gone to a movie or watched a TV show might recognize, but no one would know his name. The character actor had been admitted with the diagnosis of severe acute pancreatitis. Basically the guy's pancreas was digesting itself thanks to an overabundance of enzymes, in particular trypsin. His history of alcohol abuse—according to Dr. Williams, the doctor who'd been the attending doctor for Carey, and who she had enormous respect for—had made a major contribution to his current condition. However, according to the doctor's admitting notes, they would do studies to rule out bacterial or viral infection as a possible source as well.

Carey found the computer notes fascinating, and Dr. Williams had left no stone unturned. She'd even commented on the fact the man was almost fifty and still extremely buff. Probably because of his need to stay fit for the action/adventure roles he normally took, Carey decided. But getting back to the doctor's notes, she intended to consider his possible use of steroids as well.

To add another angle, when Carey did the admitting interview, the actor, who also did his own stunts for most movies, told her he'd had an accident on the job and had sustained blunt abdominal trauma. Well, that wasn't how he'd put it—*I got kicked in the gut*—but Carey's notation was worded that way. She put a call in to Dr. Williams to inform her.

Carey often thought how the practice of medicine was like a huge mystery where patients arrived with symptoms and the doctor's job was to gather all the evidence and figure out what was going on. Carey knew the clinic staff's job with this patient would be to watch for fluid and electrolyte imbalance, hypotension, decrease in blood oxygen, and even shock. This guy with the affable smile but pained brow was not to be taken lightly. Like many in the clinic, he was fit and healthy looking on the outside but a mess on the inside. These days, Carey could relate perfectly to that, too.

He'd been complaining of severe abdominal pain for a day or two, and had assumed it was because he'd been kicked in the gut, as he'd described it. Carey noted his abdominal guarding when she made a quick but thorough admitting physical assessment, and found his abdomen to be harder than usual. Of course, that could be due to the fact the man looked like he did hundreds of crunches a day. He'd said his symptoms had gotten worse in the last twenty-four hours, and had told her he felt "sick all over" so he'd come to the clinic's ER. After a few more questions he'd also admitted to going on a drinking binge a few days back. Yet somehow the guy was tanned and youthful looking for his age, until she looked closer. The saying about the eyes seemed true, and they were the mirror to, if not his soul, his health. There she could see the lasting effects of his living extra-large for many years.

His admitting labs showed his amylase and lipase levels were over the top, and that alone could have gotten the guy admitted. Add in the bigger picture, and this actor's next gig turned out to be the role of a hospital patient.

Carey inserted an IV to be used for medications as well as parenteral nutrition since he was on a strict NPO diet. Next she needed to perform a task no patient ever wanted to go through, at least from her experience as an RN. She had to insert a nasogastric tube.

"This is more to help relieve your nausea and vomiting than anything else," she said calmly. "You'll thank me for it later."

He gave her a highly suspicious stare, especially when she gave him a cup of ice chips.

"Suck on these when I tell you," she said as she manipulated the thick nasogastric tube with gloved hands and approximated externally how deep it would need to go to reach his stomach. "Okay, now."

He took a few ice chips and sucked at the exact time she used his nostril to insert the well-lubricated tube and push past the back of his throat and down into his esophagus and all the way to his stomach. His sucking on the ice would prevent her from going into his lungs. He gagged and protested all the way but didn't fight her. He gave no indication of the tubing mistakenly going into his lungs by having shortness of breath or becoming agitated, but she did the routine assessment of the placement anyway. She listened through her stethoscope as she inserted a small amount of air with a big syringe into a side port of the NG tube, hearing the obvious pop of air in his stomach when she did so.

"You did great," she said as she taped the tubing in place on his cheek and attached the external portion to his hospital gown, then connected the end to the bed-side suction machine. He gave her the stink eye, but she knew he was playing with her so she crossed her eyes at him. "It's one of the perks of my job. You know most nurses have a tiny sadistic side, right?"

That got a laugh out of him, and she figured she'd tortured the guy enough for now, even though she knew he was lined up for all kinds of extra lab work and additional tests in the next twenty-four hours. So she made sure the side rails on his bed were up and the call light was within his reach, then prepared to leave. "Get some rest."

"Like I can!" he managed to say.

"Carey?" Anne, the ward clerk she'd covered for while she'd gone on vacation called her name just as she exited the patient room.

"Coming." Carey marched to the nurses' station to see what her co-worker needed, only to find a huge vase of gorgeous flowers sitting on the counter. Lavender asters, golden daisies, orange dahlias, and roses, oh, so many perfect roses! "Wow, where'd these come from?"

"They're for you!"

"What?" Joe? What was he trying to do, make up for bailing on the parenting class? Why go back and forth like this, mixing her up even more? Ever since he'd said all those things about not confusing their living situation by getting involved with each other, and especially after the Fourth of July when he'd introduced her to his family, and especially later when they'd shared that significant moment during the fireworks, he'd been avoiding her like crazy. It'd stung and confused her, and she was only just getting her bearings back, thanks mostly to having the new job and not seeing him nearly as often. Was he feeling guilty for leading her on or letting her down? Both? She wanted to pull her hair out over his inconsistency.

Carey searched for a card, but all she found was an unsigned note.

These flowers are as lovely as you.

Sorry, Joe, but that is just inappropriate. Either you want to be involved with me or you don't. You can't have it both ways!

Hadn't he learned in the parenting class that hormones during pregnancy made every emotion ten times stronger? This tug-of-war with her feelings had to stop.

"Do you mind if I take a short break?" she asked one of the other nurses who'd begun to gather around the spectacle of colorful blooms, admiring them. The more she thought about those flowers, the more upset she got.

"Sure. I'll cover for you."

"Thanks." Carey marched to the elevator and pressed the "down" button, got off on the first floor and headed toward the ER. It was after two, and she knew Joe had been avoiding her by working the afternoon shift from two to ten p.m. in case he actually thought he was fooling her. Her eyes darted around the room until she spied him over by the computers, so she trudged on, determined to get some things straight.

"You got a second?" she asked.

"Sure. What's up?" His hair was a mess. Had he not even combed it? Her first thought was how endearing it made him look, but she stomped it out the instant she thought it. There was no point.

She had to admit the guy didn't have the self-satisfied look of a man who knew he'd just surprised a lady with flowers. "Did you send those flowers?"

He pulled in his chin, brows down, nose wrinkled. "What flowers?" He wasn't an actor and, honestly, he couldn't have made up that reaction.

"Are you horsing around with me?" Her frustration growing, she needed to be sure.

He raised his hands, palms up. "Honest. I don't have a clue what you're talking about. It wasn't me." Now he looked curious. "You got flowers and no one signed their name?"

She nodded, racking her brain to figure out who besides Joe would do such a thing.

Now he looked perturbed. "You must have an admirer."

"Oh, come on." Where did he get off, making such crazy statements?

"You don't think guys watch you?"

"I'm *pregnant*, Joe."

"You wear those baggy scrubs, and you're only just now starting to really show."

"You've got to be kidding. I don't encourage anyone. I mean I smile at people, I'm nice, but that's just being polite." If not Joe, then who? And, honestly, she was disappointed they hadn't been from him, and, she wanted to kick herself for even allowing the next thought.

Was that a look of jealousy on his face?

Joe hadn't felt this jealous in a long time. He'd skipped the jealous part with his wife, going directly to fury once he'd found out she'd gotten pregnant with Rico. But this was different. This feeling eating through his gut right now was good old-fashioned jealousy.

Who the hell had sent Carey flowers?

He looked suspiciously around the department. He'd introduced Frank to her at the party on the roof, but surely he could tell Carey and Joe were more than roommates. Plus they hadn't spoken two words to each other beyond, "Hi, how are you?"

It was time to get honest with himself. What could he expect? Carey was stunningly beautiful and he'd noticed admiring glances around the hospital whenever she passed by. At first it had given him great satisfaction to know she was living with him, and no one knew about it. It had been his big, fun secret. The gorgeous woman who'd come in as Jane Doe was his housemate. Now someone had the nerve to make a move on her. And it really ticked him off.

If—no, *when* he found out who it was he'd have an in-your-face moment and straighten out any misunderstanding. Carey was off-limits. Got that? Did he have the right to do that? No. But he felt unreasonable whenever things involved her, and he was being honest with himself. He. Was. Jealous.

"Um, I've got to get back to work. My shift's almost over," she said.

"Sure. Okay. If I find out anything, I'll let you know."

"Thanks."

He watched her leave, her hair high in a ponytail that swayed with each step. When he noticed one of the ER docs also watching her, he wanted to cuff the back of the guy's head. Carey was off limits. Was he being territorial when he had no right to be? Yes. Hell, yes. He folded his arms across his chest, the anger soon turning to self-doubt. How could he honestly expect loyalty from Carey when he wasn't even prepared to come clean with her about the truth of his past?

In a frustrated fit he flung his pencil across the desk. His EMT lifted a single brow at him.

Don't dare ask, if you value your job.

Back home that night, the more Carey thought about it, the more upset she got about the flowers. She tried to remember giving anyone the slightest misconception that she was interested. Beyond Joe, that was. But what bothered her more was that Joe seeming to run hot and cold with her. She still didn't put it past him to send those flowers and pretend he hadn't. Surely he'd noticed how down she'd been lately, since they'd been forced to change their relationship. But wait, they hardly saw each other anymore. Maybe he hadn't noticed anything about her mood swings.

One thing she knew for a fact, she'd gone and ruined everything by kissing him and coming on to him that night. She was a runaway, pregnant with another man's baby. Did she expect Joe to be a saint on top of everything wonderful about him and welcome her into his life with open arms? She should have left well enough alone.

She took the bouquet home and put the vase on the coffee table in the center of the living room. Might as well enjoy them since someone had spent a lot of money on them. She chewed a nail and stared at the flowers. Had their one incredible night together been worth all the confusion and heartache it had caused?

She thought for a couple of seconds and shivered through and through with some incredible memories. Hell, yeah!

Dejected, she went to the bathroom and washed her face and was getting ready for bed when she heard Joe let himself into the house.

There was no way Joe could avoid those flowers when he came in. They may not have been from him, but they sure would be a perfect catalyst to force them to have a long-overdue conversation about a few things.

She needed answers to the question that wouldn't stop circling through her mind, especially since seeing how jealous he'd been earlier: *Where do we stand?*

He'd said he didn't know who had given the flowers to her, and had seemed not to care. He'd even suggested that she'd unknowingly flirted with someone and might have encouraged the gift, which really annoyed her. Like it was her fault. And come on, she was pregnant! Why the hell would she want to get involved with a new guy now?

Precisely! That was what he'd hinted at the night he'd leveled with her. They had no business getting involved.

But she couldn't get Joe's expression out of her mind from when she'd confronted him at work and he'd sworn he hadn't been the one to send the flowers. It had been a look of pure jealousy, until he'd quickly covered it up. He still had feelings for her, as she did for him.

What a mess.

All revved up, she headed straight for the living room and the man who'd just come home. "You know what I don't get?"

"Well, hello to you, too." He looked more tired than he usually did, coming off his shift, like maybe he hadn't been sleeping well. Join the club! Or maybe work had been more stressful than usual.

"If you don't want anything to do with me anymore, why were you jealous?"

"Jealous? What are you talking about?" Now, on top of looking tired, he looked confused.

"I saw your eyes when I told you about those flowers." She didn't need to point them out. He'd obviously seen them the instant he'd walked in. His demeanor shifted, having more to do with her accusation than the flowers.

"I'll admit, it took me by surprise. And I still don't like the idea of some guy hitting on you in such an obvious way."

"But you have no right to." She folded her arms across her chest, having just then remembered she was in her pajamas. "You made it very clear we aren't allowed to have feelings for each other. It's for the best. Remember?"

He went solemn, watching her, and she made it clear she intended to have it out right then and there. Too bad if he was tired or jealous or whatever else. Now was the time. Finally. "If you don't care about me, why were you jealous?"

In an instant he'd covered the distance between them, and his hands were on her shoulders, pulling her toward him. Time seemed to stand still for a moment as they looked deep into each other's eyes and both seemed to know—without the benefit of a single word, just using that damn communication thing they had going on—that once again they were about to do something they'd regret. But it didn't stop Joe from planting a breathtaking kiss on Carey. And it didn't stop Carey from kissing him back like it might be the last kiss she'd ever get in her life. From Joe.

The kiss extended for several seconds, turning into a getting-to-know-you-all-over-again kind of thing. Her breasts tingled and tightened as she felt the tension from Joe's fingers digging into her shoulders while he continued to claim her lips. With them, a kiss was *always* more than just a kiss. She sighed over his mouth, searching with her tongue, soon finding his.

Joe's breathing proved he was as moved as she was, but then just when they were getting to the really good part he stopped. And stared into her eyes, a combination of desire and seething in his.

"Because I *am* jealous. Damn it." He'd finished with her, and now gently pushed her away.

She felt foolish standing there, her breasts peaked and pushing against the thin material of her pajama top, exposing exactly what he'd just done to her. "You can't do this to me, Joe. I don't understand why you act this way. It's not fair to keep me all mixed up like this."

He looked back at her, considering what she'd just said, and then, as if he'd made a huge decision, his expression changed to one of determination. "Then you'd better sit down, because if you want to know why I'm the way I am, it's a long story."

The comment sent a shiver through her. He finally intended to open up to her, and she was suddenly afraid of what she might find out. But she cared about Joe, and if it meant helping her understand him, she'd listen to anything he needed to share. No matter how bad it was or hard to hear.

She took a seat on the edge of the small couch. Joe chose to pace the room.

"How far back do you want me to go?"

"To the beginning, if that helps explain things."

He stopped pacing, stared at his feet for a second or two, as if calculating how far back he needed to go to get his story told once and forever. Then he started. "I met Angela, my ex-wife, when I took my paramedic training in an extension course at UCLA. We started a study group and things heated up pretty fast. Within the year, once we both got our certifications and got jobs, we got married." He glanced up at Carey, who hadn't stopped watching him for an instant. "You know how I love my family." She nodded. "Well, since I was married I wanted to start having kids right off. Like my parents did. I'd launched my business and things were going well, so I figured, let's go for it."

He started moving around the room again, turning his back on her. "After a year she still hadn't gotten pregnant, and we wondered if our stressful jobs might have something to do with it. So we took a two-week vacation to Cancun. Still nothing." He cleared his throat and glanced sheepishly back at Carey. She continued to train her gaze on him, so he turned around and faced her. "We decided to get fertility tests done. But I've got to tell you, things were really tense between us around that time, too." His hand quickly scraped along his jaw. "You know how you hear stories all the time about people who can't have kids, then they adopt a kid and the woman gets pregnant?"

Carey nodded, her heart racing as he came to what she suspected would be a key part of his story.

"Well, Angela got pregnant." He lifted his hands. "Great, huh?"

Somehow she knew it hadn't been great.

"I was thrilled, of course, and we went on our merry way, planning to be parents."

She read anything but happiness in his words, and especially with the tension of his brows and tightening in his jaw she understood he was in pain. Wait a second, she also knew Angela had left him for his best friend. He'd told her that much. But with his baby? Oh, my God, how horrible. And here she'd been dragging him to her parenting classes! If she'd only known.

Making him repeat the entire history for her benefit was cruel. "Joe, you don't have to—"

"Nope. I said I would, and I want you to hear the whole mess. Okay?" He looked pointedly at her, like it was her fault for making him begin and she needed to hear him out.

Carey tried to relax her shoulders but felt the tension fan across her chest instead. "Okay. Go on, then." She could barely breathe in anticipation.

"So we're all thrilled and planning for our baby and five months into the whole thing, out of the blue my fertility results show up in the mail. We'd completely forgotten about them because we were pregnant!" He made a mocking gesture of excitement, and it came off as really angry. "Where they'd been all that time, I didn't have a clue, but, bam, one day the results were there. Angela wasn't home when I opened them." He stopped, needing to swallow again. "And the thing is, it turned out…" He glanced up quickly, if possible looking even more in pain, and then, dipping his head, his eyes darted away. "I'm sterile."

How could that be? He was a healthy, magnificent specimen of a man, but she knew to keep her thoughts to herself.

"I did some research after I got that diagnosis because, honestly, I couldn't believe it. Evidently my sperm ducts are defective from multiple injuries in high-school baseball and from kick boxing. It's the only explanation the doctor could come up with when I finally followed up. Who knew high-school sports could do a guy in?"

Carey stared hard at Joe as she bit her lip, hoping her eyes wouldn't well up. Angela had been pregnant and living a lie under his roof. Of course, now she understood why her being pregnant seemed difficult for Joe. Oh, God, what he'd been through. And she'd rubbed his nose in that memory every single day she'd lived here. She wanted to cross the room and hug him then apologize, but every unspoken message he sent said, *Stay away. Leave me alone. Let me get this out once and for all. You asked for it!* So she stayed right where she was, aching for him and crying on the inside.

"My life stopped right then. All the happy future-parents hoopla came crashing down. My wife was pregnant—but not by me." His words were agitated and the pacing started up again. Carey understood how hard this must be for Joe, but he insisted he needed to tell the entire story. So he paced on, and she waited, nearly holding her breath. "I thought it had to be a mistake. I called the fertility clinic, suggesting they'd mixed things up. They'd obviously lost my results, since it had taken so long to mail them. But, nope, I was one hundred per

cent sterile. Said so right there on that piece of paper."
He flashed her a sad, half-dead excuse for a smile.

"So I had to confront my wife." He'd lowered his
voice as if this part was solemn, or someone had died.
"Angela insisted it was a mistake, because I hadn't
told her I'd already called to make sure. I watched her
squirm and avoid looking at me. I never felt so sick in
my life." Joe gave a pained, ironic laugh. "Oh, she swore
the baby was ours, that it had to be. I listened to her
lie. Then she finally broke down and confessed that if
the baby wasn't ours it was Rico's." Joe's fist smashed
into the palm of his other hand. Carey started to understand the importance of his punching bag. Yet all she
wanted to do was rush to him, hold him and kiss him.
He'd been betrayed by the two most important people
in his life after his family.

"My best freaking friend." A hand shot to his forehead, fingers pinching his temples as if he'd suddenly
gotten a headache, reliving the story. He sucked in a
ragged breath. "Evidently, just before we'd gone to Cancun, when things had gotten really intense here, she'd
gone to him to cry on his shoulder, but a hell of a lot
more than that wound up happening. Turns out my *best*
friend had an unusual way of consoling *my* wife."

Anger and sarcasm mixed as his agitation grew. She
wanted to tell him to stop, not say anything else, but
kept silent, sensing his need to purge the full story at
long last.

"Angela swore she'd been too racked with guilt to
tell me, especially when she didn't know who the real
father was. Can you believe it? If she could have gotten away with it, she would have tried. And I got to
think I was the future father of a beautiful baby for five

months before we were forced to face the facts. What a fool I'd been."

Carey shook her head, feeling responsible for his pain right now. "You don't have to say anything else, Joe."

"But wait, it only gets better! Angela told Rico and he wanted her to get a paternity test! Yeah, he turned out to be a real prince. So there I was looking at this stranger who was supposed to be my wife, and she's telling me about this bastard who was *supposed* to be my best friend, and the only thing I could think of saying was, 'You can leave now. You're welcome to each other.' Yet part of me couldn't bear to kick out a pregnant woman, and I was about to take it back when she got up and called Rico." A look of incredulity covered his face. "Right in front of me she told him I knew everything, and she needed a place to stay."

Joe nailed Carey with his tortured expression. "They've been together ever since. Have a baby girl and seem to be doing fine. Or at least that's what I hear from other people I used to know."

Carey's hand flew to her chest. Joe had lost his wife, child and best friend in a single moment. And to make matters worse, he also knew he'd never be able to have a child of his own. What torture that must have been for a guy who'd wanted a big family. Yet when she glanced at him she saw a man suddenly at peace.

"As you can imagine, relationships have been off-limits for me for a while now. I mean, what's the point? I'm not into one-night stands, and I can't give a woman what she'd want most if we got serious—children of her own. Not unless I send her over to Rico."

"That's not funny, Joe." Carey had heard enough, and she'd realized why Joe was the distant man he was for so many reasons. Why he blew hot and cold. It went against his natural personality to be bitter, though, which had always confused her, but now she understood why. "I'm so sorry this happened to you. Now I see why you overreacted to me getting those flowers. I mean, it makes perfect sense..."

"Nothing *ever* makes perfect sense, Carey." He sounded desperate, tired and defeated. He went into the kitchen and filled a glass with tap water, then drank. She followed him there, wishing she could love away his sadness and anger, yet understanding why he deserved to feel that way. Why he needed to keep her at a distance.

"Then I show up on your doorstep pregnant and homeless, and you're too nice a guy to toss me out. I get it. The last thing I should have done was come on to you, but I believed and still believe that it's mutual attraction. There's something real between us, Joe. You couldn't have faked that night."

He swung around, some of the water slopping out of the glass. "It doesn't matter what happened that night. It can't ever happen again. There's no point. Besides, you're all set up now. You've got a job, an income, you're back on your feet—hell, someone even sent you flowers."

"Joe, that's uncalled for."

"Is it? Ever heard the phrase 'been there done that'? I can't do it again. Won't."

Pain clutched her chest when she realized what he intended to do. Every secret hope she'd held on to was about to get dashed by a guy who'd been beaten up by love and never wanted to open his heart or life to love again.

"Look, Carey, you're a strong woman who knows

what's best for you and the baby." Now he sounded like he was pleading for her to let him go. For her not to torment him by dangling love and sex in front of him by living under his roof. "You'll be an amazing mother. Truth is, you don't need me anymore. You're ready to move on."

"Please don't push us away…" her lip trembled as she spoke from being so racked with emotion "…because you're afraid you'll get pushed first. I'm not that girl. I'm not Angela."

"And I'm not the guy for you. Sorry."

He'd shut down completely, going against every single thing she knew in her soul about him. He wanted to be the scarred guy who could never feel again, but he lied. She'd seen and felt his love firsthand. He hated that his wife had once lied to him, but now he was lying to *her*. He wanted her to leave, and she couldn't argue with a man who'd just turned to stone in front of her eyes.

"Please listen, Joe."

Something snapped. Anguish mixed with fury flashed in his stare. "Don't you get it? Every time I look at you I'm reminded what I can never have for myself. I may be stuck in the Dark Ages, but I can't get past that."

She'd heard his deepest hurt. Joe had pretended, but he really hadn't survived his wife cheating on him with his best friend, on top of finding out he was sterile. That was a total life game changer; he was broken and she couldn't fix it. He'd just said her presence only made the pain worse.

He may as well have stabbed her, and the jolt of reality nearly sent her reeling backwards. Lashing out, he'd wanted to wound her, too, and he'd done a fine job. Her eyes burned and her hands shook.

She'd promised herself she'd never beg a man the

way her mother used to beg her father. And even though her world, the new and improved version of her world since she'd come to California and met Joe, had just been ripped from her, she wouldn't beg.

A sudden surge of anger and pride made her jaw clamp shut and her shoulders straighten. Joe was damaged and wasn't open to reason. There was just no point in trying to get through to him. "I'll be out by the end of the week."

She could scarcely believe her own words, but now that she'd said them she'd have to make sure she'd carry them out. No matter what.

CHAPTER NINE

NEXT WEEK AT WORK, Carey still reeled from her final confrontation with Joe. They'd been avoiding each other like a deadly disease ever since. What a mess. She'd promised to be gone by the end of the week, and had put the word out with the nurses on her floor for any leads on small apartments to rent.

She sat in a corner, scrolling through all of her assigned patients' labs for the day, insisting on giving them her full attention. Afterwards, she'd do her morning patient assessments then pass their meds. Sometimes putting her life on hold for her day job was a relief.

"Carey?" Dr. Di Williams stood behind her.

"Yes? Anything you need, Dr. Williams?"

The middle-aged doctor offered a kind smile. "I hear there's something *you* need."

Carey quirked her brow. "Sorry?"

"An apartment?"

"Oh. Yes, well, something will pan out, I'm sure." She prayed it would because it was Wednesday and she'd promised Joe she'd be out by the weekend at the latest.

"I've got an in-law suite at my house. No one ever

uses it. It's got a private entrance and even a small kitchen. It's yours if you'd like it."

A few people were beginning to realize she was pregnant. Unfortunately, Stephanie had seen her go to the Parentcraft class, so probably the whole clinic knew by now. Obviously, Dr. Williams knew from when Carey had been her patient. "That's very kind of you, but—"

"It's a nice place. My partner and I have a house right here in the Hollywood Hills. Lisa made sure the place was comfortable and inviting, but her parents won't come to visit, and I've given up on mine coming around for years now. So what I'm saying is you're welcome to live there. I know you've had a rough time and I'd like to help you out."

Touched to her core, Carey jumped up and hugged Dr. Williams, who looked both surprised and uncomfortable. "You're a godsend. Thank you."

It was the first time Carey had ever seen the doctor grin. "We thought about adopting once, but our jobs are so demanding we decided it wouldn't be fair to the baby. Plus we're both, well, you know, getting older." She gave a self-deprecating smile. "So we'll enjoy meeting your bambino when the time comes."

She patted Carey's stomach, and Carey fully realized the reality that, yes, her baby would be born, and that after tomorrow, when she'd had another sonogram, maybe she'd even know the sex. Which made ner think how Joe had always called her baby little Spencer. It hit her then. She *really* needed a place to live. She was ready to "nest," as she'd learned the word in her parenting class. She wanted this, and the good doctor had just solved her problem.

"But I have to insist on paying rent."

Dr. Williams tossed her a gaze that perfectly expressed her thoughts—*Please, I'm a rich doctor and do we really have to negotiate money when we're having such a good moment?* "Whatever you want to pay is fine. Money isn't an issue for us. In case you didn't know, Lisa's a doctor, too."

"I'll be in great company." Carey beamed while she talked, never having felt more grateful in her life. Well, after her unending indebtedness to Joe, of course. She gave an amount she felt she could afford, nothing close to what the place would be worth, she was pretty much sure of that. But she was being honest, though, not wanting to insult the doctor by going too low, since she'd have to live on a tight budget. Especially as she'd have to return the rental car soon and would need to find a used car for transportation. *One step at a time, Carey.* Thank goodness she'd banked some unused vacation time at her hospital back in Chicago and they'd sent the final check to Joe's address last week.

"That works for me," Di said. "I'll bring the key tomorrow and you can start moving in right away."

The doctor turned to walk away, but Carey grabbed her hand and shook it, well, over-shook it, because she wanted to make her point. "You and Lisa are lifesavers. Thank you, thank you, thank you."

"Like I said, it'll be fun." Before right this moment fun would never have been a word she would have associated with Dr. Di Williams. Who knew?

Along with the warmth Carey felt for the incredible kindness of others, especially from Joe, and now from a woman Carey hardly knew, she felt new hope for her and her baby. She just might be able to pull this off, start a new life in California and move on from her past once and for all. One sad and nagging point kept her from full elation.

Joe.

She loved the guy. And she'd never get to tell him. But she'd learned her lesson in life well. Just because you wanted something, it didn't mean you'd get it. It would be too much to ask of him to love her and to accept her child, too. Not after everything he'd been through. She understood that now.

She sighed, a bittersweet thought about leaving Joe's sweet little house for her new and as yet unseen place nearly making her cry. She'd gotten so used to living with him she hated thinking about not seeing him every day. Was this really happening? Maybe she was still in a coma and this was one big Alice-in-Wonderland-style dream. The thought amused her briefly.

But she had labs to look at, and one of her assigned patients had just put on their call light.

Thank heavens for the distraction of her day job.

In order to avoid Carey and every disturbing thought she dredged up in him, Joe worked several extra shifts during the last week she lived with him. On Friday he'd even stayed on for an extra night shift so he wouldn't chance seeing her move out. The thought of watching her go would only widen the gaping wound inside him.

He'd finally opened up and told her everything, and she'd seen how messed up he truly was. Even then he'd felt her need to comfort him, but he'd held her off, pushed her away, then, once she'd seen there was just no point, that he'd never let her in, she'd agreed to move out. Whatever they'd once shared had breathed its last breath, and all the CPR in the world couldn't revive it.

It had been a crazy evening on the job with nonstop calls, and truthfully, Joe was grateful for the constant distraction.

James had thought of everything when he'd set up the hospital for his private and exclusive clientele. One perk was an emergency box in every home that went directly to The Hills emergency department instead of the more general Los Angeles system.

At two a.m. another call came through, this one from an affluent area, the Los Feliz Hills, east of The Hollywood Hills Clinic. A woman reported her husband in sudden pain that was shooting down his left arm. The emergency operator sent the message to Joe and he grabbed his team and hit the road within two minutes, siren switched on.

The five-mile distance would take fifteen minutes, thanks to the winding roads in both of the hilly communities. While they drove, the emergency operator stayed on the line and gave instructions to the wife of the patient, in case she needed to begin CPR.

Once in front of the ornate house Joe's team grabbed their emergency kits and EMT Benny rolled in the stretcher. A young housekeeper waited at the front door to the huge several-storied home and directed them up an open stairwell to the master bedroom. Joe couldn't help but notice the largest chandelier he thought he'd ever seen in a home. He quickly recalled the Hills ER operator having mentioned that the patient was the head of one of the movie studios in town.

Joe found the white-haired patient on the floor, unconscious, his wife kneeling over him in near panic.

"He just passed out," she said, fear painting a frightened mask on her face.

"Does he have a history of coronary artery disease?" She nodded.

Joe rushed to the patient's side, finding him unresponsive. He checked his airway and found him to be breathing, then he checked his carotid artery for a pulse.

"Let's get him on the stretcher," Joe directed his team, taking out the portable four-lead ECG machine and hooking up the patient for an initial reading as they applied oxygen and rolled him onto the adjustable stretcher. Then, in an effort to save more precious time, he started the IV as they transported the man down that huge stairwell. Once that IV was in place, he checked the initial four-lead heart strip, which showed possible ST elevation. Once Benny and his partner got the patient in the back of the emergency van, Joe jumped in, immediately switching the man to the twelve-lead EKG for a more thorough reading. Applying the leads, Joe was grateful the old guy wore loose-fitting pajamas, making his job a little easier.

Time was of the essence with MIs and seconds after securing the stretcher in the safety lock in the back of the van Benny and the other EMT shot to the front, turned on the emergency lights but not the siren, as a courtesy not to add stress to the heart patient, and sped down the winding hills.

Now with proof the man was in the midst of a STEMI, thanks to the twelve-lead EKG but still maintaining a decent enough blood pressure—he was even coming around a little bit, giving occasional moans— Joe added a nitroglycerin IV piggyback, gave him morphine through the IV line and aspirin under his tongue. He might not be able to stop the ST elevation myocardial infarction, but he hoped to at least help decrease the patient's pain. All this was done while the ambulance tossed and rolled around the hills, heading for Los Feliz Boulevard and onward toward Hollywood and the clinic.

Without the benefit of lab reports, he couldn't treat the patient more aggressively. And since the definitive treatment for an MI was catheterization, Joe's one job was to keep the guy alive.

The man looked ashen and his breathing had become more difficult. Joe repositioned his head for better airway and increased the oxygen one liter. oxygen sats stank. Then he checked his blood pressure, which was even lower than previously, but assumed it could be due to the nitro and morphine.

The heart monitor started alarming. Damn it, the guy was crashing. At times like these Joe felt frustrated with his role as a gap-filler until the patient got to the ER and could be hit with all the fancy lifesaving drugs. If only the ambulance could get there faster.

When the monitor went to flatline, Joe immediately started CPR, and continued to do so for the last five minutes of the ride to the clinic and the ambulance entrance where the medical big guns waited.

Unfortunately for the patient, medically the future didn't look too bright. In an oddball nonmedical way, Joe could relate.

Joe parked the car in his garage, closed the door, and headed into his house from the backyard entrance on Saturday morning. He hated how the house had felt since Carey had moved out yesterday. Had it only been yesterday? It seemed more like a month or a year even since he'd last seen her. Before, there had been this incredible life force radiating from her room. Today all he felt when he walked near it was his energy getting zapped by pain and regret. Well, he planned to save himself the angst and head right to his room to sleep.

After the stress of that morning, with the Hollywood

movie tycoon who'd wound up dying despite all emergency measures, he felt dejected and needed to sleep. It seemed typical of issues of the heart, and maybe even a metaphor for his own life lately, especially where his relationship with Carey was concerned, and with all the practical training in the world he still couldn't fix his own messed-up heart. Come to think of it, he might tear a page from Carey's story—a short-term coma would be a good thing right about now.

As usual, with any downtime, Carey was foremost on his mind. The word "coma" brought unwanted thoughts about a lady he'd once sat vigil for at her bedside. What had he done? He'd lost her. Sent her away. He unloaded the contents of his cargo pockets onto his dresser top then dug out his cell phone.

Wait a second. He'd worked all night and hadn't turned on his personal phone so he'd missed a text from Carey. He was so tired he squinted to read it.

It's a girl. Latest sonogram. Yes!

The words nearly brought him to his knees. Little Spencer was a girl. Carey didn't have anyone in her life to share the news with but him. A sudden feeling of sadness punched his gut. He'd been so selfishly focused he hadn't considered what moving out had meant for her. She'd volunteered to go and, like a wuss, he'd let her.

She deserved so, so much more. Yet, with all the bad things life had dealt her, she insisted on being upbeat. Yes! she'd written. The text was short but so touching, and all he wanted to do was find her and hold her and tell her how he really felt.

It wasn't going to happen. It wasn't possible.

He should leave well enough alone.

His house had never felt so big or empty since she'd moved out. Only yesterday! Damn, it already felt like a year. How would he go on without her?

"You did the right thing," he said aloud, glancing into the mirror above his dresser. He had to believe it because otherwise he'd go crazy. He was so messed up. Carey and the baby only would have left at some point anyway, so it was better it had happened sooner rather than later, and as *his* idea, not hers. In a childish way he admitted it felt better to have forced the change because he couldn't have survived Carey leaving him. By his spin, sending her away had been the most unselfish thing he'd done in his life.

Besides, she deserved a man with more to offer, someone without baggage like his. Anger, mistrust, suspicion, yeah, he was good at those sorry emotions. She'd had all of that tossed in her face long before she'd met him, beginning with her father and ending with that scumbag Ross. It was Carey's time to catch a break. He'd given it to her by pushing her out the door. Because he knew she was the special kind of woman who would have stuck around, put up with his sorry attitude, and tried to make the best of things if he hadn't made her leave. Beyond a laundry list of the ways she'd be better off without him, the main reason still stood out. He'd come around enough to know that Carey was nothing like Angela. He could trust what she said and did. She was as stable as they came, despite her tough life before coming to L.A. The issue was still with him.

He thought about her ultrasound and the fact her baby was a girl. The crux of the matter was that he would never know what it was like to have a woman he loved carry his baby. A kid who might look like him. And he was too damn messed up to get over it.

Better to set her free now before it got even more difficult because, honestly, he hadn't been prepared for the level of pain her leaving had unleashed. Sometimes he could barely breathe.

He thought about what he'd said to her the other night and cringed. He'd been harsh, insisting he couldn't get past his wife cheating on him, and he'd held it against a completely innocent person. What sense did that make?

He flopped, back first, onto his mattress, hands behind his head, praying sleep would find him and put him out of this torture, if only for a few hours. He'd tried to make peace with his decision about letting Carey go, but deep down something still didn't feel right.

Why, even now—when she'd found a great place to live, from what he'd heard floating around at work, and when she had nothing but good things to look forward to, a solid job, the upcoming arrival of her little baby girl, a bright future—things didn't feel right to him.

Why did he still have the foreboding sense she needed his protection?

He squeezed his eyes tight. *Go to sleep. Just go to sleep. You're getting delusional from lack of rest.*

He was bound to settle down soon because his body was completely drained and his mind so weary he could barely put two coherent thoughts together. Yeah, he'd get some sleep today, he promised himself. But first he needed a glass of water. So he hopped off the bed and headed to the kitchen for a drink.

Carey wanted to scold herself for accidentally taking Lori's clothes along with her when she'd packed the few meager possessions she owned and had moved out. Joe's sister had been nice enough to loan her some jeans and tops when she'd first moved in with zero belongings left to her name. Now she'd have to face him again, as painful as that would be, to return them. Truth was it had hurt to the core when he hadn't even bothered to reply to her text about her baby being a girl. She guessed he'd already moved on. Didn't care. Hadn't he said all she did was remind him of what he'd never have?

An ache burrowed deeply into her chest, not only for herself but for him, too. She still loved the guy. Had she imagined every good thing about Joe, or was this just how it felt to lose him? She was positive she'd never get over him, and had missed him every second since she'd moved out.

Mid-morning, she parked the rental car across the street from his house on the small cul-de-sac, thinking the car was another topic she had to bring up with Joe. As soon as she found a used car she could afford, she'd make sure this one got returned to Mr. Matthews. She wanted to make sure Joe knew she didn't expect to keep this car forever. Just for a little longer. She promised.

She reached around to the backseat and grabbed the tote bag with Lori's clothes inside. Carey had gotten the bag from the clinic the day she'd been discharged and Joe had taken her in. She'd almost slipped up and thought "home" the day when Joe had taken her home. Because that was how it'd felt when she'd walked through that door with him. She glanced at the small sage-green house across the street. Yes, he'd been a stranger then, but he'd saved her life and then kept vigil beside her hospital bed, and she'd never felt more protected or safe in her life than when she'd lived with him.

With the bag in her hand, she got out of the car and battled a feeling of half hope and half fear that Joe would be home. She'd left her house key the night she'd moved out. If he wasn't home now, she'd leave the items on the porch and make a quick getaway. On second thoughts, he'd been working so much it was possible he was sleeping and the last thing she wanted to do was wake him up. Maybe she'd just leave the bag on the lounger on his deck and not even attempt to face him right now. If she snuck off without seeing him, she'd save her lovelorn heart a whole lot of grief.

She started down the driveway, getting halfway to the kitchen-window area when she caught herself. This was cowardly. She was a big girl now. She needed to face him if he was home, though there was no sign of his car so she made a one-eighty-degree turn and headed back toward the front of the house, stunned to find a man she'd never expected to see again only a few feet away.

Ross.

How had he found her? How had he known where she'd been living? A chill zipped down her spine and her stomach felt queasy.

Then it hit her. He was the one who'd sent the flowers. How had he…? Oh, wait, he knew how to manipulate people, especially women, and had probably gotten the work address out of Polly in the employee relations department back in Chicago. Carey had been in touch with her regularly since she'd arrived in Hollywood— first to let the hospital know about her situation and to take a leave of absence, then to set up receiving her backdated pay checks, and eventually to give notice on the job and to collect her unused vacation pay. What a fool she'd been to think he wouldn't find her.

She'd thought she'd been so careful, but nothing seemed to be beyond Ross's reach. The bastard. After the quick flash of fear at seeing him she went directly into anger. The creep had another thought coming if he planned to mess up her life again. She was in control now, in no small part thanks to Joe, and Ross was powerless.

He kept his distance. Even held his hands up, all the while watching her, like a prowling animal waiting to pounce. "I know what you're probably thinking," he said, trying to sound appeasing. "What am I doing here?" He gave a poor excuse for a smile that looked more like an insincere politician's than a former lover's.

"I don't want to see you. Leave. Now."

Quickly his expression changed to that of a mistreated puppy. "I'm sorry. I've come to tell you I'm sorry. I love you. We can still be happy together. Make a life together."

"Ha! That's rich. You wanted me to get rid of my baby. That's not going to happen. There's nothing further to talk about."

She looked at Ross, tall, dark, and had she really used to think he was handsome? All he looked like now was a creep she needed to get rid of. Fast. He'd abused her, both mentally and physically. Had wanted her to have an abortion, had shoved money into her hand to do it, too.

She thought about Ross's polar opposite, Joe, and all he'd tried to do for her. How hard it must have been for him to show up at the prenatal appointments, to be the first one she shared the first sonogram with, when never being able to become a father had still been eating away at him. The moment he'd slid into that chair beside her in the parenting class had nearly made her heart burst with gratitude. He'd acted the part of being a father, even when he'd believed he would lose her and the baby, as if his past was bound to repeat itself. Yet he'd shown up and stuck with it, for her, and had never let on about the pain he must have suffered because of it. Oh, God, he was her true hero—a man to be worshipped, adored and loved. With all of her heart. And she did. She loved him.

Facing Ross, right now, she knew without a doubt what her true feelings were for Joe. Yet Joe had convinced her to walk out on him. And she'd gone because he'd looked so tortured by her being there.

She stood before Ross, a shadow of a man standing by the driveway hedge, feeling completely alone. All she wanted to do was go inside Joe's house where she'd always felt safe, and close and lock the door. Forever. On Ross.

She kept her distance, not trusting him for one second, but Ross took a single step forward.

She'd never let herself be a victim again and he'd have to hear her out. "You need to know I've finally experienced a good relationship. I know for a fact there are good, loving and caring men in the world who put their partners first. I never learned that from you, but now I have faith in the world again. In myself." She touched her heart. "You wanted to control me and tear me down to keep me under your thumb. I may have let you before but I never will again." To show how serious she was, and to prove she wasn't afraid of him anymore, she took a step forward but still kept safely out of his reach, then stared him down. "You need to leave L.A. I'll never go back to you. Never."

Ross's expectant-puppy expression soon turned to one of defeat. Did he think he could just show up and everything would be fine again? Was he that out of touch with reality? Or had it proved once and for all how he truly had zero respect for her.

Something she'd said must have gotten through to him because he actually turned to leave. Carey took a breath for the first time in several seconds. But just as quickly he turned back, lunging toward her with the look of pure rage in his demon eyes.

His first mistake had been showing up uninvited in California. His second mistake was to grab her wrist and clamp down hard enough to cut off her blood supply, then raise his other hand ready to slap her.

Instead of pulling away, fighting mad, Carey growled and steamrolled into him. Catching him off guard, her knee connected full force with his groin, the V of her free hand ramming with all her might smack into his larynx. Everything Joe had taught her about self-defense came rushing back with a vengeance.

Ross doubled over in pain, unable to gasp or shout. And, of course, he'd let go of her wrist. Shocked she'd actually pulled it off, Carey stood there dazed for one second, her body covered in goose bumps, staring at him while he writhed in pain on the driveway.

Well, plan A had worked like a charm. What was she supposed to do next?

Run! Run for the car and get the hell out of there. She turned to make her getaway, but slammed into a brick wall of a man.

CHAPTER TEN

JOE CAME FLYING out of the kitchen door the instant he'd seen the man lunge for Carey. He'd watched the whole encounter between the guy who must be Ross and Carey, the woman he loved and his new superhero, from the window above the kitchen sink.

He'd known Carey needed to face down her demon once and for all, and he'd been ready to pounce if she'd needed him. So, as hard as it had been, he'd stayed on the ready just around the corner and waited. She'd stood up to the man, not wavering for a second. When twisted reasoning hadn't panned out, the guy had lunged at her. Joe had rushed through the back door and flown outside, but she'd beaten him to the punch. Like a pro, she'd taken down her attacker. It had impressed the hell out of Joe, too. Great going.

Pride for Carey mixed with pure fear that she could have been hurt by the bastard from her past made him take her in his arms and hold tight. She didn't fight it either, just leaned into him.

"You okay?"

She nodded, then pulled back to look into his eyes. "Did you see that? I decked him! Thanks to you."

He laughed, all the while watching Ross, who slowly began to get onto his hands and knees.

"Do as Carey says, just stand up and leave. Don't ever come back," he said, with Carey safely tucked under one arm, ready, if necessary to take the matter into his own hands if the guy made so much as a hint of a move in the wrong direction.

Now Ross stood, anger still plainly carved in his face.

"The police will be here shortly," Joe said. "I called when I first saw you. She's also got a restraining order out on you in case you ever get any ideas about coming around again. Consider it your 'go-straight-to-jail' card and this is your final warning."

Ross took one look at Joe, saw the don't-even-think-about-messing-with-me stare and took off, running to the street and back toward Santa Monica Boulevard.

With arms still wrapped around each other, they watched him disappear round the corner.

"I don't have a restraining order out on him," Carey said.

"He doesn't know that."

"And the police, are they coming?"

"Again, he doesn't need to know I was just about to call when I saw you kick his ass, so I hung up to help you." Joe flashed Carey a proud grin. "You were the bomb, babe."

She laughed. "You taught me everything I know."

He pulled her near and hugged her tight. God, he'd missed her. To think he'd almost let her get away sent shivers through his chest. "You're all right? Let me see your wrist, it looked like he had a firm grip." He checked out the area around her thin wrist, which was reddened and showing signs of early bruising. Like a dope, he kissed it because it was the only thing he could think to do, and he wanted more than anything for Carey to understand how precious she was to him. "You need to know something. I said things the other night that were horrible and not true. The only person you remind me of is you, and I never want to lose you. Or your daughter."

She disengaged her wrist from his hands so she could stroke his cheek. Looking into his eyes with her soft green stare, she smiled. He got the distinct message she had a few things to clear up with him, too.

"I never want to lose you either. Standing up to Ross just now made me realize he was the one who should feel ashamed, not me. That dark past I dragged out here needs to stay in Chicago with that loser. It shouldn't have any influence over me or my future. I've started over again. That ugly shadow is gone for good."

He believed her, too. She stood before him a woman of conviction, nothing like the frightened victim he'd first met two months ago.

She went up on her toes and delivered a light kiss. He matched it with a kiss of his own, and damn if it didn't feel like a little piece of heaven had just tiptoed back into his life.

"I meant what I said to him, too," she said, her arms lightly resting around his neck. "You've given me faith again in love. You helped me learn that it's not weak to open myself up to someone and to love again. Even if you didn't want me to." Her eyes dipped down for a second then swept back up. "I couldn't stop myself from loving you. I do, Joe, I love you."

Now he felt like the coward, well, until five minutes ago anyway, when he'd watched Carey confront her biggest fear and kick its ass, and Joe finally knew without a doubt that he loved her, too. No matter how hard he'd tried, he hadn't been able to stop himself from falling in love with her. He'd pulled out every old and sorry reason to keep from loving her, but she was meant to be loved, and he was the guy to do it. And for someone whose thoughts sounded suspiciously like a caveman's—*Me Joe. You Carey. We love.*—he had yet to voice the most important words he'd ever say. He just stood there, staring into her eyes, stroking her hair, loving her in silence.

"It's especially nice when you love someone." She cleared her throat to draw his attention away from her eyes and back to noticing all of her. "If that someone loves you back."

Hint, hint! There was that tiny mischievous smile she'd occasionally given when making an obvious point, and he'd missed it so much.

The ball was clearly in his court, and it was time for him to say what he felt and mean what he said. Without a doubt he loved Carey. So, still being in caveman mode, he bent down, swept her up into his arms and carried her up the steps to his front door.

Once inside he planted another kiss on her, and got the kind of reception he'd hoped for. But he knew he couldn't get away with a mere display of affection. If ever a person deserved, or a time called for, words, it was now. So he gently released her legs to the ground, snuck in one last quickie kiss, and stepped back.

"Please forgive me for pushing you away. I was hurt. And afraid. Still am. And if you don't think that's a huge thing for me to admit, you don't know me like you think you do."

"I totally understand how huge that is." She groped around his shoulders and chest. "Just like the rest of you."

He went along with her making light of things, because the topic was difficult and heavy and loaded with old habits that needed to be set free. They'd both been through so much lately, but he had one more thing to say and he needed to say it now. He cupped her face between his hands.

"I'll understand if you can't see a future with me, because I'm sterile and I can't make babies with you."

"Stop right there," she said. "You really don't get it, do you? Did you not hear me say I love you? You may not be the biological father of the little lady here, but you've acted nothing short of a true, loving, and beyond decent father. Actions really do speak louder than, well, other actions in this case, I guess." She screwed up her face in a perfectly adorable way, having briefly confused herself. Right now there wasn't a single thing she could do wrong. "I know, terrible analogy."

He laughed lightly, while understanding exactly what she'd meant, because that was part of what was so right about them, they always *got* what each other meant, spoken or not.

"But it's all the family we need," she added, and he loved her even more for her generous thought. But the truth was a small family could never be his style, that's why he'd decided to never be in the position to have a family at all. Until Carey had shown up and changed everything.

"You don't want her—what are we going to name her?—to have sisters and brothers? How about Peaches?"

"Name my daughter after a piece of fruit?" she playfully protested.

"Our daughter, you just said it, so that gives me equal naming privileges. Besides, I thought Peaches might be significant since I'm planning to make the famous Matthews ice cream just for you after dinner tonight."

"You're making me peach ice cream?"

"How else can I make sure you'll never leave me again?"

"Ah, your father's secret ingredient."

"Yes. That. Plus the fact you have no idea what a hellhole it's been here since you left, and I'll never let you go again."

"And…?" she encouraged him.

"Because I love you and can't imagine my life without you." He kissed her again, because there was no way he could say what he just had without needing to touch her, with the best expression of love he knew. Physical touch.

"Neither can I," she said. "And if we want to give, well, I'll agree to give her the nickname of Peaches, but honestly we'll have to come up with something better than that for real. Anyway, if we want to give her siblings in the future, first one step at a time and all, right? Let's see how this little one turns out. But, honestly, in this day and age, if we want more children, we can find a million ways to do it. Right?"

"Right, as usual. Sorry I've been so dense about that topic for so long. I've been too busy wallowing in my pain."

"And *that* should never come into play with us again. Okay?"

"You got it. Because I intend to spend the rest of my life showing both of you how much I love you."

She sighed her joy and nuzzled into his neck, which felt fantastic. "That works out perfectly because I intend to spend the rest of the afternoon showing you exactly how much I love you."

For a guy who'd been up all night and who earlier could hardly keep his eyes open, Joe suddenly felt full of life, love, and, right this instant, intense desire. He pressed his nose into her hair and inhaled the smell of fresh coconut shampoo, thinking how he could contentedly spend the rest of his life simply doing this. He smiled widely, knowing she had a far better idea. "I like your plan."

She gave him a long and leisurely kiss in case there was any mistaking what her intentions were. He loved how well they communicated.

"For the record," she whispered into the shell of his ear, "you had me at homemade peach ice cream."

* * * * *

MILLS & BOON®

MEDICAL ROMANCE™

THE ULTIMATE IN ROMANTIC MEDICAL DRAMA

A sneak peek at next month's titles...

In stores from 16th June 2016:

- **Taming Hollywood's Ultimate Playboy** – Amalie Berlin
  and **Winning Back His Doctor Bride** – Tina Beckett

- **White Wedding for a Southern Belle** – Susan Carlisle
  and **Wedding Date with the Army Doc** – Lynne Marshall

- **Capturing the Single Dad's Heart** – Kate Hardy
- **Doctor, Mummy...Wife?** – Dianne Drake

Lynne Graham has sold 35 million books!

To settle a debt, she'll have to become his mistress...

Nikolai Drakos is determined to have his revenge against the man who destroyed his sister. So stealing his enemy's intended fiancé seems like the perfect solution! Until Nikolai discovers that woman is Ella Davies...

Read on for a tantalising excerpt from Lynne Graham's 100th book,

BOUGHT FOR THE GREEK'S REVENGE

'Mistress,' Nikolai slotted in cool as ice.

Shock had welded Ella's tongue to the roof of her mouth because he was sexually propositioning her and nothing could have prepared her for that. She wasn't drop-dead gorgeous... *he* was! Male heads didn't swivel when Ella walked down the street because she had neither the length of leg nor the curves usually deemed necessary to attract such attention. Why on earth could he be making *her* such an offer?

'But we don't even know each other,' she framed dazedly. 'You're a stranger...'

'If you live with me I won't be a stranger for long,' Nikolai pointed out with monumental calm. And the very sound of that inhuman calm and cool forced her to flip round and settle distraught eyes on his lean darkly handsome face.

'You can't be serious about this!'

'I assure you that I am deadly serious. Move in and I'll forget your family's debts.'

'But it's a *crazy* idea!' she gasped.

'It's not crazy to me,' Nikolai asserted. 'When I want anything, I go after it hard and fast.'

Her lashes dipped. Did he want her like that? Enough to track her down, buy up her father's debts, and try and buy rights to her and her body along with those debts? The very idea of that made her dizzy and plunged her brain into even greater turmoil. 'It's immoral… it's blackmail.'

'It's definitely *not* blackmail. I'm giving you the benefit of a choice you didn't have before I came through that door,' Nikolai Drakos fielded with a glittering cool. 'That choice is yours to make.'

'Like hell it is!' Ella fired back. 'It's a complete cheat of a supposed offer!'

Nikolai sent her a gleaming sideways glance. 'No the real cheat was you kissing me the way you did last year and then saying no and acting as if I had grossly insulted you,' he murmured with lethal quietness.

'You *did* insult me!' Ella flung back, her cheeks hot as fire while she wondered if her refusal that night had started off his whole chain reaction. What else could possibly be driving him?

Nikolai straightened lazily as he opened the door. 'If you take offence that easily, maybe it's just as well that the answer is no.'

MILLS & BOON®

Mills & Boon have been at the heart of romance since 1908... and while the fashions may have changed, one thing remains the same: from pulse-pounding passion to the gentlest caress, we're always known how to bring romance alive.

Now, we're delighted to present you with these irresistible illustrations, inspired by the vintage glamour of our covers. So indulge your wildest dreams and unleash your imagination as we present the most iconic Mills & Boon moments of the last century.

Visit **www.millsandboon.co.uk/ArtofRomance** to order yours!